Call of a Distant Shore

Corinne Hoebers

To Karin
Hope you enjoy
Corinne

www.callofadistantshore.com

This is a work of fiction. Names, characters, scenarios, and places may be the product of the author's imagination or have been used fictitiously. While based largely on historical facts of the time, any resemblances to actual persons, living or dead, or events is entirely coincidental.

Library and Archives Canada Cataloguing in Publication

Hoebers, Corinne, 1953-
Call of a distant shore / by Corinne Hoebers.

ISBN 978-1-897530-02-3

1. Germans--Nova Scotia--History--Fiction. 2. Lunenburg (N.S.)--History--Fiction. 3. Snow Pearl (Ship)--Fiction. 4. Nova Scotia--Emigration and immigration--Fiction. I. Title.

PS8615.O34C34 2008 C813'.6 C2008-905038-X

Old Block House, Lunenburg, c.1800
Nova Scotia Archives and Records Management
Photo Collection: Places: Lunenburg.
Artist: anon
Original image altered for the use of this publication by 4th Floor Press, Inc.

Published by 4th Floor Press, Inc.
www.4thfloorpress.com
1st Printing 2008
Printed in Canada

Dedication

To Mum, Isabelle May Smith (nee Hartley), who shared my passion for the family tree; who never said no when asked to join me in searching through church records and trekking through cemeteries; who always had a story to tell me about herself and my grandparents. This book is for you.

Author's Note

Call of a Distant Shore is a work of historical fiction. It is based on my maternal ancestors, who emigrated from Germany to Nova Scotia in 1751 on the ship *Snow Pearl*.

My distant grandfather, Michael Hirtle, lived in Hochdorf (old German spelling Hohctorf), Germany during the first half of the eighteenth century. Though the background of the novel is based on actual historical events, the storyline of the Heber family is pure conjecture.

At the time, England wanted the inhabitants of Nova Scotia to be loyal to it. The difficulty lay with the French Acadians who settled in the Province from France during the mid-17th century.

The Acadians refused to swear unconditional allegiance to the English crown. They possessed French culture, French language and were all Roman Catholic. Although they did not take up arms against the English, they would not take up arms against the French in Quebec. They only wished to be left alone to farm their land.

The British Government hatched a scheme in the hopes that there would be increased loyalty to the old country from those other than the French. It hired an agent by the name of John Dick to convince those of the Protestant religion from England, as well as Europe, to emigrate to Nova Scotia. Twelve ship loads from 1750-1752, mainly German, arrived in Halifax and Dartmouth, founded in 1749 and 1750 respectively, to further colonize the new land.

The Hirtle family actually lived in Dartmouth for two years before sailing with a new flux of some 1453 German and Swiss Protestants to settle the Town of Lunenburg in 1753. After extensive research, I found numerous gaps in documented records. For the purpose of this story, I filled in the blanks where necessary and took the Heber family as close to my ancestors' journey as possible. For example, I was unable to ascertain which of the two flotilla of ships they arrived on in Lunenburg; therefore, I placed the Heber family on the first flotilla, which sailed into Merligash Bay on June 8.

There are many non-fiction books on the founding of Lunenburg. I have yet to see a *fictionalized* novel to express the immense trials these determined souls endured in a hostile land. Through my imagination, I take the reader into the minds and emotions of the Heber family to get a better sense of the reality of this harsh wilderness, as they eke out a bare existence through threats of Indian attacks and meagre food rations.

Since 1753, German was spoken in the town well into the 1800s. In 1995, the historic Town of Lunenburg was designated a UNESCO World Heritage Site, recognizing it as the best surviving example of a planned British colonial settlement in North America.

Michael Hirtle died on 10 May 1777, and was buried on 13 May 1777 in Old Bayview Cemetery in Mahone Bay, Lunenburg County, Nova Scotia.

Part 1

CHAPTER 1

Germany, 1750

Snow blanketed the hilly countryside around the River Fils in Upper Swabia. Although it did not lay deep, October was too early indeed for such a landscape. The old narrow road, marked only by a single thin wagon track, wound its way through the valley and into the tiny village of Hohctorf. The road forked on either side of St. Martin's Church. The weathered stone structure still stood rooted as it had for many centuries. On this autumn day, as in ages past, the steeple bells rang clear and crisp, albeit not joyously. Under the dense gray sky, the Heber family stood in a tiny graveyard.

Beside Michael's feet lay a crude wooden box holding his daughter's body, Margaretha. She hadn't reached her thirteenth birthday. The pastor solemnly prayed a few words, while his sons, Jakob and Christian, lifted the coffin and slowly lowered their sister into the ground.

Michael's eldest daughter, Elisabeth, hugged her rough woollen cloak tighter around her. A sudden gust of wind gained momentum, swirling great clouds of snow in and around the weather-beaten cemetery markers. Elisabeth held on to his wife, Anna, until the squall died down. Anna Maria was eight months pregnant.

The first snow of the season, and Margaretha would have loved it, Michael solemnly thought. He stared numbly as his sons dropped the ropes atop the coffin. "Margie," he whispered.

Through the howling wind, Michael could swear he heard her sweet laughter around him. It was music to his ears, but at the same time it sent a shiver through his body. The sharp sound of a crow cawing brought him back to reality. Lifting his eyelids, he saw one very large raven perched on the crooked limb of a great chestnut tree. Michael stared at the ominous creature as it swooped down and landed on a broken wooden cross in the corner of the graveyard. The bird sat there and cawed again, returning Michael's intense stare. He hated crows. They are morbid and sinister, he reflected, as he gazed at the motionless coffin six feet down. The crow gave a shudder, tossing what moisture had gathered on its wings. It took off, only to be swept away by another bluster of wind; an imprint of claw marks were left behind in the snow.

A tiny hand reached up into Michael's and held as tightly as it could muster. Hanna, only five years old, did not understand. Elisabeth had explained to her that Margaretha was asleep and would never wake up again. Fresh tears pricked Michael's eyelids as he pictured Margaretha's nightly ritual of telling imaginative stories to little Hanna. Hanna eagerly went to bed every night as Margie tucked her in. She started to sob. Michael lifted her up and nuzzled her into his neck. His bristly beard scratched her a little.

"Shhh, my lamb," he muttered, glancing at Anna. The sobbing ate into his heart.

After the service, Michael lingered behind a few moments alone, while the rest of the family walked on ahead. Pastor Krumer stood beside him. His long black robe billowed out with a slight gust of wind.

"Michael," he said, holding on to his wide-brimmed hat, "I can find no words to soothe your pain. May you find comfort in the knowledge that God is with you. Trust in Him."

Michael searched his face bewildered at his pastor of twenty years. "What God?" he murmured, and slowly turned to leave. He felt Pastor Krumer gently touch his shoulder, but he shrugged it off.

Michael walked back to his waiting family and noticed a commotion just outside the gate. Upon hearing "Papa, come quick," his slow step quickly picked up speed. Anna was beside the wagon, doubled over.

"It's the baby, Michael," she uttered through her pain.

She wasn't due for another month, but the stress of her daughter's illness and eventual death had finally taken its toll. As she gripped her belly, Michael crouched beside her.

"Jakob!" he shouted to his eldest. "Help me!"

They carefully lifted Anna onto the wagon. Elisabeth climbed into the back, bunching more hay around her to keep her as warm and comfortable as possible. Michael lifted Hanna into Christian's lap and jumped up beside them.

"I'll ride on ahead, Papa, and bring Doktor..." Jakob started.

"*Nein*, get Rosina," Anna interrupted breathlessly.

"But Mama, Doktor Gessler is better qualified. Remember Barbara, it's..."

"Do I have to listen to this impertinence!" she blurted. "You heard me, get Rosina! I'll not have a man touch me."

Jakob turned on his heels and stormed off, his face coloured against his red hair, his green eyes blazing. He mounted his horse and headed towards the Haug farm. Michael gave a quick snap of the reins and the wagon jerked ahead.

****

It was snowing heavier now, the thick flakes creating depth as the storm progressed. Daylight was ending sooner than usual. Riding at a hard gallop, Jakob felt the bone-chilling wind bite through his coat. The snow stung his face, numbing the skin. The sound of Blitz's hooves were muffled on the road as he raced towards the Haug farm. How can Mama be so blind? He had it in his mind to bring Doktor Gessler instead, but he knew he would answer to her quick temper. He could never willingly defy her.

Rounding the bend in the road, Jakob spotted the farm and slowed his horse to a trot. He rode through the opening in the small hedge that grew along the front of the house. Blitz stopped just outside the door of the house, snorting and stomping his hooves. The humble dwelling was dark, except for a single candle in the front room.

He dismounted, and gave the door three hard raps. This house immediately dredged up cold, unnerving emotions. He hadn't seen nor spoken to Frau Haug since his wife and son had died. He shivered.

As he held his cloak closer, the wind howled around the corner of the drafty-looking shack she called home. If she doesn't hurry and answer this door, it will be too dangerous to travel, he cursed. He blew into his hands to keep them warm. Just as Jakob raised his hand to pound again, the door opened a crack. "Who's there?" said the cautious voice.

"Mama's pains have started and she's asked for you."

The door creaked open wider, to reveal what looked liked Frau Haug's face. A hand held up a lantern to get a better look at her intruder. The light on her face contorted her features, but he could not mistake her. Her face had aged abnormally in the one year since he had seen her. Her brown hair, which was now almost white, framed a face etched with jagged lines.

"Are you sure you want to be seen with the likes of me?" she grunted.

"Trust me, this wasn't my idea, and what I think is not important here. Mama has asked for you, so I intend to see you safely to our farm," he said sharply.

The door closed, and after what felt like a tedious long time, Frau Haug finally reappeared wearing a tattered black coat and carrying an equally frazzled-looking bag. As much hatred as Jakob had towards this old woman, he couldn't help but feel pity at the same time. He hitched his horse to her wagon, which she kept in an old shed, helped her onto the bench, and they were on their way in cold silence.

****

Anna lay on the bed writhing in pain, worried that Rosina wouldn't arrive soon enough. Great relief would follow when she did come. Elisabeth sat on the bed holding her mother's sweaty hand. The cool cloth her daughter was applying felt so soothing in the stuffy room. The window was shut, as fresh air would be harmful to a newborn. Anna listened for Rosina but could only hear the wood crackling in the hearth. Suddenly, another pain took hold of her and she gripped her daughter's hand.

There was something different about this labour, something terribly wrong. Through her anxious thoughts, Anna breathed a sigh of relief to hear Rosina's voice. Now she was sure everything would be fine. She closed her eyes and forced herself to relax. Elisabeth stood to open the door and motioned for the midwife to enter.

Rosina confidently strolled in and placed her bag down on the floor at the foot of the bed. "How's your mama, Elisabeth?" she whispered.

"Not good. She's in a lot more pain this time."

"Do not worry, little one," she said, cupping Elisabeth's chin with her thin hand. Rosina sat down on the small stool close to Anna's head.

Slowly, Anna opened her eyes. "Oh, Rosina."

"Shhh, Anna, concentrate on having this baby."

Anna gripped Rosina's hand, pressing her fingernails into her palms until she thought a trickle of blood would ooze from the pressure. Within moments of her contraction, Anna felt a warm sensation between her legs. Water gushed from her, soaking the sheets and straw beneath her.

"My water," Anna said.

Rosina threw back the blankets and examined her. "Elisabeth. Soak some cloths with warm water and bring them to me now."

Rosina said it with such urgency in her voice that Elisabeth practically ran from the room. She closed the door behind her and quickly grabbed two clean cloths of linen that were laying on the large wooden chest. Her papa was pacing back and forth. A grin crossed her lips as she thought of how Papa had done this through seven children. Elisabeth had one other older brother who had died about ten years before, one sister who died ten days after she was born, and now Margie, who they just buried that afternoon. Elisabeth's grin slowly turned downward as she thought of her mama in the next room.

At the hearth, she picked up an iron hook and grabbed the swinging crane from which a large black pot hung over the fire. Soon after coming home, she had readied the fire to ensure that there was plenty of hot water for the midwife. The crane was a new invention that was attached to the inside of the hearth and could be swung away from the fire to avoid scorching your face or getting smoke in your eyes. What will they think of next, Mama had said. Carefully, she dipped the iron ladle into the steaming water and scooped it into a large bowl. She added a small amount of cool water so the cloths could be hand held. As she immersed the linen, her papa startled her by creeping up beside her.

"How is she?" Elisabeth had never seen him so troubled. The

lines in his forehead were deeply furrowed. His eyes were heavy. She was never really close to her papa. It was impossible for her to comfort him. For Margie, it would have been easy. She was nearest to his heart. But even so, Elisabeth couldn't help but reach for his hand, giving it a gentle squeeze to reassure him.

Papa sat down but was quickly up again and back to the routine of pacing. I guess that is what he does best in times like this, Elisabeth mused. She quietly strode back into the room, handing over the linens to Rosina, steam rising off them. Rosina lifted Anna's gown, and laid the hot fabric on her swollen stomach.

"Your mother's not fully dilated for the baby to come out. The warm cloth will help widen the birth canal." Rosina reached down and brought out a small bottle.

"What's that?"

"It will help widen the cervix and speed up the delivery." Ergot, widely used by the midwives in Hohctorf, is derived from the fungus that grows on rye stalks. "This is most powerful, Elisabeth. This small amount," Rosina held up a pinch between her two bony forefingers, "can give life and also extinguish it."

Elisabeth shuddered and watched with amazement as Rosina sprinkled the pinch of ergot into a cup of water.

Anna groaned in pain. "There's something wrong. I can feel it."

Rosina carefully lifted her head onto her arm and held the cup to her lips. "Drink this! It will quicken the delivery."

Anna allowed the liquid to seep between her lips. She abruptly pushed it away, spilling some of its contents and almost knocking the cup out of Rosina's hand.

"Drink it. It is for your own good, and the babe's."

Elisabeth pressed a cloth to her mama's hot brow. Anna stared up at her daughter, who gave her a reassuring nod. Rosina cradled her head once again, pressing the cup to her lips. This time, Anna swallowed two small gulps with an equal amount dribbling down the side of her mouth. Again, she pushed it away. Elisabeth looked anxiously at Rosina.

"Not to fret, I think she had enough to help."

Anna stiffened as another wave of pain overtook her whole being. She cried out in agony as she thrashed about. This one lasted what seemed like an eternity. When it finally diminished, she lay exhausted as more beads of perspiration broke out on her forehead and face. Elisabeth gently wiped her dry.

****

Long hours had passed since bringing Anna home. Earlier, Jakob had taken Christian and Hanna to the Beck farm a mile up the road and soon returned to be with his father. His thoughts kept going back to his now departed wife and infant son. He was reliving the horrors all over again. Jakob prayed there would be no difficulty in his mother giving birth.

His father sat silently staring at the latch on the door. Finally, it creaked ajar. He was on his feet immediately, a wide smile disappearing as quickly as it came.

His daughter shook her head. "Papa, the birth is so difficult. Mama's losing her strength."

Suddenly, before she could stop him, Jakob burst into their parents' bedroom, startling Rosina. He was repulsed by what he saw. The baby was obviously not positioned correctly for the birth, and one small red hand was protruding. The midwife was standing over his mother reciting, "Lazurus, come forth, the Saviour calls thee."

"How dare you intrude! Get out!" Rosina screamed. Michael rushed in past Elisabeth to survey the horrible scene.

"You've killed my wife, you'll not take Mama too!" Jakob

shouted.

"Enough!" Michael yelled. "Leave this room at once!"

"She's a witch, I tell you! A witch! I came upon her reciting incantations. Look what she's done to your babe." Jakob's voice quivered, his eyes brimming with tears. Michael followed his son's accusing finger to behold a sight that so repulsed him he could only avert his eyes.

Elisabeth stood frozen with her feet rooted to the floor, too stunned to move. Jakob brushed past her and donned his cloak.

"I don't give a tinker's damn what Mama wants now. I'm getting Doktor Gessler."

No one moved to stop him as he rushed out the door.

****

It seemed an eternity since Jakob had left. Elisabeth sat with Anna, holding her hand and stroking her now wet hair as it lay limp over the pillow. Anna couldn't speak. Her eyes were slits. Even through more contractions, the baby was dormant. The labour seemed futile.

Elisabeth glanced up when she heard raised voices outside the door. An unfamiliar male voice was speaking roughly to Rosina. It was dark out, so Rosina needed to be escorted home, but she now preferred to wait until daylight.

Doktor Gessler made his way through the door, shutting it behind him and leaving Rosina on the other side. Even though he was a man, Elisabeth felt somewhat comforted by the fact that he was there. Male midwives were a new concept in the village, and as narrow-minded as her neighbours were, it was difficult to gain their confidence. Witnessing Rosina's skills, she now was willing to put her full trust in him.

Doktor Gessler put his bag down and knelt at the bottom of the bed. He lifted the coverlet to reveal the devastating results. Male midwives usually worked with arms and hands under the covers, keeping their eyes averted to respect the mother's modesty. But Anna was in no condition to care.

"Elisabeth, hold your mama," he asserted. "This will be painful for her."

Anna was having another contraction. "She's fully dilated," he said. Anna soon relaxed and Doktor Gessler inserted his hand to turn the baby so the crown of the head was in perfect alignment. Anna's cry was such a piercing scream that it brought Michael racing into the room.

"Michael, get over there and hold her still!"

As Doktor Gessler moved the infant, he said, "I feel another contraction coming on!" Quickly but gently, he removed his hand. "Anna. Push!" The crown of the baby started to emerge. "Push again, Anna!"

She was too weak. Her breathing was an effort for her. He raised himself off his knees and reached for a large set of tongs in his leather bag.

Michael had never seen anything like it before. They were about eleven inches long, made of a metallic substance covered with leather. He grabbed the doctor's wrist.

"What are you doing? Get away!" Doktor Gessler jerked at Michael's tight grip. "Your wife's much too weak to deliver. She needs help to bring the baby into this world quickly."

"Not on your life! You'll not touch her with that!"

"Let go of me," he hissed. "I haven't got time to stand here and argue. Your wife will die if I don't do this now!"

Michael stared at Anna, so feeble and in obvious agony, barely hearing her mouth his name through her parched lips. He released his hand.

Delicately, the doctor inserted a blade on either side of the infant's head. Another contraction came, one more, then yet another, and gently he brought the baby forth. After he cut the cord, he handed the newborn to Elisabeth, who washed him. The infant had a lusty cry in him.

"He's no worse for wear, Elisabeth," Doktor Gessler said. "He has a healthy set of lungs there." He smiled.

Elisabeth wrapped the infant in a warm woollen blanket and laid him beside his mama. Anna, as weak as she was, still managed to break out into a warm smile. Looking up at her husband, her eyes gently closed.

CHAPTER 2

The day dawned bright and crisp. Michael opened the shutter a crack, catching a breath of fresh air as he rubbed his hands briskly. There was no wind, just a tiny wisp of air that could barely move a leaf. There was a thin layer of frost on the window ledge, and a puff of white bellowed from his nostrils as he exhaled. "What a beautiful morning," he murmured.

He quietly closed the shutter and attempted to sneak across the creaky wooden floor. He didn't wish to wake the *doktor* who lay asleep by the hearth. The last pieces of wood smouldered red hot. He stoked it with a poker, then, added a few more logs. It had been too late for Doktor Gessler to return home, so Michael had offered him a cot for the night. This was for the best anyway; he had preferred to stay and monitor Anna.

Rosina had stayed also, sleeping upstairs in Elisabeth's room. Things will be tense when the two of them meet again this morning, Michael mused. The sooner one of them leaves the better. He tiptoed over to the closed door where Anna slept. He hadn't wanted to disturb her, so he slept the last few hours this morning on the bare floor by the fire with only a thin blanket to cover him. Turning the cold handle, he peered in to where his wife was still sleeping peacefully on her side. He crept over to the cradle. The smallest babe he had ever seen lay swaddled in a dark woollen blanket with only his face and a small tuft of blonde hair peeping out. His eyes were closed tightly shut and his eyebrows were so faint Michael was sure his son had none. Stefan's nostrils flared a bit as he breathed rapidly through his tiny pug nose. The coverlet moved as he stirred slightly. He tenderly stroked Stefan's tiny red cheek with the tip of his finger. Anna stirred in their bed.

"*Guten morgen*," he whispered, and sat down beside her on the edge of the bed. Anna blinked her eyes to focus and tried to raise her head. He gently pushed her back against the downy pillow.

"*Nein*, Anna, you just lie there and rest today."

Normally she would have strongly protested but not today.

"Hand me our son," she said proudly, "I want to see him." Gingerly scooping up the sleeping infant, Michael laid him beside his wife. The top of his head cradled in her arm.

"Michael," she said. "Don't let Doktor Gessler leave until I've seen him."

"*Nein*, I won't." He snuggled the blanket around Anna to keep her and Stefan warm, then left them alone.

He moved to the table where the heavy bible lay, and sat down. It had belonged to his family for over one hundred years, passed from son to son. Opening the small latch at the side, he bent the worn leather cover back. He thumbed to the third page, which revealed the birth and death of Martin Heber, his grandfather. His father's name was there, his name, and his children. The fourth page was blank. Michael dipped his quill into a tiny bottle of ink and proceeded to write.

"In the year 1750, the 18th of October, Stefan Christoph Heber was born in the morning between two and three o'clock." Joy and pride overwhelmed him. Anna and he had decided on this name, should it be a boy, after her brother. With his head bowed, he dipped again and continued to write. "In the same year, the 16th of October, Margaretha died in the evening between seven and eight o'clock at the age of twelve years, five months. God grant her eternal rest."

Michael carefully laid the quill down and sat in silence.

Staring down at the sacred book, he went over in his mind a favourite verse that his father used to recite to him when he was a small lad. "To everything there is a season, and a time to every purpose under the heaven. A time to be born, and a time to die." He was taught to love but fear God, and in time, learned to accept things when they happened, as His will. But how could he calm this gnawing ache in his heart? How could he accept that God needed Margie more than he needed her? He just couldn't accept it. But for now, there was a new baby that needed protection against anything that might threaten his existence in this cruel world. Today he thanked God for sending him his son, when only yesterday he was overwhelmed with his hate for Him. Life was just too harsh and unforgiving, he frowned.

His eyes moved slightly as he heard rustling from the straw beneath Doktor Gessler. The man stretched and let out a grunt.

"*Guten morgen*," he said, turning to look at his host.

Voices floated down from upstairs. Doktor Gessler looked up. "Is *she* still here?"

"I couldn't very well send her away now, could I? No matter how much you and Jakob wished it. You know it isn't safe on the roads at that late hour with beggars and soldiers about."

He snorted, "*Ja*. But I'm afraid if I set eyes on that witch again, I can't be responsible for my actions."

"That's the second time in less than twenty-four hours Rosina has been called a witch. What proof do you have? You can't accuse her of such a cruel title without some kind of evidence," Michael retorted. Rosina had been a long time friend of the family, more Anna's than anyone else's, but this was a serious accusation.

"In the village, they say Rosina's never appeared before the Council at the Rathaus to take the oath of office, to swear to avoid any superstitious practices."

"*Awch*," Michael waved his hands, "tis just a rumour. You had better be careful of what you speak here."

Doktor Gessler examined Michael's deep-set, icy blue eyes, held prominent against his ruddy complexion. "Are you protecting her?"

Michael ignored the remark.

The *doktor* swung his legs over the side of the cot and pulled on his boots. "She's been seen in the village by the night guard in the wee hours whispering with the beggars. Now, if that's not strange..."

"If the night guard was suspicious, why didn't he arrest her?" Michael interrupted.

"Rosina always gives Jeremias the slip, so he's never caught her. That should tell you something, Michael. Nobody escapes that feisty old night guard."

"You're just speculating. You can't expect me to condemn someone on this kind of evidence."

"Then, what about the incantation? If that doesn't tell you her true character, what more proof do you want?"

Michael was about to reply, when Elisabeth and Rosina stepped down from the bottom step of the staircase. He didn't know how much of the conversation was overheard, but by the look on their faces, it was evident they heard enough. Michael asked Rosina if she would like to breakfast with them before Jakob took her home.

"*Nein,*" she answered. "Under the circumstances, it is best that I depart immediately." She eyed Michael with hurt in her eyes. Turning to the *doktor*, she glared at him with contempt, but only succeeded in looking like a frightened rabbit.

He averted his eyes from the midwife. The silence now was awkward, but Michael broke it.

"Then it will only be a few minutes. I heard Jakob hitching the horse to the wagon."

Leering once more at Frau Haug, Doktor Gessler turned quickly to go into Anna's room to check on her. Jakob walked in, then escorted Frau Haug outside without a word spoken.

Elisabeth stood closer to her father. "Why would Doktor Gessler call her a witch?" she asked. "I've heard of women in Goppingen who were accused of practising witchcraft, and they were burned at the stake."

"Let's not speak of such things," he said, as the *doktor* returned. "Come now. Prepare us some food, for I'm famished."

Elisabeth hurriedly prepared breakfast.

"Your wife is going to be just fine, Michael. I want her resting for the next few days though."

"You don't know my Anna. She'll be up today if she can. I don't think we can keep her down too long." Doktor Gessler smiled in agreement.

"Please stay with us and have some nourishment before moving on."

"*Danke*. And call me Georg."

****

The crude rectangular table must have been used for a couple of generations, he thought, as he sat down to a surface full of deep pits and scratches. Georg Gessler was famished and eagerly tore into the dark rye bread after the cheese was passed around. Elisabeth set a large, steaming tureen of thick cornmeal porridge in the centre of the table. His mouth watered as he scooped a few ladles into his bowl.

"Georg," Michael said, passing some more cheese, "your method last night with Anna and the babe, I've never heard of such things.

Where did you learn this?"

Georg took the food from his host's hands, which were noticeably calloused. "I've recently studied in Strassbourg."

"Oh," Elisabeth interrupted, "what's it like in Strassbourg?" Michael gave her a sharp look, but she continued speaking. "I've never been outside of Hohctorf. Jakob has been to nearby Goppingen. Are the buildings higher? Are there lots of people?"

Seeing Michael's embarrassment, Georg put his mind at ease. "I don't mind at all telling her anything she wants to know." He gazed at Elisabeth and beheld an amazing wonderment in her sparkling green eyes, not like anything he had seen in other girls. Refreshing, came to his mind. No, he thought, invigorating. She had the most beautiful blonde hair that flowed in waves over her shoulders. Georg couldn't help but grin.

"Is it true that there are women and men so rich that they buy their own clothes ready made?" she queried. Michael shot her another sidelong glance.

"*Bitte.* It's okay, Michael. Really. There are people who have their own tailors to make their clothes for them, and when it rains, there are some that carry an umbrella."

"An um...what?" she sputtered, getting her tongue twisted.

"An umbrella, Elisabeth. A device that fans out and you carry it over your head to keep yourself dry. You might also see sedan chairs, where a covered chair is set on two very long pieces of wood, carried by two men, one in the front and one in the back. In Frankfort..."

"You've been to Frankfort?" Elisabeth blurted. Her face turned crimson. Georg smiled.

"Now, Elisabeth, that's enough. Give him time to finish his food."

"But, Papa..."

"Truly, Michael, it's all right." He put his hand up to stop the protesting. "When you first visit Frankfort, you would be overwhelmed by this enormous wall from which turrets arise. This surrounds the whole town, and one enters through a very large gate that was built hundreds of years ago to defend the town. The great bridge over the Main was my favourite place for walking, with a beautiful stream meandering above and below the bridge. It always filled me with delight to see the gilt cock on the old cross over the bridge glitter in the sunshine. On the other side of the river I would love to watch the arrival of the market boats, with their colourful and varied cargoes. Following along the inside of the city walls, I could catch a glimpse of the lovely gardens and courtyards of the rich." Georg gave a slight sigh, realizing he felt a little homesick now. He stared at Elisabeth and noticed how enthralled she was with her chin cupped in the palm of her hand, hanging on to his every word.

"You speak of Frankfort like you would an old friend," Michael said.

"I must apologize for rambling on like this. I must be boring you. I was born in Frankfort, and you are right, I miss it like you would a long lost friend."

"What brought you to Hohctorf?" Michael asked. "It is such a small village. Wouldn't your skills bring you a much higher pay in Frankfort?"

Lowering his eyes, Georg spoke in a voice so low it was barely audible. "My wife and two *kinder* were taken away from me. There was a dreadful epidemic of smallpox two years ago."

"I'm so sorry," Michael replied. "I certainly didn't mean to upset you."

"I wanted to go someplace where there were no memories. For a few months, I lived in Goppingen with my *onkel*. Then I came here when I heard Hohctorf was in need of a *doktor*."

Michael thought it strange a man of his credentials would settle in such a small village, but he didn't want to pry further. There was a bit of an awkward lull, when suddenly the door flew open with a bang. A litany of colourful oaths spewed from Jakob's mouth.

"Jakob!" Michael said sternly, trying to hold his own temper. It had been difficult having his son move back a couple of weeks ago after Jakob's small farm had burned to the ground. His eldest was difficult to tame again. "In my house, young man, you'll curb that manner. I presume Rosina is safely home?"

Jakob sloppily scooped up a few spoonfuls of porridge. "I just heard...I cannot believe that Prince Eugen is visiting Goppingen again! He's encouraging everyone to air their grievances; as if that is going to do us any good."

"It will! It must!" Michael added, suddenly forgetting his son's outburst and focussing on the Prince.

"Well, I have a few grievances I know he's going to hear," Georg said. "The rumblings amongst our people are loud and will continue to be so until something is done. The taxes are too heavy a burden and most of us can't pay."

"The nobility, or *gentleman,* as they prefer to be called," Jakob stated, "have no obligation to pay taxes, and they're exempt from entering the military service. We're forced to enter when need be." Jakob's voice had started to rise.

Georg nodded. "That inexperienced juvenile knows nothing of running the states. He was much too young to fill his *fater's* shoes at sixteen, and here he is six years later and things are getting worse. Because of his elaborate extravagances, we must dig deeper and deeper into our already empty pockets."

Michael grunted and tapped the table with his index finger. "I've heard that Eugen's tastes have leaked over into France. So much so, he employs a full-time consultant in Paris whose sole responsibility is to supply him with all the new French publications, court circulars, and manuals of architecture."

"His most recent project is to build a palace in Stuttgart," Jakob added. "And you know how he'll get the money! That's probably the real reason for his visit next week. He wants to hear our grievances? Well, he'll hear us!" Jakob's fist came crashing down on the table with a loud thud, making Elisabeth jump. The veins on his neck stood out.

Elisabeth promptly stood up from the table to clear the dishes. Georg continued the conversation.

"I barely have enough to pay my rent to the landlord. They can't get any more from me."

"If you won't pay, Georg, they'll find ways to get it from you," Michael said. "I must give two thirds of the crop I harvest to the lord. The crops are exported, and I'm sure the money he gets is spent on luxurious goods for his house and family. We don't see a single *kreuzer*."

"I heard there's been an ordinance posted in the village asking all the farmers to pull down their fences and hedges again so as not to impede the chase in the hunt next weekend when Prince Eugen and council arrive," Georg remarked.

"This is absurd, Papa! Why should we stand for this? We should be doing something about it, not sitting on our asses while they manipulate us like puppets!" Jakob's voice was rising again.

"Son, we're too powerless to resist. What can a handful of poor farmers do?"

"I agree with Jakob," Georg interjected. "We are barely existing; a dog has a better life than we do. At least a dog has the freedom to do as he likes. One voice is but a drop in the pond; however, the whole village will make the sound we want. I know our neighbours Herr Weber, Schultz, and Beck are on our side."

"No gain can be made by an angry mob," Michael answered,

raising an eyebrow.

“But Papa, we cannot go on like this.”

Crashing his hands heavily on the table, Michael rose, toppling his chair onto the floor. “You’ll not get involved, Jakob Heber!” he shook his fist in his son’s face.

Michael had never been so angry. He was usually even-tempered and calm, never really getting upset about anything.

“I’ll not bury another child of mine.” He was breathing heavily. “Do you hear me!”

Jakob didn’t move. Elisabeth stood frozen, watching.

“I said, Jakob,” his voice increasing in tone and determination. “Do...you...hear...me?”

Georg slowly moved in closer beside Michael. “Calm down, Michael. It’s okay. The subject’s closed. We won’t talk about it anymore.” Michael turned around, away from his son so as not to hit him.

CHAPTER 3

What is all that racket outside, Elisabeth muttered to herself, as she finished braiding her hair into one long plait. It sounded like arguing, but she couldn't make out what it was all about. She thought she had heard a wagon roll up, then the sound of small feet running up the path. Doktor Gessler had just left a few moments ago after a heated discussion with her papa. He had refused to receive any payment for delivering her brother. Jakob and Papa were now in the stable tending to the few cows and pigs they owned. Peering out the upstairs shutters of her small bedroom, she saw Hanna running ahead, her black hair in complete disarray. She laughed as Christian chased after her, yelling at the top of his lungs to stop.

What a noise to be making so early in the morning. But it was good to have the two young ones home again. The house felt empty without her brother and sister. "Keep it down, you two!" Elisabeth whispered aloud.

Christian and Hanna fell through the front door with a crash that could've woken the dead.

With the ruckus of her younger siblings, Elisabeth almost didn't notice that it was Peter Beck who had brought them home. When she laid eyes on him, her heart started to race and she felt an unusual feeling in the pit of her stomach. Elisabeth could never determine if this was good or bad. All she knew was that she didn't feel complete without him and ached to be always near him. Although they had been friends most of their lives, somewhere along the way her feelings started to change towards him. Everyday, this new-found emotion was getting stronger, and she didn't know if the same love, if indeed she dare call it that, would be reciprocated. At times she felt Peter noticed her with the same wonderful sensations as she had, but then other times, it was like nothing had changed.

She had a glimmer of hope once when a couple of weeks ago, in the village, she caught Peter staring at her in a different manner. When she questioned him, he just ignored her and walked away. Men! She thought. She couldn't figure them out. It was all a game, neither knowing what the other was thinking. She hated it!

"*Guten morgen*," Peter called up to her with a smile.

"Hello, Peter," she answered coolly. Even though Peter was tall and lanky, he always looked dashing in his black knee-breeches and colourful woollen stockings that his mama had embroidered.

Elisabeth then popped her head back in, closed the shutters, and tried not to run downstairs and appear too anxious. She wanted to be absolutely sure what he felt before she announced her love. Even if she had wanted to rush, Elisabeth would've been stopped by her siblings clamouring up the narrow steps, almost knocking her over.

"Beth," Hanna called her sister, as she never could pronounce her full name properly, "Christian says we have another sister."

"I did not!" Christian chimed in. "I said Mama had a baby. I don't know if it's a brother or a sister, silly. And if it's one like you, I hope it's a boy. Two sisters are plenty," and he pinched Hanna's arm, sending her squealing to the bottom of the stairs again.

"Ssshh, you two," Elisabeth whispered as loud as she could. "We now have a baby brother. If you behave properly, I'll take you to see him before you go off to school today." Elisabeth grabbed hold of Hanna's hand before she could scamper off noisily into Mama's room.

"Elisabeth," Peter piped up, "I'm on my way to the village now.

I can drop them off on the way."

"That's fine, Peter. Do you mind if I come along? Mama has asked me to buy some salt at the market today." Hanna tugged her hand hard, grasping her chubby hands around her sister's fingers. "I won't be long."

"*Ja*, that would be just fine," he said.

"Wait here a minute." Elisabeth followed her brother and sister into the bedroom.

Inside, Anna was lying back on the pillows nursing Stefan. Hanna broke loose from Elisabeth's grip and ran to her mama. She put her arms on the side of the bed and leaned into where the baby suckled. Putting her right arm over her youngest daughter, Anna motioned Christian to come closer. "What do you think of your new brother?"

"He's awfully small," Hanna said, crinkling her small nose.

"He'll grow soon enough," Anna answered softly.

Christian smiled down at the baby.

"Where did he come from?" Hanna asked.

Elisabeth gave a sidelong glance at Christian, who suddenly looked uncomfortable. He was shifting his feet from side to side, staring at the floor, and his cheeks were now pinker than when he first entered the room.

Anna patted the quilt, inviting Hanna to crawl up beside her. "Hanna," she started, "do you remember a long time ago, Papa put a wagon wheel way up on the roof of the barn?"

"I 'member. Papa fell down into a big haystack." She chuckled, putting her tiny hand over her mouth to stifle her laughter.

Anna smiled. "*Ja,* Hanna. Do you remember what it was for?" Hanna shook her head, frowning.

"Well, Papa put that wheel up there so a stork could build a nest, and when the time was right, the stork brought Stefan to us." Anna explained, nuzzling Hanna a little closer to her side.

Hanna's eyes were wide. "But why a stork?"

"A stork brings good fortune to the family. A Mama stork loves her children and her parents very much, and she takes good care of them if they are sick. There's a legend that they show great tenderness towards the blind and old people, carrying them around on their wings and feeding them."

"Come now, Hanna, time to get ready for school," Elisabeth interrupted. "Mama needs her rest."

"But why can't she get up?"

"You ask too many questions, my little *liebling*," Anna said, embracing her closer still. "The stork bit my leg and I have to stay in bed till it's better." She said winking at Elisabeth.

Hanna's mouth opened as wide as it could. "But why, Mama? Can I see?"

Grabbing her sister's hand, Elisabeth grinned. "Okay, that's enough questions. Time to get ready, or you and Christian will be late for school. Quick! Run outside. Peter's waiting. I'll be along shortly."

"I don't like that old bird. He's too mean and I'm telling God tonight," Hanna said. Then she stopped in her tracks. "Anyway, why do I have to go to school? You don't go, Beth. And I heard Papa say Christian soon won't have to go either."

"We've been through this before, Hanna. You know Papa will be fined if you don't go. It's the law and you only have to go till you're fourteen." Anna sighed. "And besides, you like Herr Unger." This teacher was very kind, which was unusual. Teachers were often very cruel.

"Scoot!" Elisabeth patted her sister's behind, and out she ran after Christian. It was a strange closeness between the two of them, Elisabeth mused, considering there was nine years between them.

Wherever Christian could be found, Hanna wasn't far behind. Christian loved being doted on by someone so young. He returned Hanna's love tenfold by looking out for her.

Elisabeth turned back into the room. "Mama, I'll be going into the village to buy that pound of salt you wanted. Jakob and Papa are in the barn. Will you be okay?"

"Don't fuss over me so, Elisabeth Maria Heber," she snapped. "I'll be up and around this afternoon. Sooner if need be."

"In your condition, Mama, I'm sure Pastor Krumer would be more than happy to do the baptism here."

"Not on your life, young lady. I'll not have anyone seeing that happen. Why, you know Catharina would have a fit if she saw the pastor here instead of at the church. The perfect gossip she is, that one."

It's no use even trying to reason with her when she gets like this, Elisabeth thought. She just nodded and smiled.

"Open the chest and bring me the leather pouch. I believe it's down at the bottom, in the right hand corner," Anna laboured to pull herself up on her elbow.

Elisabeth did as she was told, kneeling down and lifting the heavy lid of the wooden chest. A musty smell escaped. This was the first time she had been allowed in there. On top was a quilt Mama had made to give to her when she eventually married. Many hours were painstakingly sewed into each patch.

She carefully lifted the edge of the heavy cloth and put her hand right to the bottom, pushing her way through the numerous linens. The light was poor so she could only feel her way until she found the pouch. She gave it to her mama and then picked up Stefan, who was now fast asleep, and laid him in his cradle.

Anna shoved one finger into the centre of the drawstring and pulled it apart. She turned it upside down and a few coins fell out onto the bed. Of the ten coins, Anna counted out three *kreuzers a*nd handed them over to her daughter.

"This will pay for the salt. And get to the village early," Anna demanded. "Herr Schultz arrived from Goppingen on Saturday to sell at the market today. It'll be crowded."

"I'll leave this very minute. Peter offered to drop Christian and Hanna at Herr Unger's house for school, so I'll go with him to the village."

"That's fine." Anna closed her eyes and murmured something that was completely inaudible to Elisabeth's ears. Leaning over and lightly touching her lips to her forehead, Elisabeth took the pouch from her hands and put it back in the chest.

"*Adieu* Mama," she whispered, and softly shut the door behind her.

****

The ten minutes it took to drive to Herr Unger's house seemed like an eternity to Elisabeth, especially over the rough road. And Peter seemed extra quiet, which made the ride seem that much longer. She glanced at him out of the corner of her eye. He stared straight ahead and hadn't said two words to her since they had left the house. Sometimes she felt like yelling at him to let him know she existed. She tucked the wool blanket around her hips, when a magpie flew right in front of them. It almost touched the tips of the horse's ears, which flicked at the sound of the bird's wings. The bird settled in a nearby oak tree on the side of the road.

"Oh, Peter, what a beautiful bird," she exclaimed. "Isn't he handsome with his lovely long black and white tail?"

"*Awch*, you're crazy. They're nothing but scavengers," Peter answered.

"Well, you do have a tongue in that head of yours."

"What do you mean by that, girl?"

"You're very quiet this fine morning. Do you have something on your mind?" Maybe it's me he's thinking of, she dreamed, or maybe that was too much to hope.

"*Nichts*, Elisabeth."

"Come now, we've known each other since we were children. Don't you think I've come to know you by now? I know when something is bothering you. Give over, Peter." Maybe he wants to talk about us; if there is an us, she thought. She leaned into Peter's ear and whispered, "Hanna and Christian cannot hear us; they're sitting at the back of the wagon."

"I'm not worried about their ears listening in..." he paused.

"*Ja*, Peter." Elisabeth's voice had a kind of lilt to it, and she laid her hand over his, feeling the strength of his hand as he steered the horse with the leather reins. Elisabeth felt bold with this first move.

"Elisabeth, what in God's name are you doing? Your sister and brother will see."

She quickly removed her hand. "Peter, I've had enough of this. Are you to tell me what's wrong or not?" She didn't raise her voice but talked firmly, though what she really wanted to do was scream at him.

"I'm moving with my family to the New World," Peter blurted out.

Elisabeth thought she had heard wrong and asked him to repeat it. Hearing it a second time didn't make it any more real or believable. She sat there, unable to move or speak. Peter gave the rein a hard tug and resounded a sharp, "Whoa!" They had arrived in front of Herr Unger's house. Peter jumped down from the wagon and lifted Hanna to the ground. She ran to the house after her brother. "*Adieu*, Beth," she shouted, but Elisabeth kept staring straight ahead, oblivious to what was going on around her. Her world seemed to have crashed in on her. It can't be true, she reflected.

The wagon lurched forward towards the village. Peter looked over at Elisabeth. "Are you okay?"

"How can I be after what you just told me?" Elisabeth had so many questions that needed answering, she didn't know where to start. "How...why...when," she stammered.

"Have you not heard the talk in the village? There's an agent named Herr Kohler who's been recruiting people to emigrate to the New World. I overheard Papa say that there's many more opportunities in this new land than we could ever dream about here in Hohctorf."

Elisabeth had heard Jakob and Papa speak of such a land, but she had never paid much attention to it. It didn't affect her private little world. But she was wrong, terribly wrong. Her dreams of being with Peter had just burst like a fragile bubble. How could he do this to her? Is he so dense he cannot see how she feels towards him? How could he leave her? The anger in Elisabeth was welling up to a point where she didn't know if she could control it.

"When will you be leaving?"

"In about four months."

Elisabeth's heart sank even lower.

****

As Peter and Elisabeth arrived in the village, they noticed a bustle of activity in the centre of the square. They stopped near the first stall where the salt was sold. The stall was just the beginning of a string of about seven booths selling everything from linen to vegetables to wine.

Peter helped Elisabeth down from her seat. She didn't know

what else to say to him, and the longer the silence, the harder it was to find the words.

"I've business here, too. I'll meet you back here in about an hour."

She couldn't look at him. She nodded, managing to let a weak "*Ja*," escape her lips. She turned in the direction of Herr Schultz's salt stall.

There was a crowd around the booth, and all the women were pressing hard against each other trying to jostle to the front of the line. The pushing and shoving moved Elisabeth right beside Frau Catharina Spillman, the last person she wanted to see. Besides being a very coarse woman she was always sticking her long nose into everyone else's business. But one had to admit that besides being the biggest gossip in the village, she had a heart of gold. Even Elisabeth couldn't help but like her a little. But today was not the day she felt like speaking to anyone.

Frau Spillman wrapped her large arm around Elisabeth to protect her from the crowd. She continued to elbow her way to the front where Herr Schultz stood. One woman screamed, "Get back to the end of the line," only to be met by Catharina's, "Shut up!" Elisabeth was so embarrassed.

"*Guten morgen*, Herr Schultz!" Frau Spillman thundered, trying to raise her voice above the shouts of the women she cut in front of.

"*Guten morgen,*" he answered. "And since when are you so formal? You always call me Schutze."

"I'll reserve my judgement for after I hear the price of your salt."

Schutze gave a toothy leer. "How much salt are you buying today?" The crowd's voices lowered to rude mutterings; they were well aware of who they were up against.

"Three pounds." She turned to Elisabeth. "How much for you, my little *liebling*?"

"Just one pound," she replied.

"For three pounds, fifteen *kreuzers*; and one pound, five *kreuzers*."

"You're a crook, Schutze!" someone shouted from the back.

"That's highway robbery. It shouldn't be allowed!" cried another.

"We'll not pay those high prices," echoed Catharina, as she shook her fist in Schutze's unshaven face.

"What do you want me to do about it? I have to make money too. I bought this two days ago in Goppingen at four *kreuzers* a pound." Schutze stood his ground and eyed Catharina. With her glaring back at him, her face beet red, Elisabeth thought she would do the unthinkable and hit him.

"Buy it or leave. I'm not lowering my prices for you or anyone else here." He eyed the angry crowd. "There's plenty of other villages who'll buy." Catharina and Elisabeth had no choice. They needed the salt, like the rest.

"I only have nine *kreuzers*. Will you give me two pounds," she bargained.

"I said my price was final." He spoke so the crowd would hear him. Schutze turned to Elisabeth, "And you? How much do you have?"

Elisabeth answered that she only had three *kreuzers*. Even though the air was cool, Elisabeth was feeling almost faint by the closeness, and she was sure her face was flushed. It looked to her that Schutze was about to back down.

"I have to live too, Catharina. I have a family to support. I'm sorry." He handed a cloth sack with a pound and a half for Catharina and a half a pound for Elisabeth.

Elisabeth counted out the coins as Catharina threw hers. One rolled off onto the dirt.

"Good day, Herr Schultz," Catharina said as she pushed her way to the back of the crowd. Elisabeth did her best to follow her through the angry cries of the now larger mob: the commotion attracted the rest of the bystanders.

Once in the clearing, Catharina continued to amble, mumbling under her breath. "I'm going to report this to the village Council!"

When Elisabeth didn't answer, she continued. "Are you all right, my child? Was the crowd too much? You do look a little pale. Are you sure you're all right? Come here, sit down and you'll feel better." Not waiting for any answers, she steered Elisabeth towards a small round stone wall that stood in the centre of the market square.

As Elisabeth sat down, Catharina settled down beside her and continued to ramble on about the price of this and that, how even the price of linen has gone up, then leaping to another topic of how pigs shouldn't be allowed to roam freely in the village, with the God-awful smell of their dung heaps strewn all over the road. Elisabeth subconsciously turned a deaf ear at this point, concentrating hard not to faint. Catharina still rambled on as she ambled her way to the well, then let the bucket drop to the bottom, echoing a splat when it hit the water. With Catharina's strong arms it only took two or three yanks to pull the bucket back up. She dipped the ladle into the water and hurried over to Elisabeth's side, spilling some along the way. It felt so nice and cool to her lips as she let the water trickle down her throat.

"Are you feeling better now?"

"*Ja*. A little, *danke*."

"You've been through a lot, you and your family. That's why you're not up to the crowds today. I'm so sorry to hear about Margaretha. How's your mama doing, Elisabeth? With all the stress and strain of Margaretha's illness, I'm surprised the babe hasn't come already."

The village gossip that you are, I'm surprised you didn't know already, Elisabeth wanted to say, but restrained herself. She smiled. "The babe has come. A boy. Early this morning, he was born."

"Ah, I told you so. Well, I'm not surprised. I suppose the babe will be baptized today. And what name will your mama give him?" Before Elisabeth had a chance to answer, Catharina raised her large knobby hand. "*Nein*, *nein*, don't tell me. It's bad luck to announce the name before he be baptised, you know." She then engulfed Elisabeth's hand and stroked it gently.

Lifting her head, Catharina's eyes danced when she saw Peter coming towards them. Her laugh lines around her eyes were accentuated by her wide smile. "Now there, Elisabeth," she patted her hand again, "there's a fine young lad for you. Get yourself with him, settle down, and have a litter of *kinder*, why don't you? I remember when I met my Leonard, God rest his old soul."

Peter trotted over to where the two women were sitting and announced that he had finished his business earlier than he expected, and if Elisabeth was ready he would take her home now. Elisabeth quickly agreed. They bade their farewells to Frau Spillman and strolled toward the wagon.

"*Awch*, Peter, you came none too soon. My head ached with her prattling on so. Thanks for rescuing me."

Peter grinned knowingly and looked down at Elisabeth's hands. "That doesn't look like a pound," he said.

"The prices have gone way up. I could only get a half a pound."

"I'm not surprised, Elisabeth, and things will get worse. Over at the pub, the men there were saying a group from the village is rallying against the prince when he comes this Saturday. They're not taking any more. They've had it up to here with the crock of shit."

"Peter Beck!" Elisabeth shouted, hearing such words.

"Well, Papa's not taking it. That's why he wants his children to have a better life in the new land."

"I don't want to talk about your leaving here, Peter Beck. I won't listen. I just won't!" She had tried to forget what he had told her earlier. She quickly changed the subject. "What business did you have in the village, Peter?"

"*Nichts*. Tis not important," he said, as he helped her back into the wagon.

"It's always nothing with you! You're too secretive. Are you hiding something?"

Peter didn't answer, as they started their journey home.

CHAPTER 4

It was a fine day for the christening, but Anna still felt extremely weak since the birth two days before. Stefan Christoph Heber, she thought. "Tis a grand name for one so small. I know you'll do the name great justice. I feel it," she whispered to her sleeping son.

It was a very long day, and as much as she loved the company, she'd be glad when they had all gone. Anna glanced around the small room in their house. As always the men were grouped around in one corner, while the women mingled amongst themselves near the hearth. Michael stood tall in the centre, still looking handsome, she thought, in his Sunday best. His reddish blonde hair was tied neatly back and stood out as it lay down the back of his short black jacket. The hole she mended that morning on his blue stockings couldn't even be seen where his grey breeches ended below the knee. He handled the steins of beer he had ladled, while Doktor Gessler and Hans Beck joked about who was going to drink Michael dry.

"Maybe it will be our good Pastor Krumer," Jakob quipped, slapping him on the back.

The pastor was not a drinker, rarely finishing one stein, except once when he dipped his ladle into the keg a few times too many six months ago and never lived it down. At Jakob's remark, Anna thought the house was going to shake on its very foundation with the laughter. It was good to see them laugh again, after so much talk of the hated Prince Eugen's upcoming visit in a few days. Anna caught her husband winking at her as he toasted their newborn son, raising his beer stein while the others clinked into his.

"My, my, Anna," Catharina said, leaning into her. "Stefan showed us quite a set of lungs in church today. As soon as the water hit that tiny face of his, he wailed. That shows, Anna, he'll grow to have quite a singing voice. Here, let me take the lad. Give you some rest."

Anna could never say no to her. There was an unbridled kindness under that thick skin of hers. Catharina gathered Stefan into her arms and walked away, talking to him as if he understood.

"Sometimes I think she lives in her own little world."

Anna looked up. It was Maria Beck speaking.

"I'd trust her to look after any of my children," she answered. Maria nodded in agreement.

"Come, Maria, help me finish cutting the bread and meat." Anna grabbed the knife off the table, only to have it whisked away from her.

"Here, Elisabeth and I will do that. Sit and rest."

"Sit and rest, sit and rest," Anna mimicked. "I'm sick and tired of hearing that. If you want to help, fine, but you'll not kick me out of my kitchen."

Maria smiled at Elisabeth, while Anna paced back and forth in front of the fire. Watching nervously as her mother raised her arms in frustration, Elisabeth eyed the *kucheln* on the end of the table that almost toppled onto the floor as Anna whooshed by. Those sweet round cakes were her favourite. There were never enough made for her liking, only on St. Nicholas Day and special occasions. Maria and Hans, Stefan's godparents, had brought the usual *allerseelenspitz*, a beautiful diamond-shaped sponge cake glazed with smooth icing. It lay next to the *kucheln* and almost met the same fate. Suddenly Hanna reached up on her tiptoes, about to stick her chubby little finger into the side of the cake, before Anna shooed her away.

"Maria, you always bake such delicious cakes," Anna said, moving the cake a little closer to the centre of the table so small prying fingers couldn't reach.

"*Danke. Awch*, they're getting expensive to make. We can only afford to be godparents once a year. Making too many of these cakes would put us further in debt." Anna's cheeks blushed. Maria quickly added, "But you know we'd never refuse you and Michael. We're proud to be Stefan's godparents...it's just that..." Maria stumbled.

"It's okay, I understand." Anna gently laid her hand over her friend's. "We're all having trouble making ends meet in these trying times." She and Maria went back together many long years. Having grown up like sisters, there was nothing either of them wouldn't do for each other.

Anna quickly turned to her daughter. "Elisabeth, take Hanna to the chest. Time to light the christening candle." Clapping her hands in two sharp smacks got her children scurrying like mice. Elisabeth opened the elegantly carved box and carefully unwrapped the candle. She handed Hanna the exquisitely-embroidered cloth that covered it.

"For each child that is christened, the candle is lit," Elisabeth explained to her younger sister. "Of course, it was much larger when Jakob was born." She laid the lopsided candle on the table.

"Gather round," Anna announced, clapping her hands again. "Tis time to light the candle."

All the children assembled around the table in front of the adults. Elisabeth lifted Hanna up so she could see better. Michael pulled a long straw from the broom, held it over the fire until a small flame caught, and carefully lit the candle. Catharina handed Stefan over to his mother, while Jakob and Christian moved in behind their sisters.

"May I present the newest addition to the Heber family: Stefan

Christoph. Stefan, chosen for Anna's youngest brother, and Christoph after her *fater*. May God rest his eternal soul." The foamy broth splashed onto the floor as the steins sailed up into the air in unison, followed by a loud cheer.

****

Jakob overheard Hans Beck speak about the New World just as he rounded the corner of the staircase. The house was becoming more crowded as a steady stream of friends from the village stopped by, dipping into the stout keg that stood outside the front door. Jakob didn't know everyone. Tradition allowed all, whether it friend or vagrant, to drink from their hospitality. The women, some standing, others sitting, were gossiping about things that never interested Jakob. The remaining flame left burning in the fireplace had a blueish tinge to it as it flickered and licked the bottom of the blackened iron kettle. He was about to add more wood but became more interested in the bits of Hans' conversation. Forgetting about the task at hand for the moment, he joined the tight circle of men that surrounded his papa's friend. Hans was so ecstatic that he couldn't get the words out fast enough.

"Where is this new land you speak about, Hans?" Jakob interrupted.

"Across the ocean, far to the west of here, a land called Nova Scotia. Here, Jakob...here," Hans replied, unrolling a piece of paper, cracked around the yellowed edges. By the looks of some missing corner pieces, it had been well read...numerous times.

"I'm surprised you didn't see it when you were in Goppingen a few weeks ago. Everyone's talking about it. It was nailed on the front door of the Rathaus."

Jakob held it down by a candle to get a better look at it. He had heard some talk of it but had paid no attention. The words "Public Notice" stood out as he glanced down the page. It read: "Whereas his Majesty's Commissaries of Commerce to the Colonies have already in the last year transported a large number of people into the Province of Nova Scotia in North America, for which purpose they have nominated and appointed Mr. Johann Dick, merchant in Rotterdam, to engage all such German Protestants and others who are anxious to remove and be settlers in the said Province and become subjects of great Britain."

Hans leaned in over his shoulder. "Here, skip that," he interrupted, pointing his stubby finger to the most important part. "Look what they're willing to give."

Jakob's eyes followed to where Hans pointed. He was about to read, when Hans anxiously broke in again. "They'll give each person fifty acres of land free of all rates or taxes whatsoever for ten years."

Everyone's immediate reaction was belligerent and snickering, muttering at Hans' naivety.

Martin Schultz, the salt seller, chimed in, "*Awch*, you don't believe this trash do ya, Hans? No one's about to give away land to just anyone that comes along. You're being stupid." Others nodded in agreement, including Jakob.

"*Nein*, Schutze," Hans started, raising his voice to be heard. "I was there in Goppingen and heard Herr Kohler..."

"Kohler?" Schutze interrupted again. "Who is this? Probably one of Eugen's crooked men behind all this. Up to no good that Catholic is." His voice rose as he shook his head. Schutze's hatred for the prince was evident.

"*Bitte*." Hans said, "Just hear me out."

"Let's listen to what Hans has to say." Michael nodded to his friend to continue once the hodgepodge of gab ceased.

"Herr Kohler's the agent recruiting people to emigrate to this land. He works for Dick." He tapped the paper with the back of his hand. "He says, besides the fifty acres, each person, including wife and children, will receive ten acres. And for the first year, we'd be maintained after our arrival."

Jakob's attention was no longer on the piece of paper he held. "What do you mean 'our'?"

"*Ja*, and why the sudden interest?" Schutze queried.

"I'm taking my family away from here to a better land." He stood up straight and blinked nervously.

Schutze was speechless for the first time in his life. Michael and Jakob glanced at each other in astonishment, then stared back at Hans again. Georg, who was quietly listening to the discussion at hand, finally spoke.

"But, Hans, do you know what you're doing? To leave the *Faterland* where you've been raised? Your *fater* and his *fater* struggled on the very earth you farm. Are you willing to risk leaving everything you know to a land that's probably hostile? Don't rush into this!"

Michael found his voice. "How can you be so sure of all this? What if the land is barren...overrun with savages?"

"You have more than yourself to think about Hans. What about Maria and the children? Consider them," Schutze added. "Things are bad here, but nothing compared to what you might face in Nova Scotia."

Hans shook his head, lips pursed tightly. "I can't believe what I'm hearing from you, Schutze. You of all people I thought would sympathize with me, knowing what we've both been through, w-w-what with the uprisings against the State, the constant hiking of the taxes, n-not to mention your land, Schutze."

Hans was stuttering, as he sometimes did when he was overcome with frustration. "H-how many times have you been ordered to tear down your fences or anything that might impede the chase when Eugen and his men are out on a hunt, ruining what's left of your land? A-and you, M-Michael, didn't you just receive your orders to do this very thing? Well, don't just stand there, a-a-answer me. Michael? Schutze?" Hans glared at Schutze. He took a step towards the man.

It was all true. All stood in silence.

No one wanted to admit defeat by a Catholic ruler on their own land, or to appear weak and unable to fight back. Hans had brought to the surface the rage these men felt towards Eugen. In these anxious days, it didn't take much.

"And after this news, I suppose we can't count on you this Saturday," Schutze hissed. "You don't give a fig now about the *Faterland*, now that you're leaving it. What do you care?"

Hans was about to answer, but Michael stepped in. "That's enough, both of you." Michael then lowered his voice as the women had already taken notice of the commotion. "I've heard enough from you, Schutze, you can stop right there. I'll have nothing to do with this revolt you've been scheming, and I'll hear of no talk of such things in this house."

"Stop protecting him. You're just as bad as Hans, Michael," Schutze mocked. "You'll let Eugen walk all over you."

Jakob couldn't hold his tongue any longer. "You've no right after all Papa's done for you. After your crop failure this year, where would you be if it wasn't for him?"

The others stepped back as Jakob moved closer to Schutze. Jakob's face was so close to Schutze, he could feel his heavy breathing and smell his foul breath through the beer.

"You ungrateful little..." Jakob was clenching and unclenching his fists, contemplating if it was worth hitting this inept excuse of a man.

"That's enough, Jakob." Michael quickly yanked him back.

The women stopped their chattering altogether. Anna stood up and motioned to Elisabeth to move away from the ensuing brawl.

"I've had enough of this, Jakob," Michael continued. "One of these days your temper will land you in jail. Go outside and cool off! Come back when you've settled."

Jakob unwillingly donned his cloak and stalked out, slamming the door behind him.

"And you, Schutze, I'll not have you scaring the women by your talk of uprisings. There's been enough grief this week without you adding to it. It's all nonsense."

"Nonsense, you think? Well, Michael Heber, you just wait and see. You've never seen how belittling he can be. You've never experienced Eugen and his hounds racing across your land destroying what's left of it. And all for his pleasure, just so nothing stands in his way of the chase. You sympathize when you see it happening to others, but do you really mean it? Maybe you can take it, but I won't, and many others are with me on this, including your son. And yours, Hans."

He lifted the latch on the door, swinging it ajar. The cool outside air permeated the hot room. With his wide body frame standing in the doorway, Schutze moved slightly sideways blocking the stream of sunlight. Turning, he looked back at Hans.

"Maybe you're doing the right thing in emigrating, but we still need you to help those who are left here to fight." The door then banged shut.

No one spoke. All eyes moved towards Anna as she collapsed in the chair.

"Michael, what does he mean about Jakob and Peter? What's going on?" As soon as she spoke, the room was abuzz again with this news.

Michael was instantly by her side. He kneeled at her feet to soothe her fears.

"Anna, Schutze's right, the whole village is rising against Eugen and his men. Jakob, Peter, Georg, and..."

"You?" Anna queried, her voice almost inaudible.

"*Nein.*"

She felt powerless to stop her son. She had no impact on Jakob anymore. They were cut from the same cloth, same convictions, same temper. But ever since his wife and son's deaths, he had worsened, to the point that it scared her, and she knew it frightened Michael. Anna couldn't stop Jakob, but she could influence her husband. She felt relief when Michael denied his involvement, but she couldn't shake the dread of her son's commitment to fight.

Elisabeth needed fresh air and asked Hans if she could speak to Peter alone. He nodded, excusing himself. "Please join me for a walk," she said. "I need to talk to you."

"*Ja,* but you're not to talk me out of my joining the cause. My mind's made up," Peter said. He spread her cloak across her shoulders. Elisabeth walked out the door ahead of him.

Once outside, the cool air felt inviting. Her small home had become so intolerable, Elisabeth could hardly breathe. She was sure it was from all the conversation over the cause, as Peter called it. It was all too much for her to take in, hearing about Jakob's involvement in a revolt, and Peter moving so far away. When he had first mentioned it to her, she brushed it off as one of his pipe dreams. When he insisted on speaking of it, she ignored him and quickly changed the subject. Anything to not believe it. Elisabeth didn't want to think about it...couldn't think about it. But when Herr Beck spoke of it earlier, it was all that more real. Real enough that now it caused her much anguish. Real enough that she may never see Peter again. Real enough that this was not one of Peter's dreams. But now, something worse had happened. With him fighting at Schutze's side, it became more evident that Peter could be killed. If he moved far away, she'd never see him again. If he stayed, Elisabeth could still lose him.

Even though the air was cool, the sun was warm enough to make Elisabeth shed her heavy cloak. Peter tossed it over his arm.

"The weather changes so drastically," he said. "Just two days ago we were in the throes of an early snowstorm. Now look at it. It feels like spring again." Elisabeth didn't answer him.

They continued their walk away from the house, past the barn, toward a narrow lane that ran along a stone wall and edged the Heber land a bit before it turned into a tall hedge. The sun had rapidly melted the snow since yesterday, leaving only a trace of white - a few spots here and there were protected from the warmth of the sun's rays, but nothing more.

"You're awfully quiet for someone who wanted to talk."

"Huh," she uttered. "Sorry, Peter. What did you say?"

"What did you want to speak to me about?"

"Oh...nothing, Peter. I just wanted to get away and be here with you alone where no harm can come to us."

Peter stopped in his tracks, turned slightly, and laid his hands on her shoulders. Elisabeth looked up; he was a full head taller than her.

"Don't you worry about me. Nothing's going to happen. Look who's on our side! Schutze!" Peter smiled widely.

"If that's supposed to make me feel better, Peter Beck, it doesn't," she answered, her head bowed so he wouldn't see the tears.

He cupped her face in his gentle hands, and stroked her wet cheeks, wiping away any trace of sorrow.

She noticed that he was looking at her differently this time, and it made her feel weak from the thought of what he might be considering. This is what she longed for, for him to show his true feelings. But not out here in the open for all to see! Her embarrassment quickly melted away as he bent his head over hers and gingerly touched his lips to her cheek. One kiss, two kisses. Elisabeth tried to lower her head, but he held it up again, gently but firmly, so she could not move while he kissed her tenderly on her lips.

Eagerly she kissed back, standing on tiptoes to get even closer. Peter searched her mouth anxiously with his tongue, then, she lay her head against his chest. The sound of his beating heart made her feel safe. For the moment, she'd relish in it, she thought, as she felt him stroking her head. All will be fine, she reflected.

Peter guided Elisabeth under the large tree, whose stark branches spread across the width of the lane. Her great-grandfather had planted the oak many years ago, and her papa had proposed to her mama near this very spot. Mama called it the kissing tree, where so many couples became engaged in the summer under its leafy foliage. Now without its leaves, it looked like great claws reaching out to pick up anything that walked near it.

"You know, Elisabeth, I don't have to go. I could stay here with you. I'm sure Schutze would take me under his wing. With only two daughters, he could use the help on his land since he's gone into the salt business." He smiled. And when Peter smiled, his eyes seemed to dance.

"You'd do that for me?" she said. "Leave your family?"

"I'd do it for us."

Elisabeth reached up and planted a kiss on Peter's cheek which felt warm to her soft lips. Then, hearing someone giggle, she raised an eyebrow at him. He put his finger to his lips, as he silently crept towards the wall. Lifting her skirt so as not to snag a bush, she followed. Peter waited until she was beside him, again pressing his finger to his lips. Both peered over the wall. Christian and Hanna were crouched down, trying hard to stifle their laughter. So absorbed at what they saw, they never noticed they had been caught.

"What're you doing!" bellowed Peter in a gruff voice. Christian almost jumped out of his skin and Hanna squealed with fright.

"Wait til I get you home!" Elisabeth yelled.

Relishing the sight of Christian's sudden burst of energy as he sprinted towards home, his baby sister close behind, Peter and Elisabeth collapsed in laughter.

****

"So, Hans," Michael started, "pray, tell me more of this venture you propose." They all sat around the wooden table in the kitchen. Michael and Anna were seated across from Hans and Maria. Stefan slept soundly in his cradle beside the hearth. The get-together for the christening had come to an abrupt halt after the tense scene between Jakob and Schutze. All had departed quickly, leaving just the four of them deep in discussion.

Hans covered his wife's hand with his to protect it, gently rubbing and squeezing it. "There's not much to say, Michael, except I've made the decision that I want to give my family a better life," he said.

"When are you leaving?"

"The ship sails from Rotterdam the first week in May. The orders are to register and be aboard the *Snow Speedwell* two weeks before. We'll be departing from Hohctorf by mid-March to sail up the Rhine."

Maria looked over at Anna with apprehensive eyes, then, slowly lowered them.

"What about the stories we've heard of families returning from

Philadelphia where they emigrated not a year since?" Anna said, wringing her hands. "You can't do this to the children. Have you really thought this through?"

Hans stood up. "Don't you think I've thought of that? I've been going over and over in my mind the danger I could be putting my family in. The pros and cons of it."

"What pros?" Anna said, her voice started to rise. "The ocean crossing itself is dangerous enough without thinking of what's on the other side."

Michael rose abruptly and rested his hand on Anna's shoulder. Turning to face Hans, he questioned, "How much is this all going to cost? Surely, a trip of this nature will be enormously expensive."

"Seventy-three *gulden,*" Maria answered.

"Wha'?" Michael slowly sat down again and stared at the floor. Then glancing up at Hans said, "But how do you propose to pay that? You don't have two *kreuzers* to rub together, let alone a *gulden.*"

"Well, that's the beauty of it." Hans said, stepping closer to Michael. "Herr Kohler said they are so anxious to get new immigrants that they are willing to let us work off the passage fare in Nova Scotia on the public works."

"You're being very naive about this, Hans. Those families in Philadelphia were split up, taken on as slaves to work off the passage. Some never saw each other again. I'd say you'd fare much better here despite the uprisings. At least here you have the dignity of working your own piece of land, not indebted to some stranger's."

"*Nein*, you've got it very wrong." Hans pulled out the paper again from inside his well-worn breeches. "Remember, we're being given the land, fifty grand acres of it. The labour for the public works is to construct such things as fortresses in Nova Scotia, work at whatever is required by the government."

"And how long is this to take?"

"About four years. You're paid about one and a half...now what was it Kohler said?" Hans rubbed his forehead. "Scillings, I believe he said. *Nein*, it was shillings. That was it—one and a half shillings per day. That's about forty-five *kreuzers*."

Hans looked up into Michael's apprehensive eyes now heavily crinkled from reading the notice over and over again by candlelight. Stefan stirred and started whimpering just before letting out a loud cry, startling Michael. Anna picked her son up, muttering cooing sounds to quiet him. Finally, she put him to her breast.

"Why don't you and your family come with us?"

"Never!" Michael declared. I will not leave this land that my *fater* sweated for and his *fater* before him. I couldn't even think about it, no matter how bad things got here. *Nein*," he said again, with Anna nodding in agreement. "Pray, Hans, think this over again."

"I've done enough thinking. My mind's made up and no one can change it. Not even you." Hans put on his coat as he walked toward the door. "Come, Maria, we've overstayed our welcome here."

Anna was rocking. She sat there silent and tight-lipped as she suckled the small infant. After they bade their stiff farewells, Michael picked up the paper that Hans had left behind and sat down heavily in the tall-backed, ornate chair his papa had made for his wedding twenty years since.

Hearing the rumble of the Beck's wagon roll past their house and fade into the distance, Michael gazed at the document he was holding. Breaking the almost deafening quiet, he uttered slowly and distinctly, "I could never leave the *Faterland*."

He crumbled the paper into a tight wad and threw it aimlessly against the wall. It settled behind the stack of freshly cut wood.

Anna kept her silence, as she watched her husband rubbing the palms of his hands so intensely over the arms of the chair.

CHAPTER 5

The moon sat high in the sky, a full moon that seemed brighter and larger than any Peter and his papa had seen in a long time. It shone with such brilliance that it lit their way as they walked briskly along the path to where Schutze and the others were waiting. Every few minutes the clouds dimmed the light on the road as they sailed past the moon's glow, but it never hindered their vision in the least. There was a warm breeze tonight. If this good weather holds out, Peter thought, it will be in our favour.

So engrossed in their own expectations, Peter and Hans continued their journey in silence. Both were thinking hard on the skirmish that was planned Saturday in Goppingen, but Peter's mind strayed at times to Elisabeth. How would he break it to his papa that he wanted to stay here in Hohctorf and not travel to Nova Scotia? He was jerked back to reality, when Hans spoke. "We're here, son."

Looking up ahead, he could see a small timber dwelling that certainly didn't appear very liveable. Taking longer strides now, trying to keep up with Hans' quickened pace, Peter found it hard to believe this was where Schutze lived, in the middle of nowhere. The building was in a very bad state of repair. The only part of the structure that looked solid were the timber beams. The wattle and daub between the beams had probably made the dwelling quite handsome at one time. But now? Where the clay once covered the woven rods and twigs, it now lay bare over most of the construction. Where once there was thatching on the roof, now had great bare patches revealing the planking underneath. The door was partly ajar, and Hans gently pushed it open to reveal a very crowded room, about twenty-five of the villagers and neighbours they knew were present. Most turned as the door swung open.

"Hans, what're you doing here? I didn't expect..." Schutze started, but Hans cut him off.

"I know you didn't, after yesterday. Even though we won't be living in Hohctorf much longer, we believe in fighting for what's right. Count us in."

Schutze smiled and motioned them to shut the door. Scooping up some ale from the keg, he handed them each a stein dripping with froth.

"Were you followed?" Schutze queried hastily. "Georg overheard that Jeremias was tipped off about this gathering tonight, and the Council will be quickly squashing any hint of a revolt."

Even though Hans and Peter assured them they were not followed, tension and worry were written on everyone's faces.

"How do we know that they aren't behind the Council?" piped one. All eyes turned on them, and another voiced, "Can we trust them? After all, why should they care? They won't be amongst us for long, leaving before spring."

The grumbling was increasing, so Hans and Peter backed off as they were stared down. Schutze stepped in.

"That's enough! Any more of this will pull us apart. We need them, and we need you. If there is anyone here who wants out, there's the door." Schutze pointed. He halfheartedly expected a few to follow his advice but no one moved. Hans could hear Schutze's laboured breathing. After a few tense seconds that felt like minutes, he said, "All right then, let's stick together. We've a lot to get organized before sun up."

Just as they were about to discuss their strategy, the door bolted open. There stood Jakob trying to catch his breath, his broad chest heaving rapidly up and down.

"They're onto us!"

Schutze bolted upright, knocking his chair backwards against the fireplace. "What?" Schutze exclaimed. "What's going on?"

"It's the Council! They know! They're on their way now. Jeremias tipped them off. Now the Privy Council has cancelled the hunt."

"That little weasel!" Schutze hissed.

"The prince is still coming, but the plans are changed. He'll be arriving in Hohctorf instead to hear the people's grievances tomorrow, rather than next Friday." Jakob's panting calmed somewhat, but he still talked very rapidly. "I was only about ten minutes ahead of the Council. We've got to get out of here!"

The whole place erupted. Schutze stood his ground attempting to calm the group, restraining those who pushed their way through the door.

"Hold on, hold on...hold on! Wait..." He turned to Jakob. "They've nothing on us. Nothing can be proved. The Council only has Jeremias' word. He's drunk most of the time. You know that. He can't even stand up some nights. He's worthless," he continued.

"Are you daft?" Georg said. "You know what they do to those who hold such meetings. They don't have to prove anything. It's illegal to have any type of gathering like this unless they know what it's about. Do you want to land in the Rathaus?"

"Not me," shouted another. "I'm not rotting in jail."

And with that, Georg and the others rushed past Schutze and Jakob, leaving them standing eyeing each other. Jakob darted after, without another word to his friend.

Watching as Jakob's back disappeared into the woods, Schutze heard Jeremias' voice and others. Slipping out quietly, he closed the back door behind him, and disappeared into the darkness.

****

The next morning, St. Hubert's Day, word spread like wildfire that the prince was now holding his grievance meeting before the people of the village at one o'clock sharp. Speculation ran rampant of why Eugen's plans were suddenly changed. The usual pomp and ceremony that the prince demanded had to take a back seat this time. The market square where he would be speaking would need to be set up in such a way that he could be well heard and seen by his subjects.

Jakob rode in on Blitz to a scene of much ado over the building of this stage. He noticed Schutze strolling into the tavern with Georg on his right. He shouted to them but wasn't heard over the loud banging and hammering. Motioning his horse to the tavern door, Jakob started to dismount before Blitz came to a full halt.

Walking in, he eyed the two of them in the corner of the room hunched over the table conversing in what looked like hushed voices. Schutze's back was to him. Georg was facing him with his back against the window. Jakob inclined his head to a few of his neighbours as he brushed past them to the table.

Georg glanced up just as Jakob slapped Schutze on the back, making him jump.

"Jakob," he said, relaxing a bit but still edgy.

"That was a close call last night," Jakob answered, not caring to keep his voice down like his companions. Even though he had panicked the evening before, he still relished the excitement.

Jakob slid in beside Georg as Schutze motioned him to keep his voice down. "Relax. No one can hear over these noisy simpletons. Look at them, they're half drunk now, and St. Martin's clock hasn't even struck ten yet. They're going to make a great impression on the prince," he quipped.

Georg scanned the room as Schutze strained his neck to see. Jakob started to laugh, then more boisterous when his two companions joined him.

The tavern owner, Herr Weber, acknowledged Jakob's nod with a beer. Schutze raised his stein up above his head and cheered aloud so others could hear, "Here's to the Duke of Wurttemberg, Prince Carl Eugen."

They eyed Schutze suspiciously. But after a sidelong glance and a wink from their friend, they, too, sang their praises to the Duke.

Walls do have ears, Jakob thought.

An hour later, Hans and Peter spotted the three of them in the corner, and joined in. They grabbed a couple of chairs, and invited themselves into the conversation.

Peter was the first to speak. "The Council has implicated the person who headed the resistance against the prince last night."

"Who is it they're accusing?" Georg asked.

Hans looked down at his hands.

"Well, speak up! Speak up, Hans!" Schutze said.

Hans didn't reply, nor did he have to. It was written all over his face as he stared at Schutze.

"*Awch*, nonsense. They can't arrest me until they've proved it. If they're about to take Jeremias' word, then the Council is the bunch of idiots I always knew they were."

"That's not all," Peter continued. "I heard from a very reliable source that the hunt is going as planned, after the grievance meeting."

"But this time, the chase will be through the Spillman and Hurdlin farms. They've already been ordered to dismantle any fences or brush that would impede the chase," Hans added.

Schutze rubbed the stubble on his chin as he inhaled deeply.

When he exhaled, a high-pitched whistle escaped from the space between his two bottom yellow teeth.

"We can still do it," he finally said, after what seemed an eternity of silence. Bringing his voice down to an almost inaudible whisper, he said, "Georg, ride hard over to the Spillman and Hurdlin farms and tell them the plan is still on. Tell them not to take down anything. Do you hear me? We're going to stop Eugen dead in his tracks. Hans and Peter, you go and get word to the rest. Jakob, come with me," he ordered, as he swung his legs over the bench, knocking the bottom of the table with his muddy boots.

Jakob did as he was told and followed Schutze out, his adrenalin pumping again.

****

The clock at St. Martin's chimed a resonant one o'clock; Jakob quaked at the sound of it. He glanced around the already assembled crowd and spotted Schutze's bald head. Schutze was short, but Jakob was tall enough to see over the crowd. He called to him as he pushed his way through. Upon approaching him, Hans and Peter arrived at the same time.

"Well, Hans?" Schutze asked. "Did you get word around?"

He nodded. "*Ja*. But we're on our own. Everyone's scared of the Council and backed out, except Hurdlin and Spillman. I spoke with Georg, who is at Spillman's now, and they're behind us all the way."

"Jesus Christ," Jakob blasphemed. "Those lily-livered bastards." He swore that if he just had one of them here standing in front of him, he would have strung them up by their balls.

"Damn it! Keep your blasted voice down," Schutze said. "There are eyes everywhere, watching our every move. If this is the way those scoundrels want to help us, we don't need 'em."

"Hans, Jakob, stay here. Peter, ride over to Spillman's and wait for us there. After this is finished, we'll join you and wait for Eugen. Don't look so worried, Peter, everything's under control." Schutze patted the left side of his jacket.

Peter turned on his heels and disappeared through the crowd. Hans gripped Schutze's arm so hard his knuckles turned white. "What's that in your coat?" he questioned Schutze.

"Just a bit of reassurance," he answered through his tightly-clenched jaw.

"We agreed, Schutze, no violence."

"No, you imbecile, you agreed," he sneered. "And if this game is too rough for you, get out now!"

They were face to face, so close that Hans could smell Schutze's sour breath made worse from the ale this morning. Schutze's lips were wet with his spittle and the fire in his bloodshot eyes scared him.

Jakob backed off, deciding to let the two of them fight it out. To his relief, and he was sure Hans' too, the prince arrived and stepped up to the platform. Schutze violently jerked his arm from Hans's vice grip.

The prince was average in height, round faced, and fair-skinned, which seemed even fairer under the white powdered wig he wore. On his head, he wore a wide-brimmed, black velvet hat with a very large ostrich feather which protruded back on the left side. Any whisper of a breeze sent the feather flush against the rich material. Under the black coat, also velvet, his waistcoat and breeches were in the Catholic colours of red and yellow. His breeches ended just below his knees and rested at the top of fine dark brown high leather boots. Despite his small stature, he exhibited such a grandiose and proud image that his subjects were in awe of him. A small part of his

Privy Council, numbering three, stood on each side of him with one behind. Their height made the prince look like a mere child despite his twenty-two years.

Until a couple of months ago, Eugen's Council was dominated by Bilfinger. After his death, Friedrich August von Hardenberg replaced him. He stood behind the prince, his eyes darting back and forth anticipating any trouble. He was against Prince Eugen mingling with the people. It just wasn't done. It was much too dangerous.

The mayor of Hohctorf, the Burgermeister, stood on the platform with Eugen. He opened his fat little mouth to welcome the prince, when one lone voice from the back of the crowd jeered, "How much longer are you going to continue taxing the blood from our very souls, oh foul one?" That was all that needed to be said. The Town Council quickly swarmed in ready to carry the old man away. The prince raised his hand and motioned for the arrest to stop.

"Gentlemen, I have come here today to help you understand that these taxes are to assist me and my Council to make a better life for you and your families," he started.

"Help us?" another questioned. "Help us with what? I've seen nothing but poverty and misfortune here in our village. There are so many tolls on the roads that I can't send my wares across the country to trade. I cannot afford to pay the *gulden* you and your damn henchmen are asking. How in God's name do you expect me to feed my family when I can't even travel fifteen *stundens* without having to pay?"

Eugen started to speak, but his voice was drowned by the increasing crescendo of mumblings that reverberated throughout the multitude.

Ignoring the prince, another spoke up, agreeing with the first. "I have a wife and seven children to support, three of them are over thirteen years. And now you are about to introduce a new poll tax which states that anyone fourteen years and over has to pay! I couldn't pay you the land tax last year, when your Bilfinger threatened to evict me and my family. How the hell do you expect me to pay more? You can't get blood from a stone," he barked. The crowd's muttering got louder, agreeing with the second.

"*Bitte,*" Eugen pleaded, "*Bitte.*" The crowd was getting out of control.

Still a third voice was heard, this time from Schutze. "Eugen," he yelled, "you tax us so you can line your own silk pockets in those fancy breeches of yours. You want our able-bodied sons to help fight your battles that we don't want anything to do with. Tell me, Eugen," he emphasized the last word, as he edged closer to the front of the crowd, "why don't you recruit the nobility, the rich? Why are we taxed more than them? Haven't you enough money coming into your private account from King Louis of France? Isn't it true that the king is paying you to recruit and train infantrymen?"

Schutze stopped, realizing that the crowd was silent this time listening to what he had to say. This last part about the French king was not common knowledge. Everyone waited to hear what the prince had to say.

"Answer me, damn it!" was all Schutze could say. Beads of perspiration gathered on Eugen's brow.

"From where did you obtain such knowledge?" the prince queried.

"What does that matter?" Jakob chimed in. "It's common knowledge that you deal too much with the French. No clothes will satisfy you or the nobility that do not come from France."

Schutze interrupted Jakob. "French scissors trim our German beards. You'll buy their watches because they've been made in Paris."

"Maybe the reason is that the quality is much more superior than the German craftsmen," the prince answered adamantly.

Roars of protest thundered aloud. In one mass movement, the crowd shoved their way towards Eugen.

"Well, maybe if you didn't put such high tolls on the roads, we would be able to afford to work with better grades of tools and materials to surpass the weak French, so all you fine gentlemen and your precious ladies can parade in exquisite garments," Hans added.

A few of his neighbours screamed in agreement.

"Are you ashamed of your people? Are you ashamed of the *Faterland* and what it should stand for?" Schutze was now becoming hoarse from shrieking.

"What *Faterland*?" the prince shrieked. "I *am* the *Faterland.* You are nothing."

Schutze saw red. Everything happened so fast, Jakob and Hans couldn't have stopped him if they tried. A gunshot pierced the air. The prince reeled backwards against von Hardenberg, blood squirting from his shoulder where the bullet penetrated. Amidst the shouts, the Town Council charged through the crowd and made their way towards Schutze. Another deafening shot resounded, but this time from von Hardenberg's pistol as he stood over the prince's prostrate body. Hans leapt out in front of Schutze to protect him, taking the bullet in his stead. Jakob caught Hans just as he was about to crumple to the ground, oblivious to the mayhem around him. Neither saw the Council drag Schutze away.

Hans' head was cradled in Jakob's arm. As he let out a long groan, Jakob slipped his hand under Hans' shirt and felt the warm blood ooze over his fingers. The bullet had infiltrated the area of his heart. To his disbelief, he heard Peter's anxious voice, "Papa!" Peter was supposed to be with Georg.

Kneeling beside Hans, Peter's tears streamed unchecked. Hans, barely audible to either of them, clawed at his son's coat, beckoning him closer.

"Son, t-take care of your *mutter.*"

"You'll be okay, you're going to get better," Peter whispered. Then with eyes pleading, "Jakob, please tell Papa."

"*Nein.* I w-want," he said and coughed, "I want you...to promise... me. Finish my dream. Take your mama...and sister...to...the new land."

"Papa. You're coming too." Peter implored Jakob for reassurance.

"Promise me, Peter...promise me..." he swore, trying to lift his head. Jakob did all he could to choke back his own emotion.

Peter hesitated, then relinquished, "I promise." His quivering voice hardly got the words out.

Hans attempted a smile, then gently closed his eyes as if to sleep.

"Papa!" Peter fell on top of the limp body, weeping uncontrollably.

CHAPTER 6

FOUR WEEKS LATER

The huge fiery ball began to sink on the horizon, appearing to sit on the far edge of the Heber's farmland. The sky was streaked with bright reds and purples. It was the most spectacular sunset Elisabeth had ever seen. She wanted to linger with the shutters open, but the chill of the oncoming winter sent a shiver through her thin body as she stood in her nightgown.

Oh, she thought, I hate the cold. I wish it could be warm all year round. Then, she changed her mind. Deep down she truly loved all the seasons, especially the festivals and dances that heralded the various times of the year. She loved to celebrate the harvest games in the autumn and Rejoicing Day in the summer. Elisabeth's particular love was May Day, dancing around a tree whose bark had been peeled off in spiral patterns. How she loved to dance. The wreath hoisted to the top was laden with fragrant flowers and colourful ribbons, and inside the wreath were small presents. Last year, Peter climbed up to get one of those presents for her. It was the prettiest blue ribbon. She cherished it, wearing it in her hair only on special occasions. But for Peter it meant nothing, merely a gesture of friendship then. Earlier that day, she had been so disappointed not to find a *Maien* under her bedroom window. Her best friend Kristina found one underneath her window from her beau, Martin. It was beautifully made of birch twigs and flowers. Peter may not have shown his feelings then, but that has all changed now, she mused.

Elisabeth sat down on her bed, shifting her weight until she felt comfortable enough so as not to feel the few ends of straw that always prickled her backside. She tried to be as quiet as possible so she wouldn't wake Hanna, though she couldn't tell whether she was asleep or not. Hanna all to often pretended, afraid of missing anything.

Papa had sent Elisabeth to bed early tonight because tomorrow was *Andreasnacht* (St. Andrew's night), and she was allowed to stay up until midnight. There was a dance in the village that her parents would take her to. Maybe she would see Peter again. She picked up her hairbrush, and stroked the closely knit bristles through her long, thick hair.

Peter, she thought, her lips parting a little, almost uttering his name aloud. Her mind wandered back to the day of his papa's funeral. He looked horrible; she was sure he hadn't slept for days. She just wanted to take him in her arms to ease the terrible pain he was feeling. Seeing him again about a week ago, so long after the funeral, reinforced her worries. He was worse, more withdrawn.

Things will get better, Elisabeth contemplated. They've got to. After all, we love each other, she said to herself. I'll see him tomorrow night and everything will be back to normal. She tucked her hair underneath the bed cap. She shoved her cold feet underneath the blanket that was now toasty warm from the hot stone her mother had placed there earlier. She couldn't stop thinking about Peter's ramblings to avenge Hans' death. That's just sadness and bitterness talking, Elisabeth deliberated. Time will heal.

She was so engrossed in her thoughts that she was totally unaware of the sudden increase of the wind howling around the house, until a tree branch snapped and hit the shutter, startling her. Leaning over the side, Elisabeth peeked at Hanna who was still fast asleep in the trundle bed beside her. She whispered a silent prayer to

God, snuggled under the cover, and drifted off to sleep, dreaming of her future with Peter.

****

The next evening, excitement coursed through Elisabeth's veins as her parents escorted her and Christian to the dance. Jakob decided to stay home with Hanna. Ever since the shooting on St. Hubert's Day, living with Jakob and her papa was almost impossible. The obvious tension between the two of them was unmistakable to all who were close. Another blow occurred tonight just before leaving the house, resulting in her brother refusing to come. Papa knew that his son was involved in the uprising, but Jakob thought the suspicion laid upon him was uncalled for.

Well, Elisabeth wasn't about to let that ruin her fun. She was here to have a good time. At least, as best a time as she could under her mama's watchful eyes. As the wagon pulled up outside, she could hear the alluring music dancing on the frosty air. Jumping down from the wagon before it came to a complete halt, she was met with Anna's voice.

"Elisabeth! Stop right there! I'll not have any daughter of mine rushing in there like a common beggar. Settle yourself properly and wait."

"But, Mama."

"No buts, young lady. You'll wait for us."

"*Ja*, Mama," she stopped and sighed, then she eyed the front door and inched her way closer.

Christian leapt from the wagon behind her, and sniggered, "Elisabeth, why *are* you in so much of a hurry? Peter's probably not here."

Elisabeth wanted to hit him, but she restrained herself and opened the door to a crowded room of lively music and dancing.

The beer and wine that were flowing freely were forbidden to Elisabeth. But since it was *Andreasnacht* and one week before St. Nicholas' visit, Mama had promised she could have a small cup of wine. After all, she was sixteen, a young lady.

Elisabeth scanned the room. Christian was right, Peter wasn't there. She knew most everyone, but the most important didn't show. Or at least, not yet. She still had hope, although she had overheard Mama say to Papa earlier that Frau Beck was still grieving and couldn't bear to come. But that doesn't mean Peter wouldn't make it, she pondered, as she straightened her coarse woollen dress, patted her hair, and rearranged her blue ribbon to perfection. Glancing around, she noticed everyone was in their Sunday best. The girls' colourful skirts, embroidered around the hem, and their full-sleeved linen blouses under latticed bodices were only rivalled by the men's gayly decorated stockings.

Doktor Gessler spotted Michael and strode over to where the Hebers were standing.

"*Guten abend*, Michael. Anna." And to Elisabeth, he smiled and cocked his head.

"*Guten abend,* Georg," Michael answered.

They proceeded to engage in some small talk, which Elisabeth had no interest in. With wine in hand, her attention was on the music, watching the musicians that even included Pastor Krumer. His foot tapping to the sound of the violin he played was contagious. She couldn't help but move her own foot to the beat, until she felt a nudge from her mama to act properly. It didn't go unnoticed by Georg, and he turned to her. "Fraulein, shall we?" He politely bowed his head and held out his hand to lead her to the dance floor.

For a split second, Elisabeth thought her mama would protest, but instead she noticed a nod of her head and a smile.

"*Ja*, Doktor Gessler," she answered, and was escorted to the centre of the room. Upon reaching the others, the music stopped.

"Time for the *Kisseltanz*! Grab your partners," the band leader yelled.

All of a sudden, the women and girls each grabbed a cushion, piled up in a corner of the room. Elisabeth proceeded to walk away. She couldn't dance the *Kisseltanz* with someone she didn't know that well.

But instead, Georg gently pulled her back.

"You would do me great honour to dance this with me."

With her eyes downcast, she turned to leave but was still met with resistance. Finally looking up at him, she noticed a pleading look in his eyes that she couldn't refuse. Just then, the music began, so Elisabeth ran to snatch a cushion and met him back on the dance floor.

Standing in front of her partner holding the cushion in the palms of her hands, she circled and danced around the *doktor*. Elisabeth was so enthralled with the lively steps, she quickly forgot about her embarrassment, until it came time at the end for all the cushions to be set upon the floor in front of each girl.

The sudden realization of what happens next made Elisabeth blush. Doktor Gessler knelt on the cushion waiting for the kiss that ends the dance. Elisabeth leaned over and planted a peck on his right cheek. She started to giggle but noticed he looked at her with such intent that it made her feel extremely uncomfortable. Without a word, he straightened and escorted her from the floor, all the while giving her sidelong glances while the others continued the dance, changing partners. Then to her comfort and surprise, Elisabeth noticed that Frau Beck had arrived with Peter, and none too soon.

"Peter!" she called. He turned and said a few words to his mama. Anna glanced over at her and smiled. As Elisabeth watched him walk towards her, she wanted so much to wrap her arms around his neck and hold him, but of course she wouldn't. It would cause such a stir. If only they could be alone. She was sure Peter felt the same way.

"Who did I just see you kissing there in the middle of the dance floor?" he teased.

"Why, Peter," she slipped her hand in his, "I do believe you're jealous." She guided him towards the dance floor.

The music was livelier now with the sweet sound of the violin in the foreground, which delighted Elisabeth. Once again, she stood in front of her partner, but one that she much preferred this time. The dance began.

This time the couples glided apart and Elisabeth spun around to the music with her skirt flying out, while Peter leaped and stomped, whilst slapping his knees and ankles. The noise was so deafening that it almost drowned the music. Elisabeth was ecstatic and showed it with her constant laughter throughout the whole dance. However, with the wine she had earlier, the spinning was beginning to make her dizzy, almost sick. Thankfully, Peter grabbed her by the hand, and they sneaked through the side door without their parents noticing.

The air was cold, and to Elisabeth's delight, Peter willingly gave up his jacket to her and held her tight. In their embrace, he started to shake. He buried his face in her thick hair and wept. Not saying a word, she stroked his head and held him until he quieted down.

After what seemed an eternity, she gently lifted his head to witness the pain through his tear-filled eyes. "Shush, my *liebling*. I know, I know," she cooed.

"I feel my heart is being ripped from inside," he said, his voice quaking. "I miss *fater* so. I have such hatred for Schutze that it scares me, Elisabeth."

"But why? He didn't kill your papa. It was just an accident."

"If Schutze didn't have that gun on him..." he paused to regain composure. "It was supposed to be peaceful. No weapons! We all agreed!"

"We? Whose we?"

"Jakob. Georg." And he continued with other names from the village and surrounding farms familiar to her. But she tuned Peter out when she heard her brother's name.

"Jakob?" she exclaimed. "Then Papa was right in accusing him."

"Didn't you know?"

"*Nein. Ja. Nein*!" she shook her head. "We didn't know for sure. Nothing could be proven. Jakob's been closed-mouthed about the whole thing, just heated words with Papa, who has suspected from the beginning. But Peter, nothing can prove he was involved, especially in the shooting. To the authorities, he was just an innocent bystander."

"Your brother was Schutze's right hand man in this. He was into it up to his neck. But don't get me wrong, Elisabeth, Jakob never agreed to violence."

Putting her arms around Peter's waist, she felt him rest his chin on top of her head. She had difficulty taking all this in about her brother's involvement, so she chose to ignore it.

Glancing up, she said, "Promise me you'll stop talking such nonsense of avenging your papa's death. It hurts me to hear you say such things. Are you listening to me, Peter Beck?" Her voice raised to a pitch.

Manoeuvring his head back again, he tried to look away from her, but she implored, "Promise me?"

When he still didn't answer, Elisabeth dropped the subject. It was no use talking to him when he was like this. Instead, she gave him the support he needed to hear. "We'll get through this together."

Peter embraced her tightly. "I love you so much. Don't ever leave me," he whispered. He held her head between his hands, kissing her so deliciously hard and long that it left her wanting more.

****

As the evening wore on, talk seemed always to return to that fateful day. Talk of the prince putting a halt to his visitations for a while throughout his estates. Talk of Schutze's escape from prison. Talk of where he might be hiding. Sympathy towards Maria Beck and Peter.

The increasingly serious tone of the evening changed at midnight. It was time for all the young girls to line up with their backs a few feet away from the door. Everyone, including Elisabeth, took off one shoe and flung it towards the door. If the toe of the shoe pointed outward that meant a young man would come within a year and take the girl out of the house. To Elisabeth's delight, her shoe pointed outward. She smiled at Peter, who grinned in return.

Before leaving with her parents, Peter again pulled Elisabeth aside. "We've got to talk somewhere private," he told her.

"Not now, silly." Elisabeth was sure he wanted to ask her to marry him and talk about when the announcement would be made. She was just as anxious, but now was not the right time.

"Elisabeth, we have to talk soon, very soon." The urgency in his voice made her stop and listen to him more intently. "There's a dance next Sunday."

"Dance? Don't be so foolish, you know very well that the Council doesn't allow dances on Sundays," she said, putting her hands in her woollen muff.

"Not here. In Steinbach."

"Are you insane? You know we could go to jail for that, not to mention what Papa would say if he found out. I would be beaten from here to Goppingen. I cannot." Anna called out to her, and she proceeded to walk away, but he held her back.

"Elisabeth, I need you..." he implored. "And don't worry your pretty little head about getting out of the house undetected. Leave that to me. I have a plan. Please, I need to spend some time alone with you so we can talk."

Elisabeth actually felt weak-kneed. She didn't know whether it was because Peter needed her, or the thrill of going to Steinbach without anyone knowing about it. She did love to dance and she wouldn't be alone.

"Okay, Peter. When did you say it was?"

"As I said before, next Sunday," he snapped.

"What?" Elisabeth gasped, suddenly realizing something. "That's on St. Nicholas Day. I couldn't poss..."

"Never mind then. Forget it!" Peter turned to go.

"Okay, I'll go with you."

He squeezed her hand and walked her to the wagon. As he helped her climb up, he bid her adieu. Elisabeth glanced at him, not speaking but worrying what kind of idea he had to pull this off. She couldn't help but think it would never work. However, she had enough faith in him to know he'd never do anything to harm her.

CHAPTER 7

For the next five days, Elisabeth was edgy and high-strung, which certainly did not go unnoticed by her mama. But Anna attributed it to the excitement of the upcoming holiday, and also a little to the fact that Schutze was still on the loose and the authorities didn't know where he was. This had the whole village uptight and nervous; no one felt safe.

Enough of this, Anna remarked to herself, as she manoeuvred her needle in and out, putting the finishing touches on Elisabeth's apron. This is a time of happiness.

Outside was a biting cold wind that chilled her to the bone, but the warm fire inside made her feel safe and secure from the outside elements. The night had descended suddenly due to the heavy snow that was falling and Anna's eyes were becoming weary from the tedious work she was trying to finish by candlelight. She set down her sewing on her lap and glanced up at Michael, who sat opposite her carving the finishing touches on a piece of wood that would hopefully look like the doll Hanna had been wanting since last St. Nicholas' Day. Anna had finished the doll's dress last week out of some scrap material she had in her chest.

The children were upstairs and they were told *Sunnerklas* wouldn't come to the house unless they were quiet. When they heard a knock at the door, they could come down. This had been a tradition since Anna was a little girl, so she carried it through to her own family. Jakob was upstairs also, and he always made it that much more believable just for Hanna.

"I'm surprised you're allowing Elisabeth to spend tomorrow with Peter." Anna broke the silence.

"Huh?" Michael looked up from the carving. "It's only for the afternoon. Elisabeth will celebrate with us in the morning. Peter wants to talk to her about his decision to now leave. She doesn't know yet."

"I wonder how she'll take it. I always thought they would get married one day. How things change. I was sure all had been settled when Maria and Peter decided not to go." Anna sighed. "I thought for sure Maria would forget this nonsense when Hans died. I couldn't believe it when Peter spoke to us yesterday to say they decided to go after all. I don't think..."

Just then Hanna tiptoed downstairs, holding onto the wooden railing while rubbing her eyes with the back of her hand.

"And what are you doing up, my child?" Anna said, lifting herself out of the chair. "Let's take you back upstairs. By the looks of you, you fell asleep waiting for *Sunnerklas*."

"Don't wanna, I'm scared. Beth said that if I was bad I won't get anything from *Sunnerklas*," Hanna whimpered, still rubbing one eye and peeking at Anna with the other.

Michael lifted her up. "Well, little one, you won't have anything to worry about now, will you? You haven't been bad." He pushed his finger into her chest, tickling her. Hanna wriggled. He lifted her higher onto his shoulders and proceeded up the steps.

Anna picked up her sewing again and sat down to finish off Elisabeth's present. Michael only got to the second step, when a knock came at the door. Hanna looked at her mama with wide eyes, speechless. Elisabeth, Jakob, and Christian came racing down the stairs and almost knocked over their papa in the process. Jakob opened the door to reveal a very large man with a bushy, but well-kept white beard. A tall red hat sat perched upon his head. Over a long white gown, a plain red cape flowed to the ground. In his right hand, he clutched a long staff that towered above his head, while the bottom tip rested on the ground beside his large feet.

"Shall we invite him in to warm his cold bones?" Jakob put the question to his baby sister.

Hanna hid behind Michael's head but peered out every now and then. She hesitantly nodded. He set her down, and she scampered to her mama, partially hiding behind her skirt.

Sunnerklas walked in, and behind him was a mean-looking man dressed all in torn black clothing with a fur draped over his shoulders. He was carrying a sack and a birch twig. He was known as *Ruprecht*, *Sunnerklas'* helper. He raised a chain above his head and shook it, scaring Hanna into hiding completely behind Anna's skirt. Michael let out a roaring laugh. "Come now, Hanna. There's nothing to be frightened of." He paused. "If you've been good!" Hanna reluctantly allowed her papa to take her hand and walk her over to the white-bearded man. He smelled of smoke and cold air. The snowflakes that showed up so well on his red cape were now melting.

"Have you been good, Hanna?" *Sunnerklas* asked, bending down to her level.

Hanna nodded slowly.

Sunnerklas straightened up and asked her older siblings, "Have you prayed diligently?"

"*Ja*!" they answered simultaneously.

"Have you been well-behaved towards your parents and teachers?"

Elisabeth and Jakob looked to the floor.

Then, "*Ja!*" They all laughed in unison.

"Have you now?" *Ruprecht* asked, opening a bulky book, the

largest one Hanna had ever seen. He ran his bony finger down the page then stopped midway. "Hmmmm," he said, making his lips form a very straight line and his cheeks puff a little. "It says here you've been teasing your sister," he growled.

Hanna stepped back and turned to run, but Michael stopped her.

"Do you see this?" *Ruprecht* raised the birch twig in his right hand. "Do you think I should use this?"

Anna now recognized *Sunnerklas* as Pastor Krumer but couldn't make out who was dressed as his helper.

Hanna didn't lift her head, only her eyes, and shook her head slowly.

"Do you promise not to tease your sister again?"

Hanna nodded her head. *Ruprecht* stood up straight, opened his sack, and gave Hanna, her sister, and brothers an apple each, with a few nuts.

Hanna giggled with delight and ran to show her mama. Jakob opened the door to show them out so they could continue on their way to the next farm.

"Okay, up to bed." Michael clapped his hands together. Jakob picked up Hanna and carried her off to bed. She held as many nuts as she could in her tiny hands.

****

Elisabeth arose the next morning with a queasy feeling in the pit of her stomach. Today Peter would come by before noon to pick her up. She had never lied to her parents before, and she wasn't sure if she could do it. The plan was that her parents would think she was spending the day at the Beck farm with Peter, while his mama assumed he was here with her.

It will never work, she reflected. How could it? Things like this never work for me. She pulled the covers up to her chin. If only she could just stay here in bed and feign an illness. *Nein*! She couldn't do that either; Mama would have her drinking the worst-tasting medicine. It was chilly in her room, and she could hear the wind whistling through a crack in the shutter. It sounded very ominous.

"Beth! Beth!" Hanna yelled, as she came crashing into the room. "Mama wants you downstairs now." She tugged at the cover on the bed.

"*Ja, ja,* Hanna. Go. I'll be down in a minute."

It was cold and Elisabeth dressed as fast as she could. Halfway down the stairs, she could feel the warmth of the hearth hit her cool face. The meal Mama always prepared on this special day permeated the whole room. Everyone stood around the table.

"Come, Elisabeth. *Schnell*!" Anna called. "Papa has an announcement to make."

Elisabeth did as she was told and found a place to stand between her brothers.

Michael straightened his back and walked around the table to where Christian stood. He stood behind him and leaned his hands heavily on his son's shoulders. Christian buckled a bit from the sudden weight on his thin frame. Everyone was staring at Papa, anticipating what the important news could possibly be.

"Your Onkel Gottlieb has been kind enough to offer Christian an apprenticeship into his trade. Christian will study and learn the trade of a weaver." Michael slapped his son on the back. He was beaming with pride to be able to give one of his sons this grand opportunity. Normally, Michael could never afford this, but his brother Gottlieb offered this chance because his own son had died not a year since.

All eyes were now on Christian. Instead of the expected elation, Christian was disheartened. He stared back at his papa in disbelief.

"Well! What do you think?" Michael turned Christian around so they were face to face. "Speak up!"

His first words were almost inaudible, but he eventually spoke when he coughed up enough courage. "But, Papa, I've always thought I would be a farmer like you. Take over the farm."

"Christian, you know the farm will go to Jakob. He's the eldest. What made you think it would be any different?" Christian shrugged his shoulders. Michael added, "You should be happy to get this chance to make a better life for yourself."

"I don't want it, Papa."

Those words seemed to echo around the room over and over again. No one dared talk back like that and get away with it. Papa never hit any of his children, but you never disobeyed him.

"What did you say?" His voice was tense and cold. Elisabeth quickly grabbed Hanna's hand and trotted up the stairs.

Weakly, Christian answered, "I don't want it."

Michael glared at his son. Christian's knees felt so weak he was sure he would crumble to the floor. But he would never let Papa see this. He collected all the courage he had with amazing fortitude. With head held high, he spoke, albeit shakily.

"Jakob doesn't give a tinker's damn about the land. I do." Christian gave a sidelong glance at his brother. He spoke the truth and his brother knew it.

"I'll not hear anymore about it, Christian Heber," Michael said calmly. "We leave early tomorrow for Goppingen."

"But, Papa." Christian begged, then backed off. He could only push so far.

Michael stared down at his son sternly.

"*Ja,* Papa," was his only reply.

****

The rest of the morning was spent busily doing chores around the house until Peter came. Elisabeth thought the knock on the door would never sound. When it did come, she felt surprisingly excited. Her parents wished her to pay their respects to Frau Beck. She felt guilty, but not as much as she thought she would when the time came to go.

Peter helped Elisabeth onto the wagon, then wrapped the large homespun blanket around her legs and up to her waist. He eyed her. The sudden look chilled her. When they started out, it had begun to snow again, but within a matter of minutes, the huge white flakes turned to a light drizzle. Much of the journey was in silence.

Elisabeth turned her head to look at him and mumbled under her breath.

"Pardon? Did you say something, Elisabeth?"

"*Nein.*"

"Are you warm enough?"

"*Ja.*"

The ride was a long one over a road that was no more than a path. As they jostled from side to side, Elisabeth wondered if they would even survive this trip, let alone the wagon. She hadn't long to find out, when the right side of the wagon lurched in the back. At the sound of a loud crack, she let out a shriek as she lost her balance. She fell sideways into a drift of wet snow.

"Elisabeth!" Peter bolted from his seat. Darting to the side of the wagon, he plunged into the drift beside her and lifted her up. "Are you okay?" he asked.

"I think so," she answered, rubbing the back of her head. Peter took off her hat to make sure there was no blood.

"You must have hit your head on this rock. Here, let me help you up. Can you stand?"

She felt a little woozy, but stood with Peter's help, leaning into him. The two of them surveyed the damage. The right back wheel must have hit a deep rut in the road, as it was bent outward in such a contortion that it looked as if some great force had pushed from atop the wagon to cause the wheel to splay out.

"What're we going to do now?" Elisabeth asked anxiously. "We're too far from Steinbach to walk."

"Not to worry. We passed an inn about ten minutes back. Are you strong enough to walk?" He felt the back of her head where quite a lump was rising.

"I think so."

He snatched the blanket, shook off the snow as much as he could, and wrapped it around her. Though it was damp, it would still keep much of the wet from soaking her clothes. However, the drizzle was now turning to a heavier rain.

Five minutes into their journey, the same road that they had just travelled on was now slushy, and the deep ruts were turning into pools of water. Still feeling dizzy, Elisabeth thought she missed one of these pools but landed ankle deep into icy water. Lifting her foot out, she shook it and continued on. They soon spotted the small refuge in the distance and arrived at the front door, both soaking wet.

The inn was situated about halfway between Hohctorf and Steinbach. Travellers from farther north needing fresh horses usually stopped there before continuing their journey south. About three yards in front of the inn stood a well-worn sign that had probably, at one time, displayed the proper title of the establishment. Neither of them could make out the name. The weather-beaten wood with chipped paint swayed with every gust of wind, making an eerie creaking sound on its hinges. They ducked under the overhang. Peter knocked loudly on a dilapidated door. When it opened, an elderly, gray-haired gentleman warmly greeted them. He was much shorter than Peter, but larger in stature. His rotund belly was accentuated by the stained apron he wore.

Reluctantly Elisabeth stepped inside and found it to have quite a pleasant ambiance. The innkeeper introduced himself as Herr Muller and commented on how strange it was to have someone knock on his door where travellers usually come and go as they please.

"Mama!" Herr Muller called out. A little wisp of a woman, as tiny to the extreme as Herr Muller was fat, ran briskly down the steps. She immediately called the pair her two lost waifs and adopted them as her own.

"Here, my *liebling*, take off your coat and let me dry it by the fire. Oh, you poor thing," she continued, helping Elisabeth. "You must be soaked through to the skin. Come, sit by the fire and warm yourself." She guided Elisabeth past a couple of patrons drinking ale. "Come, come, you too." She gestured to Peter with her thin little hands.

"*Danke.* I'm fine. I need your help to fix my wagon before nightfall. The back wheel needs repairing. Can you help me?" Peter queried to Herr Muller.

Peter knew the innkeeper looked upon him with suspicion. Young Protestants often went into Catholic Steinbach to drink and dance since it was forbidden in their own village. He hoped the fat man would not think as such and help them.

"Mama," he called over. "I'll be back, hopefully in a couple of hours. I'm going down the road to where this young man left their wagon." He threw off his apron and it landed on a nearby table.

"You be careful," she answered, as the two of them closed the door behind them.

Elisabeth held her pounding head. "Are you all right?" she heard.

"*Nein.*"

"Come, I'll help you upstairs to one of the rooms." Elisabeth protested as she had no money to pay her kind host.

"Don't you worry your pretty little head. Come, come," she urged.

Not feeling well at all, Elisabeth objected no more. She allowed herself to be assisted up the steps to a quiet room at the end of the hall. Frau Muller stripped her of the wet clothes and put a wrinkled but clean nightgown over her head. It was much too big for her, but it felt warm and dry against her damp skin. It was the prettiest she had ever seen. The daintiest lace skirted the collar and around the cuffs, and even more elaborate lace followed the buttons down the front of the nightgown. Elisabeth didn't object when Frau Muller gently pushed her back onto the pillow and tucked the blankets around her. She shivered a bit, then the warmth of the fire next to her bed quickly overwhelmed her as she fell asleep.

****

It seemed like only a few minutes when Elisabeth awoke with a start. For a moment she forgot where she was. She didn't know how long she had slept, but the room was still light, and she could hear the wood crackling in the fireplace. She felt groggy. She looked out the small window beside the bed; the rain was lashing harder against the window pane.

Her head had stopped pounding, but she could feel a large lump on the back of her skull that was very sore to touch. She slowly sat up and swung her feet over the side of the bed. She took one step to walk over to where Frau Muller had hung her clothes to dry, when she heard Peter's voice coming up the steps. Hastily she crawled back into bed just as he opened the door and peeked inside.

"Elisabeth, are you awake?" He entered the room and shut the door behind him.

"I am," she muttered sheepishly.

"How're you feeling?"

"Much better. Is the wheel fixed?"

"*Ja,* it is. It's really bad out. The road is very muddy but not impassable. For now though, we might as well stay here until our clothes dry, then we'll turn around and go back home. It'll be too late to go to the dance now."

"You're not sleeping here! Go to another room!" Elisabeth pointed to the door.

"I can't, it's the only room left. All the others are taken."

"What will Herr and Frau Muller think of me?"

"Don't worry about that, Elisabeth. I already told them we just got married."

"You what?" She jumped out of bed to give him one wallop with her fist, until she came to the sudden realization that she wore only a nightgown. She swiftly retreated back under the covers. "How dare you, Peter Beck!"

"Herr Muller gave me this cotton nightshirt to wear until my clothes dry." Peter started to undo his belt.

"Get behind my clothes that are hanging there," Elisabeth demanded, turning her back, even though she could only see from his knees down behind the damp clothes.

Peter donned the nightshirt. It did not hang to the floor as it should but above his knees, as the innkeeper was much shorter than he. "I'll stay on the other side of the bed, if you'd like."

A few moments passed unspoken. Then, breaking the unbearable silence, Elisabeth spoke. "Peter, you said last Monday you wanted to talk to me. What about?"

"Now's not the time. We'll talk later."

Sitting straight up, she argued, "It's never a good time with you. You can't tell me one day you have to talk and then forget about it. Tell me now."

Peter sat down beside her on the edge of the bed without answering.

"Well?" Elisabeth said again. She knew it had to be about announcing their engagement soon and then the wedding plans. He was probably too shy to discuss it. If she stood firm with Peter, he would eventually tell her what she wanted to hear.

"I'm still going to Nova Scotia. With Mama and Kristina." He didn't look her in the eyes. "Papa never knew that I planned to stay behind. With his dying breath, he made me promise to take them."

Elisabeth lay there with a lump in her throat, unable to speak. She felt her whole world crash down around her. Tears burned her eyes and trickled out of the corners down into her ears. Shutting her eyelids tightly so no more would leak out, Elisabeth covered her ears to drown out his voice. She couldn't stand to listen any more.

"*Awch*, Elisabeth, please don't. You know I hate it when you cry."

"How could you! How could you? How..."

"Shh, they'll hear downstairs. I have no choice. Don't you see? I promised him."

"What about your promise to me?" Elisabeth turned her back, her shoulders quivering. He touched her arm, and even though she tried to shrug off his hand, he pulled her towards him.

Elisabeth stared into his dark brown eyes and knew he was going to kiss her. She didn't have the strength to stop him. She didn't want to stop him.

"I love you so much, Elisabeth." He breathed heavily.

His kisses were short but lingering pecks on her eyelids, then her nose, her cheeks, then finally he opened his mouth on hers, slowly moving his tongue inside her mouth. Elisabeth felt such a tingling sensation between her thighs that she wanted him desperately to continue. She kissed him back, searching his mouth with her own tongue. Crawling into bed beside her, he continued to kiss her. She felt his hand slip under her nightgown and caress her breast ever so softly, making her nipples stand erect from the mere touch. He moved down over her hip, raised her garment, and slowly rubbed the inside of her leg. She felt something hard pressing against her.

"Ahh, I need you," he whispered, as he wet the inside of her ear with his tongue.

The tingling between her thighs grew so intense that she arched her back so his hand would press harder where it lay. Gently, Peter pulled her nightgown up to her waist, then threw his nightshirt onto the floor. Awkwardly, he tried to penetrate her. After several attempts, he finally found his way into that warm, dark, secret place of a girl.

Elisabeth was in horrible pain. She tried to protest with every thrust that went deeper and deeper into her. He was oblivious to her agony, pumping faster and faster until he exploded. He lay on top of her exhausted.

"Elisabeth, I'm sorry, I'm so sorry..." She didn't stop crying. "I'm sorry," Peter said, rocking her back and forth as he held her in his arms.

CHAPTER 8

"Peter! Peter!" The voice was panicked and shrill, almost to the point of screaming. There was a loud beating on the door. Anna had been busily preparing supper when she heard the commotion outside. She was alone in the house with Stefan, who was sound asleep in his cradle, and she wasn't about to open the door to anyone. The banging persisted as the voice yelled again. "Peter!"

"Maria?" she called through the closed door. Anna then opened it to reveal her friend. Her daughter, Kristina, appeared calm, while her mother was clearly in a state of frenzy.

"Anna! Where's Peter?" Maria tried to peer in through the door.

"Come in, come in. You'll catch your death standing there. What in the world is going on to get you in such a state?" It was raining again and the dampness sent a shiver through Anna as she pulled her inside.

"I must speak to my son. Where is he? I must see him. *Bitte*."

"What are you talking about? Peter was here late this morning to pick up Elisabeth to spend the afternoon with you and Kristina."

Upon hearing this, Maria let herself drop in a nearby chair, while Kristina stood with half a grin on her face. Her mother is emotionally distraught, and she isn't the least bit interested in trying to comfort her, Anna thought. She could have slapped that silly grin off her face, even though she was sixteen years old. Anna never understood how Kristina could ever be a part of the Beck family. She certainly was not the caring soul her parents were.

Maria looked up, constantly moving and wringing her hands. "I knew it! I just knew it!" she cried. "I didn't want to believe it."

Anna knelt down and held her friend's hands, trying to suppress the desire to shake the information out of her. "Believe what? What's wrong? What has happened? Do you know where they are?"

"They're in Steinbach."

Anna couldn't believe her ears. "What are you saying? Surely, you must be wrong."

"Steinbach, Anna. Steinbach!" she repeated. "The Council came to the house an hour ago looking for Peter. He was spotted with Elisabeth on the road going south. Oh, Anna, I'm so frightened. What will I do? Once the Council gets a hold of him..." At this, she broke down into tears.

"Oh, Mama, they just went dancing," Kristina said, and rolled her eyes.

Anna couldn't hold her tongue any longer. "How dare you, you... you little vixen. You have no inkling of the severity of this situation. Do you?"

Kristina raised her eyes upwards, ignoring her.

"Your brother could end up in jail. And if the people in the village get word of this, you'll have a mob at your door in no time. They'll take matters into their own hands. Not to mention what this will do to Elisabeth's reputation. Don't you turn your head, young lady," she said firmly. "Look at me. Have you forgotten that you did this very thing last year, and where did it get you? Shall I refresh your memory, Kristina?"

"Anna, don't." Maria stood up. "She didn't mean it."

"I'm sorry, Maria," Anna replied, but she wasn't about to apologize to Kristina, she'd had it coming for a long time. Kristina sauntered over to where Stefan lay, peered into the cradle, then plunked herself down at the kitchen table, expressionless.

"Oh, how I wish Hans were here. He had no business dying like he did, did he, Anna?" Maria said, tears streaming down her face.

Anna put her arms around her friend, trying to comfort her as best she could. She was never good at that sort of thing. Oh yes, she was always concerned when someone was in trouble and she never had any problem consoling children, but adults? That was a different matter. "It's okay. Michael will be home soon. He'll know what to do."

She no sooner had the words out of her mouth when her husband strode through the door. His frame almost filled the entire doorway. In fact, as tall as he was he had to duck his head a wee bit so as not to knock it against the top frame.

"Brrr, it's cold out there this afternoon. I think it might turn to snow again." He shook his coat as he removed it. The raindrops danced onto the floor. "Ahhh, *guten tag,* Maria. Kristina." He inclined his head. "What brings you over here on such a dreadful afternoon?" Michael saw Maria's wet face and looked at Anna. He raised his thick eyebrows, querying her without words.

"Tis Peter and Elisabeth."

"What about them?" He walked over to Anna, looking down at her and then at Maria. "What's wrong?" His voice rose a little.

Anna interceded. "They went to Steinbach."

It was hard to determine whether what she said had really registered or not. It was always hard to read her husband most of the time. Since Margaretha's death though, he was prone to more fits of outrage than usual.

Michael turned away for a moment then back again, looking at each woman in turn. "How do you know? Has someone seen them?"

"*Ja.*" It was Maria who spoke now, somewhat more composed.

"Don't know who spotted them. The Council wouldn't say."

"The Council?"

"They were over to our house an hour or so ago, questioning Peter's whereabouts. Oh, Anna, what am I to do? If Peter ends up in jail, where will I be then? I need my son, Anna. Kristina and I cannot make the journey to America by ourselves."

America! Anna thought. She couldn't believe Maria still had it in her naive little head to continue with this ridiculous notion. But, this was not the time to discuss it. She would talk to her later.

"Shhh," Anna cooed, walking over to where Maria sat rocking.

"There'll be no talk of that here. Peter's not going to jail," she continued, eyeing Michael for more encouragement.

"Anna's right. He won't be put in the Rathaus. The Council must be getting their information second-hand. I'm sure it's just a case of mistaken identity."

"Come, Maria. Help me make the supper I've started," Anna said, thinking that busy hands would help her. "You and Kristina stay and eat. Wait here till the two of them get home. Kristina, set the table."

Kristina had ignored everyone up till now, sitting quietly on the bench. But she obeyed without a word, and Anna was sure under duress. Michael stood staring out the window as the skies started to darken. Night was falling.

****

Elisabeth and Peter had left the inn about an hour before dusk, but it was now dark as they turned onto the road that led to Elisabeth's house. Neither of them had spoken much since their departure from the Mullers. It had turned colder, and had begun to snow.

Elisabeth had the blanket wrapped tightly around her legs as she sat almost on the edge of the bench. She was too nervous to sit any closer to Peter, though the jolting all over the road made it almost impossible to sit farther than a few inches from him anyway. Getting closer to her house, she saw Frau Beck's wagon. The sight of it made her stomach knot instantly.

Elisabeth shrieked. "Peter, your mama's here? Everyone knows now. I knew it. I knew we'd get caught."

"Stop it! Calm down."

"Calm down?" she screeched. "I knew I shouldn't have let you talk me into it. I can just hear Mama now."

"Look, they don't know where we've been. I'll just say we were on our way back to my house and we met Pastor Krumer. *Ja*, that's it. He invited us in and we never realized how much time had passed."

"It won't work. It just won't."

Just as the wagon slowed to a halt in front of her family's stone house, they were met by Michael standing in the doorway.

"Where the hell have you two been?" he said, stomping out to meet them. Michael grabbed Elisabeth by the waist and lifted her down with such force it almost took her breath away. The blanket she had wrapped around her legs snagged on the wheel and tore.

"In the house now!" Michael grabbed Peter by the scruff of the neck, forcibly leading him inside as Elisabeth scurried in front. Peter was met at the door by Maria, who scrambled to embrace him. Michael was not so lenient and didn't waste time letting his feelings be known. Elisabeth was surprised. She had expected it from her mama instead.

"What the hell do you two think you were doing?" he started.

"Herr Heber, I don't know of what you are speaking," Peter said. "Elisabeth and I were on our way back to my house when we were met by the pastor, who invited us to visit with him, and..."

"You're lying through your teeth, young man!" Michael's tone caused Peter to step back warily. "You were seen driving to Steinbach and reported to the Council."

Elisabeth felt so weak she thought she was going to faint. She sat down on the chair next to her mama, who was unusually quiet and didn't even look at her. Frau Beck stood crying and doing her usual fretting, while Kristina just sat there with a smug look about her.

"But sir, we never went to Steinbach," Peter said.

"Liar!" Michael retorted.

"Tis true, Papa. We never did get there."

"Elisabeth, upstairs. I'll speak to you later."

"But, Papa," she begged, frightened of what might happen to Peter.

"Now!" She ran up the stairs sobbing.

Michael turned back to Peter. "I want the truth and I want it now," he said, a bit quieter this time. He pushed Peter hard on his chest until he sat in the chair involuntarily.

Elisabeth had no intention of going to her bedroom and stopped at the top of the stairs. She crouched down, out of view, and watched with impending trepidation. She could see Peter sitting with his head bowed, clearly trembling, while her papa towered over him. Without raising his head, Peter blurted out the whole story, obviously leaving out their private moment at the inn. After he finished, the silence was deafening. Elisabeth saw her papa walk out of her view. Peter looked so desolate.

"Peter, do you have any idea of the dire consequences of your actions this afternoon? Did you ever think to consider the danger you put yourself and my daughter in returning at this time of night? Schutze is on the loose! Or did you just forget that? What if you met up with him? Do you realize what you've done?" When Peter wouldn't look up, Michael repeated himself, "Do you?" he demanded, grabbing his chin so hard Peter had no choice but to stare him in the eye. He slowly nodded.

Michael let go of his chin with a jerk, leaving a red mark where he had held it. "*Nein*," he said slowly but with intention, "I don't think you do. The Council can have you thrown in jail, and the way I see it, I am the only one who can willingly save your skin."

"But sir, anyone in Steinbach who was at the dance could vouch that we weren't there."

"Do you think any of the young people in that Catholic town will jeopardize their silence to save you? I don't think so."

"The inn," Peter started again. "Ask the innkeepers."

"*Ja*, you're right. But to the Council, you still could have continued on your journey to Steinbach, unless I tell them what time you arrived here tonight."

What was he trying to do? Elisabeth couldn't imagine why he was acting like this. She bolted downstairs, "Papa! You cannot allow this. Only you can tell them. Don't let them put Peter in jail. Mama!" she pleaded, but it fell on deaf ears.

"How dare you disobey me! Back upstairs. Now!" He pointed a shaking finger.

"Papa..." Elisabeth had never stood up to him before, and she could only imagine what the consequences would be if she did. But there was no backing down now. She couldn't stand silent any longer while he battered her beloved. "I'm sorry for going with Peter, but you can't allow this to happen."

"*Pardon* me? Am I hearing you right? Do I have to remind you what happened to Kristina last year?" He gestured in her direction. "Do you want to be reminded of the humiliation she caused her family? Being branded a whore?"

That ugly word seemed to echo over and over again in the small room. She stared at Kristina, who now stared back at her with pity.

Anna spoke, breaking her long silence. "That's what we don't want to happen to Elisabeth. If Peter goes to jail, word would spread in no time and her reputation would surely be tarnished. Michael, I'll not have what happened to Kristina happen to our daughter. You can do something," she stared at him, her eyes softening.

"Peter," Michael said, calmly now, "I forbid you to see Elisabeth again."

"*Bitte*, Papa." Elisabeth cried, grabbing his arm. "You cannot. We love each other."

"I can and I will," he released her hold.

Her rage got the better of her, and she glared at him viciously. "I'll never forgive you for this."

"Elisabeth!" It was her mama who spoke.

"I hate you, Papa! I hate..." The slap of her mama's palm stung her right ear. Elisabeth turned on her heels and raced upstairs sobbing, leaving the room in awkward silence.

CHAPTER 9

"Whoa! Whoa!" Michael held on tight to the reins, trying to control the horses. The wagon on which he and Christian were sitting came to a dead stop while the horses whinnied and reared up. Eight huge hogs ran across their path, and two more raced along either side of the wagon. Christian grabbed the reins as his papa leapt down to clutch the bridles. He tried his best to hold the horses still until the small stampede passed. Christian was small in stature for his fourteen years, at least smaller than Jakob was at his age, and he found the strength of the horses almost too much to handle.

After the last snorting hog stomped by, the master was not too far behind. With a long staff in his right hand, he was frantically waving his left arm over his head and shouting. The middle-aged man was so overweight that it was difficult for him to keep up with the herd. As he ran on his large chubby legs wheezing and shouting blasphemies, the situation became more humourous than serious. Michael broke out into a wide grin, which made it seem all the more amusing until he couldn't contain his laughter any longer. Onlookers joined in, much to the chagrin of the master.

So this is Goppingen, Christian mused. It was so much different from his small village—the noises, the smells, the people, and the general hustle and bustle. As much as he hated the thought of studying to become a weaver under his uncle's tutelage, for a few brief moments, it was all forgotten as other fascinating sights unrolled before his eyes.

Soon the onlookers dispersed and Michael carefully manoeuvred the wagon through the crowd. Stall owners, selling various wares, screamed at the top of their lungs to attract the buyers over to them and away from the neighbouring booths. The spicy, almost pungent aroma of sausages and the pleasant smell of roasting chestnuts seemed to hang over Christian. His stomach gurgled and his mouth watered. The bread and cheese he had been munching on and off during the journey that morning was now mundane.

At the start of their trip, the sun kept Christian warm enough against the chilly air. But now, large grey sombre clouds filled the entire sky, threatening to burst forth thousands of snowflakes. He blew into his hands, rubbing them hard to keep warm as Michael guided the horse down an even narrower street. The houses were so close together, mostly three stories high, with just a few smaller two storey buildings. Michael pulled up in front of a three-story, half-timbered house, and Christian's excitement suddenly left him as quickly as it came. He had never met his Onkel Gottlieb, or not that he remembered anyway.

Michael was already knocking at the door when he motioned him to quickly dismount. There was a commotion going on inside that sounded like arguing, but it abruptly ceased when the door swung open to reveal a short, unusual looking man. He greeted Michael with open arms, giving him a great bear hug. He eyed Christian up and down and commented how he still would have recognized him as his nephew; he was an exact replica of Michael when he was a boy. Putting his arm around his brother, Gottlieb pulled Michael inside and shut the door.

"How went the journey, Michael? You're earlier than we expected."

"We made excellent time, considering the roads. Where's Marie?" he queried, peering around the room.

"My, my, look at my manners. Go over to the fire and warm yourselves. You must be chilled to the bone. The weather has certainly turned since early this morning. I think we're in for some snow." Gottlieb urged them forward.

"*Danke*, Gottlieb." They quickly moved in closer to where the warmth emanated. "Where is Marie?" Michael questioned again.

"Oh, she just went to the market to get a few things."

That seemed to settle Michael's mind, or if it didn't, he certainly never showed it, Christian thought. Already, he was feeling uneasy about this situation; both he and his papa distinctly heard loud arguing just before they were greeted. Onkel Gottlieb seemed kind enough, but Christian certainly would not have guessed that he and his papa were brothers. He was much shorter and stouter. His head was balding on the top, making him look like a monk, and what little hair he did have was gray and wispy. He looked much older than his fifty-five years. His large bulbous nose had small red and purple veins that travelled down either side and meandered over to his cheeks. And when he talked, his nose seemed to wiggle a bit, which made Christian want to laugh.

"Come, Michael. Christian," he said, motioning them to the back of the house where the kitchen was. "Before she left, Marie prepared something hot to eat. Come, come," he gestured, practically running into the kitchen. He turned suddenly and put his hands on his nephew's shoulders, looking him squarely in the eyes. Christian could see they were bloodshot.

"I'm sure we're going to get on just fine, my lad." His uncle's grin made him recoil and want to run away, back to the comfort of his home and family and to the dream of working on the family farm. He just knew he was going to hate it here.

****

The *kartoffel* soup was watery, not thick like his mama's. The potatoes were mushy and tasted bad, almost musty, but it was hot and it quickly warmed them both in a matter of minutes.

Since they sat down to eat, Onkel Gottlieb hadn't stopped talking, shovelling bread and spoonfuls of soup after every sentence. Christian looked at him with disgust as some of the soup dribbled down over his stubbly chin. The usual pleasantries were expressed about Anna, Elisabeth, and how the rest of the children fared. In the same breath, Onkel Gottlieb also extended his sympathies to Michael over his niece's death. Christian noted it did not seem genuine. Michael quickly changed the subject. "How's business been these days, Gottlieb?"

It was the first time Michael's older brother had stopped feeding himself. He chewed away the large bulge in the right side of his mouth. Swallowing, he said, "*Schrecklich*. Very bad." Michael raised his eyebrows in surprise as Gottlieb continued. "At one time, the worst I had to worry about was my neighbour selling his wool cheaper than mine. I wish it were that simple now. The Guild can't fix this problem. The fine ladies and gentlemen have a preference for French-made clothing."

Michael didn't answer.

Gottlieb leaned on the table with both hands and lifted himself up. He walked over to the oak sideboard to grab a printed newspaper that was only four pages. He read aloud. "'No clothes will satisfy us Germans that do not come from France. Watches run better if the Germans in Paris have made them, for the air there is more favourable for their manufacturers than at Augsburg...' And it goes on to say that the same goes for varied articles such as combs, boots, shirts, stockings, etc." Gottlieb threw the newspaper down, which, because of its thinness, floated to the floor.

"I can't believe this. You're the best weaver in these parts. Why, everyone comes from miles around to buy your cloth from as far as Frankfort and Nuremberg."

"That's no matter. With Prince Eugen more in touch with France, there is a much more discriminating demand than us old-fashioned craftsman can satisfy. Paris, for instance, is using much more elaborate tools, and the guild is too stringent to admit such quality of wares to equal them." He stopped for a moment and took in a deep breath. Exhaling, he continued, "I can't keep up with the new machinery that puts out clothing cheaper and more rapidly than I."

"But the quality cannot be the same, Gottlieb. Surely your clients don't think that a machine could produce better."

"Well, right now I'm holding my own. My old clientele have been loyal so far. But eventually they'll probably go where it's cheaper. One of these days I may have to secure a *Verleger*."

"And that is?" Michael furrowed his brow.

"A merchant that would advance me money to buy the tools I need to equal those in Paris, and he in turn would sell my goods."

Michael began to protest at the thought of his brother having to borrow, especially now that he had taken Christian in for the next four years as his apprentice while also paying his Guild fees.

"*Awch*, not to worry, brother. It hasn't gotten that bad yet. Besides we don't want to worry my nephew, do we?" He ruffled the top of Christian's head. Christian, up to this point, wasn't really listening and pulled his head away from his uncle's stubby hand. Giving his nephew a sly look, Gottlieb continued to talk about another subject that interested Christian even less.

Christian turned to look out the window and saw a small boy peering in from out in the courtyard. He quickly left the table and wandered outside. The boy was still standing near the window and turned when hearing Christian speak.

"*Guten tag*."

The skinny boy stared at Christian with large eyes that seemed to fill half his thin face. He had never seen such beautiful yet sorrowful eyes before. The boy looked out from under a mass of tangled curls that hung in small ringlets over his brow. His breeches were full of dirt, with thin patches on the thighs that showed hard wear. The small lad shivered as he wrapped a much too big coat tighter around him. Christian shook as well as he had walked outside without putting on his own. They stood staring at each other.

"*Guten tag*," Christian repeated.

"Shoo! Get away now, you dirty beggar." It was Onkel Gottlieb startling them from behind. "Away with you!" He clapped his hands. "Before I get my switch." The boy took off, running as fast as his thin legs could carry him. Christian saw the fright on his face and would never forgive his uncle.

"Don't let me catch you near that boy. He's a beggar's son. Always in here after any scraps that are thrown out for the dogs."

Michael was right behind his brother. "Where does he live?"

"I suppose in some rat hole," Gottlieb quipped.

"I'd best be heading back to Hohctorf while I've still some light left," Michael said, and embraced his brother. He then gave Christian a longer one. Christian couldn't believe his papa was actually going to leave him there. He felt abandoned.

"*Danke*," Michael added, as he looked at Gottlieb. "Remember what we talked about," he said to Christian. Michael had told him he should be thankful for this opportunity, but he still had a hard time accepting it.

"He'll be fine," Gottlieb remarked, and was about to tousle his nephew's hair again. Instead, he held him hard to his side with his hairy arm, much to Christian's abhorrence.

As they heard the clip-clop of the hooves on the cobblestones as his papa drove away, Christian did everything in his power to fight back the hot tears that threatened to roll down his face.

CHAPTER 10

"Get away from that loom!"

Gottlieb shoved Christian to the side and he fell on his backside, slamming his head on the edge of the wooden loom on the way down. He rubbed the side of his temple as he tried to get up, but his uncle dealt him two hard blows to the side of his head that left his ear ringing. A burning sensation stung his ear and a trickle of blood oozed from it.

His hatred for his uncle had grown over the past couple of weeks as each day slowly melted into the next. He wasn't allowed near the looms, and if he was, he answered to it like today. Christian felt more like a slave than an apprentice, dealing with the day-to-day drudgery of polishing his uncle's shoes, washing the floors, emptying the slop buckets for the night women to collect and dump into the sewer. The worst task of all was when he was ordered to bring home his aunt, who was frequently out to a neighbouring house drinking.

Two nights ago, he had found her sitting on the side of the street shouting profanities at passers-by. However, when his aunt didn't stink of brandy, she was always kind towards him. Christian's heart went out to her when he would see her staggering up the side alley towards their house. She so rarely found her way home.

Christian stared back at his uncle defiantly as he raised his arm to deliver his nephew yet another blow. But Christian flinched, protecting himself with his arms from any further injury. To his surprise and relief, Gottlieb lowered his arm, sputtering, "Go and get your aunt. Now!"

Christian scrambled to his feet and ran out the door, thanking God that he got off easy this time. The last time his right ear was boxed so hard, it pained him for days. He bolted like a rabbit and never stopped until he was a safe distance from the house.

It was dark and the streets were deserted, except for a couple of misplaced beggars huddled in doorways to keep themselves warm. Christian rushed past them and turned down an alley towards the house where his aunt spent most of her days. Usually he went late in the afternoon when it was still light, but today was different, and the darkness frightened him. Slowing his pace through the alley so as not to trip, he stepped methodically over the deep, frozen ruts made by the various wagons and feet of the townspeople. A large cat darted across his path so suddenly that his heart pounded against his chest. He hated this part of town. The houses were so closely knit together. And with the second stories jutting out, it left little room for any moonlight to penetrate. It wasn't too much farther, just a couple more houses and he would be there.

Christian had an uneasy feeling that someone was following him. He quickened his pace, but the steps behind him seemed to match his own. His heart beat faster. Just before he broke into a run, he got up enough nerve to turn around long enough to see a small boy dart against a wall, out of sight. Briefly, in the little moonlight that was allowed to infiltrate, Christian thought he recognized him as the one he had first met outside his uncle's house. Figuring he was probably harmless, he retraced his steps to where he thought he saw him disappear into the shadows. He found him against the wall, eyes bulging with fright.

"Don't be scared. I'm not going to hurt you," Christian soothed. "Didn't I see you a couple of weeks ago?"

The boy nodded his head slightly.

"What's your name?"

"Philip," he answered, barely audible to Christian's ears.

"Do you live around here?" Again the boy motioned his head up and down. He couldn't be more than seven or eight years old, Christian thought. "Where?"

"Where the hell are you, you little brat!" Christian snapped his head around in the direction of the gruff voice. A man of medium-stature came barrelling towards them.

The man elbowed Christian out of the way and grabbed Philip by the scruff of the neck. "I've been looking all over town for you. Where in hell's creation were you? What've you got for me? I'm starving. Empty your pockets!" The intruder then roughly rummaged Philip's pockets. He pulled out the lining in the first pocket, and left it dangling with its frayed hole exposed when he came up empty-handed. The second one had four *kreuzers*. The man smiled impishly and then glared down at Christian, who couldn't help but notice he had one tooth missing.

Christian's heart skipped a beat. He couldn't believe it. It was Schutze, or at least he thought it was him. This man had a full beard; Schutze had always just had stubble. On second thought, however, Christian couldn't be mistaken. He recognized the small close-set eyes and the one tooth that was missing showed a gaping hole when he spoke. And of course, he was sure Schutze recognized him. His mouth opened to speak, but nothing came out as he watched the intruder skitter away into the shadows with Philip chasing after him.

****

Christian bolted straight up in bed, blinking his eyes and panting hard. For the past three nights, he had been dreaming that Schutze was chasing him, and each time Christian had been able to dodge him. But this time, he felt Schutze's hand come down on his back, and that's when he woke. It was still dark but out the window a red-streaked horizon grew in the distance. The sun would be up soon. It was time to put the fire on for Aunt. Instead, he lay still, shivering through the thin worn blanket that he held up to his chin.

He felt a snowflake land gently on the tip of his nose. Peering up, he could see a few flakes drifting down through the hole in the roof and onto his small bed. Initially, sleeping in the attic frightened him because it was the first time he had ever been alone. He was used to sharing with Jakob back home and in a bed not too much bigger than the one he had now.

He let his mind drift to the few nights before when he had met Schutze. Questions were darting in and out of his head faster than he could determine, but one kept reoccurring. How did Philip get involved with such a demon like him? Christian must warn him that he's an escaped convict. But how? He didn't even know where the young lad lived. Well, first things first. He would look for him on his usual errand to get Aunt.

He leapt out of bed, ducking under the clothes dangling above that his aunt had hung to dry, but dry they didn't. They were frozen stiff, miniature icicles dangling at the bottom of his uncle's clothes. As fast as he could, Christian donned his stockings, shirt, and breeches. They felt like ice.

After accomplishing most of the chores that morning, his aunt had asked him to run to the *Brunnen* to fetch more water. Christian was amazed to see her. The customary routine was to meet her friends for "needlepoint" and drink. Onkel Gottlieb was out, so she was left to take care of the shop selling the linen, which was done from the ground level of the house. The shutters opened horizontally onto the courtyard. The bottom shutter served as the counter while the one from above acted as shelter. His aunt wasn't paying too much attention to her nephew as she sat at the counter speaking with a passer-by, so Christian slipped on his coat and stepped out into the fresh air.

The sky was a mass of blueish-gray clouds threatening still more snow. Nature had waved its magic wand during the night. A beautiful dusting of white covered the houses, roofs, and streets. Christian ran with the two wooden buckets, one in each hand, losing his footing now and again in the small drifts. The trees that surrounded the fountain were completely laden with snow, with only a miniscule of dark, wet bark tracing the branches.

Christian kicked the snow from the stone steps and knelt down. Leaning over the small stone wall, he broke through the thin layer of ice with his fist. The skin on his knees itched as the snow melted its way through his wool breeches. It was quiet here; most of the townspeople were mulling about the marketplace wheeling and dealing with the craftsmen.

Just as Christian was dipping the bucket into the frigid water, he heard voices. Glancing in their direction, he saw a tall broad-chested man who wore a long black velvet coat. It was open, revealing a waistcoat with gold buttons that stood out on the scarlet cloth. Standing beside the man was Philip. Now was his chance to warn him about Schutze. He continued filling his pail but watched them on the sly. He'd go after the boy as soon as the stranger left.

The gentleman leaned to one side on his walking stick, and Christian could see the gold knob he was clutching through his fingers. The voices increased in volume. He tried to hear what they were saying, but to no avail. Then suddenly, the man grabbed Philip by his tattered coat. The stick rose up above Philip's head. Christian didn't think twice; if he had, he wouldn't have been so hasty in his decision.

He lifted the pail that was now full and stole his way over to where they stood. The fellow was totally unaware of the dire circumstance creeping up to him, though Philip was quite alert to the scene that was about to play out. Philip ducked when Christian gave his assailant a hard kick from behind.

Christian threw the bucket of water over his head, and in the commotion, they bolted, leaving the victim cursing after them. They ran into the marketplace and lost themselves in the crowd. A few minutes later, out of breath, they turned a corner just outside a shoemaker's shop. They slowed their step to a normal pace once assured they were out of danger. Christian spoke first.

"What happened back there?" he said between short breaths.

"Oh, he caught me begging and wanted to turn me over to the authorities."

Christian had heard his uncle talking about beggars being arrested and sent to convents. For the next few minutes, they walked in silence until they found themselves outside a shop with a small window that displayed a box crib. Christian had never seen anything like it in his life. Both he and Philip stopped to have a better look. What a wondrous sight! He couldn't believe his eyes. As if by magic, the shepherds and the three kings made their appearance while the little animals were moving.

"Look at that, Philip," Christian exclaimed with delight.

"They're amazing, aren't they? My parents had a similar scene like that, but it didn't move. A coin sets these figures in motion. See," he pointed, "Oh, now it's stopped."

Christian wished he had a coin to give the shopkeeper.

"Don't your parents have one anymore?"

Philip lowered his eyes and walked on ahead. Christian quickened his step to catch up.

"Where are your parents? Do they not live here?"

"They're dead."

Christian thought he had heard wrong. He couldn't imagine anyone having no parents, no one to love or take care of you. His papa had spoken about orphans in Goppingen. They would drift from town to town, and after being picked up from the gutters, they were either kicked out or ran away from the convents. Not knowing what to say, he continued to stare at Philip and was relieved when his new-found friend finally spoke.

"I never knew my mama. She died giving birth to me. We lived in Nuremberg, where she was born, for about two years after her death. Papa's from England, and he always promised me we'd go there one day. Papa had no relations in Nuremberg, so Mama's aunt tried to take me away. She said that Papa couldn't raise me proper. Even the authorities were trying to split us up. He was a tailor, and one day we packed what little we had and moved from town to town, staying only as long as it took for Papa to do all the tailoring that was needed."

Even though dozens of questions were flitting in and out of his head, Christian didn't interrupt for fear that Philip would stop. He studied him as Philip's voice waivered. He could see that it was becoming increasingly difficult for him to speak about it.

"About a year ago, we were in Augsburg," Philip started after a brief silence. "Papa was delivering some clothes he had just made and was struck down by a runaway cart." His voice shook and tears welled up in his eyes.

Christian put his arm around him. Philip tensed, so Christian awkwardly removed his arm and shoved his hands in his pockets. "How did you end up here in Goppingen?"

Philip ran his dirty sleeve across his eyes and sniffed at the same time. "The authorities caught me sleeping in a doorway, and the owner of the house reported me. I was taken to a convent with other orphans. I ran away and met up with a couple of craftsmen. We ended up here."

"How old are you, Philip?"

"Nine, almost ten," he said, pushing his shoulders back and holding his head higher.

He seemed small for his age, Christian thought. "Where are you living?"

"Here and there, wherever I can find a warm cubbyhole. But lately, I've been taken in by a kind old man."

Christian felt relieved that at least Philip had protection from the harsh weather.

"Remember a couple of nights back when we met again?" Philip asked.

Christian nodded.

"That was him."

"Schutze!"

"Schutze? *Nein,* his name is Jeremias, Jeremias Schmid!"

Christian wrinkled his brow. Maybe he was mistaken. *Nein*, he said to himself, as he remembered the recognition in Schutze's eyes. It's impossible. It had to be him. It made sense that he would be under an assumed name to dodge the authorities.

"I know him. Not as you say, but as Martin Schultz. He goes by the name Schutze. He's escaped from prison. The authorities are looking for him after he tried to kill Prince Eugen in Hohctorf."

"*Awch, nein*! It must be someone else. Jeremias is from Goppingen and hasn't been outside this town. You're mistaken. 'Sides he's been good to me, taking me in like he has and all."

"The way he was roughing you up the other night, it doesn't look like he's so good to you."

"Well, he's never hurt me all the time I've known him. We takes good care of each other. It's kinda like we're two peas in a pod now. Jeremias makes sure that I don't get carted off to the convent, and I looks out for him that he don't get sent to the Rathaus for his fighting, which he does when he gets to drinking too much. 'Sides he's real kind to me when he's sober. He was just drunk when you saw him." He then said, "You know, I don't know your name!"

"Christian."

"Christian," he repeated. "That's a nice name, I like it. It's the last Thursday afore Christmas. What say you and me go knocking tonight? I'll meet you here."

All of a sudden it dawned on Christian that he'd been gone far too long to fetch the water. He wasn't afraid of his aunt, but he had to get back before his uncle returned from his errands. There was no telling what he would do when he got into his fits of rage.

"I have to go, Philip."

"What about tonight?"

"I can't. I'll see you later." He sped off back to the *Brunnen* to get the buckets he had left.

****

That night, Christian sat on the edge of his bed, fully clothed, cradling his chin in the palms of his hands. He was thankful that his uncle wasn't home yet. Being chastised by his aunt verbally was nothing compared to a whipping. The chill of his room was painfully evident as he crawled under the blanket, hoping to alleviate some of the cold. He shivered. The snow was falling again through the roof and a few flakes found their way atop a brown mouse. It squealed in surprise and skittered away across the floor.

He could hear noises in the street of knockers going from door to door, throwing beans or small stones at the windows. He had fond memories when he, Jakob, and his sisters used to sing a song of praise at a house, stick a pitchfork through the doorway, and the owner of the house would stick something nice to eat on the end of it.

A tapping sound interrupted his reverie. Christian didn't bother to look up; it was probably a knocker at the house or maybe the mice again. When it got louder and more distinct, he sat up; Philip peered in through the window. He rushed to swing it open and saw his friend trying desperately to balance himself on a branch of the great oak tree that stood alongside the house.

"What the hell are you doing here? How'd you find me?" Christian whispered.

"After you left me this afternoon, I followed you here. Come on. We'll go knocking together."

"I told you earlier, I can't."

"Come on, Christian, no one will even know you're gone. We'll only be gone an hour."

It was tempting. He could climb down and be back without them even knowing. Besides, they never looked in on him after he'd gone to bed.

"I'll come." He grabbed his coat, climbed out of the window, and shimmied down the tree after Philip. Surprisingly, Christian wasn't frightened. He was excited to do something without his uncle's watchful eyes.

The hour had passed quickly. They now sauntered down an alley, feeling quite content and eating some gingerbread given to them. Actually, Christian had done the knocking while Philip hid around the corner of the house. It was too obvious he was a beggar.

Philip munched greedily on the gingerbread. "When Papa and I were in Munich, he would always buy me one of these from the Christ Child's Market that was always set up before Christmas."

Goppingen had been exciting for Christian, but listening to

Philip talk, it paled in comparison to Munich. He had heard of the Christmas markets in the larger towns, Nuremberg being the most talked about. "You've been to Munich?" he queried.

"*Ja.* You should see it. The whole market place is covered with stalls, with all kinds of goods for sale. You can buy anything you need for Christmas: decorations for the tree, candles, or cribs like the one we saw this afternoon. Papa always said the Christ Child buys his wares there. The one here isn't nearly so grand."

It was a busy night with the knockers out making lots of racket. But as a light snow began to fall, there was a sense of tranquillity that made Christian dread the thought of going back to the house. He knew he had to before they noticed he was gone. If they ever did check his room – he shivered at the very idea of it.

"I must get back."

They turned around and ran all the way. Philip laughed as he tried to keep up with Christian.

"Shhh, be quiet. I can see Onkel through the window. Get down and keep out of sight."

Christian leapt up to the branch above and lifted himself up with his arms, swinging one leg over the next branch. Climbing as quietly as he could, he stepped onto a smaller branch. It snapped off. He caught himself, but to his dismay the bough fell against the window below.

"Quick, Christian! I see him. He heard!" Philip's face was panicked.

"Go, Philip, run before he sees you." Without another word, his friend obeyed and quickly sped off into the night.

Christian continued to climb, and swung open the partly ajar window. He crawled inside and quickly threw off his clothes and put on his nightshirt. Just as he was getting into bed, his uncle appeared at the doorway. His stomach churned at the sight of him.

"Where the hell have you been, you ingrate?" he spat. He stormed into the room, throwing back the clothes that hung in his way, some falling into a heap on the floor. In his hand, Christian saw the bough that had broken and hit the pane.

He had no time to answer before the branch came down hard on his thighs. He covered his face and screamed. His uncle continuously thrashed him over his arms, chest, and legs, leaving red welts that instantly puffed up on his white skin.

"This is what you get when you disobey me!"

The words kept ringing in his ears as it was repeated over and over again. Christian could feel a warm stream run down his leg.

"You'll kill him! Don't, Gottlieb! Stop it!" His aunt suddenly appeared and tried to grab her husband's arm. She had to duck so as not to get the sting of the weapon.

"Get away, woman!" he growled and shoved her, almost knocking her over. "I'll teach him, and this is the only way he'll learn."

Christian didn't know what made him stop, but when he turned his gaze back to him and their eyes met, he threw down the bough and walked away. Marie ran after him.

Shaking and aching all over, Christian slowly pulled the coverlet over his head. He trembled from fear more than the cold. He wanted desperately to run away. But there was no telling what Gottlieb was capable of if he found him. At first, as he lay in the wetness of his bed, the shame overwhelmed him and he gave in to crying. Then he angrily ran his hands over his eyes. The hate that welled up in him left no room for tears. He would get out of here. He'd find a way.

CHAPTER 11

Elisabeth awoke suddenly from a deep sleep. The abrupt realization that she was going to be sick made her leap out of bed to a basin set in the corner of her room. Her eyes watered when she purged the little contents that she had from her belly. Inhaling deep shallow breaths, she waited for another heave but it didn't come.

She slowly stood up and felt her way in the dark to the water basin. Her index finger poked through a layer of paper-thin ice, and she dipped the cloth in the frigid water. As frosty as the room felt, her forehead and face still felt sweaty. The coolness felt soothing as she pressed it against her warm cheeks.

She heard Hanna stir and quietly tiptoed back to her bed, silently slipping under the covers so as not to further disturb her. Her baby sister asked so many questions, and she definitely didn't want her running to Mama blurting out that she was sick.

It wasn't the first time she had vomited. Since Christmas she had been nauseous every morning but not always retching. She had been very quiet and moody of late, and her monthly flux had not occurred. Remembering her mama's symptoms, she was sure she was pregnant. Her parents noticed her temperament but told her she would soon get over Peter in time.

Elisabeth cringed at the thought of what would happen when her papa found out, yet she was elated to be having Peter's baby. Now Peter would have to marry her, and Papa couldn't stop it. He certainly wouldn't stand for any daughter of his having a child out of wedlock.

Her thoughts darted from one direction to another. Peter couldn't go to America now. How could he with this babe growing inside her belly? She had not seen him since that awful night they were forbidden to see each other. Seeing him at a distance at church or the market didn't count, as either one parent or the other would always hurry her along. Mama and Papa just didn't understand. They loved each other so much, and she knew there wasn't much time now. Peter and his family were leaving in a couple of weeks to meet the *Speedwell* in Rotterdam.

She would have to plan something quickly. Elisabeth's stomach was more settled now, which made her relax. There was another hour left before the house bustled with activity, and she started to become drowsy considering how she could see her beloved privately. It would take some scheming to deceive her parents, who seemed to be never out of her sight. Maybe Jakob would help her, she reflected, as she allowed herself to slip back into slumber.

****

It was easier than she thought. Surprisingly, Jakob accepted the task even though they weren't as close as they used to be. It was her chore to always get the eggs in the morning from the hens in the barn, and the cowshed was far enough from the house that no one would hear or see anything. Promptly before daybreak, she snatched the basket and the lantern, and donned her coat. She set off towards the barn. Her stomach was turning somersaults at the thought of getting caught, and of seeing Peter alone for the first time in eight weeks. The sun wasn't even peeking over the horizon yet as she carried the lantern. The only noise in the early morning silence was her feet crunching through the snow. She slowly opened the door; it scraped noisily in the crisp air. Stepping inside, she soon realized he hadn't arrived. She hung the lantern on the wooden peg and began to extract the eggs from under the hens, laying them gently in the basket.

Her mind was certainly not on the things at hand. She wondered if Peter would indeed show his face, if he had been able to sneak past his mama, or his sister for that matter, who relished in squealing on her brother. Even though she liked Kristina enormously, she was such a tattle-tale. She had rehearsed over and over in her mind what she was going to say. She was sure that when he heard, he would do the right thing and marry her.

"Elisabeth?"

Her heart leapt in her mouth as she turned and dropped the two eggs she was holding. One cracked on her boot and the other fell to the dirt floor. White and yellow fluid oozed from both as it intermingled with the straw. Peter was standing behind her. For how long, she didn't know. She felt nauseated but knew it wasn't from her pregnancy this time.

"Peter! My goodness!" She could see her foggy breath clouding the chilly air as she spoke.

"I've been here for an hour already. Up there," he pointed to the loft of hay above their heads.

"Why didn't you make your presence known to me? Now look at what you've done. Mama will have a fit; the hens haven't been laying many lately." She bent down and tried to wipe the yoke off her boot with the straw.

Peter took her by the arms to stand her up and gazed into her eyes. Elisabeth felt weak-kneed and everything she had rehearsed was for naught. She couldn't remember a thing. Without a word, he took her in his arms and squeezed her so tightly she couldn't breathe. She could feel his hot breath on her ear.

"Elisabeth, I missed you so," he whispered, then held her at arm's length.

"And I you, Peter." Then to her surprise and shock, she started to cry, which she told herself she wouldn't do.

"Shh. I'm here now."

Elisabeth let her feelings go completely out of control.

She was so angry at herself. He bent his head, kissing her hard. She responded with equally-frenzied passion. It felt good again and so right. He started to move his hand inside her coat, but she pushed him away.

"I'm with child." Elisabeth didn't know where the words came from. They hung there frozen in mid-air on the cold February morning.

Peter's eyes grew large.

"Your seed grows within me."

"Are you sure?"

"I'm as sure as you're standing in front of me. I've been sick almost every morning. And my flux..." Her voice lowered in embarrassment. "It hasn't come. It's overdue," she continued quietly, bowing her head.

Turning and walking away from her, Peter never uttered a word, until, "What are you going to do?"

This isn't right, she thought. He was supposed to take her in his arms and ask her to marry him. He was supposed to be happy. This can't be happening.

"What am *I* going to do? I can't believe you're saying this. I thought you missed me...the night you bedded me...didn't it mean anything?" Her eyes stung with tears. She brushed past him and clutched the latch on the door.

"Elisabeth, don't! Don't leave like this. You know I have a commitment. We leave in two weeks."

She stopped short and spun around, her shawl slipping off her head and falling onto her shoulders. “What about us? You have a far bigger commitment here, our baby.” Her voice cracked.

“Elisabeth, come with me. Marry me and we’ll go together, start a new life.”

Marry him was what she wanted to hear but not away from her home and her family. She couldn’t. “I’ll marry you, Peter. I love you so much. But I’ll not move away from here. Don’t go, stay here with me. I have nowhere to turn. When Papa finds out I’m to have a baby, there’s no telling what he’ll do. *Bitte...*” She sobbed hysterically.

Peter gathered her up in his arms and held her close to his chest. He smoothed her hair. “I’ll stay.”

****

For the next ten days, Jakob acted the messenger between the two lovers. Elisabeth still had not mustered up the courage to tell her papa that she was planning to marry Peter. But she couldn’t ignore the inevitable any longer. She was more than eight weeks pregnant. The sooner the deed was done, the sooner the two of them could get married. Of course, by her parents’ calculations, the baby would be born too early, but she would worry about that when it happened. First things first, she thought.

****

The village was abuzz with activity as two families, the Becks and Ehrhards, were starting out at first light tomorrow morning towards the Rhine, which would take them on their long journey to where the *Speedwell* was docked in Rotterdam. Every time Elisabeth would broach the subject with Peter, he would change it. He was always so closed-mouthed about things that were hurtful to him. And Elisabeth was sure it must have been the hardest thing to tell his family that he was going against his papa's wishes. The last couple of days she had seen him, he was very moody. Yesterday morning, after their usual clandestine meeting in the cowshed at dawn, they finally decided to approach her parents together the next day after church. There was going to be a special service for the two families before starting on their journey.

This morning Elisabeth's family rode to St. Martin's to see their friends for the last time. Feigning illness, she was glad her mama put it down to her flux and didn't question her further. As soon as she heard the wagon pull away, she hurriedly dressed herself. Peter would be here soon. They needed to talk about their plans and how best to tell her parents.

An hour went by and there was still no sign of him. She started to pace the floor, sat down in her papa's rocking chair, then stood up again. All of a sudden, a horse whinnied outside and she rushed to open it. It was Jakob.

"What are you doing here? Where's Peter? Do you know where he is?" Upon seeing his solemn face, she demanded, "Jakob, answer me!" Her brother handed her a piece of paper. She stood staring at it, not wanting to touch it. Jakob thrust it into her hands. She slowly walked to the lit lantern on the table and opened it.

"Dearest Elisabeth," it started. "By the time you read this, I'll be on my way to the Rhine. I'm so sorry. I can't abandon Mama after my promise to Papa on his deathbed..." She couldn't read any further. She let the letter float to the floor.

Jakob picked it up, and read aloud. "I'm so ashamed to be abandoning you when you need me most." Jakob looked at his sister in bewilderment. He continued, "I'll be back. Wait for me. B*itte*."

Elisabeth was deaf to his words. What was she going to do?

Where could she turn? She fell to her knees and was oblivious to the tears that now wet her cheeks.

Jakob crouched down in front of his sister as she rocked back and forth. He held her hands tightly. "Elisabeth, what did he mean 'abandoning you when you need me most.'?"

Her brother was the one person she could confide in. He deserved that for what he had been doing for her over the past couple of weeks. Sniffing back her tears and gripping her belly, she blurted out the whole sad story. "I'm going to have Peter's baby." His eyes softened and he hugged her tightly.

"I love Peter so much. He'll come back, he's got to," she said, choking back the tears, "He must."

"I hope so." He rocked her back and forth, trying as best he could to comfort her.

In the distance, Elisabeth could hear the faint ringing of St. Martin's church bells. The families had already left Hohctorf.

****

For the next few nights, she didn't sleep a wink, tossing and turning. The decision to tell her parents was difficult; however, there was an easy way out—be rid of the baby. Her mind went back to Frau Haug when her mama was in labour. She needed that plant, or was it fungus? Now what was it Frau Haug had called it - ergan, no, ergot. That was it, ergot! It can give life or take it away, she once told her. One night she would say yes to doing this terrible deed, and then another, she couldn't bear to think about it. Desperation took over.

Finally the decision was made. She just needed a plan to get to Frau Haug's house. On this particular morning, the last day of February, luck was with her. It must be right; things were falling into place so systematically. After the circumstances with Stefan's birth, no one would dare bring Frau Haug's name up in the house again. But Mama was still loyal to her, and Elisabeth thought, maybe in a way felt sorry for her. Mama never really got her full strength back after the birth, and that morning she asked Elisabeth to drive over to the midwife to get some herbs. Of course, without Papa and Jakob's knowledge. But first she would stop in the village with her basket of eggs to sell. *Ja*, she thought, she was sure of this decision. She couldn't live with the disgrace of having a baby out of wedlock, not to mention her Papa's devastation. She would be branded a whore. This was the right thing to do.

****

Jakob reined in his horse hard as it reared up at a flock of large woolly sheep crossing the road in front of him. A black and white dog barked profusely to keep his charges in line, while his master walked farther behind the flock carrying a large wooden stave. Concentrating on matters at hand, the farmer was unaware of Jakob's presence at first. Upon hearing his observer's "*guten morgen*," he briefly acknowledged him with a wave of his free hand and a smile.

Carefully picking his way through the confusion, Jakob continued his journey into the village. It was another beautiful spring-like morning, as it had been the past couple of weeks. The season was arriving too early. Maybe this is just one of Mother Nature's tricks, Jakob thought. Tomorrow we could be back in the throes of winter again. However, there was evidence to the contrary. Jakob had seen a lone barn swallow this morning, who must have thought Spring was here also. Just yesterday, he was not mistaken when he observed a large black stork with its red bill and legs. Birds perceive things and follow their God-given instincts that are unexplainable to man. Even the smell of Spring seemed to permeate Jakob's nostrils as he and Blitz cantered down the straight dirt road, which heaved in spots from the winter frost. He was sure his mind was playing tricks when he saw the buds on a nearby chestnut tree swelling to burst forth their new leaves.

As he approached the village market, his back felt very warm from the sun. He meandered through the crowd that mingled in and around the stalls, dismounting at the tavern. He tethered the reins to the post outside the door, and walked in. Being mid-morning, the place was abuzz with the locals. The smell of beer wafted in the stale air. Villagers stood with their earthenware mugs, some seated shoulder to shoulder on benches. Upon spotting a familiar face, he squeezed his way through the crowd over to Georg's table.

Georg waved to his friend. He slid over on his bench to give Jakob what little room there was.

He sat down in the corner, facing backwards toward the window, one worn leather boot balanced on the ledge and leaning back against the table. The proprietor carried a tall icy stein, thick with froth, to where they were seated. The usual greetings were exchanged before the owner carried on with his duties.

"What are you doing in here, Georg? I would have thought you'd be busy with your patients."

"I have a few, but not as many as I would like." His voice sounded bitter. "Not that I want everyone to be sick. It's just difficult breaking into a new village after the locals here are accustomed to the barber-surgeon from Goppingen. And the women won't let me near them to deliver their children."

Jakob couldn't help but smile as he remembered his mama being too sick to retaliate. He understood what Georg was saying. The village was set in its ways, especially the women. Stubborn!

"In fact, I've just returned from your mama's."

"Oh?" Jakob lowered his mug, wiping his lips. He was unaware of any problems, other than his mama's complaints of being tired.

"Not to worry, my friend. It's nothing serious, or at least I don't think so. That woman won't let me near her." Georg's lips formed a straight line in frustration. He set his beer down so hard that the contents swished to the rim of its container. "Do you know she chased me out the door waving a large spoon over her head?"

Jakob let out the most uproarious laughter. "*Awch*, Georg," he remarked. "I wouldn't lose any sleep over that one. You can keep trying, but I very much doubt you'll get anywhere with Mama."

Georg eyed him, then joined in his laughter.

Because of the close proximity of the other patrons in the tavern, they could not help but overhear various conversations. "I can't believe everyone is still talking about Eugen's close brush with death," Jakob said. "Time to let it rest! Of course, they're equally wagging their tongues about the lunatics sailing across the ocean."

"I spotted you a couple of weeks ago at St. Martin's, seeing off those families. I couldn't get your attention with all the commotion." Georg fell silent for a brief moment, contemplating his next thought. "You know, Jakob, I've been thinking that emigrating isn't such a bad idea after all."

"Are you daft? Do you really want to sail three months across the dangerous ocean? Why, the journey alone from here to Rotterdam takes two, two-and-a-half months. Not for me, uh-uh." He shook his head.

"I'm sick to death of this Godless land; the Catholics and Protestants up in arms. Raising taxes again! Trying to get more tariffs from us, instead of bleeding the rich. Why, I couldn't even travel from Frankfort without a bloody permit. It's ludicrous!" His voice started to get louder and more high-pitched. "*Awch*, this poor land! It hasn't been the same for a hundred years since the wars ravished it. It's left so few people."

"Lower your voice, Georg. You don't have any idea who has big ears."

"My whole point, my friend. I'm sick and tired of the secret meetings, the unrest, the hatred, and the road tolls. I could go on and on." Georg waved his hand in defeat. "I wish to God that blood-sucking prince had met his death."

"If you don't lower your voice, both of us will get thrown out of here. If not that, we'll get thrown in the Rathaus. Besides," Jakob lowered his voice to a whisper and leaned into the *doktor's* ear, "you know I share the same views as you. The faster that pig dies the better."

They eyed each other and smirked.

"I know exactly how you feel," Jakob continued. "Did you hear yesterday that Caspar Heckman's been drafted into the army? He's my age! It won't be long before they get me, but they're not."

"I don't know how, but so far I've escaped the dreaded army. But not for long. That's why I want out of here. In the new land, they'll certainly be in need of a *doktor*. Then there won't be any problems keeping busy."

"Ja," Jakob nodded. "With the poisonous snakes and savage Indians, the immigrants will be too hard up to be fussy about who heals their wounds." He chuckled but soon stopped when he noticed his friend wasn't joining in.

"That's just gossip spread around by the Council to keep us here. Can you imagine if they had no one to manipulate or kick around?" He smiled at that statement. "Besides you don't have any hard evidence of what things are really like over there. No one's ever returned to Hohctorf since the emigration started almost a year ago. It's all hearsay. Hell, Jakob, it can't be any worse than here. Right?"

He nudged him with his elbow.

A few moments passed in silence, each one pondering what it would be like to start a whole new life.

"By the by, I just saw your sister leave the village in the family cart alone. It looked like she was heading in the direction of Frau Haug's house."

"Damn! Why would she go there? How long ago was it?" Jakob stood directly. Then it dawned on him.

"About an hour ago. Just before I got here." Georg stood up, eying Jakob. He was a full head shorter than his friend. "What's wrong? You look like you've seen a ghost."

"Why didn't you say something?" As soon as Jakob uttered the words, he realized how unreasonable he was being. His companion couldn't possibly know what was going on. For the past ten days since Elisabeth had confided in him, he'd noticed her becoming more withdrawn. She had told him that she was considering not telling their parents about the baby. She had also become increasingly interested in Frau Haug. Jakob didn't understand at the time, but now things started to make sense. After explaining the sordid story of what he knew, he ran out the door, pushing his way through the crowd. Georg bolted after him.

****

Elisabeth sat on the bench seat of the wagon, waiting to summon up enough courage to knock on the door. This was the first time she'd been here. The dwelling was smaller than she imagined: run down and set in the middle of nowhere without one tree around the property.

Staring at the lead-pane window, Elisabeth thought she detected a slight movement of the curtain. Now she would have to go in;

Frau Haug must have seen her. Slowly she stepped down from the wagon and made her way to the door. Elisabeth suspected that Frau Haug was aware of her presence, but still it startled her when the door opened.

Rosina didn't hesitate to invite her in. She was beckoned inside to the only room where cooking, eating, and sleeping were done. Elisabeth had to adjust her eyes to the dim light. Directly in front of her was a small dirty table with one chair whose seat sagged in the middle. A tiny motley cat was curled up into a ball fast asleep. Elisabeth could see its tail twitching from side to side. The room was sparsely furnished with only a small cot set up on one side of the room under the shutters. There were numerous bunches of drying herbs dangling from the beams in the ceiling. One large cauldron was set inside the opening of the fireplace, steam rising from the contents. The smell certainly wasn't appealing, but it was overpowered by the fresh dried herbs that hung by their stems upright above Elisabeth's head.

"Come in, child. Tis good to see you. How's your mama faring these days?" Frau Haug guided her farther inside. "I'm surprised she lived after that ordeal; your brother, bringing in that despicable *doktor*." She rambled on without waiting for any reply from her visitor. "After all, I delivered you and all your brothers and sisters, didn't I?" Her voice became more rigid. "How's the new babe? He must be growing big, *nein*?"

Elisabeth simply wanted the herb potion for her mama and the ergot for herself. If she dawdled any longer, she'd lose her nerve.

"Mama's fine. Just feeling a bit tired. She sent me here to see if you have anything to gain her energy back."

"Well, my child, I have just the thing." Walking over to a small clay container with a broken lid, she pinched some herbs, crushing them back and forth in the palm of her hand. She sprinkled them into a small dirty piece of cloth and said, "Now, tell your mama to put a tiny amount about the size of a *kreuzer* into a glass of fresh milk and drink it once a day for about a week. You mark my words, child, she'll be feeling herself in no time at all." She tied the four corners of the cloth together with a piece of twine and set it into Elisabeth's outstretched palm.

After putting the object in her coat pocket for safekeeping, Elisabeth stood there silently, trying to get up enough nerve to ask for her more important need.

"What is it, child? Speak up! Is there something else you haven't told me about Anna?"

"*Nein*!" she answered abruptly. "I want some ergot..." Her voice was shaky and the last word was barely audible.

"What did you say you wanted?"

"Ergot."

"Whatever for? Who for?"

Involuntarily, her eyes filled with moisture.

Frau Haug put her arm around Elisabeth and guided her to a chair. "Shoo! Scat!" she said to her pet. With a hiss, the cat slinked to the floor. Elisabeth sat down on the lone seat, warm from the animal. The whole story came out — about Peter promising to marry her, her being with child, and then her abandonment.

Frau Haug crossed herself. "You poor thing. Why, you're just a babe yourself." She stroked Elisabeth's yellow hair back from her red-rimmed eyes. "And you've come here to be rid of this child?" Elisabeth nodded her head. "Are you sure you want to go through with this? Elisabeth, have you thought this through long enough? I know your mama and papa well. Of course, they'll be upset at first, but they'll come around, child."

"Oh, Frau Haug, I have to, I must get rid of it. I hate Peter for leaving me. I can't go through with it. Don't turn me down. You've got to do it, *bitte*." Tears streamed down her face, big drops trickled onto her coat.

"But your mama and I are friends. I couldn't do this..."

Elisabeth stopped crying and jumped up, shrugging off Rosina's hands that held her. "Fine! I'll go somewhere else. I'll find someone to help me even if I have to go to Goppingen," she shouted. She knew she had nowhere else to go, but she was desperate and hoped the threat might change Frau Haug's mind.

"I'll do it," Frau Haug said. "In my hands you'll come to no harm; but, some other butcher of a midwife could very well kill you."

She walked over to her cupboard, mumbling things Elisabeth couldn't comprehend. "We won't use ergot; much too dangerous." She thought she heard her say 'savin bush,' then saw her shake her head.

"Aha," Frau Haug uttered under her breath. "This is it, child: rue, or ruta graviolens. This isn't dangerous and it'll do the job." Rosina took three roots of rue about the size of her finger, sliced them up, and put them in water that was already boiling over the fire.

It was much later before Frau Haug spoke again. Elisabeth had lost all track of time. Taking a large spoon, she stirred the contents in the black pot. "See, it's been boiled down to the perfect amount, about three cupfuls." She poured it into a bowl, letting it cool a bit before handing it to her.

"Now drink this all at once," she said, blowing into the bowl to further cool it and passed it to her. "You'll abort in about two days."

Elisabeth hesitated, then, sipped it. It didn't taste so bad, so she proceeded to gulp it. It was a lot to drink and she paused halfway through.

The door smashed open just as she was ready to down the rest.

She dropped the bowl and spilled its contents onto the floor. Jakob rushed towards Frau Haug. Her brother's face was so red with rage that it blended into his red hair. Georg darted in immediately after her brother.

"What's the meaning of this? Get out of here!" Rosina pounced at Jakob, then recoiled at the sight of Georg. "And take that godless viper with you!"

"Out of my way, old woman." Looking in Elisabeth's direction, he said, "Are you all right?" He eyed the wet floor and the upside down bowl at her feet. "What are you doing here, what's this?" he pointed at the floor.

Georg dipped his finger into the puddle and tasted it. He inclined his head slightly to Jakob giving him some sort of a signal.

"You cursed witch! You killed my family, but, by God, you'll not hurt my sister!" Jakob screamed. "Why, I just might..." He lunged at Frau Haug, who was now backing away from her accuser.

"It's not her fault." Elisabeth clawed at Jakob's arm. "I forced her to do this. I begged her. Jakob, don't!"

"You expect me to believe that?" he snapped. Jakob knocked Frau Haug over with his arm, and with such force that she reeled backward and hit her head on the stone hearth with a sickening crunch. Blood immediately gushed from the back of her skull. She didn't move. His chest heaving up and down, Jakob was frozen to the floor. Georg rushed to the lifeless body and examined it. Feeling no pulse, he leered at Jakob, horrified.

"My God, Jakob! What have you done?" Elisabeth screamed.

"She's dead," Georg uttered in disbelief. He grabbed a blanket to cover the gruesome sight.

With her hand over her mouth, Elisabeth let out a stifled scream, gagging at the same time. Jakob backed his way to the door.

"Give me a hand and help me get her into the wagon. Grab that other blanket." At hearing no response, Georg repeated, "Jakob!"

He kept backing up, almost tripping over the chair.

Elisabeth could see beads of perspiration breaking out on his face and forehead. He never once took his eyes off the body now lying limp in Georg's arms. Blood dripped onto the floor.

"Help me, now!" Georg demanded. "Snap out of it! We've got to take the body into the village. Report it, and..."

"*Nein.*" It was Elisabeth speaking, panic in her voice. She didn't even know how much time had lapsed. It seemed forever, as if time had stood still. "We can't. They'll arrest him. He'll be hanged. Why not just leave her on the floor? Whoever finds her will think she has fallen. No one ever needs to know we were here."

"Come to your senses, girl. There's no bloody way the Council will believe there was no foul play. They'll investigate. *Nein,* we're doing the right thing in explaining the whole story. We're witnesses. We'll say it was an accident."

"My God, I killed her," Jakob muttered. It was the first time he'd spoken, and Georg and Elisabeth stared at him. He kept repeating it over and over again, then turned quickly out the door.

"Jakob!" Elisabeth ran after him. But it was too late, he had already mounted Blitz and galloped off at a neck-breaking speed.

****

For the next two days, Elisabeth was in agony. Even though she had only drunk about half of the rue, she felt its terrible effects. It had started as soon as she arrived home, after leaving Frau Haug's. First the nausea, then the sharp pains in her belly. Elisabeth was beginning to wonder if this was really worth it. For the last twenty-four hours, she had not been able to keep anything down. She wasn't even sure what day it was now. She vaguely remembered her mama putting a cool hand on her face and stroking the hair back from her forehead. Was that Jakob she saw? She wasn't sure. Elisabeth was so hot, and everyone in the room seemed to be moving so slowly.

She awoke some time in the afternoon just as the sun was streaming through the window onto her bed. She felt weak from the ordeal, and her sheets were damp from where the fever must have broken. She blinked a few times to focus.

"Mama?" Elisabeth touched her mama's hair softly as she slept beside her on a stool, her head resting on the quilt. She saw Doktor Gessler also sleeping in a chair, his head bent forward onto his chest. She puzzled over why he was here; her mama had banned him from ever entering the house. Elisabeth scanned the room to find her papa dozing in the same manner.

Anna jolted awake. "Elisabeth! Oh, Elisabeth! Doktor Gessler, she's awake. Oh, my *liebling*." Her mama stroked her head.

Georg stretched and leaned over his charge. He laid the back of his hand on her cheeks. "You're looking much better. How do you feel?"

"Weak."

"And you will for a while. I just want you to rest here for the next few days and stick to eating only clear broth to settle your stomach and get your strength back."

Her papa was on the other side of the bed, staring down at her. He seemed much older than usual. "Where's Jakob?" she asked him.

"I'll go downstairs now and bring you that soup." Anna left the room, closing the door quietly behind her.

"We'll talk later when you're much stronger," Michael replied, smiling. He eyed Georg. "I'll see you out." Michael walked ahead, leaving Georg alone with Elisabeth.

"What's going on? Where's Jakob? I saw him in this room."

"You couldn't have, Elisabeth. You were running a very high

fever, you must have been hallucinating." She was about to protest, but Georg stopped her. "You must put all your energies into getting better."

Suddenly she realized - the baby! Had she lost it? She couldn't say anything since Jakob was the only one who knew.

"You didn't lose the baby. I don't know how, but, for what you just went through, it's a miracle. God must want you to have it. It's your destiny."

Doktor Gessler must have read her mind. Before she was able to ask the next question, he volunteered, "Your parents know. You rest."

She was devastated. How could she face them again? She lay alone in her bed, terrified.

CHAPTER 12

For the next few days, Elisabeth gradually regained her strength. She had been fully bedridden for the first two before attempting to move about. Lying in bed gave her time to think and worry about the baby and her parents. Ideas of running away flashed before her eyes, but where could she go? Her mama had been her usual attentive self, fretting over her; but Papa had been silent, only popping his head in once to see how she was feeling.

She could hear whispers between her parents, which ended the moment she would enter the room. She knew they were most likely discussing her situation. Elisabeth thought of directly asking them, but she knew that would only make the situation worse. Papa would discuss it in due course and not before he was ready. She thought of maybe getting around Mama, but she was now acting differently. It would be better if they would just scream at her, punish her, get it over with, rather than this strained silence. The silence was draining.

She considered drinking the potion again, but there was no one to go to now. Frau Haug was dead. Remembering that horrific day of the macabre scene with her lifeless body on the floor and Jakob running away was too much, and she tried to shove it to the back of her mind. Where was he? Maybe that was what all the whispers were about and it wasn't her at all, but she doubted it.

On this particular day, Elisabeth was feeling stronger and decided to prepare the *spatzle* for the *fladdle* soup that bubbled over the fire. Mama was sitting on her stool spinning wool, her foot pumping busily up and down. Stefan was napping next to her in his cradle, while Papa sat in his chair carving wooden spoons. She was sure this was at Mama's insistence, as the old ones were perfectly good in his eyes. The platters they ate from also needed replacing, and during the long winter months, Papa and Jakob would sculpt them diligently. These were the days for fixing, repairing, and making anew. Up until now, they spent most of their time in the barn fixing the scythes, rakes, and other tools.

The silence was still too hard to take, especially the empty spot where her brother should be sitting. Hearing Papa clear his throat, she nervously glanced up from the table where she was mixing the dumplings. Things seemed to be climaxing the last few days, so she was trying to prepare herself for the inevitable. What that was, she didn't know.

"Elisabeth?"

"*Ja*, Papa." Her mama continued spinning, clap, clap, with her foot. It was nerve wracking. Something was amiss.

"Are you ready to tell us what happened?"

She didn't know if he was speaking about the baby, Jakob, or Frau Haug's untimely death. How much did her parents know, and what had Doktor Gessler said? Oh, she wished she had asked him what had transpired during her illness. "About what, Papa?" Her voice was barely a whisper.

"You know damn well what I mean, young lady." He was standing now and his fist came crashing down on the table. The wooden bowl she was mixing the *spatzle* in jumped and tipped on its side. "I want the whole story! Everything! You were there at Frau Haug's. You saw the whole thing. What happened, girl?"

Her mama raised her head in Elisabeth's direction. The click-click of the peddle stopped. The spinning wheel was motionless. Elisabeth wished with all her heart that she was anywhere but here.

Remembering what the *doktor* said on that day, she blurted, "It was an accident, Papa!" Her lower lip quivered. Then the whole story came out: why she was there, Jakob and Doktor Gessler showing up, the argument. But she twisted the story to Jakob's favour, saying that Frau Haug had slipped and fell backwards.

"Do you know where Jakob is?"

She slowly shook her head.

"You said he came to see you the night you took ill. What did he say? Did he say where he was going?"

"I don't know." Her lips trembled. I will not cry, she told herself stubbornly. She had talked herself into thinking that seeing Jakob was all a dream. It didn't seem real.

"You must know! Think! You said he came here to your bed. Tell me!" His fist hit hard directly in front of her. She jumped back.

"*Nein*, Papa! I tell you I don't know! *Bitte!*" She started to cry heart-wrenching sobs.

"Michael!" Anna pleaded. "Don't browbeat her so. She doesn't remember. She had a high fever. We don't know for sure she saw him."

Michael walked to the hearth and leaned his hand on the stone frame above. He stared down into the fire, visibly trying to regain his composure. "The Council was here the day after Doktor Gessler took Rosina's body into the village. He told them what you just said, that it was an accident. However, they still suspect foul play, especially since Jakob's been missing for over a week now." He turned to look at his daughter. "And you're the only one who might know. Think, child! You've got to remember if Jakob said anything to you as to where he might be going."

Elisabeth went back to the deepest recesses of her mind, trying to remember something, anything, but it was all a blur. Except lately, the Rhine kept echoing in her head, and she couldn't make sense of it until now. She kept silent though, not letting her thoughts be known to her parents, or to anyone for that matter. As long as she and Doktor Gessler kept to their story, it could never be proven. God speed, Jakob, she reflected briefly. She was staring blankly, when her papa suddenly brought her back.

"Child, this is all your fault! All your fault," he repeated accusingly. "You're carrying Peter's baby. Peter!" he screamed. "The one I strictly forbade you to see again. How long have you been seeing him behind our backs?" He didn't wait for an answer. "How far along does this child grow inside you?" He paused. "Don't just sit there, answer me!"

Elisabeth was too embarrassed to look him in the eye. She turned to her mama for reassurance, but instead was met with two thin lines for lips and a furrowed brow. "Ten or twelve weeks," she eventually muttered.

"Elisabeth, whatever possessed you to attempt such a thing?" Anna's voice was strained. More gently, she added, "God be praised, child, it's a miracle that you are still alive and the babe still grows within."

"I'm so sorry, Mama. I didn't mean for this to happen. I don't know what to do, I..."

"I know what you're going to do, daughter." It was her papa speaking. "You can't have this baby out of wedlock. Your mama and I have been discussing that, and it's in your best interest to have you marry...and soon."

Elisabeth stared, trying to decipher what he was getting at. What could he possibly mean? Marry? To whom? Peter was no longer here, and even if he was, she had doubts that her papa would allow such a marriage. She sat dumbfounded, unable to find any words. She was sure she'd wake up from this nightmare.

"Doctor Gessler has been showing interest in you for the last couple of months. He's a gentle man. He has a substantial means to keep you, and he took the initiative to ask me for your hand. Considering the circumstances, we agreed."

Elisabeth couldn't believe what she was hearing. She didn't love Doktor Gessler; Peter was the only one and always would be. How could she marry someone she didn't care for? She eventually found the words. "I will not, Papa!" She stood, to better hold her ground with him. "I refuse. You cannot force me."

Michael's back was to Elisabeth. He turned slowly, ominously. "Oh no? The Council is not aware of your presence that day at Frau Haug's, and I'd like to keep it that way."

She observed her mama. She was backed into a corner and no one was there to open a door to escape.

"You'll do my bidding?" he queried.

"But, I can't..." She began to cry again.

"You can and you will." The words were softly spoken yet so tense and foreboding that she feared worse repercussions if not obeyed.

****

The birds were chirping on this last day of March, a beautiful, cloudless morning. Elisabeth sat on the windowsill of her bedroom, the warm sun upon her face, dreading the day to come, her wedding day. She had always looked to this day with elation, but with Peter.

Plans had been made more quickly than the normal six to eight weeks between the betrothal announcement and the wedding. Getting married during Lent was another bad omen, and the quick ceremony was much to the delight of the local tongue waggers of the village. But she didn't care about the old gossipers. She wasn't concerned about anything nowadays. Papa had hardly spoken a word to her over the past couple of weeks, and Mama was trying to make the best of a terrible situation, saying that it was a daughter's lot to obey her *fater*. And Doktor Gessler, or Georg, which she found strange to say, was nine years her senior. She refused to call him by his first name. He may as well be twenty years older; he felt ancient to her.

Elisabeth had only spent a little time with her intended, and the few little hours that did pass between them showed him to be very kind, but it didn't help matters; she didn't love him. A day didn't go by without thoughts of what Peter might be doing. As she prayed fervently every night for his return, she willed that he must be able to sense her anguish across that vast expanse of water. Laying her hand on her belly, she felt a funny feeling like butterflies, and wondered if it was nerves or just the movement of the baby.

Oh Peter, she reflected, why! At first, she hated him for leaving her, but anguish brought back her old feelings. Closing her eyes, she felt her lids prickle with hot tears. "I'll always love you. I may be forced to marry that *doktor*, but I'll not love him," she vowed. "I'll promise you that. I'll be true to you always."

A light tap on the door snapped her out of her thoughts. She hastily wiped her face with both hands and cleared her throat. "Come in." It was Mama, bringing the wedding dress that was hers and her mother's before her.

"*Awch,* child. You haven't even started to ready yourself. Come, come," Anna waved her hands. "Now stop that pouting."

Elisabeth thought if she kept up this attitude, she would just scream. And sure enough, "You've brought this all on yourself, young lady," her mama said, laying the dress out on the bed. Elisabeth bit her tongue at the sight of it. She had never seen it before. It was lovely. She half-listened to the ramblings about the baby, Peter, and the devil's temptations. "You should consider yourself lucky to have the likes of Georg want to marry you, you not a virgin and with child!"

Elisabeth couldn't believe what she was hearing, especially since her mama had never made any bones about how she felt about him. "How can you say that, Mama? You wouldn't let him near you when he came around after Stefan was born."

"Hush, child. That's different. Just because he's doing a midwife's job and shouldn't concern himself with such female delicacies doesn't mean he won't make you a good husband, especially in your condition." She draped the garment over her daughter's head. The whole piece was a heavy linen with a light blue bottom. The bodice was a flowered brocade of velvet closely laced by narrow ribbons of different shades of blue and black. The full sleeves were ivory and gathered into an embroidered cuff. "You're very lucky. God is shining down on you today. I was worried this dress wouldn't fit you, being four months gone, but I think you're much smaller than I was with Stefan. But I can see it's fine. Just fine."

Elisabeth didn't feel very fortunate. She could hear the mingling of some of the guests downstairs already, and the butterflies increased in her stomach. The smell of the wedding soup was becoming stronger now as it drifted upstairs.

"Come here, child, and help me with the belt." The belt was comprised of small heart-shaped plaques connected with three silver chains. The two end plaques had her grandmother's initials carved in them, indicating only the first owner of this ornate item. Alternating with the heart-shaped medallions were small garnets. This was the only thing of value that Mama had from her side of the family, and she cherished it. From the belt flowed six flowered ribbons down the front of her skirt. The fullness of the skirt hid any indiscretions.

Elisabeth stood solid as a statue, expressionless. Her mama continued to flitter here and there about the room. Finally, Anna showed her the homemade headpiece. Even Hanna had helped make it. She wasn't allowed to see it until now, and if she could have seen past her heartache, the crown of twigs and flowers would have touched her very soul. Anna placed it on her long blonde hair, braided into two plaits. With the onset of early spring a month ago, they were fortunate to add some fresh daisies and tiny blue flowers. Hanging from the back of the bridal crown were three long ribbons that reached the middle of her back, almost as long as her hair.

Anna held Elisabeth at arm's length. "You're the most beautiful in all of Upper Swabia, child. *Awch*, I must stop calling you that. You're a woman now." Anna, on rare occasions, gave way to tears and this was one of those times. Her eyes glistened. She blinked rapidly and started to fix the wisps of hair off Elisabeth's face. She smiled at her daughter. Elisabeth managed to force one too, without breaking into tears herself.

"You'll be fine, my *liebling*," Anna coaxed. "Remember to obey your husband at all times, help him, and always be there for him." Elisabeth's eyes welled up. "Elisabeth," she stroked her face with the back of her hand, "love will come in time. You'll see."

****

After the general compliments about the bride, Elisabeth made it through the morning soup amidst the din of her guests and family. Georg arrived at the house soon after everyone had eaten to collect his intended, but Elisabeth refused the tradition of hiding while the groom searched for her. This was not the happiest day of her life, so she wasn't about to play along with the games and gimmicks that were so customary. Together the two of them rode in the wedding cart to St. Martin's Church. The night before, her parents had helped Georg decorate his wagon with a multitude of ribbons and a few early spring flowers. Along the way, some of the boys from the neighbouring farms seized their horse and forced them to pay a toll, which was a typical ritual of all weddings.

At the small church, the wagons were parked every which way, in no particular order. Bringing the horse to a halt, Georg jumped down and offered his hand to help Elisabeth to the ground. She deliberately attempted to climb down on the opposite side. He looked disgruntled, but she didn't really care. Aiming her foot blindly for the step, she couldn't see with all the frills and flowers on her costume. Elisabeth's foot found the top of the wheel but slipped, then, caught herself before she fell. Georg had quickly come to her rescue just before she landed safely on the ground.

"Next time, take the help when it's offered," Georg said, trying not to laugh.

"Hmph," she grunted, smoothing out her skirt and rearranging her headpiece. Walking on ahead of him, she ignored the mocking display of his arm in a sweeping motion as he backed away from her.

He caught up to her and grabbed her arm. "I think it appropriate if we do this together. You wouldn't want the village tongues to wag again!"

Keeping her eyes straight ahead, she said, "I may be forced to marry you, but by God, I don't have to love you." Georg let go of her arm and opened the church door to a crowded interior.

Walking up the aisle, Georg kept his eyes to the ground as tradition dictated. He was not to look about or he would make eyes at other women when married. Elisabeth tried to keep her head down but couldn't help but stare at her papa. She would never forgive him for ruining her life. She noticed again that he seemed to have aged so much in the past couple of weeks since Jakob's disappearance. She hadn't seen much of her papa. He had been travelling to nearby towns and villages, hoping to find her brother. Frequenting taverns and inviting himself in on conversations, he hoped to pick up clues to his eldest's whereabouts. The last she had heard from her mama was that a travelling craftsman had met Jakob once or twice when visiting. Tomorrow at first light, her papa was going to the town.

Elisabeth didn't remember too much of the actual ceremony or even if the church was decorated or not. But when she and Georg knelt to be blessed, a flood of emotions overcame her – fear, sadness, then outrage. Mostly the latter for what she was forced into. Also anger at her mama, who Elisabeth thought should be on her side. But the only reason Mama was for this marriage was not to disgrace the family. Now she had the traditional walk back home with her husband to look forward to. The bride and groom never rode after the ceremony but went on foot so the two could spend some time alone before the party continued. Ridiculous custom, Elisabeth brooded. Georg tried very hard to make conversation, but she didn't attempt to acknowledge him. The whole journey was very long for both.

Even though the rest of the day and evening were spent in conversation, dancing, and eating with their guests, Elisabeth was content to spend most of it with her mama. Papa was in his own little world and never even attempted to kiss her after the ceremony, which was just as well.

At midnight, Elisabeth was blindfolded, the wreath on her head removed by the married women of the village, and a special bonnet placed over her hair as a symbol of her new state. The kitchen table was moved to the side to leave room for three candles to be placed on the floor. Normally, she would have to dance around the candles with her husband's male relatives, but since Georg had no living family that he ever spoke about, Elisabeth danced with two of her uncles. Halfway through the dance, two of the candles blew out, and she didn't need an absurd custom to tell her the marriage wouldn't be smooth. It was a given. She noticed her papa give a slight nod towards Georg.

He walked to the centre of the floor and placed his arm around her waist. She immediately stiffened at his touch as he raised his arm and toasted his new bride. “May our new-found happiness be carried with us across the vast ocean.” No one raised their steins. Everyone looked at each other with noisy mutterings.

“What?” Elisabeth cried.

Georg stared dumbfounded at his father-in-law, then looked back at his new wife. “Didn’t your *fater* tell you?”

“Tell me what?” Elisabeth glared at her papa.

“I’m sorry, I thought you knew. We’re going to the new land. I made the arrangements just after I spoke to your *fater* about my intentions to marry you.”

“Michael, you never uttered a word. How could you!” Anna cried. All eyes in the room were on Michael.

“This isn’t the time nor the place to discuss it. We’ll talk later,” he said.

Michael walked into the next room, his daughter shouting after him, “You never loved me, have you, Papa? Margaretha always was your favourite!”

“Elisabeth!” Anna cried, and slapped her on the face. A red mark was left for all to see. “Where are your manners, child? You have guests.”

Elisabeth saw her papa turn around before closing the door between them. She realized that this time she had gone too far. But, what about her feelings? Had anyone once thought about her? The room was so quiet, it was smothering. She felt trapped. She ran from the house to where the cart and horse were ready to take her to her new home. Georg followed on her heels with their coats.

“Here, Elisabeth, you’ll catch your death,” he said, draping her shoulders with the garment. She was so angry that she shrugged the coat off in defiance. She felt alone and it hadn't ended yet. There was still the wedding night.

She was frightened and didn't know what to expect from him. The minutes passed too quickly, and before she realized it, they were in Georg's house and preparing for bed. She was thankful that he allowed her to undress in private. Her stomach was churning as she lay on her side. She didn't even glance at him as he undressed. Her heart pounded harder as she felt him crawl in beside her. Turning her over, Georg kissed her gingerly, and gently placed her hand between his legs. Elisabeth instantly recoiled. Then to her surprise and relief, he turned over onto his back.

"I'll not push you. It will be when you're ready," he whispered. Then promptly, he fell asleep.

Breathing a sigh of relief, she couldn't believe her luck, for tonight anyway. The time would soon come when she'd have to do her wifely duty. Her life was over. What had she to look forward to now? Not only was she married to someone she didn't love, but now she was moving far away from her family to a land she had no desire to go to. She turned over, not to sleep, but to release her emotions quietly into her pillow.

CHAPTER 13

Schutze snatched Christian from behind and dragged him kicking up a dozen rickety steps to where he lived with Philip. It was dusk and the air had started to chill as soon as the sun went down, but Christian could feel the hot air of his assailant breathing down his neck. Schutze's breath was foul, reeking of stale liquor, and, Christian was sure, a few rotten teeth. Once inside the small room, he bit Schutze's hand so hard he was sure he must have drawn blood. Schutze howled a vile oath.

"Why you little scoundrel! Want to play tough, eh?" He seized Christian by a clump of hair and threw him onto the bed. The one candle that was lit on the table was producing tall shadows, and Christian eyed a black rat silhouetted on the stained dirty wall. The racket Schutze was causing made it skitter away into a nearby hole.

With his eyes squinting down at Christian, he clutched at his shirt with both stubby hands. "Have you told anyone of me, Heber?"

"*Nein*," Christian choked, shaking his head repeatedly. "*Nein*!" Schutze yanked him closer to his bearded face, glowering into his frightened eyes. Christian turned his head but was forced to face him again. Schutze's nails dug deep into his skin.

"If I ever hear that you've blabbed to Philip or anyone, I promise I won't miss this time as I did with that princely pig. Trust me, Heber, you'll never see the light of day to tell about it." He spit as he spoke.

"Leave 'im be, Jeremias. Or should I now call you Schutze?"

Philip spoke from behind.

Schutze released Christian. "How long've you been standing there, you bastard?"

"Long enough. Are you all right, Christian?"

Christian coughed and raised his hand to indicate he was okay.

Schutze immediately began gathering the few meagre pieces of clothing he owned into a ripped satchel.

"What the hell are you doing?" Philip asked.

"Leaving. If the likes of him recognizes me, it won't be long before the Council finds me. And who's to say *he* won't rat on me anyway?"

"But where will you go?"

"Nova Scotia," he said, as he kicked Christian's feet out of the way to look under the bed. "If I'm to catch the *Speedwell* in May, I've got to leave now. With all those tolls on the Rhine, it'll take the full four to five weeks to sail down it." He found nothing but dust and cobwebs. He stood clumsily, "There's at least thirty custom houses alone from Heilbronn to Holland."

"Take me with you, Schutze."

"You don't need to go with him, Philip," Christian interjected.

"Shut your trap," Schutze spat.

Philip shrugged his shoulders. "I have no choice. I'll be picked up for begging." Then to Schutze, "If you don't take me, I will turn you in. Up till now, we've been silent, but..."

Schutze eyed him maliciously, then, gave him a quick nod. He turned to Christian. "And remember, if the Council catches up with me, I have Philip here. I can see you've made friends and you wouldn't want any harm to come to him, would you?" His dirty face was inches from Christian's. "I know we can steal those horses that your *onkel* has, right?"

"Just steal those two we always see in the next alley," Philip said.

"Ha! They're worth nothing. We'd be lucky if they could get us to the edge of the forest. *Nein*, we need his *onkel's* horses." Schutze squinted at Christian again. "Take us now, scoundrel." He grabbed Christian by a fistful of hair and carted him back down the stairs, Philip behind them.

At his uncle's, Christian led them to the small stable at the back of the house, and opened the right half of the large doors. Gottlieb owned two horses, but only one was idly munching on hay. His *onkel* was out with the other one.

"Quick, take it before Onkel Gottlieb gets back," Christian urged. He was sure his uncle would find some way to blame him and beat him again.

Grumbling, Schutze quickly saddled up and mounted with Philip straddled in front. Gottlieb trotted in.

"What the...? Thieves!" he shouted, and quickly dismounted with whip in hand. He bolted to grab the reins of the fleeing horse. Schutze kicked his horse hard. It reared up and knocked over Gottlieb. They escaped in a cloud of dust.

Christian watched and didn't attempt to help his uncle up. When he stood and dusted himself off, Gottlieb squeezed his nephew's arm and swung at him across the head. He tried to protect himself as best he could from the blows.

"Gottlieb! What on earth! You'll kill him!" His aunt screamed from the house. That was enough diversion for Christian to get up and race to the saddled horse. He mounted and galloped out as fast as he could, amidst numerous oaths that were hurled after him.

Christian was sweating profusely and his chest pained from his pounding heart. He rode at a breakneck speed, not glancing back. It was a couple of hours before he allowed himself to slow down to a trot. He was so engrossed in getting as far away as possible, he suddenly realized that he hadn't passed Schutze and Philip. He should have on this road.

When he felt safe enough, he decided to dismount and rest. He tied the horse to a tree, and leaned his wet back against the hard bark. He nodded off unintentionally, only to be woken to a commotion. Schutze was riding off with his horse. Foolishly, he raced after him. He saw Philip glance back as they galloped away.

It was still dark and he was frightened. He had no idea how long into the night it was, so he limped over to an abandoned barn he had seen earlier and settled down till daylight. He was so sore. He wasn't sure if it was from the horse ride or the beatings he had endured.

He awoke later with a start. He was dreaming of Gottlieb standing over him with a horse's whip, ready to strike him. He stretched, then lay there a few minutes, shivering and stomach growling. Getting up, he started his long walk back home to Hohctorf. It was dawn and the sun was just ready to burst on the horizon. He walked on for hours before he finally reached the River Fils just outside his village. Everything suddenly cluttered his mind. What would he say to his papa? Would Onkel Gottlieb send word of what happened? Maybe he wouldn't, he was sure his *onkel* was glad he was gone.

As he crossed the stone bridge over a narrow gushing stream, he thought about the farm. Slowly climbing the hill to the top, he surveyed the beauty as far as the eye could see. As tired as he was, he sat down in the dirt and thought about how much he wanted to be a farmer. Jakob doesn't care a fig about this land, he thought. Land as far as the eye could see, dotted with clumps of trees and rows of hedges separating each farm from the next. From where he sat, Christian could see a farmer tilling his earth to make ready for planting oats and barley or maybe even potatoes. It was very common now to see potato fields since King Frederick forced everyone to plant them about ten years ago. And next to it was a smaller field, probably to grow cabbage and hemp for his family's personal use. Christian dug his fingers into the damp cool soil, scooping some into the palm of his hand. He loved the smell and feel of it. He could see his house and knew he had to convince his papa to pass the farm to him.

His energy suddenly returned with a vengeance. He threw down the dirt, stood up, and cut across the Beck farm, which stood empty now. He found the road that led to home. As he approached the house, he noticed two untethered horses he didn't recognize nibbling on grass. His first thought was that the authorities were there already for the stolen horses. But that was impossible; they wouldn't have gotten here so fast.

Christian could now hear loud voices and furniture scraping across the floor. The door was partly ajar and he peered in. His mama and Hanna were huddled together at the kitchen table. He could hear a shouting voice that wasn't his papa's. Christian was just about to make a quick getaway. To where, he didn't know, when a heavy hand seized him and marched him inside.

"Christian!" Anna cried, and attempted to stand, but was roughly pushed back into the chair.

"Stay right here! You, come here!" he pointed to Christian. Where's the money kept?"

Christian didn't recognize the two men but noticed the badge on their vests meant they were sent by the prince, probably to collect the taxes. His papa usually paid on time once a month to Eugen's collectors in the village. He had heard of people who never paid and it only had to happen once.

"I don't know," Christian answered, which was immediately met with a backhanded slap across the face, sending him onto the floor.

The second intruder kicked down the door of his parents' bedroom. His baby brother wailed at the top of his lungs. Again, his mama tried to struggle to her feet, but was shoved against the wall. Her eyes were wide were fear. Hanna ran and buried her face into the folds of her skirts. Inside the bedroom, the mattress was turned upside down and clothes were strewn over the floor. The man opened the oak chest that stood at the foot of the bed and rummaged through the contents inside.

"Aha! I found it!" He pulled out the leather pouch that his mother had so diligently hidden. Ripping the opening apart, he spilled the coins into the palm of his hand. "Not much here, but it'll have to do. For now!" He glared at Anna.

The two assailants fled out the door and mounted their horses. Christian could see them from the window, and as soon as they were out of sight, he turned to his mama. She was already in the bedroom trying to calm Stefan. As he tried to comfort Hanna, Michael suddenly appeared.

"Anna!" he cried. Michael stopped dead in his tracks upon seeing Christian, but stood in disbelief at the scene before him. Hanna was now sobbing into her brother's arms. Both benches were overturned on their sides; clothes from a cupboard were strewn in disarray, some still partially hanging out of the drawers. Logs that had been neatly piled in one corner now spilled over in a disorderly manner.

"Anna!" He observed his wife cradling their infant son in the doorway of their bedroom. "What's happened? I saw two men gallop away."

"Eugen's men, looking for the tax money," Anna said, calmly. "Shh," she cooed at Stefan, rocking the infant in her arms.

Behind his wife, Michael surveyed the disaster. Her voice now shaking, Anna said, "They've taken all we have. There's nothing left." Her eyes welled up. "What are we going to do now?"

Michael had no reassuring words for his wife as he held her in his arms. Remembering Schutze's words a few months ago, he thought about the other families that had felt the wrath of the prince. He always tried to be sympathetic to their hardships but had never experienced it firsthand. Now that he had, he could feel the hatred for the prince that others displayed openly.

****

The sun had all but sank behind the horizon. Anna was sleeping with Hanna pressed up beside her. After the ordeal they went through, it was difficult for their youngest to lie down alone in her own bed.

Michael's mind was racing. He had gone yesterday morning after hearing a rumour that he could find Jakob. But it was a dead end. Over the course of time, he hung onto every word that circulated in the village as to the possible location of his eldest. It was amazing how one person could just disappear without a trace. Michael aggressively pursued every lead from anyone who said they may have seen him. The latest was a travelling craftsman who thought he saw a man of Jakob's description a few days ago between Plochingen and Esslingen.

Initially, the Council had harassed Michael and his family as to Jakob's whereabouts. Even now, they were hard-pressed to surmise that he would hide their son and endanger his family. Up until now, the Council had not tracked him down, and the latest rumour they discovered was that Jakob was making his way to the Rhine. Michael was beginning to fathom they were on the right track. After all, he was trying to imagine what he would do if he were in his son's shoes. He'd escape also and catch the *Speedwell* on her next sailing.

He gazed at his field, waiting to be tilled and readied for planting over the next few days, and he realized that maybe his long time friend, had been right to take his family from this sordid life. He felt saddened when he thought of Hans' unfulfilled dreams. At least his surviving family had the courage to follow his dying wishes.

So much had happened over the last few months. Hans killed, Eugen's near-death, Jakob's disappearance, which surely showed his guilt, Elisabeth's baby, and now her and Georg sailing soon to the new land. And then, Christian's sudden appearance. Michael's first reaction had been to take him back in the morning, until he saw the cuts and bruises. It was all too much for one human to take in the short space of five months since Margaretha's death.

He turned away from the window and buried his face in his hands. His mind reeled at today's events. There were no tears, just despair and deep, heart-wrenching hopelessness. He stooped down to pile the logs that had spilled from the earlier chaos, and spotted a wad of paper. It was the notice that Hans had given him. He had seen it posted in every village and town throughout his searches. He read it again. "Fifty acres of land free of all rates or taxes for ten years."

Michael had sworn he would never leave the only home he had known, but he wasn't so stubborn as not to consider it when his family was threatened. It was a quick decision, but in his heart, he knew it was right. He would take his family to safety.

Part 2

CHAPTER 14

With the crowds pressing in around her, the hot, damp air made it all that more unbearable. Elisabeth ran her hand over her face, brushing the wisps of wet hair from her forehead. Her husband, Georg, was ahead of her, trying desperately to make a path for them to the gangplank. The baby was kicking, and not lightly either, which made her stop temporarily until the sharp stab subsided. They had lost sight of her parents, Christian, and Hanna after they registered in a small stifling building that had hardly any air in which to breathe.

Elisabeth was shocked when she found out her family was also emigrating, but she certainly understood the reason. And she felt relieved that she wasn't leaving them behind after all. So far, they had travelled over two hundred *stunden* from Hohctorf since leaving at the end of April. It was now June 25, and it had taken over six weeks to travel down the Neckar and Rhine rivers. If it wasn't for the toll stations, the trip on the *schippers* probably would have been much more pleasant and faster.

Elisabeth reached for her husband's hand and he pulled her through the masses to the plank, where she could now see a wooden sign, "Snow Pearl." This would be her home for the next eleven or twelve weeks to a land God knows where. She was hearing both damaging and respectable reports of emigrants that had gone on before them. The worst was at one of the toll stations on the Rhine, where an agent was desperately attempting to steer those destined for Nova Scotia to go to Pennsylvania instead. Crops that don't grow and poisonous snakes were a couple of the reasons that particularly stuck in Elisabeth's head. A few of the fearful passengers were persuaded to go to the accusing agent.

Farther down the pier, Elisabeth could see another ship much larger than theirs, but she couldn't make out the name, only its destination: Pennsylvania. She had never even heard of this town until a few weeks ago and wondered if Georg should have been convinced also to settle there instead of Nova Scotia. After all, Pennsylvania was now an established settlement, much more civilized was what she had heard so far.

Staring up at the *Pearl*, she craned her neck to see two large masts. The large canvases had been raised up and tied loosely to the masthead. Georg still had a hold of her hand as he guided her onto the gangplank.

"Doktor Gessler, I am quite capable now of making my own way up." She jerked her hand out of his.

"I don't doubt this," he replied. "But I'll not have a crowd of onlookers sneering that I refuse to help my wife up this plank. And please, do dispense with calling me Doktor Gessler. We are husband and wife now."

"In name only." She certainly didn't want to give the impression that she would willingly bed him. Over the past couple of months since their wedding, she was able to ward off his advances, feigning illness due to her condition. So far, he'd been patient with her, but for how much longer, she worried. She couldn't bring herself to call him Georg; to her it indicated that she had accepted their marriage. It was like cheating on Peter. Everyday she refused to give in to what her papa had forced her into. Elisabeth would never forgive him. Never!

"That could be easily remedied, my dear Frau Gessler," he smiled.

Elisabeth eyed him with disdain, lifted her skirt, and stepped onto the plank. Holding onto the ropes on either side, she picked her way up the wooden incline. The green water lapping against the hull of the ship made her feel dizzy and light-headed. She refused to let her husband see her weakness, so steadied herself and continued without even so much as a downward glance. Once on board, the smells of rope and wood intermingled with the salt air. It was not at all unpleasant. Whether it was the sheer adventure that appealed to her or the anticipation of possibly finding Peter again, she couldn't determine. There were already many passengers on board, some in similar dress as herself, but others? She wondered where they were from as she admired their unusual attire. The ship's working crew all wore gray jackets with brass buttons, and their bare calloused feet appeared awkward and clumsy from beneath their wide breeches that hung freely just above their ankles. Some wore tarred, wide-brimmed hats on their heads as they either scrambled up ropes or balanced on the edges of the hull above her. One odd fellow could be seen at the very tip of the mast, which made her feel queasy at the very thought of him being so high. The sailors were rolling large wooden casks down below deck. She could only assume they contained food and water. Elisabeth almost bumped into one such object and would have fallen if it hadn't been for Georg.

Upon registering earlier, they were assigned a specific berth and stopped one of the ship hands for direction. By the expression on the young boy's face, it was obvious he didn't understand. Georg retrieved a piece of paper from his pocket and placed it in front of his face. The sailor mumbled something unintelligible and motioned them to follow him. Even though the ship was in dock, Elisabeth could still feel the slight rocking motion, which became more prevalent as they descended the few steps to each deck.

Their escort pointed to the low beam above, which came much

too late for Georg, who did himself minor injury. He swore loudly; the first time Elisabeth had ever heard him do so. Stifling a giggle, she continued to turn corners down the steps to their dingy deck. As it was, she only had a couple of inches clearing for her own head.

Once her eyes adjusted to the darkness, she could see nothing but berths tiered one on top of the other, three deep. Each berth was about six feet long and only two feet wide, though some were as wide as they were long, making them appear square. Some of them already had belongings strewn out. The sailor waved his hand towards two separate smaller berths, one above the other.

"This won't do," Georg remarked, still rubbing the bump on his head. The sailor departed without a word. Elisabeth smiled inwardly.

An elderly, balding man was lying on his side with his head propped up by his hand. "Those larger beds are for families."

"Huh?" Georg squinted in the direction of the voice.

"You can't go about taking a bed for two, when it could fit three or four easy. And I don't think your young wife would care to sleep with a stranger." He stood up and walked closer to where they were standing. "Besides, with the close quarters as they are here, you'll not be wanting to get too friendly, if you know what I mean." He winked at Georg, and Elisabeth felt her face flush hot.

"Here, whoever you are, I'll..."

"Johann...Johann Korber. And who might you be?" He extended his hand.

"My name's of no consequence to you. I'll not have you speak in such a rude manner in front of my wife."

"I'm sorry. Didn't mean anything by it, but since we're going to be living together here over the next few weeks, let's not get off on the wrong foot. Truce?" Johann extended his hand again. It was missing two fingers.

Georg hesitated at first, then nodded his head and shook his hand. "Georg Gessler. And this is my wife, Elisabeth." She nodded and smiled apprehensively in Johann's direction.

"Where are you two from?"

"Hohctorf, in the district of Wurttemberg. And you?"

"The district of Palatinate, from Oppenheim."

"*Awch,* that explains why your speech sounded familiar to me. I know that area well. I'm originally from Frankfort, but my parents were born in Oppenheim and they took me there frequently when I was a young lad."

"Then I'm sure we'll get along quite famously. I'll leave you two to get settled a bit, though you'll have plenty of time to do it." Georg looked puzzled. "Not all the passengers have arrived. There are still some coming down the Rhine the last I heard. We'll probably be here the next five days or so." And he left them alone.

****

Johann was right. The few remaining passengers arrived the next five days and the ship finally sailed on the last day of June. During this time, Elisabeth discovered her parents and siblings were one deck above them that was laid out identically to theirs – rows and rows of berths with barely over five feet between decks. Both Christian and she took after their mama in height, so the cramped space didn't bother them. But her papa was so tall; she wondered how he was managing. There had to have been at least 250 people, not only from her homeland, but from Switzerland and even Holland.

The ship stopped at Gosport, England, and was delayed a week because of customs, and the newly-installed ventilators needed to be inspected. She had overheard Georg speaking with Johann about these ventilators. Because of the high mortality rate on the ships that had gone on before them a year ago, it was ordered that ships following were to have such equipment. It was so stuffy and close where they slept, she wondered if they were working at all.

As one day slowly melted into the next, the air became more stale below deck, and all she had been able to smell since settling in was a biting vinegar that penetrated and stung her nostrils. Even though she hated the pungent aroma, it was better than the stench that was increasing with each passing day. The closeness of so many bodies, along with the heat of the summer, caused the perspiration to linger and mingle with the stink of vomit. Her only escape was the time she was able to spend on deck. Everyone had turns in small numbers, and her little group was usually up on deck once in the early morning and at dusk.

On one particular morning, a couple of weeks after leaving Gosport, Elisabeth was above leaning against the side of the ship with her face to the wind. It was exhilarating, she thought, breathing in the fresh salt air and listening to the ship cutting its way through the waves, the hull gently listing from side to side. So far, they had been blessed with fair weather for the crossing. The air was so different out here. The dampness and salt clung to her skin and clothes.

"You make a good sailor."

Elisabeth turned to the voice; it was Sophia, Johann's wife, who was the same age as Elisabeth, sixteen. During the voyage, they were finding that they had a lot in common. They both married a man who was older than they, though Johann was thirty years older, where Georg was only nine. Neither one of them loved their husbands.

"*Ja,* I love it. I find it invigorating," Elisabeth replied, filling her lungs with deep breaths. "It's good to see you up on deck. Are you feeling any better?"

"A little. The fresh air seems to make me feel not quite so ill."

Sophia was still pale, and she hadn't moved from her berth since they had left Gosport.

"You must get up here when it's your turn, no matter how sick you are. You'll feel better. Doktor Gessler says it's much healthier for you. The stench down there is enough to make anyone ill."

Sophia knew the story about the baby and Peter. She understood why her new friend insisted on calling her husband formally, although she herself had always called her husband by his first name.

Smiling faintly, she asked, "Where is Georg? Doesn't he usually come up with you?"

"Since Gosport he's done nothing but administer to the sick. He's been given special dispensation to come on deck whenever he gets a chance. I consider myself one of the lucky ones to not be so susceptible to the motion of the ship."

Looking past Sophia at the vast ocean that lay ahead of them, she could see large dark clouds beginning to form. She thought of Peter and where he might be at that very moment, wondering if he was thinking of her. If she thought long and hard, she was sure he was.

Sophia reeled slightly before her, snapping Elisabeth back to the present. "Come on, Sophia, let's get you below. You're still very weak. Rest today and get your strength back. Unfortunately, our time up here has ended. *Awch,* here comes that awful sailor again." One of the crew in charge of dispersing passengers off the deck for the next group was always gesturing wildly with his arms to make himself understood. "One of these days, Sophia, he's going to wave himself right off this ship and into that ocean, never to be seen again." Elisabeth laughed and her friend grinned. "Are you sure you're fine? Your face is quite flushed, which you never had before," she said, laying the palm of her hand against her cheek. "You're very warm."

"Don't fuss over me so. You're like a mother hen, surely. Tis the weather changing. It's become much more humid."

And that it was, Elisabeth thought. Since coming on deck an hour ago, the air was hotter and more sticky. Looking out, she could see the waves rising higher than before. The two of them stayed at the back of their group to breathe in as much salt air as possible before being subjected to the horror below. How she dreaded the time there.

The thick air hit them like a suffocating blanket as the putrid odours of vomit and excrement wafted through the stale air. By the time they reached their own deck, the stench had worsened. Elisabeth helped her friend to her bunk and sternly told her to rest, at least for the remainder of the day. The few brief minutes that Elisabeth was down below made her wet with perspiration. She felt small droplets of sweat trickling between her breasts. As her husband was tending to the many passengers, she decided to try and sneak up to where her parents were.

Before leaving port, it was abruptly told to everyone that the captain wouldn't have everyone mingling about freely. With the commotion of the next group going up on deck, Elisabeth thought this would be a good time to slip by unnoticed. She had to get away from all this moaning and groaning before it started to take its toll on her.

Her parents' level wasn't any better; just as many were sick. Only a quarter of the bunks were empty with those up on deck taking their turn for air. Seeing her papa, she walked to the very end, steadying herself by clutching the tops of the bunks as the ship listed to one side. She could feel her head lightly brush against the ceiling of the cabin. The situation between Elisabeth and her papa remained strained. Not many words had been exchanged since leaving their home.

Her mama was lying down, which was strange. The seasickness hadn't affected her since the onset of the voyage. Stefan was lying beside her, looking restless and flushed in the face. Christian and Hanna were sitting up on the bed across from them, staring, neither of them affected by the motion. Her papa stood with his head and shoulders bent out of necessity to the awkward quarters. It was impossible for him to stand perfectly erect. The nape of his neck crammed against the ceiling made the deck seem all the more confined.

"She's much worse this morning, daughter." Michael spoke without emotion. Not, Elisabeth was sure, because he wasn't concerned for his wife, but because of the strain between the two of them. He had begun to use the term daughter more frequently. "Anna won't eat. She's complaining of severe pain in her head. And now Stefan's refusing to take any food."

In her restless state, Anna was groaning and continually throwing the blanket off her. The baby was crying beside her. "I'm sure everything's fine. It's just the seasickness that's affecting mostly everyone. Papa, go up and get some fresh air. It's too long between our turns on deck." She turned to her siblings. "And that goes for you, too. Shoo!" Elisabeth clapped her hands. Maybe Sophia was right, I am a mother hen, she thought fondly. Hanna ran giggling, her brother close at her heels.

"*Nein*," her papa spoke firmly. "My turn is with your *mutter*. There's something wrong, I can feel it." And he set himself on a small stool beside the berth, watching his wife intently.

"Papa, they'll be fine. Some are just harder hit by this than others." Elisabeth knew her words were falling on deaf ears and her comfort was futile.

The ship was pitching so much more now that she had to hold on to keep from losing her balance. No sooner had Christian and Hanna left, they were back. "I thought I told both of you to go up on deck," she asserted.

"No one's allowed out now," Christian replied. She could hear the commotion from the returning passengers and shouts from the crew to stay below to weather out the storm. With a lot of banging, the doors slammed, shutting them in their hold. Then, sounded the loudest clap of thunder, making her flinch nervously.

"And you should see the waves, Beth. They're this high." Hanna reached her tiny arm as high as she could above her head.

Elisabeth wasn't hearing her sister. They were trapped like the rats she so often saw scurrying about the ship. She hated it down here, but just knowing that the hatches were open and that they had their turns on deck kept her sane. Now, it was different! They weren't allowed out at all now.

Anna grabbed Elisabeth's hand, "I knew we shouldn't have come. It's God's judgement for leaving our homeland, leaving Jakob. Oh-, Jakob," she moaned, turning her head and staring above her. "My son! Jakob!" she screamed hysterically. Papa leaned in to hold her still.

Anna had refused to leave Hohctorf, until the Council discovered that Jakob was seen in Rotterdam. Michael was just as stubborn about leaving as he was before in staying. Once he got an idea into his head, it was difficult to shake him of it. With the remote possibility that Jakob could have gone with the influx of emigrants to America, Michael succeeded in convincing his wife. What Jakob did made perfect sense: he put as much distance between him and the *Faterland* as possible.

"I'll go get Doktor Gessler," Elisabeth remarked. She knew she couldn't stay still. She'd have to keep busy, to keep sane until the storm was over.

****

The baby was very active, kicking away in her belly, making her feel even more uncomfortable in the heat. The one or two lanterns here and there gave little light as Elisabeth picked her way back to her deck. She was besought by people in her quarters extending their hands, pleading for help. Her pathway was an obstacle course of bedding and personal belongings and buckets that had tipped over their contents of excrement that had not been properly disposed of in time before the storm. She could see and hear the clanging of the pails rolling across the floor as the violent pitching increased. The perpetual lamenting from the sick would not let up. If only it would stop! She wanted to scream! She covered her ears, as she was sure she would go mad. She lost her balance and fell to one side just as Georg caught her.

"Elisabeth!" Her husband's voice sounded so distant as he guided her to bed. "Lie here and rest before you do the baby great harm," she barely heard him say. She willingly conceded and fell asleep. She didn't know how long. When she awoke, the storm was still ravaging outside with fierce lightning and tremendous bangs of thunder. Even though they were three decks below, she could hear the crashing of the waves above her. The moanings had let up some, possibly giving way to sleep.

"Well, well, how's my *liebling*?" It was her husband hovering over her.

"I'm not your *liebling*. How long have I been asleep?" She propped herself up on her elbows.

"A good five hours. You must've needed it. Your baby requires you to rest more than you're willing to give it."

"That's right, Doktor Gessler. It's *my* baby and I'll take care of him as I see fit. I don't need you telling me what to do." Elisabeth realized her words were too sharp, but she didn't care. After all, why should she? He knew right from the start where he stood with her. She wished at times Doktor Gessler wasn't always so good to her. Hating him would be much easier if he was mean to her like a lot of husbands she knew who beat their wives unmercifully. Come to think of it, her husband was much like her papa, who never believed in such atrocities.

"Elisabeth, something horrible has happened." He sat down beside her. The way his gaze met her, she realized they'd have to put aside their differences for now.

"This is not just seasickness we're dealing with here. The symptoms are becoming much more severe. It's typhus."

"Typhus!" Elisabeth blurted.

"Keep your voice down. I don't want this to get around. It'll only create more havoc in an already depressing situation."

"How many are affected?"

"So far, I've noted eleven cases; three of them on our deck. Sophia is one of them."

Elisabeth couldn't believe her ears. She remembered her papa telling her and her brother stories of the awful devastation in towns and villages north of them about twenty years ago. Hohctorf had only a slight infection, with only two or three dying. "You must be mistaken. Surely, it must be the seasickness. You've said yourself that some people are affected more than others."

"I would give my right arm to know I'm wrong. But there's no mistaking the symptoms. The high fever, severe headache, and a few have already shown the rash." He tenderly held his wife's hand, but she quickly withdrew.

"Mama!" Her voice trembled. She had completely forgotten why she came below earlier. "My God!" she screamed.

"Get a hold of yourself. What's wrong?"

"I saw Mama this morning. Papa said she's been complaining of pains in her head since last night. Didn't you see them when you did your rounds?"

"I haven't gotten there yet. I was on my way just as you were waking up." Pressing down on his wife's arms to try and calm her, he pried for more information. "What other symptoms were there?"

"She's burning up with fever and was delirious. And the baby, he's also fallen ill this morning. He won't eat. I told Papa it was just the ship's motion. From what you've just said, they must have typhus, and it's all my fault. I should have told you as soon as I..."

"Stop it! Calm yourself. I'll go to them now. You stay here," he ordered, eyeing her belly. But she followed anyway. They found Anna in a worse state than just a few short hours earlier. She winced with pain in her back and legs. The fever raged leaving her weak and agitated. After examining Anna, Georg said, "The rash is just starting to appear on her shoulders. See," he pointed, "small pink spots that disappear upon pressure with my finger. In the next couple of days, the rash will spread and become purple in colour, then brownish red, then finally brown."

"What are you talking about, Georg?" Michael said, anxiously.

"It's typhus."

Georg lifted Stefan up and cradled him while he examined the nine month old infant. Babies usually didn't survive typhus, but if he was lucky and the infection wasn't as severe, maybe.

Stefan lay in his arms limp as a rag, his skin clammy with fever. The rash hadn't appeared on him yet.

Elisabeth thought about what her mama had said. This was God's judgement for leaving their home. Maybe she was even the cause of all this: carrying a child that wasn't her husband's, Jakob on the run for murder.

"The only thing you can do is try to get a little liquid down both of them, and any food they will take," Georg said. "Even if Anna can't keep it down, continue to encourage her. Keep cool wet rags on her to reduce the fever. I'm going to see to the rest of this deck." Georg disappeared quickly into the poorly-lit shadows of the hold.

****

"Come. Come with me to eat," Georg said. For the last couple of days, he was bringing what little food his wife would eat so she could keep up the vigil over her mother and brother. Now he thought it best to remove her from the situation for a while. The fever was still running rampant and the rash had spread to the back of Anna's hands, palms, and soles of her feet. Stefan had just started showing the first signs of the pink spots. Georg fretted over the baby; he hadn't eaten for two days and now refused everything remotely considered food. With the vomiting and diarrhoea, Stefan was dehydrated, and he didn't know how much longer he could last. He was sure he'd most likely die of starvation before the infection took him. As for the rest of the people infected, there had already been one death.

The storm that tossed the ship around like a loose bottle in the ocean had finally abated yesterday. For the first time in two days, Georg suggested to his wife that they both go up for fresh air. But she had refused to leave Anna. Now, the suffering was even starting to take its toll on him.

"Michael will come for us if there is any change in their condition. Now come, think of the baby." Michael nodded his assent to his daughter, and Elisabeth wearily stood up and leaned into her husband. She hadn't eaten much the last two days. Of course, even if she was hungry, it was difficult to consume anything, as the food was getting worse as the voyage progressed.

Every morning, the ship's cook alternated with a bowl of either barley or oatmeal. At first, Elisabeth thought it rather tasty even though it wasn't as palatable as what her mama used to make. But considering the circumstances, it would have to do. And the water! It had become so foul that vinegar was added, just to overcome the putrid smell and taste. The last few mornings, she had been trying to force it down for the sake of her baby. It was Thursday, and tonight would be pork. There was so much salt in it for preservation that Elisabeth had to drink to quench her thirst. Up until now, there was beer to wash the food down, but Doktor Gessler said it was now so rotten it couldn't be drunk. That left the water.

She sat down on a stool once Georg handed her a plate. There was one very large slab of pork and a chunk of ship bread, which wasn't at all 'normal.' It was hard as a rock. She cut into the pork and took one bite. All she could taste was salt. She snatched at the water to wash it down, but it was so revolting she almost gagged. She stabbed the meat again with the knife, revealing a small white wiggly worm. She screamed and the plate went flying across the deck.

"What ever is wrong, child?" The old woman next to her was hungrily feeding herself, oblivious to what might be squirming inside her meal. "Go ahead, eat some of mine," she said, pushing some into her face.

Elisabeth was glad to see Georg return. "I can't eat that!"

"Here, at least have some bread. You've got to eat."

"You call that nourishment? The water smells like the floor of a barn and pork is riddled with maggots!" Elisabeth shuddered at the thought of it while nibbling at the bread. It was tasteless, but at least it was edible.

"This is all there is and you've no choice in the matter. Here, mine is free of worms so far, have a bite." Elisabeth recoiled at the thought of it and backed away.

"Georg! Quick! It's Anna! She's delirious. I can't quiet her." It was Michael. They immediately ran after him.

Anna moaned relentlessly, muttering inaudible words. Georg could hardly detect her pulse. Her hands and feet were cold to the touch, yet she was still burning up with fever. The infection seemed to be quickly running its course. She was now displaying the last stages before death. He stared at Michael and didn't say a word. They all knew.

"I'm staying. I'll sleep in that berth, Christian and Hanna can sleep in mine," Elisabeth ordered, as her brother and sister clung to each other. They look so thin, she thought. Georg whisked them away from the terrifying scene.

After they left, Elisabeth wrung out more rags. She wiped the beads of sweat from Anna's face and laid a cloth across her forehead. Anna was unaware of Elisabeth's care as she drifted in and out of a fitful sleep. Stefan lay beside her sleeping, as he did constantly now. She kept the cool rags on his small face as well. Michael sat helplessly on the stool watching and waiting. At times, he rocked his son in his arms, while clutching his wife's hand.

About an hour later, Georg returned with a bowl of watery, but hot broth he had bribed the cook into putting together. It wasn't much, just a piece of leftover pork with water and dried peas boiled together. "Try and get some of this into her."

Holding Anna's head, Elisabeth eased the cup to her blistered lips. More broth was coughed up than swallowed. "*Bitte.* Drink, Mama," Elisabeth coaxed. "You can't die, you just can't." Tears wet her cheeks. Anna sipped a little more, then pushed it away. Georg left them alone while he checked on his other patients. There had been four more cases in the past two days. Elisabeth knelt down beside her mama and silently pleaded to God.

CHAPTER 15

Elisabeth didn't know how long she had been asleep, or whether or not it was morning, but she could see that most people were still sleeping. She could barely make out Georg in the darkness, administering to one of his patients a couple of bunks down. Does he ever rest? Watching him, she felt a slight tenderness towards him. He is a very caring soul, she pondered. She then felt a warm hand on her arm and jumped.

"Elisabeth," Anna whispered.

"Mama? Doktor Gessler, it's Mama!" She stood aside as her husband leaned over Anna. Michael awoke with a jolt.

Georg felt his patient's face. It was cool to the touch. And her hands and feet were warm. "I don't believe it! The fever's broken. The worst is over. You're on your way to recovery, Anna." A wide grin lit up his face. Michael and Elisabeth collapsed against each other in relief. "You'll be weak for a while, so I'm prescribing lots of bed rest."

"What's a body to do to get something to eat?" she said feebly.

"You'll wish you never said that," Elisabeth grinned, her eyes glistening with tears. "Oh, Mama, we'd thought we lost you."

"You'll never be rid of me that easily." Anna closed her eyes, drifting off to sleep again. She was completely unaware that her infant son lay beside her, stricken with the same illness.

****

"Oh my God! Stefan! Wake up!" she shrieked.

Elisabeth awoke to the scene that would be etched in her memory for the rest of her life. Sitting on the edge of the bed, Anna cradled her brother's limp body, his head pressed against her wet cheek. Michael sat on the floor staring blankly in Elisabeth's direction, unaware she was watching. Anna mouthed the word 'Stefan' without a sound. The infant's arm relaxed, his tiny fingers brushing the top of Michael's head.

****

Her brother was the second fatality, and Sophia soon followed that morning. Elisabeth had not spoken with her friend since that morning on deck. Never in her wildest dreams did she think it would be the last time. She had helped her husband with the caring of his patients, paying particular attention to Sophia. At times, Elisabeth stole a few precious moments from her mama to soothe Sophia's delirium. After Stefan died, she went down to see her friend again, but it was too late. She watched Sophia's husband lightly brush her eyelids closed and cover the body with a gray, dingy blanket.

Now as she stood on deck with her family, she watched numbly as a sailor tipped the planks with one tiny package and one larger one. They slid into the frothy brine below. Anna rushed to the edge of the deck to watch as her son sank from view to his watery grave. Elisabeth could not bring herself to look as she stood wearily beside her papa.

Georg was absent as the number of passengers near death had increased during the night. Dreading the return to her berth, Elisabeth lingered behind as the others quietly disappeared below. The groups that were allowed on deck at specific intervals were diminishing to just a handful. It was almost August, and the warm humidity was pressing in around her. The cool salt air in the evenings did nothing to penetrate the squalor below.

Leaning against the side of the ship, she closed her eyes and filled her lungs with the fragrant sea air. Removing the pins from her hair, she let it fall loose to allow the breeze to blow through her tangled tresses. A crystal clear image appeared before her of Peter, whom she had not thought of for the last few days. Oh, how she missed him. Her heart ached for the feel of his arms around her. She laid her hand gently on her stomach. A light but firm hand caressed her shoulder. "Peter," she whispered, and slowly turned around.

"Elisabeth?" It was Georg.

"Oh." Peter had seemed so real to her a moment ago.

"What did you call me?" He glared at her.

"What is it you want?"

"I need your help. Christian's doing his best to empty the buckets as fast as they fill up. The disease is out of control. Now it's running unchecked from deck to deck. Up till now, family members of the sick have been taking care of their own, aiding me when I can't be in two places at once."

"But what can I do?"

Georg's face was withdrawn and pale from lack of sleep. His empty eyes stared back at her as if his very soul had been wrenched from his body.

"You can make the patients as comfortable as possible, feeding them what might stay down, cooling their hot brows," Georg replied abruptly. "You're a better help to me down below than up here dreaming of the impossible."

"I don't know what you're talking about, Doktor Gessler." Elisabeth walked past him, but her arm was caught by the tight grip of his hand.

"You know damn well what I'm speaking about," he said in a harsh whisper so as not to be overheard by the few passengers mingling around them.

"You're hurting me," she squealed, as she tried to wriggle free. A few heads turned in their direction.

Georg released her. "I'll expect to see you shortly."

"I hate you!" she hissed through clenched teeth. Rubbing her arm, Elisabeth watched him disappear down the steps two at a time.

****

Christian dumped two more buckets of sickness and excrement into the ocean. He swore he had developed muscles in his young arms as they ached severely. There was a tremendous apathy in what he was doing as he moved numbly from deck to deck, cleaning and doing what he could to help Georg. Until now, he had only been looking out for Hanna on this voyage. He jumped at the chance to assist his brother-in-law in anything that made him feel more useful.

The terrible ordeal with his uncle was tame compared to what he was enduring on this ship. The food was wretched and his throat was persistently parched, not so much from the salt caked into everything, but by refusing to drink the horrid water. But some days, he knew he had to force it down. He was filthy from lack of proper cleanliness, and, at first, was embarrassed. This soon gave way to an acceptance as he was no different from anyone else on board.

****

Another week trudged by and Georg's exhaustion was giving way to defeat. He couldn't fathom where the strength appeared from to continue day in and day out. Twenty-four hours didn't pass now without at least one person going to their watery grave, mostly the old and the children. Thank God for Christian's help, and Anna's, who'd begun assisting him immediately after her strength returned. Anna's need to keep busy was great. Even Johann was doing as much as he could. As for his wife, Elisabeth pitched in after their episode on deck, without a word passing between them.

Georg knew full well what he was getting himself into by marrying Elisabeth. He thought in time that she would forget Peter and grow to love him. They had been married four months now and had not yet consummated their marriage. He had shown extreme patience with her, but her excuses were wearing thin. He had loved Elisabeth from the moment he laid eyes on her last October. He hadn't understood the instant attraction to this girl from Hohctorf. She was the complete opposite from his first wife, who had never spoke a cross word or raised her voice to him. Despite being nearly ten years younger than him, Elisabeth seemed so much older, and at times he forgot their age difference. But at other times, she was like a small child who he wanted to gather in his waiting arms for protection.

Georg watched his wife as she tended to the sick. Her sleeves were rolled up well past her elbows as she rinsed an unending number of cloths and applied them to the many fevered brows. For the past week, she was throwing herself into the work. As stubborn as she was, Elisabeth was the most beautiful creature he had ever had the privilege to meet. He smiled to himself. As much as he tried, he couldn't hate her.

****

Georg was receiving no co-operation from the master of the ship.

Captain Thomas Francis was keeping as far away from the afflicted passengers as possible and ordering his crew to do the same. Not speaking the language, Georg was unable to communicate with him, leaving them both utterly frustrated. He took it upon himself to take matters into his own hands. With the help of some healthy men, Georg ordered the removal and cleansing of the bedding of those who had died or survived the disease. He demanded they be spread on deck for sun and air, along with any clothing that had been worn by the afflicted.

At first he was met with resistance by those claiming that the new ventilation in the ship was spreading the fever. Georg believed strongly that the disease was spread by the bodies of men, clothes, and bedding. Through long and heated discussions, the others conceded, much to Georg's relief. Extra water was required to clean the clothes and bodies of those affected. As the dead were thrown overboard, Georg concerned himself with the living.

Only two quarts were allowed for each person ages fifteen and up, and there was no water allowance for children under four.

It was difficult for families with very little water to give any of it up. As much as he hated the thought of forcing those to relinquish any of the precious liquid they had, his convictions drove him to that end. Stopping the disease was far more urgent. The grievances, however, mounted daily and reverberated throughout the decks, manifesting itself like typhus.

"How I wish I were home. Lying with the pigs would be better than the dirt I've been forced to live with here," Georg heard one grumble.

Everyday it was the same: dealing with wormy food and filthy water. This was hard enough to bear as the small ship made its way to, for all they knew, a God-forsaken land. Now God had sent them the dreaded ship fever to suffer.

"It's God's judgment, that's what it is. We shouldn't have left the *Faterland*. We're all going to die," he heard another complain.

Georg glanced at Johann, who was at the next berth sponging down an elderly passenger recently stricken with the disease. He raised his eyebrows in hopelessness. What could they do? It was impossible to raise anyone's spirits in such pathetic and wretched surroundings. For his own sanity, he had attempted to close his eyes to the suffering, but Georg's heart bled for them. The crying and lamenting that persisted daily cracked even the most hardened hearts.

Georg covered another corpse with a blanket, lifted it, and was about to dispose of it off the main deck, when the hatches banged shut again. They were amidst another storm, which meant this corpse and others like it would have to stay amongst the living. The storm could last two or three days. He said a silent prayer to himself which was now an everyday occurrence. A necessity Georg relied upon. It was the only saving grace after being awakened from the few short stolen minutes of sleep to screams from the living who found themselves nestled between two dead bodies that had perished during the night. It had been three weeks since the onset of the ship fever, and so far twenty-eight had succumbed. Whispering another prayer, Georg implored that the disease would finally come to its own death.

"Come, Johann, Michael," he ordered, "help me clear this berth. God knows how long we'll have to weather this storm. If anyone else dies, we'll just have to lay them in this corner of the bunk. At least no one will be forced to sleep with the dead in the same bed." Georg rolled one body up against the cabin wall and lay another corpse beside it.

On the far side of the cabin near the now-closed hatch, there was a small huddle of about four or five people. One of them howled, snapping Georg's head in their direction. As he and Johann rushed towards the circle, more shrieking was heard as it started to spread from one person to the next.

"Where did you hear such nonsense?" Georg overheard one say.

"When I was on deck at daybreak, two of the sailors knew about the massacre from another ship that returned from Halifax just before we set sail from Rotterdam."

"What's going on?" Georg yelled to make himself heard amongst the loud voices.

"We're going to hell! That's where we're going, Georg. Franz here said there was a massacre by Indians in the very place this ship is taking us," a man named Joseph vocalized.

"What?" Georg couldn't believe his ears. "You must be mistaken. You've heard incorrectly. You don't speak the sailors' tongue. Couldn't you have misinterpreted what they said?"

"*Nein*! I don't have a full command of their language, but I can decipher a few words here and there."

That was true. Joseph did know a few words, enough to get by. However he couldn't carry on a decent conversation with any of them. Georg had experienced this first hand, to his dismay when he tried to use Joseph to get his point across to the captain about the cleansing of the ship.

"But don't you think you might've been confused this time? I can't see them taking us there knowing this." Georg tried to calm the others as the panic quickly spread.

"You're an imbecile! I heard what I heard. People were killed, then scalped afterwards. Hands were cut off, bellies ripped open. Screams were heard on the other side of the harbour. I tell you," Joseph continued, walking through what was now a throng of people crowding around them, "this was a grave mistake leaving our homeland. And it's not the first time a raid like this has happened. A similar instance occurred two years ago. Oh, what a terrible web we weave," Joseph lamented, pacing back and forth.

Georg examined the faces of those around him. He watched as each one of them seemed to age before his eyes. It was as if what they heard was the last nail in their coffins. He had no comforting words to offer them. What if Joseph had heard right and they were sailing to their deaths? The crowd dispersed slowly as everyone shuffled back to their bunks in silence. The depression that now descended was overpowering. Georg felt deeply for them, and let his own despair defeat him which, up until now, had taken every ounce of his energy to suppress. Sitting on a stool next to a dying old woman, he could, for the first time, hear nothing but the hacking coughs of the sick and the waves as they crashed against the hull of the ship. No moaning, no lamenting, just stillness.

****

"We're all going to perish!" Joseph screamed repeatedly, as he ran back and forth splashing as much vinegar as he could. This was his third cask. Unfortunately, the third cask wasn't vinegar, but water. "We're all going to die!" he howled again, almost mad with frenzy. Running back to the steps, he stumbled and his feet slipped from under him. Georg, scrambling after him, slipped and fell on the vinegar-drenched floor.

"Grab him!" Georg screamed. "Before he wastes any more!"

Descending the steps just as he heard his friend, Johann did as he was told, tackling Joseph as he attempted to stand and reach for another cask. Joseph lashed out at him with flailing arms, narrowly missing his eye with a clenched fist. He ducked, the arm grazing the top of his head giving him the opportunity to hoist Joseph over his shoulders like a sack of potatoes. Joseph thrashed about, shouting blasphemies at the top of his lungs. Johann threw him into an empty bunk. Joseph's head crashed against the wood with a loud crack.

"What the devil do you think you're doing?" Georg shrieked. He lunged at Joseph, forcing him to sit up as his stained shirt ripped open.

"What's going on?" Johann queried. "What'd he do?"

"Tell him, you maggot! Tell him how much vinegar you just poured in here, not to mention emptying the little water we have left. You fool! What possessed you, you..." Georg shook with outrage, and shoved Joseph against the wall with a sickening thud.

"You what?" It was Johann's turn to display his fury. Joseph dug his heels into the bed, pushing himself away from his accusers.

"I did what had to be done," he yelled at the two of them. "God knows you wouldn't. And you call yourself a *doktor*. Any good surgeon knows that vinegar will get rid of any disease. Your ways are the devil's ways. And as for the water, what good is it anyway? It's undrinkable with the green slime that floats through it like long, greasy fingers." Joseph's eyes darted back and forth in the poor light.

Their deck was almost empty, with just one or two sick in their bunks while the others were out for air. They scowled at this pathetic man who was looking more mad than frightened. The two months they had spent crowded unwillingly amongst the verminous infestations was taking a grave toll on Joseph. The cramped, intolerable quarters were enough to make anyone go mad. But as far as Johann was concerned, it was no excuse for what he did.

"You impudent little bastard! We need every ounce of that water to last us the rest of this voyage. Why, I have a mind to remove your ration." Joseph began to laugh aloud in Johann's face, showing a few blackened teeth, odd for someone as young as Joseph, a mere eighteen years.

Grabbing his throat with his left hand, Johann pulled Joseph towards him, within inches of his face. He pressed his fingers tighter on Joseph's Adam's apple. "I'll rip this from your neck and throw it to the sharks if I ever catch you near those casks again," he threatened through a taut mouth. Joseph coughed and sputtered.

"*Nein*, Johann! Don't!" Georg interfered, attempting to pry Johann's grip from Joseph's throat. "Enough!"

Johann loosened his hold but not before he threw Joseph to the wet floor, knocking over a bucket of excrement. It mixed with the vinegar and created the most abhorrent smell. "There, you low-life. There's your water ration." Joseph bolted for the steps just as the others were filtering down from above.

"Not a word to anyone about what transpired here, lest Joseph end up dead. We'd have complete chaos." His advice seemed unheeded. "Johann?"

Johann stood breathing heavily, trying to calm himself. Without speaking, he nodded in agreement.

****

It was the first day of September. Georg and Johann threw overboard what they were sure was the last body. The typhus had coursed its way unchecked over the past seven weeks. Now everyone was as healthy as circumstances would permit, and only a few people were weak but recovering. Georg was sure the disease was near its end. There hadn't been a new case for almost a week. This was a good sign, considering a day usually didn't go by without three or four displaying the onset of the symptoms. There was one family of eight that was almost completely annihilated, leaving only two; a father and his fourteen-year old son.

In all, thirty-two perished.

CHAPTER 16

Elisabeth lay awake in the dark with her knees up, hoping to relieve the pain in her lower back. Since yesterday she had this dull ache, but thought it must be from the extra weight she was carrying. Her stomach seemed to have suddenly enlarged in the ninth month. Stroking her belly lightly with the palms of her hands, Elisabeth was elated at the sudden sensation of her and Peter's baby. Lately though, it seemed that the baby didn't move as much. She worried for the little one. It couldn't possibly be getting the nourishment it needed. The last few days she was barely getting enough to sustain herself, let alone the other life that grew within her. No matter how many times she tried, she was revolted by the food, gagging at the very sight of a patch of red worms the size of a *thaler* squirming on the ship's biscuits.

More rationing of the water made it increasingly arduous to even wash her hands. The rest of her body had to remain unwashed. As each warm day melted into the next, the stench of unclean bodies hung thick in the air. Elisabeth scratched her head, now crawling with lice, and felt disgustingly foul. She was sure the mattress upon which she lay was the cause of the flea bites. Over the past few weeks, she had kept her thoughts focussed on her baby. It gave her something to live for in the intolerable conditions, but at times there were things that were impossible to ignore; the rampant scurrying and high-pitched din of the rats, for one. As she lay listening to the scratching and gnawing of one she was sure was beneath her bed, Elisabeth covered her ears with both hands to drown out the horrifying sound. No matter what she did, her attempts were fruitless, and her stomach churned at the idea of rats scampering around.

Shifting her cumbersome body to a different position to get better relief, she could feel the pains move to the front of her stomach as if a strap were slowly constricting around her middle. She drew in a long deep breath through her mouth until the pain subsided. The very idea of her being in labour was impossible to imagine. The baby wasn't due for another two weeks. Fear now gripped her. Dear God, she thought, not here! Not now! Her mind raced back to a month ago when a woman not much older than her had great difficulty in delivering. Both the mother and child had died. They were thrown to their watery graves. She was now determined to push that from her mind and concentrate on the living child within her.

She let her mind wander to other pleasant things. When would she meet Peter again? She wouldn't allow the remotest possibility that they wouldn't see each other enter her mind. She just couldn't. It was the only string of hope that stood between her loveless marriage and this voyage to a dangerous wilderness. Peter and his baby. Closing her eyes, Elisabeth's mind drifted to their future together, when she would show him their baby, they would run away together, and live in each other's love. She remembered the stolen glances, the timid first kisses in the barn back home, and their declaration of love. Smiling to herself, she opened her eyes to reveal a stark reality facing her. At the bottom of her bed, two tiny beady eyes shone at her. It wasn't the first time they had appeared on the bed looking for food.

She screamed. With her eyes squeezed shut, she kicked her legs widely to knock the disgusting creature off her bed. She didn't have the courage to see if it had indeed gone. She continued flailing until Georg, who had awoken amidst the racket, tried to calm her. Indeed, the rest of the bunk-mates on her deck were also rudely awakened.

Georg was standing now, commanding everyone to go back to sleep. "It's okay. It's gone now," he soothed to Elisabeth, crawling back into bed beside her. They had been sleeping in the same bed ever since the rats had become braver, spreading themselves from bed to bed. "Are you okay now? You're trembling," he whispered tenderly.

"Hold me."

Eagerly, Georg manoeuvred his arm around her as best he could with the child between them. Elisabeth cradled her head on his shoulder.

"I hate it here. I don't know how much longer I can cope in these conditions," she said. "I'm at the end of my rope, I tell you. To bring forth a babe in this squalor defies the imagination. It won't survive."

"Shh, don't talk such nonsense. A healthy babe will be born to you, I'm sure. And besides, what're you talking about? You're not due for another two weeks. You've nothing to fear and usually the first one is late anyway. You'll birth a healthy infant on dry land in the comfort of our new home." Hearing his wife's sudden intake of breath, Georg looked at her searchingly in the dark. "Elisabeth?" he asked. "What's the matter?" He carefully removed his arm from beneath her neck. "How long have you been in pain?"

"Since yesterday, I..."

"Yesterday! Why didn't you say something earlier? All this talk of having a baby on board wasn't just needless worrying on your part, was it? You're in labour, aren't you?"

"I really didn't think I was. For the past twenty-four hours, I've just had back pain. I thought it was due to my increased weight. It's only the last hour or so the pains have worsened. I've been awake most of the night." Of course, she didn't know what time it was, lying awake for one hour seemed like many. The night seemed to have dragged on. For all she knew, it could almost be morning. The hatch was the only means of discerning if it was in fact the start of a new day.

"I'll be right back."

"Don't leave me," she begged, holding out her hand. The thought of being left here alone in the dark with rats frightened and sickened her.

"I won't be long. I'm just going to see if I can scrounge some water and rags."

"*Bitte*! Don't leave me," she said emphatically, clutching his arm as he was about to turn away. "They'll be back for the baby." Elisabeth was a strong person, but the rats were unnerving her. He decided to stay with her and woke Johann in the next bunk.

"Korber! Come on, wake up, lazy," he said, shaking him through his grunting.

"Wha?" Johann answered sleepily, rubbing his eyes. "What's the matter?"

"Elisabeth's pains have started, and I need you to fetch me some water and rags," Georg answered, helping Johann to stand. He almost pushed his friend forward towards his intended duty.

"There's hardly anything left that's decent," Johann complained.

"Do the best you can. Here, take this bucket and go around the deck and scrape together what you can from anyone. Go!"

He turned back to his patient and lit the lantern hanging on a hook above him. Pulling the blanket off Elisabeth, he examined her. She tensed again at the next wave of pain.

"Relax, Elisabeth. Breathe deeply through the pain."

"Relax? I can't! Don't you tell me, Doktor Gessler, to relax," she said through clenched teeth. "Oh, God, I'm going to be sick," and she vomited water over the side of the bed. "Get Mama!" she cried.

A few moments later Johann was back with what water he could find, about half a bucketful. He was then ordered again to quickly get Anna on the next deck up.

"*Bitte*!"

****

"Push, Elisabeth, push!" Georg urged.

"I can't." Elisabeth's voice was barely audible. "I'm so tired." Anna was smoothing her daughter's wet hair back from her face and eyes.

"Come now. One more will do it," Georg encouraged.

"I told you, I can't," she answered weakly. "Just let me die."

"You're not going to die, Elisabeth Barbara Maria Gessler," Anna said firmly. "There's been enough death on this ship, and you," she said emphatically, "young lady, are not going to add to the toll. Now, do as your husband says and push."

"I can't, Mama." Elisabeth cried weakly.

Anna sat on the edge of the bed and lifted her daughter's back to support it against her chest. "I don't want to hear it. Push!" Elisabeth conceded.

"That's it! Again," Doktor Gessler commanded. "Once more. I have the head."

When she heard that, it seemed to make all the pain more bearable. Peter's face was now ingrained in her mind's eye. She didn't know where the strength suddenly appeared, but she pushed as hard as she could with every ounce of energy, screaming at the sheer power of it. She felt the baby gush forth between her legs. She lay against her mama, breathing heavily and listening to the wail of her newborn.

"It's a boy!" Georg held the bloodied baby up in the palm of his hands, the umbilical cord still attached.

Elisabeth stared from her baby to her mama and back again, crying in sheer ecstasy. Her and Peter's baby! Georg cut the cord with a knife and handed the infant to Anna. She wet a rag and did the best she could to clean her grandson before giving the newborn to his mother to suckle. Anna looked to Georg.

"What's his name?" Anna asked.

"Why Peter, Mama, after your *fater*. You know the first grandson in the family must be named after the *grandfater*." Anna eyed her daughter sharply.

Elisabeth glanced at her husband. By the look in his eyes, she knew he was on to her. He'll never really truly be sure, she pondered, if she had named her son after Peter or if tradition really did prevail. She gave her husband a smile but didn't get one in return.

****

"Land! I saw land!" The bearer of this great news was Christian, who came barrelling down the steps backwards two at a time. He held onto the railing screaming the long-awaited words as he went. The passengers all pressed in around him, then, proceeded to push their way up the steps and onto the open deck. He ran and gave his sister and brother-in-law a hug, then scooted back up to get Hanna and his parents.

It was now the middle of September and the last two weeks had dragged on, even with the increasing demands of Elisabeth's son to fill so much of her attention. She was caught up in the moment along with everyone else and ran up with her husband, carrying her newborn in her arms. Once on deck, the cool autumn air hit her face, rejuvenating her.

"Look, Elisabeth, over there!" Georg cried out. "We've made it!"

The deck was becoming crowded as more and more filtered up. Dozens leaned over the edge of the ship and cried in jubilation. She was caught up in it too and hugged Georg, feeling the life breathe back into her body.

Brilliant white seagulls with spotty gray on their wings screeched over the water. They circled the ship with one or two perching themselves at the top of the mainmast, and still many others swooped into the sparkling brine below in search of fish. As the ship slowly approached the headland, Elisabeth could see the harbour leading them to their new home. At the mouth was a large island that looked deserted, then a smaller one appeared farther into the bay. On this island she could see a timber fort-like structure. Sailors scrambled about shouting orders. Others shimmied up the foremast and mainmast, rolling the canvas sails up tight into the ropes. Not much farther past this small island, the ship came to rest with a loud splash of the anchor over the side.

By now the rest of Elisabeth's family had found their way through the crowds to where she and Georg stood. Christian lifted Hanna up and was beaming. He felt exhilarated.

"Welcome home, daughter," Anna smiled. Elisabeth was giddy with excitement. She didn't know if it was seeing land after eleven weeks of the worst living conditions she could imagine, or the fact that this would be where she was going to find her love.

CHAPTER 17

Reverend William Tutty's voice strained over the din of the hammering and banging of workmen. They were hurrying to finish the last of the palisade surrounding the small settlement in Dartmouth. Each picket—about six inches in diameter, sharply pointed at the top end, and standing about ten feet in height—was strung together in a rough line around the colony as far back as Elisabeth could see. The beginning and end of this security abruptly stopped at the water's edge of Chebucto Harbour.

Since arriving a month ago, Elisabeth and the other settlers never ventured far because of the threat of Indian attacks. The rumour of the Dartmouth massacre that had spread throughout the ship just before their arrival turned out to be horribly true, hence the reason for the protection of their small group now colonizing across from Halifax. The Indian raid left nothing of the established settlement from the year before. Men, women, and children were murdered and scalped mercilessly in their sleep. Others were taken captive. The handful that did escape vowed not to return, fleeing to the other side of the harbour in terror.

Those people that now occupied Dartmouth consisted of about 150 from the ship *Speedwell* that arrived in July, just two months prior to their own arrival on the *Pearl*. Most from these two ships were dispersed to Halifax. The more recent vessel, *Gale*, settled at either Halifax or the isthmus.

It was Sunday afternoon as the settlers gathered around Reverend

Tutty to hear his service in the open air at the water's edge. The congregation consisted mainly of women and children; the men were labouring on the palisade to work off their passage debts. Most of the men from both ships were working for two shillings a day until their freight was paid. Georg and Elisabeth were one of the few to have their passage free of charge. Georg's occupation as a doctor certainly worked to their advantage.

Elisabeth's arm was tingling from little Petie's position, so she shifted him to her other side. She was alone on this day. Georg was at the Orphan House in Halifax attending the sick who had just arrived on the *Murdoch* last week. Originally, the House was set up to shelter the children that were left alone after their parents had succumbed to disease or starvation on the immigrant ships. The building was now housing the old, as well as those who arrived too late to build their homes as winter was quickly descending upon them. Such was the case with the *Murdoch* that docked a week ago. Even some of those from the *Pearl* had to make do at the Orphan House until the following spring.

Elisabeth and her family were one of the more fortunate in building their log house. With Papa, Georg, Christian, and others pitching in to help each other build roofs over their heads, the structures were up in no time, to Elisabeth's relief. She couldn't bear to think of cramped quarters again after the lengthy weeks at sea.

Even though Reverend Tutty was bred in England, he gave the service in German. The former minister, Reverend Peter Burger, taught him the language before he sailed back to London a couple of months before. Unfortunately, Reverend Tutty learned very little and was unable to converse with the immigrants. He did the best he could from what he was taught and picked his way precariously through the service. It was easy for Elisabeth to become distracted as some mispronounced words filtered in one ear and out the other.

From the corner of her eye, she noticed a small boat drifting toward shore with only one occupant.

When the Reverend was halfway through, there arose such a commotion from a nearby blockhouse that it was impossible to continue. Not because he was unable to raise his voice above it, but because he was beginning to lose his audience as they slowly drifted towards the disturbance. The crowd that now gathered was milling around the one person that Elisabeth had seen disembark from the tiny boat on the beach. He was beet red in the face and walking away from a young man who, from what Elisabeth could tell by the uniform, was an ensign in Governor Cornwallis' regiment. Anna walked alongside her daughter tightly holding Hanna's hand.

"Mr. Hoffman. Stop!" yelled the young man, waving a letter high above his head. The older one stopped and turned. "What business have you here in Dartmouth?"

"You have no power to make such a question to me, Gildart."

"God damn you, Hoffman, I'll show you!" He lunged at his opponent, whereupon Hoffman stayed him with his large hand upon his chest.

"I'm the Justice of the Peace appointed by the Governor. Do you dare to question *his* authority? And the letter that has just been delivered to you is from the Commissioner of Peace, Ephriam Cook."

"Ha!" Gildart jeered. "It would have been better if Cook delivered this himself." He threw the paper onto the ground. "Seize him!" Five soldiers arrested Hoffman and proceeded to carry him like a criminal through the settlement, amongst the ridicule of some. But others siding with Hoffman attempted to follow him and were met with the end of a whip by Walter Clark, the overseer. "Back to work!" he howled.

Clark delivered a blow to Michael's left shoulder. Elisabeth saw her mother wince and about to make a move towards her husband. Her eyes shot a stern warning to her mama not to interfere. Hugging Hanna snugly by her side, Anna heeded her daughter and hurried alongside her back home.

The jaunt home was in silence and more of a saunter than a quick step, which Elisabeth was normally used to when walking with her mother. Papa had been struck before by the gaffer; there were obvious cuts and bruises on his arms and face when he returned late at night. In fact, the mistreatment wasn't centred around her Papa; others under Herr Clark's thumb were increasingly being beaten, diminishing what pride and dignity was left. Both Anna and Elisabeth were well aware of the happenings, as well as their neighbours, but it was the first time they had witnessed it. Elisabeth was astonished at how easy it was to belay her mother's unbridled desire to tear into Herr Clark. Back in the old country, a team of wild horses couldn't have stopped her.

As slow as they were walking, it still didn't take long to arrive at her parents' home. When coming north from the harbour, she always happened upon theirs first. Her and Georg's log dwelling was just three buildings away. She worried about her mama so decided to stay with her until Papa returned.

Their closest neighbours had arrived on the *Speedwell* in July and were from the Pallatine, north of their village. Elisabeth still referred to Hohctorf as home. Her parents' one-room cabin was built alongside two others that had been abandoned in May after the massacre. In fact, one of them, Elisabeth wasn't sure which one, was the scene of the most abhorrent and hideous sights that she couldn't even begin to imagine. A baby had been found lying next to its parents. All three had been scalped, their bellies ripped open and the father's brains had been dashed out. It was also said that in one of the houses near the shore, a six-year old male was found hiding under a bed in terror while his parents were lying outside in a pool of blood after being unmercifully tomahawked to death.

Four families, including Elisabeth, Georg, and her parents, all of whom lived in two of the houses that used to skirt the edge of the dense woods, were now protected by the back end of the palisade. The ten foot wooden structure did not relieve Elisabeth's fears, especially at night when she lay awake in the stillness listening to the howling of nearby wolves, wondering if they were Indians communicating to each other in disguise, planning their next attack.

Elisabeth skirted around one of many stumps that littered the land around the cabin. With everyone pitching in, including the women, it was little time before the logs were felled, cut with notches at either end, and stacked up to form the walls. The foundation on which it lay was carefully built of stone, with the chimney erected above it. After the roof was completed, moss, leaves, and mud were stuffed into the spaces between the logs to keep out the wind and rain. And this couldn't have happened soon enough. They were no sooner in their makeshift homes than the cold blew through the settlement, making the ground hard with frost. Those who did get their houses built before the winter considered themselves fortunate, even though the buildings they lived in were roughcast.

Elisabeth's cabin was similar to her parents, and most others in Dartmouth. It had a dirt floor and no glass for windows because of the necessity to build quickly before the cold. There was only one small opening for a window with paper pasted up in place of the glass. Papa had oiled the paper so that light could pass through.

Hanna stayed outside to play with the neighbouring children. There was one small girl from Switzerland, who was a year younger than Hanna. Language was no barrier to the little ones, as they became fast friends.

Elisabeth sat down on her parents' bed that was crudely set up against the wall. She laid her infant son beside her on the coarse blanket, while her mother blew into the ashes to start a flame. A large log of wood was kept burning day and night in the hearth, with the smouldering piece of timber being buried in ashes each time before retiring. This way there would always be a fire for cooking. She watched her mother in silence as she placed a large iron pot on the trivet. The change in her was tremendous, thought Elisabeth. Anna's impetuous temperament was diminishing slowly, but nonetheless was sharply noticeable. Her mama sat down on a nearby bench, staring blankly at the dirt floor.

"We should never have come," she started.

Elisabeth knitted her eyebrows together in question.

"I know now, it was the wrong thing to do. Look at what we've come to!"

Anna got up again and busied herself with supper, throwing it into the pot in jerky motions, sometimes splashing the water. The sizzling water beads slipped over the cauldron and into the fire below. Food was scarce again. Tomorrow, they would pick up more rations. Winter was arriving and they would have to rely on victuals supplied to them from the government, which was even further degradation in Mama's eyes.

"Mama, you agreed with the emigration. You and Papa discussed..."

"Lands sake, child! Who told you such nonsense? I never agreed to any such foolishness. There was no discussion. Oh! *Ja*," she expressed emphatically, tossing the dried peas in, "your papa addressed it all right, with Christian. He's the head of this household, and what he says goes." She turned around to eye her daughter. "As if you didn't know!" There was a gleam in her eye when she said this, which made Elisabeth smile slightly.

"At least we're not under the tyranny of the Prince, always being persecuted for not being Catholic," Elisabeth replied, trying to think of the positives in an almost impossible situation. "No taxes!"

"We've jumped from a hot cauldron into the fire. With the threat of Indian attacks, your papa slaving under Clark, begging for food..."

"Oh, Mama," Elisabeth had to cut in. "Stop exaggerating! You know we don't beg. We're given provisions that are due to us; it was in the agreement."

"Humph," she grunted, and started stirring the mixture, bending over to see more clearly. "The pork and beef are so salty, they're almost inedible. And when we do get bread? It's that horrid hard ship bread we had coming over here. I don't know which is the lesser of two evils, Prince Eugen or Walter Clark. No one knows how to fish, and all the men are too frightened to hunt the deer and partridge outside the palisade."

"Things will get better. Just you wait and see." Elisabeth had trouble making it sound convincing. She agreed with most of what her mama had to say. "Papa will only be under Herr Clark until the passages have been worked off.

"What better!" she cried, waving her arms. "Where's this fifty acres that was promised us? We barely have enough room, cramped in here to eat, sleep, and live. Back home, at least we had an upstairs to sleep. Look at that table to eat off. Why, it's just a piece of rough plank with a sawhorse at each end. I don't know how many times I've received splinters just scrubbing the top of it." Anna was pacing back and forth in front of Elisabeth, chattering away. Elisabeth could see the footprints she left on the floor as she walked with determination. She stopped in front of her, "*Awch,* I don't know what to do. And, your papa working on a Sunday. Terrible! Terrible!"

Petie started to cry. Elisabeth lifted him carefully, placing him to her breast. He immediately quieted.

"There's nothing we can do but make the best of it." Anna sat down beside her and stroked her grandson's forehead. "There's no turning back now. We'll just have to have faith things will get better," Elisabeth said.

"What's this world coming to?" she replied, "You, my daughter, giving me advice. Tsk tsk tsk!" She shook her head and smiled. She then frowned at her grandson. "What's happened to Jakob?"

No one in the family had brought up his name, unless Mama mentioned it first. No one wanted to upset her. Such a conversation always led Mama down the path of her thinking he was dead, or running from the authorities all over the country back home. Despite the reliable stories that he was seen on one of the ships crossing over, she refused to believe it, no matter how much everyone tried to convince her. But Elisabeth hung onto this string of rumour just as she reassured herself daily that she would one day find Peter.

Elisabeth laid her hand over her mother's, attempting to soothe her fears. "We'll find him," she said, watching her mother's eyes glisten. "Remember what you used to say to me when I was troubled?"

Anna shook her head. "God always has a special place in his heart for the troubled, and carries them through their tribulations." Her mama's difficult smile quickly melted away.

"Then Stefan wouldn't have died," she replied.

****

Michael and Christian walked through the front door, signalling that the afternoon was gone. Hanna was napping on the bed, snuggled up close to her tiny nephew, while Elisabeth and Anna readied the meal. Elisabeth could see that her papa was worn and tired, not from the physical labour he'd been used to all his life, but from the constant wearing down of his dignity.

Michael kissed his wife, poured water in a basin, and scrubbed his face and hands. Meanwhile, the table was set, and everyone sat down to eat, including sleepy-eyed Hanna. Petie was left to nap undisturbed. Anna had asked Elisabeth to stay since Georg would still be at the Orphan House in Halifax. At first, she hesitated. The tension between her and her father hadn't improved. Every time she thought of being forced into marriage, Elisabeth would seethe inside.

The five of them sat around the table, bowed their heads, and held hands while Michael said grace. Hanna had to stretch across the table as it was too big for her small arms. Michael thanked the good Lord for giving them the strength, courage, and determination needed to survive in their new lives together. It amazed Elisabeth how he had maintained his faith through the past year. When Margaretha died, his beliefs waivered, but not to the extent that he stopped believing. Tonight the grace was especially long as he thanked Him for the support and help of their neighbours. Then he ended it, thanking Him that they were still all together. Elisabeth glanced at Anna. She knew she was thinking of Jakob and the death of Stefan.

No one said anything about what had happened that morning. Dinner was eaten in silence and it irked Elisabeth tremendously. If her mama wasn't about to open the subject, she would just burst. Not until the soup was dished up and the bowls were half emptied, did Anna venture to ask.

"What was all the commotion about this morning between the two gentlemen?" she asked.

"I wouldn't exactly call them gentlemen. Well, Hoffman, *ja*, but Gildart? Not on your life. He's lower than..." Christian answered.

"Hush, Christian. I'll have no such talk in my house," Michael said, giving his son a severe stare. "Between Johann's little English and the fellow workers today, we found out that Hoffman is someone we can trust."

"I've never seen him in Dartmouth before," Elisabeth said.

"He lives across the harbour, and today he delivered a letter to Gildart with a few complaints," Michael answered. "Herr Clark's been accused of selling liquors on the Sabbath."

"Well, it's about time something was done about that tavern of his. It's not right to have such evil open on the Sabbath," Anna exclaimed.

"That's only a small part of it, Anna. Clark's finally going to have to answer to forcing us to work on Sundays: building the palisade, the blockhouses, and also for striking us without cause."

"Why, he's even had people shingling his own house on the Sabbath!" Christian added.

"I can't take the abuse you've been receiving from Clark..." Anna started.

"And that's another thing, Anna. I don't want you attempting to interfere like you were about to today." Michael held up his hand to prevent her from saying anything further. "You'll only make an impossible situation worse."

"I held her back," Elisabeth answered proudly.

"*Danke*, daughter." Michael turned and smiled at his wife. Reaching across the table, he placed his large hand so that it completely enveloped hers.

"Isn't there some way of working under another overseer, Michael?"

"*Nein*. Herr Clark is the only overseer, and all of us German picketers fall under his jurisdiction. Nought can be done about it." He saw the pain in his wife's eyes. "Anna, it's in God's hands now. He'll carry us through this," he said quietly.

"The eighteen pence you receive will take you years to pay off.

We're indebted to Governor Cornwallis, probably for the next two years, and under Herr Clark, you could be dead by then." Anna's voice cracked but she still maintained her composure.

"It won't take years, and besides, a couple of years is small potatoes when you think of what we've been promised. We'll soon have our own land with our own animals, along with our own crops. Just be patient. *Bitte*!" Eying his wife, then daughter, he said, "Christian and I are just fine. We can take care of ourselves. We've only been here a month. Things *will* get better, you just wait and see." Seeing that they still were not convinced, he continued, "Besides, just a year ago labourers were only receiving twelve pence per day for the king's work, and because of the Palatines promptly going on strike, the pay was increased."

"And that's supposed to make me feel better!" Anna cried, standing at the table.

"Anna, *bitte*!" Michael interceded, not wanting to continue the conversation in front of the children. Hanna, who had fallen asleep after eating, was awakened by the sudden rise in her mama's voice. Elisabeth looked at her brother, not knowing what to do. They couldn't go to another room like they could at home; they were in the only room of the house, and it was much too cold to stand outside.

"You're the eternal optimist, Michael. Look around you. Just look at where you brought us. There's no school for Hanna. Of course, I wouldn't let her out of my sight anyway in case of an Indian lurking about. We had to leave all our belongings behind in the old country. Everything we worked so hard for over the years was left to rot there. We're eating on a piece of board for a table that's in the same room where we sleep with both our children, or should I say with what is left of our children." Her voice faltered for a brief moment but quickly found the strength to go on. "Stefan is dead and God knows where Jakob is..."

Elisabeth had her head down but lifted her eyes to glance at her papa. The pain flashed across his face as if Mama had stabbed him through the heart. Anna stared at her husband, then her eyes darted from Elisabeth to Christian to Hanna, who all sat in silence.

"The food, Michael! The food! We beg like street urchins to get what sustenance we need to continue to live this meagre life you've brought us to."

"Stop it! Don't do this to yourself," Michael said as Anna collapsed in tears into her husband's waiting arms.

Elisabeth stared at the pitiful scene. She always thought her mother a tower of strength. And Papa! She wondered how he found the fortitude to remain calm while his wife cut him to the quick, laying such accusations at his feet. Elisabeth couldn't take her eyes off her parents, no longer two pillars of strength that were always there for her. They were now two human beings trying to make a difficult circumstance more tolerable.

****

Christian was embarrassed by the scene and was relieved when his sister suggested he sleep at her house. He'd be company for her since Georg sometimes didn't get home from the hospital until the wee hours of the morning. It was snowing and the stiff wind from the North was whipping it into their faces. Elisabeth protected Petie inside her coat, and to their surprise, found Georg at home sitting by the open hearth with his feet facing into the fire.

"Doktor Gessler!"

Christian snickered. He still found it amusing that his sister called her husband of seven months so formally. It was acceptable amongst the gentry, but at their station in life he thought it ridiculous. His grin was soon erased when met by his sister's glare.

"I hadn't expected you so early!"

Georg greeted his wife just as reservedly but friendly, more like brother and sister than husband and wife, Christian thought. "Don't worry, Frau Gessler," he stated sarcastically, "I'm only here briefly to get some food supplies."

"Don't you have enough at the hospital without having to dig into our reserve?"

"There are too many mouths to feed. It has exceeded the normal hospital ration."

"Well, ours, Doktor Gessler, is too low to share. Surely if you ask the Governor, he would extend extra victualling under the circumstances."

"We've already tried that and it got us nowhere," Georg said.

"But our rations are low now. We can't afford to give that out..."

He interrupted her. "Not really. Of late, you've only yourself to feed most of the time. I've been eating at the hospital and you breast-feed Petie..."

Elisabeth blushed at this in front of her young brother.

"Tomorrow is victual day. Surely you'll get more then."

"Precisely my point, Elisabeth. The hospital is on a separate ration list from the rest of us, and consequently, have one week to survive. Doktor Erhard brought in food supplies yesterday, and it still isn't enough," Georg exclaimed. "You're picking up more food tomorrow, so the reserve we have left will help out where it is better needed."

Without a word, but with a reproachful look in her husband's direction, Elisabeth prepared her son for his cradle. Georg piled the food into a canvas bag and Christian smiled at him.

"Can I help you, Georg?" Christian asked eagerly.

He handed him hard-tack, oatmeal, molasses, and half a sack of flour. "Every little bit will help," Georg said. "Even if it aids just one dying creature."

The snow was so wet and heavy that by the time the wagon was loaded, the canvas tarp, used to cover the foodstuffs, was completely white, and so were the two of them. Christian jumped up onto the wagon and grabbed the reins.

"Hey! Where do you think you're going, brother?"

"You said I could help!"

"With the loading of the wagon, but I never said a word about you coming with me. Come on! Off with you!" He gestured for Christian to get down.

"*Bitte*. You said there weren't enough bodies to help, and the patients were too much to handle for just you and Doktor Erhard."

"You've got more important things to do with the finishing of this palisade and another blockhouse to build before the winter becomes too severe to continue."

"By the looks of this storm, I'd say the building will be delayed tomorrow, and besides, even if I do miss a day, I can make it up. I'll just work longer hours." Georg looked as if he was about to concede. Christian continued, "You can't deny that you two are overworked, right?"

Georg nodded and gave in. "Just a minute," he said and disappeared back into the house. In a matter of seconds he reappeared, jumped up onto the bench seat, and grabbed the reins from Christian. "Come then. We're wasting our time here dawdling. And wipe that smirk off your face." The horse jerked the vehicle forward and faded into the white storm.

They arrived at the shore, and only a few minutes passed before a man of medium height emerged out of the white swirls of snow that were now whipping up a frenzy. Georg and Christian had already loaded the boat as they waited for the navigator. The waves were increasing, and Christian could hear them crashing onto the shore as the boat bobbed up and down on the swells. A man with the lantern lifted it up to see who was with Georg. Christian recognized him as Herr Hoffman.

"Come on, you two. We have little time to spare. Have to cross now before this storm makes the harbour unnavigable."

Hoffman hooked the lantern he was carrying onto a pole at the bow of the boat and stepped in, pushing the vessel farther away from the shore. Except for the little light the lantern cast, it was pitch black. Christian clung to the side of the boat as it dashed about on the waves.

Hoffman and Georg were rowing hard against the swelling surf. It seemed like an eternity before they reached the Halifax beach. The men dragged the boat out of the water far enough on shore so the increasing waves wouldn't claim the craft back for its own again. Hoffman shone the light into Christian's face.

"You're looking a little pale, young man. Wait a couple of hours and this harbour will be impossible to cross. Looks like we're in for a long one tonight."

Georg nodded. "Here, Christian, help me load the wagon." The last part of their journey was through the most populated area of Halifax, along the shoreline over rough streets of stone and tree stumps that were now hidden with the wet snow. The storm didn't seem to deter people from making an appearance at a nearby tavern, though. Other than the laughter and gaiety that emanated from the establishment, the streets were pretty much deserted, with the odd beggar swaying side to side drunk with rum.

The cart rumbled on to the outskirts of the settlement towards the hospital. As they drove farther away, Christian could hear the laughter and noisy cries from the tavern steadily decrease in volume until there was silence again. The wind was blowing more fiercely now, and Christian squinted against the driving snow that stung his face as he strained to see ahead.

"How much farther?" he yelled.

"We're almost there," Georg replied.

Christian could now see the palisade towering beside him, but they appeared to be riding outside of it and not inside. What if the Indians attacked, though surely not on a night like this, he thought. However, what a better night to come upon a couple of unsuspecting souls. He immediately pushed the thought far from his mind and concentrated on matters on hand.

The snow was making things impossible to see until one was up close. The horse was reined in as they pulled up to the Orphan House. Christian jumped off after Hoffman and Georg, then helped them carry the foodstuffs into the log building.

Christian didn't have any preconceived idea about this place, but he still wasn't prepared for what he was about to see. The Orphan House was one large rectangular room with a huge fireplace at one end. There were families young and old, some prostrate, some sitting on beds that were shoulder to shoulder against both sides of the wall, and cots straight down the middle. One couldn't see the floor for everyone's belongings. Some had blankets hung on strung-up rope between the beds to accommodate some form of privacy, as little as it allowed. Christian thought he recognized a few people from the *Pearl* but he wasn't too sure.

"All of these people are passengers that came over this year. Some are from the *Pearl,* some from the *Murdoch,"* Georg said. "Get over here before my back breaks! Help me carry these crates to the fireplace." They were greeted with cheering from the inhabitants, who pounced upon them, offering their help.

"*Danke,* Herr Henderick," Hoffman said, gratefully handing a couple to the man. "Just stack them on that side of the hearth there in the corner." All the men formed a line down the centre between the clutter to carry the supplies faster to the end of the room. Christian noticed that Herr Henderick had a pleasant manner about him, with a very kind, middle-aged face to fit his personality. The snow was making its way through the open door and building up between the cracks in the wooden floor.

"You came none too soon, Hoffman. The women were fretting something terrible, wondering what they were going to feed their children tomorrow. We're down to the last bit of scraps: a few pieces of moldy shipbread and some dried peas," Henderick told him.

"We still need to be extra careful to make this last the rest of the week, until we get more. I'll still try and scrape more together," Georg said, passing one container to Christian.

"That's the last one, everyone," Hoffman stated. "Georg, I'm going to put the wagon and horse in the stable. I'll be back shortly." He disappeared, slamming the door shut against the wind, which seemed to have picked up with such great force that Christian could hear it whistling through the hinges on the door.

"Nicolaas, this is Christian, my brother-in-law." Georg introduced them laying his hands on either side of his shoulder.

"Glad to meet you, sir," Herr Henderick said, extending his hand and smiling. "You've been a great help. *Danke*, Christian." Christian nodded and smiled, shaking his hand. He felt so grown up; no one had called him sir before. "Welcome. By the looks of that blizzard out there, I think you and Georg will be staying the night. Come and warm yourselves by the fire."

"How are things upstairs, Nicolaas?"

"Pretty quiet, actually. Doktor Erhard is up there now. A couple of hours ago, I heard Regina crying and ran upstairs. And the strangest thing, Georg, Fredrick was beside her holding her hand. He had her calmed down by the time I got there."

Georg raised his eyebrows in amazement. "Really? Tis better than finding trouble, or rather trouble finding him."

Nicolaas rubbed his chin. "Come to think of it, I think we've gone a whole day without his usual rumbles with Simon. What's the world coming to?" Georg and he laughed in unison. Christian was curious as to what else was on the second floor and deduced it was just more of what was down here.

"I'll be down in a minute," Georg said, ducking his head to miss the low beam. He ran up the steps two at a time.

"Come, Christian. Come sit with me by the fire." Nicolaas guided his new friend through the mass of people, who were obviously much relieved with the supplies.

A few of the women were well on their way to preparing stew when Hoffman rushed in the door. It flung open more by the gale than by his own persuasion. "*Awch*, it's bitter out there; not fit for man nor beast," he remarked, pushing the door shut with some difficulty. Throwing his coat down, he stepped towards the warm glow of the fire. He stood to one corner of it so as not to disturb the women busily preparing the food. He leaned in, briskly rubbing his hands together over the flames. Christian saw his balding head when he threw off his hat. What hair was left was tied back with a piece of twine.

"So, Christian, do I assume you're from Frankfort where Georg is from?" Herr Hoffman asked.

"*Nein*, Herr Hoffman, I..."

"*Bitte*, Christian, call me John," he smiled. Christian felt uncomfortable calling someone so much older than he by his first name, but nodded his assent.

"And that goes for me, too. No airs out here. Call me Nicolaas," Herr Henderick quipped, leaning his back against the crates that were piled up by the wall. He stretched his legs to soak up the heat emanating from the hearth.

Satisfied with regaining his body heat, John pulled up a three-legged stool, and set himself down beside Christian. He withdrew his pipe and pressed small clumps of tobacco inside. "So where are you from then, my boy?" he said, pushing the dry substance in with his forefinger.

"We're from Hohctorf, not far from Stuttgart."

"We? I assume you mean your family?" John said, lighting the tobacco with a lit piece of straw while sucking noisily on it.

"*Ja*, I have two sisters, one younger than me, Hanna, and one older, Elisabeth, who is married to Georg. Actually I had three sisters, but one died about a year ago."

"No brothers?" Nicolaas asked.

"One now. Jakob is still in Hohctorf." Christian didn't want to lie, especially to two men he had taken an instant liking to, but he didn't want to have to explain the circumstances surrounding the black sheep of the family.

"One now?"

"My youngest brother, Stefan, died of typhus on the ship over here."

"I'm sorry. Your brother Jakob never emigrated with you?" John asked, now puffing away with great billows of smoke rising above his head. Christian found the aroma surprisingly pleasant.

"He said he never wanted to leave the *Faterland*." Christian remembered Papa used to always say this. He was feeling unsettled and wanted to change the subject, so was relieved when Georg arrived at their small soiree.

"All's well with the regiment."

"Regiment?" Christian queried.

"Just a game that the children and I play. I'm their Colonel rather than a *doktor*."

"Children? You make it sound like there's nothing but children up there."

Georg's eyes crinkled compassionately. "They're all orphans. Their parents died on the voyages here. Some have been left all alone in this world with no siblings either."

Christian couldn't imagine being alone. It was absolutely incomprehensible. "Can I go and look?"

"Tomorrow. They're all asleep now. So, what have you three been talking about?"

"We were just discussing Christian's family," John said, talking out of the side of his pipe.

Not wanting to bring up Jakob again, Christian quickly went onto another topic. "Aren't you afraid of an Indian attack, being outside the palisade like this?

John raised his eyebrows and answered slowly. "With the darkness and the blizzard, you probably didn't see the regiment encamped up the hill just a few yards behind us." He gestured with a nod of his head.

"Actually, I could barely see through the blizzard, but I saw a few lights. This regiment can protect you?"

"Well, with Warburton's men here, we haven't had an attack yet," Nicolaas proudly remarked. "And there are two blockhouses west of us."

"I'd heard the other day that two soldiers were keeping watch one night and both of them were killed."

"They were also playing cards and should've been watching out for those savages. It's their own fault. Never knew what hit them. Brutal, just brutal it was. No one heard anything. They were found early in the morning when the new shift came on." As John was talking, he gazed into space, then, shuddered. Christian sat wide-eyed, hanging onto his every word.

"But you've no need to worry, my boy. Horseman's and Cornwallis' Forts are situated not far from here. We've got Fort George built on the highest point in Halifax as well. You can see for miles around. Those Indians won't encroach upon us before they're seen first. Don't you fret." Christian could see John's nostrils flare as he inhaled long and deep, puffing out more smoke from the side of his mouth.

Georg squeezed Chistian's shoulder. "Even if the Indians got this far, we're quite safe here. This building's musket-proof."

"But it's not fire-proof," Christian replied.

No one answered.

Nicolaas was the first to respond. "It's been pretty quiet here. Dartmouth has had no attacks since May."

"The attacks are so sporadic that you just don't know when the next one will be," John said. "The French are still supplying the Mi'kmaq with ammunition."

"What would the French prove in doing that, John?" Up until now, Christian had been avoiding calling Herr Hoffman by his first name, but now he was so at ease with him that, surprisingly, it felt right.

"The Acadians have a burr up their ass," John whispered, so the women cooking behind him wouldn't be offended. "They're aiding the Mi'kmaq, hoping the Government will give in, let them live their own lives and not pledge their allegiance to Britain."

"It's blackmail, pure and simple," Georg added.

Christian squinted, trying to follow. "You see, my boy, the problems that have plagued Nova Scotia go back about forty years, when this province repeatedly changed hands between England and France," John said.

"In fact, to the French, Nova Scotia is Acadie," Nicolaas interrupted.

John cleared his throat, loudly.

"Then for the last time, Port Royal, the tiny French capital, miles from here on the South Shore, was captured by the English and renamed Annapolis Royal. In 1713, the Treaty of Utrecht caused France to cede to Britain her claim of Nova Scotia, except for the islands of Cape Breton and St. Jean." Nicolass stopped, suddenly.

"Go ahead, Nicolaas, you're doing great." John was pretending to be annoyed, which made Christian chuckle.

"Go ahead, John. You're doing fine."

Georg glanced at Christian and nudged him not to laugh.

"What he said is correct," John said, eyeing Nicolaas to see if he had really stopped. "The British continued over the years to maintain Annapolis Royal, while the French created Louisbourg in Cape Breton - a fortress built at great expense, but the Acadians weren't anchored to Cape Breton. Over the years, they spread themselves to five or six settlements in Nova Scotia."

"So what's that got to do with them arming the Indians?"

"Patience, my boy, I'm getting to that. Also in this Treaty, the Acadians had one year to agree to become British subjects or leave the Province, forfeiting all their rights to the land they were occupying, which would pass to the British Crown. A lot of them said they would leave, and a few actually did go back to Cape Breton. The long and short of it is that those Acadians that refused to take the oath of allegiance still remained in Nova Scotia, on what they were determined to still call their land."

"The monarch in France even protested, on the grounds that anyone leaving should have the right to sell their occupied land," Nicolaas added quickly.

"Right you are, Nicolaas," John said, eyeing him playfully. "But there was tremendous dispute as to who actually owned the land and what the Acadie's boundaries actually were. They were under the old French land system, which had been seigneurial. And the Acadians were paying their rent to the French territories, when it should have been to the British Crown."

"So how could they sell something they don't own?" Christian asked.

"Ah, but you see, my boy, Acadians in their own minds did own the land under this system. So, England's Queen Anne submitted an Act of Grace, whereupon they could sell the land if they found purchasers."

"Some Act of Grace that was," Nicolaas said. "There were so few settlers, how could they find the buyers?"

"Do I hear sympathies for these Acadians?" John retorted.

"*Nein*, John, just giving the facts," he replied seriously.

Waving his hand to pretend annoyance at his lack of understanding, John went on, "And the British were strictly forbidden to buy their land. And well this should be the case. Around '28 or '29, Governor Philipps ordered all rents be made to the government at Annapolis Royal, and anyone claiming rights to land should present their cases there. It's simple. All the Acadians had to do was swear the allegiance of the Crown and the land was theirs, but they refused."

Nicolaas couldn't keep his opinion to himself. "They should get rid of the lot of them. The government is too lenient with them. They're still there occupying unauthorized land and no one has promised the desired oath."

"And they also demanded that the pledge be exempt from those taking sides between the British/French or British/Indians," Georg added.

Nodding, John puffed on his pipe some more while relighting it. Georg continued, "That's one of the reasons why the Government wanted Protestant immigrants like us to settle among the French, so we would influence them in turning away from the Roman Catholic religion. Thereby the French would become more peaceful subjects and eventually take the Oath. You see, they can keep the land they occupy if they take their allegiance to the British Crown."

"You too, Georg? You're getting ahead of my story. And that, Christian, is where the Government is sadly mistaken. The Acadians won't be swayed from their religion. Governor Shirley of Massachusetts believed that it *may* help change their attitudes, but this only over the next two or three generations."

Georg asked, "But didn't the Treaty allow the Acadians free will to exercise their religion?"

"Only if they take the proper Oath of Allegiance," John replied through a puff of smoke.

"Anyway, where was I?" John said, rubbing his chin. "Ahhh. Governor Shirley suggested expelling the French Roman Catholic priests, saying that their ministration was not guaranteed under the Treaty. He wanted to bring in French Protestant clergy and English school teachers, thinking that with intermarriage among the French and Protestants, the Acadians would become peaceful subjects of the Crown. And by their children going to English schools, the next generation would become Protestant."

"And is it working?" Christian asked.

"*Nein.* Even under Cornwallis' instructions to offer land titles to the Acadians who take the oath, and also asking for their assistance to the new settlers, they outspokenly refused to give any help to these British settlements. And of course, the Indians are Roman Catholic, and because they too have challenged the Crown's title to Nova Scotia, they are more apt to help the French against the British at a time of war."

"Where are these Acadians living now who do not claim allegiance?" Georg queried.

"Most of them stick to the marshlands in Annapolis, Chignecto, and Minas. In fact, it's Minas where the Board was hoping to make a settlement by dispersing us amongst them. But with the Acadians actively arming the Indians and inciting them against the English, the plan has been put on hold temporarily."

"And how does the situation stand now, John?" Christian said, now yawning.

"As I said before, the Indians have been relatively quiet these past couple of months and surprisingly enough, the Acadians too. Maybe now the original plan will go ahead."

Christian was growing tired and could hardly keep his eyes open. His determination to keep awake was waning, even though he was very interested in the conversation. "But what makes Cornwallis think that the Acadians will pledge their allegiance by settling some of us among them? And what makes the Acadians think they'll get their way by supplying arms to the Indians? It sounds pretty naive to me."

"You know, my boy, I think you're right." John threw his head back in laughter, disturbing a nearby person who was sleeping.

"Do you know what I think?" Georg whispered. "I think it's time to hit the hay. I can't believe it's this late. It must be past midnight. Look, we've been so engrossed in John that everyone's asleep." It was true. They hadn't even noticed that the women cooking busily behind them had gone to bed, keeping tomorrow's breakfast simmering over the hot coals.

"I agree, Georg," Nicolaas volunteered, as he stood and stretched. He left with a lantern to pick his way between the beds. The place was now in darkness, save the small glow from the fireplace.

"Come, Christian," Georg said, standing. "I'll show you where you'll sleep tonight." Taking him by the arm, he kindly guided him to his bed. As much as Christian wanted to know more, it was becoming impossible to stay awake. "Good night, John."

"Hmph," John grunted, knocking his pipe against the stone hearth. Tiny bits of ashes floated to the floor.

CHAPTER 18

Awakened suddenly, Elisabeth lay in bed listening to what sounded like a sharp object hitting the side of the house. The storm had worsened during the night. The fire had gone out, leaving the room icy cold, but she could still see a few smouldering embers. She glanced at the cradle beside her; Petie was not disturbed by the noise. She hugged a thick blanket around her shivering body and slowly felt her way in the dark to the hearth. Sending up a brief prayer, she stoked the ashes, lifting them from underneath and hoping to find a few more hot ones. Her prayer was answered. She immediately threw on some kindling.

The mysterious object continued to bang repeatedly as the wind almost shook the house on its foundation. Then came a crash and the banging stopped, leaving an eerie whistling through a crack in the door. Her heart skipped a beat as it pounded against her ribs. Elisabeth stood rooted to the spot. She didn't have the nerve to investigate outside her safe domain. Her mind started to race from one story to the next about the brutalities of the Indians. *Nein*! She tried to calm herself. If the savages lurked outside they certainly wouldn't be making themselves known, that was for sure. But what if it was a large animal and...Elisabeth abruptly cut her thoughts cold, determined to think of kinder things.

Now the kindling had sparked from a little flame to a larger one as it lapped its way around one of the logs. Lighting a lantern, Elisabeth tended to her son, who had just awakened. Petie was always a quiet baby, at times making her wonder if she actually had one. He hardly ever cried when he was wet or hungry, only whimpered - not the loud bellowing she normally heard from other babies. She never knew when he was awake. He would lay quietly until she had stirred herself.

Peering over him, his cheerful smiling eyes met hers. You look so much like your papa, she mused, remembering the last time they were together. His image was still etched in her mind and a day never passed without thinking of him. She wondered when she would see her beloved again and feel the warmth of his embrace. She would reflect on his memory so much that reality would often merge into her fantasy. One day she swore she saw him in a crowd down at the harbour, and even imagined her name uttered from his sweet lips.

She lifted their son up from his bed. Gurgling sounds bubbled up and the most innocent, pure smile radiated on his face. “I’ll find your Papa, Petie,” she said aloud, as she lifted him into the air. His face brightened into a toothless grin. Cradling her precious, Elisabeth rocked him as he fed at her breast. As the room warmed with the increasing fire, she ceased her shivering and relaxed in the contentment. The spell broke with a sharp knock on the door and a jiggling of the latch. Elisabeth’s heart instantly beat faster again as she recollected what had woken her earlier.

“Elisabeth!” The voice strained. It was barely audible over the storm. “Elisabeth!” it cried again. “Open the door. It’s Papa.”

Relieved, but her heart still beating furiously, she lay Petie back in his cradle. Quickly covering her exposed breast, she opened the door. A sudden gust of wind forced the door against her. She strained to hold on to it as her papa hurried in, stomping his feet and shaking off the clumps of snow that clung to his boots and stockings.

“Here, give over, Elisabeth,” he said, as he grabbed the door and shut it against the gale with much more ease than she could ever had done. "Tis nasty out there. The worst storm I've ever had the pleasure of meeting." Michael had recently begun to lighten the tension that persisted between them. "Not fit for the sturdiest of work oxen."

She made a slight movement of her lips that one would hardly call a smile. "My thoughts exactly. So what brings you here?" She checked on her son, and then moved quietly to the table to pour the last bit of flour into a large wooden bowl. Docktor Gessler must have missed this minuscule bit, she thought.

"A spruce tree has downed in the storm on that side of the house," he remarked, pointing to the north end of the wall. He slowly blew short sharp breaths into his hands to warm them. Elisabeth felt great relief that it wasn't the Indians her wild imagination had led her to believe. She didn't comment on it.

"From what I can tell, it doesn't look like there's any major damage to the house, but nothing can be done until this blizzard stops." Michael stopped rubbing his hands together. "As soon as Georg can remove himself away from the hospital, he, Christian, and I can pull the rest of it to the ground and chop it up for firewood. By the way, where is Christian?"

"He went with Georg to the hospital."

"When?"

"Last night." Elisabeth sprinkled more water on the flour as she mixed it vigorously.

"Damn it!" Michael let his hand drop on the table, making her flinch nervously. "Why would he go in this storm knowing he probably wouldn't make it back?"

"They left last night just as the snow started. How were they to know this would turn into a nasty blizzard?"

"We don't know what weather this land is capable of yet," he replied, walking over to where his grandson lay. Petie was content entertaining himself with the end of the blanket and half his fist in his mouth. "Christian was to help me with the monthly food rations. Such irresponsibility, damn it," he swore again. He stared down at the baby. "I certainly hope you're listening, young lad, and don't cause any grief to your parents."

Elisabeth eyed her papa maliciously. "*Danke*," she said and leaned into the table, determined not to turn around. "You're never going to let me forget, are you? Isn't it enough that you forced me into this loveless marriage?"

"Tsch! You should consider yourself lucky, daughter. Georg has been more than decent."

She sighed out of frustration and turned to face him, wiping her hands briskly on the soiled apron she was wearing. "Papa, you don't really even know me, do you? You don't even know Christian. You only worry about yourself and what other people will think of your children."

"What's Christian got to do with any of this?"

"This has to do with you, Papa. With you!" She was almost screaming at him. "Already you're thinking the worst of him. Calling him irresponsible."

"I never called him..."

"You did! Give him credit! Do you even know why he went with Georg?" She barely paused for an answer. "He helped take extra food rations for the sick and homeless in the Orphan House. Their supplies have run out two weeks before their allotted provisions." Elisabeth couldn't believe she was now sticking up for her husband, when just the night before, she had chastised him for grabbing food from his own family's mouths.

"He knew what he had to do today, and with this snow and being in this new land..."

"Stop it! You don't see the compassion Christian is capable of showing. All you care about is that he does your bidding. All you care about is you."

Michael was at his daughter's side in two strides. He towered over her as he glared down into her face. Elisabeth's legs felt weak; they were about to give out from under her, but she stood her ground, all the while shaking inside. He spoke first. "How dare you speak to me in that manner? Who was the one who ran the countryside searching for Jakob? Who gave Christian the opportunity to become an apprentice to my brother?"

"You never listen! Christian wanted the farm, not an apprenticeship."

"A fourteen year old doesn't know his own mind. I know what's best for him. The first son takes over the farm, the second learns a trade." He turned away from her. "Why, young boys Christian's age would give their eye teeth to get a start in the weaving trade."

"And what a miserable few months he had. Beaten within an inch of his life. He learned to duck the leather strap and the drunken hand that was meant for weaving fine clothes. And you wouldn't believe him." Michael turned around to face her. "You only thought about yourself and what other people would think when they found out that your son ran away, incapable of becoming an apprentice. If you hadn't decided to come here, I know you would have sent him back, and probably to his grave."

"Christian will get many more beatings as he goes through life. He'd learn by his experience as an apprentice and grow up to be a man. He's not going to be suckled like a newborn babe. He has to be tough."

She couldn't believe what she was hearing. This wasn't the loving father she remembered as a little girl. "Papa you've changed." She stepped towards him. "It hasn't been the same since Margaretha died."

He ignored her remark. "If it wasn't for me, you'd have led a disgraced life scorned by the whole village. You wouldn't be able to hold your head high without the daily snides and hurtful remarks. Could you have really lived like that?"

She had been ready to embrace him, now she backed away.

"You should be thanking me, young lady, for forcing you to marry a good, sensible man, and grateful to him for bringing you here away from any scandal. Face it, daughter, you can't keep something like that a secret." He pointed accusingly at his grandson.

Elisabeth was seething. "Get out!" She adamantly pointed to the door. "Get out! I never want to see your face here again. I hate you! I don't care about you anymore. You've ruined my life!"

Petie started to cry. Michael faced the door in silence. The snow drifted in as he opened it, and he closed it as quietly as he could against the blasts of wind. She stared angrily as the latch dropped into place.

She showed great determination not to cry in front of him, not to give in to the unseemly display of emotion. Now what was she going to do? He was picking up the food rations for her as well, and by the looks of the storm, Georg wouldn't be back, probably not until tomorrow. Her rations were gone after she used up the last little bit for breakfast. She refused to go crawling back to him now, not after all the terrible things he said. Even though it was the sensible thing to do, her stubbornness wouldn't allow it.

****

Later that morning, Elisabeth left her son with her mama. Even amid prolific protesting, she was still determined to brave the elements for the needed supplies. Anna was willing to give her some of hers to tie her over, but they wouldn't last long. The victualling took place only one day a month, no matter what the weather; and if the foodstuffs weren't obtained then, she would have to wait for the next round. And besides, Mama barely had enough to feed herself and the rest of the family. It wasn't far to go and the storm seemed to be tapering off. Only a few small flakes were falling now. But the wind was still forceful, whipping the snow around her as she carefully stepped through the knee-deep drifts. There was one saving grace: the wind was behind her, even though at times it almost toppled her over. She was sure that once she got the supplies, one kind soul would be more than happy to give her a ride home. At least that was what she was counting on; it would be impossible to walk back.

By the time she reached the store, the tips of her fingers and toes were numb and the sensation of pins and needles stung the backs of her legs. Knowing that her papa would be there, Elisabeth was hoping to be in and out as quickly as possible. She couldn't spot him however. Since he had a half hour start on her, he was probably inside already. She stuck out amid the sea of men lined up outside. She stamped her feet to keep warm, while she waited patiently for what seemed like an hour before she felt the warmth of the room. Her cheeks burned as they began to thaw.

Once inside, the line was even longer. That didn't bother her. It was much more alluring here than outside. Elisabeth glanced around the room, attempting to spot a kindly gentleman who would feel for her situation and get her home with the food, but now reality set in. It was too intimidating a venture, so reluctantly, she decided to keep silent. She half listened to a conversation amongst a group of men who stood before her. They were grumbling about the work stoppage for the winter and how it would now take even longer to pay off their passage debts.

The line was moving faster now, and before long she found herself standing nervously in front of one of the three storekeepers. The usual flour, peas, and oatmeal were all in large brown burlap sacks. A rough, burly-looking man stacked the sacks into the corner for her beside an even larger cask of salted beef and pork. Looking at the sizes, Elisabeth had to think of something fast. Obviously the storekeeper didn't care and probably wouldn't even try to understand her language.

"Next!" he bellowed.

Elisabeth stood rooted to the floor as if her feet were made of lead. The storekeeper waved her to the side. She slowly trudged over to where her supplies lay.

"You're more crooked than Hayes and Little before ye," someone yelled from behind her. She tried to peer over and through the crowd that seemed to have become more dense since she left the line.

"How dare ye hold back supplies that are rightly due us!" This time other voices chimed in unison to the protestations.

"It's not my fault you people are eating more than your share. We've run out. That's it!"

"Give over, mate, or I'll run the lot of you into the harbour," said another. Elisabeth's blood ran cold. That voice!

Straining to see, Elisabeth did as best she could to push her way through the throng. While others pushed her back, she got as far as she could go and could barely ascertain the owner of the voice. He had one of the storekeepers by the throat. There was jeering from the crowd to string him up. Elisabeth couldn't believe it. Her heart was thumping hard against her chest. "Peter!" she cried, but her voice wouldn't carry above the bedlam. Then, with one forceful shove, she managed to escape to the front of the commotion.

"Peter!" she cried again, and this time he turned, briefly catching her eye. Then, like thunder, a half a dozen men in bright red uniforms crashed in upon the scene. Peter bolted with one of Cornwallis' soldiers close at his heels.

"Don't! Stop!" Elisabeth ran after him through the doorway, past the queue that had now stood aside after the first two flew by.

"Elisabeth!" She was jolted back by a firm grip on her arm. "Elisabeth! Stop this display at once!" It was her papa. Peter disappeared ahead over the ridge and out of sight, but not before he briefly turned around, his gaze burning into hers.

CHAPTER 19

The blizzard eased up for a couple of hours, then started again. Christian wasn't sure if it was the same storm or another one blowing in. Whatever the case may be, it lasted for three days, leaving large drifts on the back and one side of the building up to the roof. On the fourth day, the long-awaited sun rose high in the bright blue sky, but it was of no consolation as it had turned bitterly cold. Luckily the snow that had continually drifted at the front door had been kept clear by the soldiers from Horseman's Fort, so there wasn't much left to dig out on the fourth day. The food supplies were holding out, but barely.

It was mid afternoon before Hoffman took Georg and Christian to attempt the crossing. Even though the wind had died down to a mere breeze, it wasn't finished. They were met by waves two to three feet high crashing thunderously onto the shore. It was much too dangerous to undertake.

"Looks like you'll not be going home today either," Hoffman said. "It'll be much calmer tomorrow."

"What makes you so sure?" Georg queried.

"The ocean always swells after a storm, causing a ripple effect in the harbour. Always seems worse the day after a storm than during. Mark my words, it'll be as smooth as glass in the morning. That's if another storm doesn't follow," Hoffman added. He slapped his arms around each of his friends, laughing. "Only kidding. Come, we'll get something to eat at Mauger's."

The snow was too deep for the horses, so they donned their snowshoes to walk through the drifts. Christian's face felt frozen, even with the woollen muffler around his mouth, but something hot in his belly certainly sounded appealing.

The pub was situated at the bottom of the hill where Fort George was located. It was in amongst a few other log buildings, a blacksmith shop, baker, and soap-maker. Christian found it strange that there was someone selling soap; his mother had always made her own. Candles were also made at home, and cabinets were built by his *fater* when the need arose. Even though the shops were open for business despite the snow, there were only a few people loitering about the settlement.

By the time the three reached the pub, Christian's hands and feet were numb. The sign looked newly carved. Stepping inside behind Hoffman and Georg, he felt the inviting warmth as it eventually crept around every crevice of his body. The pub was crowded with patrons, some standing as they talked loudly and guzzled large quantities of ale and rum. There were no seats to be had, so Hoffman led his companions through the din and smoke to the fireplace. Christian had never been in a tavern before. Georg left them briefly to get three large tankards of ale which, from where Christian could see, were dipped into an enormous keg. The steins came up dripping wet.

About a half hour later, a long bench was found unoccupied, so the three sat down to hot steaming soup. Christian was thankful for the warmth, as the drink had chilled him. The next round was rum, which he had never drunk before, but he welcomed its warmth as well. The time flew by amid deep conversation about desertions and no work, to hangings for petty burglary. All the while, the liquor flowed freely. People only intermingled, honing in on other people's conversations when it peaked their interest.

"Remember that old woman who was caught stealing a couple of copper and pewter pots, along with two brass candlesticks? Well, she escaped the death sentence the other day," one said.

"Damn lucky," Christian heard another yell. "Reverend Tutty pleaded her case and she was only branded with the letter "T" on her right hand, then thrown into jail for two months."

"If you ask me, she should've been hanged proper till dead. Getting off scot-free will only tempt others to do it."

"Well, who asked you?" remarked one old man, who was swaying from side to side.

Hoffman cleared his throat intentionally, whispering, "That's the old crone's husband." The three of them stood up to be closer to the circle that was now forming around him.

"You can blame Cornwallis for that," he sputtered, his lips wet with alcohol. "My wife w-wouldn't be in jail if we got what we were p-promised." Now the loud roar of conversation was beginning to die down as he spoke his mind. "W-weren't every one of you promised land to live on, to g-grow food to k-keep your family from starving?" He pointed his limp finger around the men who surrounded him. At one point, he almost fell until Hoffman stood him upright again.

"It's coming," Hoffman answered. "There's a lot resting on Cornwallis' shoulders with the likes of you, old man." He put his fists up, mocking a fight. A wave of laughter erupted from the onlookers.

"Don't y-you joke about it, Hoffman. You of all people should know. How l-long have you been here?" He waved his limp finger again, this time directly in Hoffman's face. "Right, then. You've been here as long as me, two years hence, and w-what have you got to show for it? Bloody hell, nothing. Because of this frozen hell we're in there's no work in the winter. How much longer are w-we going to be slaves to the government?" He eyed everyone as he swayed back and forth. "All the money we work our asses off for goes to paying our debts. You too, Hoffman. All my wife did was borrow a few things; we have nothing. I'm s-sure you too, Georg, was asked to l-leave all your belongings in the old country. Huh?"

Georg didn't say anything.

Hoffman answered him, "Come, old man. You've had enough."

"Lay your grimy hands off me," and he spun around, losing his balance into the crowd. They threw him back onto his feet again.

"You m-mark my words, all those promises were a ruse to g-get us to settle here in this God-forsaken wilderness. We're p-probably only here for those damn French!" He stumbled out the door, shouting the worst profanities Christian had ever heard.

The tavern was in an uproar of laughter, but a few had listened intently to the old man's words and were silent. "He's damned lucky Cornwallis' soldiers aren't here," Hoffman piped up. "He'd be arrested for treason and thrown in jail with his wife, if not hanged."

"I thought we left the tiptoeing around officials back home," Christian said.

"It's not as bad as that, but we still need some sort of order, and the likes of him could incite a revolt," Hoffman said, leaning in closer to Christian and Georg. "What he said back there rings true. He had the guts to say what's on everyone else's mind in here."

"Hey!" someone yelled. "Let the festivities begin!" The door flung open and Christian could see someone carrying a large white cloth figure with a rope around his neck.

"What's going on?" Georg asked. The tavern emptied in a matter of seconds. Through the window, Christian could see people running past the pub carrying torches.

"Guy Fawkes Day," Hoffman answered. "You've never heard of him?" He shook his head in bewilderment. "He was an English conspirator last century in Britain."

"Why celebrate it here?"

"The custom was brought here by the New Englanders, but as far as I can see, it's just an excuse for riots. Come, I'll show you."

Hoffman ran ahead as Georg and Christian hastened to catch up. The streets certainly weren't deserted now. There were people running everywhere, men and boys alike yelling at the top of their lungs. "Burn 'em!" Christian could hear every so often above the mayhem. There were about a half a dozen effigies. A couple were covered in tar and feathers, and men were running towards the centre of town carrying torches and pitchforks.

"The effigy used to represent Guy Fawkes, but now they'll burn anyone who is unpopular with the masses. Look over there, that one is supposed to be the pope."

Most of the snow had been trampled down by the mobs, which made it much easier to walk about. There were even a few people hanging out of their windows yelling obscenities. Christian narrowly missed a bucket of excrement that was thrown out of the window above. Steam rose above it when it hit the cold snow, turning it an ugly brownish-yellow. When they reached the gallows, three of the effigies were already strung up and set afire. All of them became one mass flame as they hung side by side. The crowd was getting completely out of hand. More effigies were carried in amongst the mob, who shouted and competed for each other's images. The liquor Christian had drunk made him feel light-headed, which now increased in intensity in the cold air. With the throngs pressing up against him, he felt deathly ill. People swam around him in circles before his eyes, and Georg's voice sounded distant until he heard no more.

****

Christian awoke groggy. He didn't know what time of day it was, and his mind was foggy as to how he got here in this cot. Looking around, he could see rows of beds with children in them. Where was he? Looking beside him, he thought his mind was playing cruel tricks on him. He rubbed his eyes and slowly lifted his head. It pounded like a dozen hammers. It looked like Philip lying asleep in the cot next to him. But how did he get here?

"Ah, I see you're awake." It was Georg speaking. "How're you feeling?"

"Where am I?" he said weakly, so as not to jar his head.

"At the Orphan House, upstairs."

"Ah." He laid his head back down on the bed. That's why he didn't recognize it. "What happened? I can only remember effigies burning, drinking some...Oh God! My head!" He massaged his brow.

Georg smiled. "You passed out cold. Can't hold your liquor?" he laughed. "Hoffman and I took turns carrying you back here last night. And light you weren't! You'll live."

"Georg, who's that?" he pointed to the bed beside him.

"Philip. He came over on the *Speedwell* a few weeks before us."

"What's wrong with him?" Christian knew that only the sick were upstairs.

"Consumption. He's had it for a while by the looks of him. I'd seen him begging in the street and brought him in a couple of weeks ago. I found him in the corner of a building shivering from the cold. He hardly had a stitch of clothing on him. He certainly would've died if I hadn't found him."

"Is he going to be all right?"

"Why the interest in this one? Do you know him?"

"*Ja.*" He continued staring at the sleeping boy.

Georg didn't question him further. "I'll get you something hot to eat to make you feel better." He disappeared down the steep narrow stairwell.

Christian carefully rose from his bed. He was still in the same clothes from the day before, which were now stained and smelled of sour liquor. He must have been sick, he thought, disgusted. Staring over at Philip, he wanted to wake him to find out what had happened since that day they went their separate ways. Philip's face was thin and sallow. Much to Christian's relief, his long-lost friend stirred and opened his eyes. At first there was disbelief, then the shock of realization.

"Christian!" Philip said weakly.

"My friend!" he answered, sitting on the side of his bed. "Is it really you? I didn't think we'd ever see each other again."

Philip smiled. "Are you sick? What are you doing here?"

"Mine was self-inflicted," he groaned, holding his head. "And you. You're so much thinner now."

"I haven't eaten much living on the streets the past four months. Doktor Gessler says once I start gaining some weight, I'll be outta here in no time."

"There are so many questions I want to ask you since we last saw each other. I don't know where to begin." Christian's head was still throbbing, so he tried not to get too excited.

"Where do I begin, Christian?"

"How about starting with how you ended up here in Nova Scotia?"

"Well, let's see. When we left you in Goppingen, Schutze and I headed down the Rhine to catch the first sailing on the *Speedwell.*"

"How did you make it past the checkpoints? Eugen's men have been everywhere looking for Schutze."

"Ah, but he's a crafty one. We came across two points with

Eugen's men but got around them. And then when we got to the Rhine, Schutze knew one of the schippers who operated the boats down the river. We got on with no questions asked, though we almost didn't make it. At one of Ruhrort's toll stations, Steadman's agents came on board threatening to throw into the river all the baggage of those who wouldn't sign with him."

"Who's Steadman?"

"He certainly wasn't one of Dick's agents, that's for bloody sure. He tried to get us to go with him to Philadelphia instead of Nova Scotia. He told everyone that the land here is nothing but fish and sand, with no one able to grow crops. We were delayed a couple of days. A small handful were won over and went with that snake, but most stayed. By the next morning Dick's agents overthrew Steadman's men." Philip started coughing.

"So you must have caught the *Speedwell* before it sailed?"

"With time to spare." Then, after a pause, "Have you seen your brother?"

"Jakob! You saw Jakob? Where?" he asked impatiently.

"He was on the same ship we sailed on. He talked of you."

"Where is he now?"

"Don't know. Jakob and Schutze became fast friends, and when we landed here, it was only a couple of weeks before they got involved with the French. Kicked me out they did, and I had to fend for myself. Haven't seen 'em since."

So his brother did make it here, Christian thought. He was anxious now to tell his family, especially Mama. Suddenly his friend was wracked with a severe fit of coughing. Christian shuddered in fear.

"Hey, you two talking? Go downstairs, Christian, and fill your belly. And you, my boy," Georg said to Philip, "must get some much needed rest."

"We'll talk later," Christian said. He left him to drift off to sleep again. But more bouts of coughing shook Philip's thin body.

Later, Christian took the opportunity to ask Georg when Philip would be ready to leave and what would become of him. He said Philip would only be leaving in a coffin.

CHAPTER 20

"Where did you see him? Where, Christian?" Anna was frantic.

"I didn't, Mama. As I said before, Philip met him on the *Speedwell* a few months ago. He doesn't know where they are now."

"They?" his papa queried.

"Jakob and Schutze."

Christian and Georg had made it back to Dartmouth that afternoon. Hoffman had been right; the harbour was calm enough for the crossing. Christian had had no intention of telling his parents about Jakob teaming up with Schutze; it was a slip of the tongue.

"My God! What will happen to my son? He's hooked up with a criminal," Anna ranted, pacing back and forth.

"Schutze?" Michael repeated. "I thought we left all that behind us. He means trouble for sure."

"I can start asking around if anyone has seen them. Maybe..."

"*Nein*. It's best we keep quiet for a while," Michael said. "Everyone within a few miles of Hohctorf knows who Schutze is."

"But surely the majority of the people were on Schutze's side," Christian added.

"In principal, *ja*. But when it turned to violence and attempted murder, almost all were out to save their own hides. They didn't want anything to do with it."

"Fickle people," he retorted.

"You're right, Christian, but they're smart. They didn't want any of their families in danger. If anyone here should find out that

Schutze is on the loose, they may take matters into their own hands. Maybe lynch him, and Jakob with him."

Anna was a bundle of nerves now. "Those two together can surely come to no good."

Michael put his arm around his wife. "Jakob's been accused of murder back home, and if there is talk of that here, an investigation will ensue."

Anna couldn't control her weeping. "Our son is not a murderer. Christian," she pleaded, "you've got to find him."

Christian eyed his papa, who replied, "*Nein*."

****

The next few months proved to be the severest winter the settlement had seen. In January, parts of the harbour along the shoreline on both sides froze solid. Snowstorms repeatedly battered the colony with gale winds that made the skin freeze if any part of it was exposed.

On February 3, 1752, John Connor was given exclusive rights by Cornwallis to operate a ferry between the two settlements. Two boats operated daily from sunrise to sunset. Christian was usually able to obtain a free passage, instead of the usual cost of three pence, only because of the frequent visits with Georg to the Orphan House.

The next month saw the first print of *The Halifax Gazette*. Bartholemew Green had arrived the year before from Boston with the first printing press. His partner, John Bushell, distributed a half size sheet with news from months-old English newspapers. When Christian first saw it, he was amazed. On each side of the title were woodcuts—a ship in full sail on one side and a fowler hunting game on the other. The news was old, but at least the colony didn't feel so isolated. The English language was no barrier, as Hoffman would translate it when a new copy came out. They would all sit huddled together at the Orphan House listening intently to what had happened. Christian would repeat what he had heard to his parents.

The first week of April led everyone to believe that spring had finally arrived. Icicles dripped profusely from the eaves of buildings and the inviting sound of water trickled underneath patches of thinning ice. But Old Man Winter refused to release his icy grip when he blew in more snow and cold. Christian thought he would never see the green grass again. He was sure it would take the entire summer to melt the endless, dreary piles of snow.

On this particular day, even though the air was chilly, the spring sun was warming his back as he chopped trees Hoffman and Nicolaas had felled the week before. With much difficulty, they dragged what they could from the forest, which was still knee-deep in snow with the odd waist-high drifts. Today they had taken the sleigh into town to stock up on their foodstuffs. Christian continued to axe the last tree into smaller chunks and stack them in the shed.

Christian stripped off his winter coat, throwing it on the nearby bench. Humming to himself, he hacked away at the tree securing his foot at one end. His mind drifted across the vast ocean that lay between him and his homeland. He thought about the springs in Hohctorf. The snow would be totally gone now and his old neighbours would be preparing their fields for the forthcoming crops.

He wondered if Herr Kasper, who lived about ten minutes away from their farm, was busy at this moment tilling his field. Maybe, Christian pondered, Herr Kasper was chosen this year by the parish cowherd to get his cattle ready for the yearly ceremony. Last year, Herr Schermuller was awoken by the loud blast of the horn at six in the morning to get his animals ready as the parish cowherd took them over. Herr Kuhn was chosen last year to change the baby names of the calves to sonorous names of cowhood, like Besse or Stern. While christening, he decorated the calves with sprigs of mountain ash.

For the first time, Christian was feeling twinges of homesickness. Easter had come and gone with none of the familiar festivities that would greet him and his family. Normally Mama would be busy making a garden of willow twigs and moss for the Easter Hare, while Hanna would willingly help with her clumsy baby fingers. This year, everything was still asleep under a thick blanket of snow.

The winter had been so hard on Mama. It was extremely painful to watch her become more withdrawn as the cold progressed. The games they used to play with Easter eggs were now considered frivolous. Papa tried to keep everyone's spirits up, but once the long winter set in, along with the growing complaints that had started to filter throughout the colony, it became more difficult. Papa's days were mainly filled with gathering wood for the fire, whittling out wooden spoons and bowls for Mama's use, and telling stories to Hanna of better days in Hohctorf. Christian was sure his papa would have much preferred to work off the passage, but the severe winter had caused a work stoppage. Hopefully it would start up again soon and he too could help pay off the debt.

Feeling a bit depressed, Christian's humming became louder. He hoped to alleviate the growing homesickness he was now sensing. He remembered a verse he used to sing with his friends during Easter week. "*Palm, Palm, Posken; Lot den Kuckuck rosken*." Then a voice from behind chimed in, "*Lot die Vuegel singen; Lot de palmen springen*." It was Georg. He sang while clapping his hands.

"Reliving your childhood?"

Christian shook his head. He was sure his face was now red with embarrassment.

"*Awch,* that's fine. Nothing wrong with that," he smiled. "With the trials we've been through, I can't say I blame you." His smile quickly turned to one of seriousness. "Christian, come. Philip is asking for you."

"Tell him I'll be there shortly," he answered, wiping the sweat from his forehead with the back of his hand. He turned back to his work. He was about to swing the axe again, when Georg laid a firm hand on his arm.

"You'd better come now."

Philip was always asking that Christian tell him stories, some fairy-tales, some real, but mostly ones that Christian thought up in his imagination. "What's wrong, Georg?"

"He's slipping away fast."

"But I just saw him early this morning. He was chattering away about how much he liked the grand new tale I told him last night. In fact, I mentioned to Hoffman and Nicolaas how much stronger he seemed. I thought maybe today he could finally rise from that bed."

"Come."

Christian couldn't believe the change a few hours could make. Philip now lay limp in his bed with his eyes half-closed and his mouth open, gasping for air. Pulling up a stool so he was closer to him, Christian stroked his hand as it lay so lifeless. It was so frail that he thought he would break it if he held it too tight. He couldn't believe he never noticed Philip's hands before.

"What's this, lying about in bed? Remember what you said this morning?" Philip slowly moved his head to one side. "You were going to get up today."

"Not today. Not ever." He strained to open his eyes, then stared blankly at Christian.

"Don't talk like that, Philip. Once spring finally shows its head, we'll get you outside in that warm sunshine again. In fact, I saw a robin today. He was chittering away in the chestnut tree."

"*Nein*." A coughing spasm racked his weak body so much that Christian thought it would be his last breath. "Christian...your b-brother. I know...where...he is."

Christian's heart first leapt with anticipation at hearing this, then shock at how Philip would know. Philip lay still for a moment with his eyes shut. Silently, Christian watched his friend's chest labouriously rise up and down. He could hear his raspy breathing and found himself voluntarily trying to inhale and exhale for his friend's sake.

"Piziquid...with...French..."

"How do you know?"

Philip could barely force a smile. He lay there quietly and what little strength Christian felt in his hand was now gone entirely. He gave it a gentle squeeze. "Philip! Answer me. How do you know?" Christian blinked back his tears. He watched through blurred vision as Georg put his ear to his friend's chest as it lay still. Stunned, Christian stared at the blank, hollow eyes that refused to shut. Then, Georg gently brushed his hand over his patient's eyes. Turning back, he left Christian alone in his sorrow.

He had never experienced anyone's dying moments, and it left him drained and devastated. He wasn't in the same room when his sister had died two years ago, nor did he ever feel that special closeness to her like he did Philip. In an almost macabre but pleasant way, he felt privileged to be sitting with him. Yet it didn't seem real. Everything was fine earlier.

****

Because the earth was still frozen, they were unable to give Philip a proper burial. Hoffman built a crude wooden box, weighed it down with rocks, and threw it off the boat into the harbour. To Christian it seemed cruel and cold, but to leave the body in a coffin buried in the snow until the ground thawed would be heartless if wild animals found it.

He had become very close to Philip during the last months of his illness and was lost without him. He missed relating stories to him he had heard in town. He enjoyed embellishing them just to watch Philip grow wide-eyed with anticipation of what would happen next. Philip had spoken more freely of his life than before, particularly about his *fater*. Or so Christian thought. It stunned him when his friend spoke of Jakob in his dying breath. Thinking back to their precious times together, he remembered how Philip would always change topics each time Jakob's name was brought up. Why was he afraid to talk to him about his brother before? Why now?

"It's simple. He knew he was dying, and loving you as he did, he didn't want to take that to his grave," Georg said, about a week later.

"Maybe," Christian pondered. "And, maybe not. I think there was something else. Where is Piziquid?"

Hoffman's ears perked up when he heard this. Until now, Christian had been quiet about Philip's dying words, and was thankful for Georg's silence as well. "Why do you want to know that?"

"No reason, just asking."

"No one asks about Piziquid. That's one of the areas in Minas that the French have settled. There have been rumours that's where the Indians are gathering to get arms. What's it to you?"

"I just overheard two men talking that Piziquid is one of the areas that Cornwallis may give us our land to settle," Christian said. "That's all."

"It'll never happen," Hoffman replied. "Too much Indian antagonism." He stuck his pipe in his mouth while searching for his tobacco pouch. "It's too dangerous."

"How far is it from here?" Georg asked nonchalantly.

"By land, much too long. It's faster by the Shubenacadie River, but even that's much too hazardous. It's a route long used by the Indians. In fact, the Mi'kmaq used that river after they gathered at Minas Basin to raid Dartmouth."

Hoffman stared at Christian. "Who do you know there?"

Christian's hands were sweating and he was sure John picked up on his nervousness. He had no intention of telling anyone, especially his family, until he knew for sure where Jakob was living. Even against his papa's wishes, Christian had to find his brother.

Looking John squarely in the eyes, he replied, "No one."

CHAPTER 21

"Mama! Mama! Look!" Hanna and Sara were running up the dusty road to where Elisabeth sat with a large bowl of raspberries outside her parents' house. Petie was content to lay beside her on the grass, while Anna was busy scrubbing clothes and hanging them to dry.

"Mama! Look!" Hanna screamed again, pointing up.

"What's all this fuss about?" Anna glanced up from what she was doing.

"It's so tiny, Mama," she said, pointing again.

"What do you see, my *liebling*?" Looking at her youngest, then to Elisabeth, Anna shrugged her shoulders.

"It's gone now." Hanna sighed, disappointed. "It was a bird, Mama. It was so tiny and I couldn't see its wings it was moving so fast. It was standing still in the air."

Elisabeth playfully eyed her mama, who was smiling and trying not to laugh at her youngest's imagination. It was the first time she had seen her smile in months.

"You don't believe me, do you?" Hanna's tiny lips protruded to form a pout.

"Of course, I believe you. Run along now and see if you can find me another one, okay?" Hanna nodded excitedly and ran after Sara, who waited for her shyly at a distance.

Mama hadn't talked much these past weeks, so it was wonderful to see her smile. Elisabeth quietly mashed the raspberries with a spoon. She had found them growing wild near the woods where the palisade ended at the harbour. There were soldiers mingling about, so she wasn't nervous picking them with Hanna in the daylight.

It was so good to feel the warmth of the July sun after such a long winter. It actually took until the end of May for the ice and snow to melt completely. Papa and Christian had been gone now for days to work on building the Peninsular Road and blockhouses at Torrington Bay, where Fort Sacvile was located. They only came home a couple of days a month. A permit was needed to travel the road because of the increased desertions from the settlement. They could have come home more often but preferred to work long hours, accepting any type of work to pay off the family's passage.

From where Elisabeth was sitting, she could see the top of the masts where the *Speedwell* and the *Betty* were anchored in Chebucto Harbour, bringing more anxious settlers. They had just arrived within a few days of each other, and Elisabeth had heard that their passages were smoother, which meant that the casualties were much lower than when she came over. Those who arrived late last fall were finally able to build houses in Dartmouth and Halifax at the first thaw. The Orphan House was now used as it was initially intended for: one part to house the orphans and the other part as a school. Georg still spent most of his time there, but with the summer upon them, it was much easier to travel across the harbour. Elisabeth now saw more of him than she had during the entire winter.

The first few months of their marriage had been unbearable for her, but as time dragged on, his presence in their bed was becoming more tolerable. Elisabeth shuddered to think of them in the accepted marital way; their marriage still had never been consummated. There were times when she would begin to soften towards him, but she wouldn't allow it, rebuking herself to stay loyal to Peter. Her parents never guessed what went on between them, but at times she was sure they sensed it.

Ever since she briefly saw Peter months ago, she prayed daily to God for his return. But her dreams were not to come true. Her imagination would play tricks on her, hearing his voice where it wasn't. She kept her ears tuned to the smallest details that might indicate if someone saw him, though she couldn't talk about it. Each day steadily slipped by while the mental picture of him slowly faded. Death crossed her mind numerous times when she remembered that last glimpse of him as he was closely pursued by soldiers. What if they had caught him? Maybe he was killed in the struggle to get away. Surely if he was alive, he would have made attempts to contact her. Elisabeth's disturbed mind was running amok. She couldn't think of such things. He's got to be alive, she prayed.

In the distance, she could hear the rumblings of people's voices. She didn't pay much attention as she tried so desperately to conjure up Peter's image. The noise from the crowd was getting closer. It was beginning to irritate her until she could ignore it no longer. Forcing herself away from her secret thoughts, she noticed a couple of men running down the road. They steadily increased in number, including women and children racing along beside them trying to keep up the pace. They were heading towards the harbour.

"What's going on?" Elisabeth asked one passerby. Wiping her hands, Anna came up alongside her daughter.

"The new Governor just arrived," the man said. Elisabeth had forgotten that today Governor Hopson was to take over Cornwallis' position. There had been a lot of talk about Hopson. He was the British commander at Louisbourg a couple of years ago before the French takeover. Elisabeth's curiosity got the better of her.

"Come, Mama," she said, picking up Petie.

"I'm not interested," Anna said, now turning her attention to her task at hand. "Why should I want to do something so foolish as that?

It won't do an ounce of good whether I see him or not. It's vain, that's what it is. Why, look at everyone tripping over each other just to get a glimpse of him? *Awch*! Foolish," she exclaimed, now rubbing Christian's breeches more vigorously on the washboard.

"Well, I'm going," Elisabeth said excitedly.

"If you know what's best for you, child, you'll stay here too. Nothing good ever comes of mobs of people congregating, no matter how innocent it looks on the surface."

Elisabeth knew her mama's bitterness stemmed from the attempted assassination back home. "Oh, Mama, you're being ridiculously overcautious. Here, take Petie so he's not in any danger then." She gently set him back on the shaded grass and ran off down the road. Anna's protestations faded away as the distance between them increased.

The noonday sun caused Elisabeth to perspire profusely. She arrived out of breath at the harbour, where everybody, she was sure, who lived on both sides of the harbour, stood mingling about. All ventured to catch a glimpse of Governor Hopson. She welcomed the delicious breeze blowing in from the ocean, and could now see the *Speedwell* and *Betty* in full view anchored by George's Island. A couple of other ships she didn't recognize were also stationed nearby, gently drifting with the least ripple of waves. One of them could be the ship that brought the new Governor, Elisabeth thought.

It was impossible to get near the water's edge. Even standing on tiptoes to catch a glimpse over the sea of heads was an impossible feat. From what she could gather from the talk now filtering through the crowd, the Governor had just stepped on shore from a small boat that accommodated, at most, four people. As the crowd became more dense, it slowly squeezed Elisabeth out, forcing her to gradually fall back. Eyeing a flight stairs at one of the storage buildings, she ran past a couple of soldiers and darted up to get a better look. But it was still impossible to see him as he disappeared into the crowd. Disappointed, she gave up and walked back down to go home. As she reached the bottom step, a figure suddenly shot in front of her. "Pete..." she sputtered, but he quickly put his hand over her mouth. Elisabeth could smell the dirt on his hand, and a few pieces of grit found their way into her mouth.

He kept his hand clamped tightly as he forced her under the stairwell and out of view of the soldiers. He let go.

"Peter!" Again the dirty hand enveloped her mouth.

"Shh. Come." He grabbed her hand and ducked into a nearby shed stocked with flour. It was dark, except for a small window letting in a stream of dust-filled sunlight. Their movement left a swirl of dust around them, making Elisabeth sneeze.

For a long precious moment, they embraced without a word, conscious only of their rapid breathing. "Peter, oh Peter. Where have you been? I thought you were dead." She gave way to weeping.

"Why would you think that?" He held her away from him.

"The soldiers...those long months ago..." she sputtered through her tears.

"Poor thing. How you must have fretted. I did get away. I lost them in the woods."

Her tears subsided as she stared up at him for the first time. His skin was browner, causing the freckles across his nose to melt away into a deeper tan. His hair was longer now, hanging past his shoulders, but not as curly as Elisabeth remembered it. Examining his face as he stood before her, he seemed to have aged ten years instead of just one. Peter wasn't the skinny boy she remembered. A man was staring down at her. He gave her one long fierce kiss that made her head spin. He moved his hand to cup her breast. She instinctively pushed him away.

"Why did you leave me without a word, abandoning me in

Hohctorf?"

"I sent Jakob to you. Didn't you get my letter?"

"You said you'd be back. You didn't even know we were coming here." She paced the floor as her long skirt kicked up puffs of flour.

"Elisabeth. Don't fret so. I'm here, aren't I?" He held her still.

"Get away from me," she said, wriggling her way clear of his embrace. "What you did, Peter, was unforgivable: leaving me and knowing I was to have your child. Your very namesake."

"My namesake? I have a son?" Peter turned her around to face him.

"*Ja.*"

"Oh, Elisabeth. I love you so." He kissed her hard at first, then through her struggling, Elisabeth gave way and melted into his arms as the kisses became deeper and sweeter.

Everything felt right. She couldn't get enough of him. Their kisses became more urgent as she gently pushed back his hair. She recoiled when she felt only part of his ear. It was hardened with scar tissue.

"My God, what happened?"

"Sit here." He sat down, pulling her beside him. He proceeded to describe the horrors after his escape from the soldiers. He had met up with a band of other deserters on their way to Fort Gaspereau at Baie Verte, and there was an Indian attack. It was a miracle that Peter had escaped with only part of his ear missing. Elisabeth's stomach churned at the sight of the most hideous scar on his neck that ran from the ear to his shoulder. He spoke rapidly about almost bleeding to death until a trapper found him half-conscious and delirious. The man brought him home to an Acadian family and nursed him back to health. It was all too much for Elisabeth to take in.

"You've not spoken about your mama and sister in all this. Where were they? Tell me you didn't desert them."

"I arrived alone. They didn't survive the voyage. Kristina took ill a couple of weeks after sailing and died within days of a fever. Mama just pined away, refusing any food."

There was a short silence between them, then, "Schutze was on that ship, and I've a score to settle with him." Peter's eyes glazed over.

"You had eleven weeks with him. Couldn't you have settled it then?"

"How could I? The ship was overcrowded with people...too many watchful eyes. Couldn't be done."

"What couldn't be done?"

"Nothing. I'm here now. Everything's going to be fine. We can pick up where we left off." Peter held her so tight she thought she would lose consciousness. "Elisabeth," he whispered, "I've missed you so much." She could feel his hot breath on her neck as he found his way to her lips again. She yielded to his passionate kisses as they enveloped her whole being. Then suddenly, he said, "My son. It sounds strange when I say it. What's he like?"

"He's a miniature of yourself. He looks just like you. His eyes are the deepest brown with dark curly hair. And he's the best baby I've ever had the pleasure to meet."

"You're just prejudiced."

"Not a word of a lie," she said, crossing her heart quickly. "I hardly ever hear him cry. In the morning, he'll actually wait until I'm up, and even then he's all smiles. Ne'er a whimper from him."

"Well, that he must get from his mama," Peter said, losing his hand in her long hair as he caressed it. "I can't wait to see him."

Jumping up, Elisabeth replied, "Come now." She tugged on his arm.

"Are you crazy? It's much too dangerous in the daylight. I'll be seen."

"What's all this nonsense about, Peter? What's dangerous? What're you running away from?"

"I've deserted."

"Deserted from what!"

"Even though Mama and Kristina died on the voyage, I'm still responsible for paying their passage as well as mine. I don't see why I have to pay for dead people, so I escaped. I don't have a permit to be on the road, so I'm always in hiding. The soldiers here already know me."

"But where will you go now?"

"I've heard that Schutze is in Piziquid. When I find him, I'm gonna..." Peter stopped.

"I'm coming with you."

"Don't be foolish, Elisabeth."

"*Bitte*," she implored. Now that she had found him, she couldn't bear to part with him again.

"Just get that ridiculous notion out of your head." She shook her head as her eyes rapidly filled up. "Now listen to me," Peter grabbed both her arms. "Let me finish this business I have to do, and I'll come back. I promise. Besides, you have our son to look after."

Trying desperately not to lose control, she said, "How will you eat, live?"

"How I've been doing it all along: stealing when I'm hungry, finding shelter in bad weather. I'll be fine. If I'm not back before winter, I promise I'll be back by next spring."

"Spring! But that's months away. I'm coming with you. I'll bring Petie and we can live together like a family, away from here."

"Listen to yourself! You're not thinking straight. Everything will work out, you'll see. Next spring is not that far off. I'll be back in no time after I've set up a place where we can live. I'll come back for you. *Awch*, don't cry. You know how it upsets me." Peter held her close again.

"You can do something to help me, though," he said quietly. "I need a few shillings to help me get by, and also any food you can bring me. Can you do that for me?" Elisabeth nodded. "Tonight, meet me here after sunset." He kissed away her tears.

Opening the door a crack to make sure all was safe, he sent Elisabeth back home. "I'll be waiting," he said.

Immediately after the sun went down, Elisabeth raced all the way back to the food shed where she had left Peter that afternoon. Georg was in Halifax working, which made it easier to go without an explanation to anyone. She couldn't leave her baby with Mama without explaining what she was up to, so she had left him sound asleep in his crib. She wanted so much to bring him with her so Peter could hold him, but she couldn't risk it. This could be the one time that her son cried out in the dead of night. Besides, she wasn't going to be gone long, Elisabeth convinced herself. He'll be fine.

She arrived breathless at the shed, seeing no one. Not even the soldiers on duty had spotted her. She nervously took one more backward glance. She was sure she heard a rustle, but seeing nothing, she slowly opened the door and was in her beloved's arms once more.

"Did anyone see you?" he asked.

She shook her head.

"Did you bring it?"

Elisabeth spilled out the shillings she had stolen from Georg's hiding place. Her husband didn't even know she knew where they were. Unknown to him, she was awake one night when she saw him count out the coins into a small tin box and quietly place it back underneath their bed. It was disconcerting to her that she now felt tremendous guilt, and even an awkward twinge of tenderness. Elisabeth quickly pushed the thought to the back of her mind; after all, it's not like it was stealing. She was helping another and Peter did say he'd pay her back.

He cupped his hands together to catch the few coins. He smiled at them as they clinked one by one.

"Here's some bread to help you get by," she whispered. "It's all I could spare."

Peter never spoke. They both stood there silently, staring at each other. "Elisabeth..."

"I'm coming with you. I can go back now and get a few things," she ranted frantically, thinking that if he left again, he would be lost to her forever.

"Elisabeth..."

"I can leave the baby with Mama. I..."

"For God's sake, Elisabeth! Don't!"

"Wait for me. I'll go now. I...I...Don't leave me again," she sobbed, burying her face in her hands. "I can't bear it."

Peter soothed, "You're not thinking sensibly. Surely you know you can't come. It's safer here." He put his arms around her, but Elisabeth resisted.

"Go! I never want to see you again!"

"*Bitte...*" he cried.

"Please go." Reluctantly, Peter opened the door to leave. He lingered, then, turned back to her. "I will be back. I promise." He disappeared into the night.

Staring out the small window after him, Elisabeth realized she couldn't mean what she had just said. Grabbing the door, she ran after him. "Peter!" she called, but there was only darkness. He was gone. "I will wait for you," she whispered through her tears.

Standing in the warm summer night, she told herself she wanted to believe him and forced herself to think of their future together. In the spring, he said. It was so far away, but the thought of being together for the rest of their lives would make the long months ahead seem more bearable. Suddenly she was disturbingly aware that she had left Petie by himself. The guilt played on her mind. She must get home quickly. She bolted into a run before the soldiers returned to the shed on their watch.

Elisabeth knew she hadn't been gone long. She was only a few short minutes from home, and her stolen moments with Peter were minuscule as she bade him farewell. At most, she was sure she was only gone about half an hour. All through her son's short life, he had always slept uninterrupted until morning. She was sure he was fine, but still, the shame coloured her face as she ran even faster. Stopping just a few short yards from her house, breathless, she noticed a light flickering. She was sure she had snuffed out that candle on the table. Panicking, she ran up to the door, flinging it open. She breathed a sigh of relief when she saw her infant son still sleeping peacefully in his cradle.

"Where the hell have you been?"

She spun around, her heart pounding as her husband stood before her. In her panic, she must have walked right past him, not even noticing him standing in the shadows. She could see that the empty box where she had grabbed the money was now lying at his feet.

"Don't do that. You startled me." She sighed, laying her hand on her breast as it heaved up and down. "I thought you wouldn't be home til tomorrow."

"Where have you been, Elisabeth?"

"Nowhere." Panic enveloped her. She had to think fast. "Oh, you mean just now," she started, hiding her nervousness by puttering around the hearth. She dared not look at him.

"I popped into Mama's. Hanna was playing here this afternoon and she forgot that clump of straw she calls a doll. Mama couldn't put her down without it. Hanna was making such a fuss, I came over here, put Petie down, and quickly popped back with the doll." Elisabeth knew she was rambling and kept her head down, unable to look at Georg.

"You're lying." He stepped closer to her. "Look at me!" His hand crushed her arm to get her attention.

She straightened up, defiantly staring back at him. "How dare you accuse me of such a thing!" His eyes never waivered as she tried to step back. Georg had never hit her before, but looking at the fire in his eyes, she couldn't be sure of him right now and tried to squirm her way free. "You're hurting me!"

"Tell me the truth, Elisabeth." His grip tightened even more. She thought her bones would break.

"I am. *Bitte.* Let go, you're hurting me!" she cried.

"What were you thinking of, leaving him alone?"

"I told you, Doktor Gessler, he was only out of my sight for a few minutes from the time it took to take the doll..."

"An hour is more like it." To her relief, he loosened his hold. She stood before him, rubbing the pain in her arm.

"I've been waiting all this time for you to come home. I should whip you to the very inch of your life, and no man here would blame me." Georg snatched her painful arm again and released her so roughly she almost fell over. "Are you going to tell me the truth, or shall I beat it out of you?"

"As I said before, I was at Mama's. I must have been gone longer than I thought."

"Damn you, Elisabeth!" Georg's fist formed in front of her face, then, crashed onto the table. She winced and ran to her son. He only stirred, whimpered, then fell back into a deep sleep again. "I just stepped off the boat from Halifax and saw someone sneaking past the guard and into one of the supply sheds. It was dark and I couldn't see who it was, so I thought it was an Indian stealing food. I was about to alert the guard when I saw another figure run behind the building." Stepping towards her, he continued. "How do you think I felt when I saw my wife prowling about in the dark like a common criminal?"

"What makes you so sure it was me? You just said it was too dark to make anything out. It could've been some foolish young girl rendezvousing with her lover." Elisabeth eyed Georg nervously as he picked up the money box and meticulously turned it over and over in his hands.

"It was you alright. As I came closer, I was sure when you stepped out into the moonlight just before entering the shed." After a few long seconds of deafening silence, Elisabeth thought she would faint from the strain of this interrogation. "Who is he?"

"Peter." Elisabeth wasn't sure it was her talking. She was numb. There was more silence. She stared at her husband, who stood before her with a deep hurt in his eyes. All the anger that he was venting seemed to instantly vanish as an inner pain replaced it. He seemed to age before her. It's his own fault, she thought stubbornly. He knew from the beginning that I didn't love him! He thought I could be broken…She felt a pang of pity and her heart softened. Damn him, she thought. He'll not manipulate me so. I love Peter and only Peter. We'll soon be together.

"Can I not trust you with our money either?" He flung the box with such force it broke at her feet, making her jump back.

Then, Georg spoke so softly, Elisabeth could barely hear him. "Why? Do you know the consequences of your actions? To leave our son defenceless?" His voice started to rise again. "Are you insane? Do you know what could have happened?"

She couldn't believe Georg was ignoring the fact that she was alone with Peter in the shed. Didn't he want to know what transpired? He's shaming her through her son. Well, she wouldn't let him. "He was fine. He sleeps through anything. Nothing would have happened."

"Nothing! Are you mad? With Indians snatching up babies, taking them captive, bringing them up as their own. Worse still, killed."

"Nein! Bitte!" Elisabeth cried, quickly covering her ears. "He's not your son, Doktor Gessler. He's not yours and don't you forget it." She knelt down beside the cradle, stroking her baby's head, tears streaming down her face.

"How could I? Your constant little reminders – christening him after his *fater*. Do you think I'm stupid? I didn't believe you for a moment that it was family tradition. But I ignored it the same way you pretend I don't exist. Ha! We must be the only couple on God's green earth that has waited this long to consummate a marriage!" His face was red, sweaty. "I love you, Elisabeth, and I'll wait as long as it takes for you to become my wife, not just in name. I won't give you the satisfaction of giving you up that easily."

She scowled at him, "You'll have a long wait then."

"When's the next clandestine meeting with your lover?" he said. His voice was like ice.

Elisabeth stood up. She reached her hand around and was about to slap him hard across his face, when he snatched her wrist. "Don't you even think it. Remember, there's no one in this land who would convict me if I beat you."

"You wouldn't touch me, Doktor Gessler. It's not in your nature."

"Try me." He stared down at her. "Forgetting the horrid things you've done tonight, I could whip you for not bedding with me. I could force you..."

"Come on then! Take me now. You want me to be your wife, then do what's expected of you. What's your problem? Don't just stand there!" Fumbling frantically at the lacing on her dress, she threw it off her shoulders, standing in front of him bare-chested. She was frightened and angry at the same time.

Georg bent Elisabeth's head back in his hands and kissed her so hard it hurt. His lips crushed hers as his tongue probed frantically in her wet mouth.

At first she fiercely resisted, but as his kisses made their way searchingly for her breasts, she felt delicious pangs of wanting more. She couldn't understand where these strange feelings were coming from. Then, determined not to enjoy it, she suddenly stiffened.

Georg sensed it and, as abruptly as he started, threw a blanket over her. "As much as I want you, Elisabeth, I'll not take you like this." He walked out, slamming the door behind him.

CHAPTER 22

The next few weeks were slow, and the times that Michael and Christian came home were less and less. They oftentimes turned down the opportunity to go on leave so they could do extra jobs for the public works. Michael would say that the more work they did before the winter set in, the shorter the time to pay off their debts.

As each day gave way to the next, Anna became increasingly depressed. She regretted the move to Nova Scotia and her deeper distress over Jakob was a constant worry to her family.

Elisabeth had hardly seen Georg since the night he left. He spent increasingly more time at the hospital. When he did suddenly appear, times were spent civilly in idle chit-chat about the newly-arrived ships and even more children disembarking as orphans. Nothing really changed between the two of them. It was as if that summer night of angry passion had never happened, and, much to her relief, Georg never discussed it. She desperately didn't want to think about those deeply hidden feelings he had briefly stirred in her. It was just as well the subject wasn't broached. It was easier to pretend nothing had happened. What would get her through the next winter was knowing that Peter was at the end of it, and she would be waiting with open arms.

The *Snow Pearl* returned again at the end of August with more passengers, mostly Germans this time. Governor Hopson had kept them on board a full two weeks longer to keep any infectious disease at bay. He allowed them to disembark at the isthmus between the Bay of Bedford and the head of Sandwich River. The *Pearl* had suffered the most casualties, until the *Sally* limped into the harbour soon after the *Gale*. Elisabeth heard that the disease that had manifested itself throughout the ship had also claimed the life of its master. The night before last, Georg had said that forty people died on the *Sally* alone, thirteen of whom were children.

This year, 1752, also saw Halifax embrace the new style calendar, and eleven days were lost. Elisabeth thought it ridiculous. Georg tried to explain it to her one day, but it fell on deaf ears. She agreed with her mama that the world must be going mad. So when the ships arrived on August 26, it was actually September 6. As for the passengers who were left on board for two weeks, some said it was due to disease, while others said the Governor had no place to house them and was frantically building temporary wooden barracks. Michael and Christian were part of the crew to build these very structures.

Hopson was a much better man for the job than Cornwallis. He was a much more competent supervisor, Georg would say. He reinforced this notion one nippy autumn evening at the beginning of October as he waved a petition in front of Elisabeth's face.

Georg knew where to find his wife. She had been spending more and more time with Anna, who was growing more despondent in her depressed state of mind. She was prone to fevers and headaches, and Georg had been unable to find the cause of them. There weren't many days where she'd dress herself, let alone Hanna. Tonight, though, she was out of bed and sitting in a chair in front of the fire, staring into the flames as she so often did. Georg was sure Elisabeth had encouraged it. Hanna was sitting at her mama's feet, and Petie was asleep on the cot by the back wall with blankets bunched around him to keep him safe from rolling off. Georg found his wife sitting beside Anna, mending some sort of clothing as he excitedly ran through the doorway.

"Doktor Gessler!" Elisabeth exclaimed, after she whipped around in her chair. "Have the sense you were born with and walk in here like the gentleman you claim to be and not the madman I now know you are." She glanced over to her son, but he never stirred. Hanna ran to her sister's side, as Anna sat there in her own world, completely undisturbed by the commotion.

"Elisabeth!" He waved the same piece of paper at her that was now annoying her to no end. "It's here! Finally something may be done."

"What's here?" she replied in a loud whisper, obviously annoyed. "And please keep your voice down." Elisabeth glanced again at her baby, still sleeping, thank God. She's had an unusually difficult time putting him down tonight and didn't want the fuss again if he woke up.

Scooping up Hanna in his arms, Georg said, "I don't care if the whole town wakes up. In fact, I won't be a bit surprised if all of Dartmouth riots, as they should. Halifax has already started."

"What are you talking about?"

"This," and he laid several pages of paper flat on the table, smoothing out the creases. "A petition! And once everyone signs it, it will be delivered to Hopson."

"A petition that can only come to no good."

"Now you're beginning to sound like Anna. This isn't Hohctorf," Georg said, his voice starting to rise to make his point. Elisabeth gazed at him warily, but he continued. "And don't look at me like that. In Hohctorf, it was a small uprising. This petition, once it gets circulated, will have every man, woman, and child marking their X, from here to Halifax and around to the basin."

Elisabeth held the first page up to the candlelight, scanning the words. It opened with the complaint about how they were forced to sell their most essential household items before leaving their old homes, upon reassurance of obtaining the same upon landing. Also, there were words to the effect of not receiving the allotted acreages that were promised, along with all the necessary building materials, implements, and household goods that they had sold. Glancing up for some sort of response from her husband, she read on, as he was now standing over her shoulder. It continued to explain how they had not had time to recover from the tedious passage, but were immediately forced to hard labour with nothing but salt provisions and maybe once, two pounds of fresh beef.

"Look here," he pointed, showing her the second page of the long document. "It also talks about the work that many have done for the New Englanders, clearing lots and cutting wood, and it has taken three times longer to get our pay."

"That's not true, Doktor Gessler. Papa and Christian have never complained about this."

"It has happened and it's still going on."

"But nothing's been said. They..."

"And they won't say anything," he whispered, looking at the pitiful figure wasting away in front of the fire who hadn't looked up once. "Why do you think the periods of time your *fater* and brother are away from here are becoming longer? The extra sixpence they are supposed to be receiving to pay off your family's passage is not being paid daily as it should. So if they can get other work, it's to their benefit. At least they'll get paid on time."

"I'm sorry, I didn't know. Does Mama know?"

"It's best she doesn't. It won't do her any good." Turning Elisabeth around with his back to Anna, he explained further. "Everyone's going to sign this, you'll see. And Hopson's a good man. He'll plead our case in London. We've all got to stick together as one. The Board of Trade in London has got to know what's going on here. The letters that have been sent to friends and clergymen in London this summer are falling on deaf ears. We're next, Elisabeth. The one year free supply of food is up. First it was those who arrived on the *Speedwell,* then the *Gale* just last month.

"This petition was probably started with the people of those ships."

"It doesn't matter who initiated this. It had to be done, and it speaks for all of us. There are people starving here!"

Elisabeth eyed him with apprehension. She knew he was right, but her mind kept flashing back to Hohctorf, when Hans Beck was murdered.

As if Georg had read her mind, he added, "No one will be killed. We've got to stand up for our rights." He held her close.

****

Elisabeth awoke with a start the next morning to the sound of rain thundering on the roof above her. She was alone, except for Petie giggling to himself in his cradle. Georg must have left early to go back to the hospital, she thought. She briskly hastened to the hearth to feed the hot ashes, still fiery red. Then quickly getting herself and Petie dressed, she readied the pot to make breakfast. It still hung from a hook over the fire from the night before.

Grabbing the sack of oats, she noticed a rustling inside and dropped it to the floor. She thrust a hand to her mouth to muffle a scream. Out of the burlap scurried two brown rats. They quickly brushed past her feet. Elisabeth's skin crawled at the feeling, and she quickly flung open the door, grabbed a broom, and started beating wildly about the floor. She was sure she hit one when she heard a high-pitched squeal. The creature scurried away into a hole beside the hearth, while the other scampered out the door. Slamming it shut, she snatched up the sack to find only a few oats left from the already diminishing supply. Not even enough to feed her son, she agonized, not that she would even consider eating them now after that vermin had feasted on it. She couldn't stomach the thought.

A sickening feeling in the pit of Elisabeth's stomach gripped her with a sudden fear. She had only a small bit of flour left over and a pound of beef. No peas, butter, or oats. Despite the repeated warnings from Georg about rationing the food to make it last longer, she hadn't been frugal enough. Some of her neighbours had warned that this was the last of the food they would ever receive. She refused to believe that the Governor or whoever was in charge of distributing the victuals, would allow anyone to starve. Elisabeth had never gone hungry in her life. Mama would always see to it that none of the children went without full bellies.

That's it! Mama has to have food. Draping her shawl over her head, Elisabeth scooped up Petie and dashed through the rain. Upon arriving, she stepped inside a cold, damp room. Hanna was sitting alone at the table with her head resting on her arms. There was no fire in the hearth, not even smouldering ashes.

"Hanna, where's Mama?"

Hanna awoke with a start. "Mama?"

"It's Elisabeth. Where's Mama?"

"In bed," she whimpered, rubbing her eye with one small hand. She pointed to the blanket that Papa had hung over a piece of twine.

Elisabeth couldn't bear the thought that her sister might have slept at the table all night. Pushing back the makeshift curtain, she found Anna shivering. A gray tattered blanket was pulled snug to her chin.

"Oh Mama! You're burning up again," she said, feeling her hot forehead with the palm of her hand.

"Don't fuss over me," she said, agitated, "just let me die."

"No one's going to die, Mama."

She turned around to call for Hanna, and almost tripped over her as she suddenly appeared behind her. "Hanna! Stay here with Petie." She set him down beside his aunt, while she gathered some bits of wood to start a fire. Then she went looking for the wood-sorrel tea that Georg had prescribed for Anna since taking the fevers. To her relief, there was a whole supply of it. She wondered if Mama had not been taking it as she should. That would explain why she couldn't shake some of her fevers. With Papa and Christian away for such long periods of time, she just wasn't taking care of herself. Elisabeth would have to keep a closer watch on her.

It seemed to take an eternity before the fire began to crackle and warm the room up. Elisabeth pushed back the blanket so Anna could feel the heat. As soon as the tea was ready, she held Anna against her chest. She fed her the hot medicine, surprisingly without a struggle. Hanna watched in fear.

"Do you want to be a big help?"

Hanna nodded reluctantly.

"Do what I'm doing and feed Mama this while I try to get breakfast for us. Okay?" Elisabeth propped the pillow against the wall and pushed Anna's back against it. She's so weak, she feared. "That's good, Hanna. Now make sure she drinks it all."

As she hunted for food, Elisabeth feared the worst until she found some oatmeal, just enough to feed the small group today and maybe for two more. Mama's food was as scarce as her own. After cooking the oat porridge, feeding everyone, and making sure that Anna got it all down, she decided to attempt to get supplies, even though she wasn't entitled to any. Maybe they wouldn't notice. Elisabeth wanted to go alone, but Mama wasn't in any condition to look after two small ones. She decided to take them along. Besides, if the officers saw her with two small children, maybe they would show some compassion. Taking her charges, she quietly closed the door behind her as Anna peacefully slipped into slumber.

The rain had stopped, but the fog that rolled in was as thick as pea soup. It was almost impossible for Elisabeth to see two feet in front of them. As usual, by the time she arrived, the line up was long, but today, it seemed exceptionally so. It wasn't an orderly line, more like a mob scene in front of the door as soldiers forcefully pushed people back. She saw one pitifully small girl crouched near the back clutching her thin baby. Tiny tracks streaked her dirty face where once tears had run, as she nervously held out her scrawny hand for food. It was a common sight that Elisabeth could not get used to.

"What's going on?" she asked a rough-looking elderly woman. She almost bordered on manly features, Elisabeth thought.

"The swine! They've refused to give out any food."

"Why not?" she yelled, hoping to be heard above the growing obscenities being thrown to the front where the soldiers were standing.

"See all those at the front there, child, shoving their way through the crowd? They ain't supposed to be here. Their victuallin' has finished. One year's up, they say. Me and some others here are entitled. We just arrived this summer. Them soldiers are saying no food is leaving that building until the others leave peacefully-like." And to the mob, she screamed, "Get your carcasses away from here and let some poor folk here get what they deserve, eh!"

Elisabeth felt a pang of guilt and was about to turn away, when she thought of the little food in her mama's house and even less in hers. Staring at her son in her arms and Hanna holding tightly to her hand beside her, she couldn't give up hope that maybe the soldiers would give in. The hard woman beside her pushed her way to the front, shouting rude obscenities.

Elisabeth stood back away from the angry mob for fear of their safety. They waited and watched uneasily. There was no progress, except more soldiers attempting to disperse the crowd. Gradually, one by one, men and women slowly gave up and wearily turned to go home. She watched with sickening horror as she saw so many thin and ashen trudge past her. Terror gripped her. Searching downwards to make sure her sister was still in her clutches, she raced home as fast as she could, slipping and sliding through the mud. Her feet were soaked as the muck seeped in through the holes in her shoes.

"Beth, slow down," she thought she heard Hanna yell. But she paid no attention amidst the now screaming baby, and didn't stop until she reached the door of her mama's house. Flinging the door open, she saw Christian suddenly rush toward them. To Hanna's delight, she giggled, screaming Christian's name over and over again as he swung her around. Michael stood by Mama. Still harbouring an unhealthy hate for Papa, Elisabeth was not glad to see him. She now blamed him for leaving Mama in this state of mind. The greeting between the two of them was cold and awkward. She turned to her brother and welcomed him with open arms.

"Come, Hanna, Elisabeth. Look what we brought." Christian held up two pairs of shoes. One for a child, about Hanna's size, and the other probably for Mama.

"Where did you get these?" Elisabeth couldn't believe her eyes. Shoes were so hard to come by, and hers and Hanna's were wearing too thin to be worn through the oncoming winter.

"The Board of Trade sent a large shipment of shoes of all sizes for the troops and settlers."

"How did you pay for such things? There's no money for food, let alone shoes." Even though Elisabeth desperately needed them, she would gladly give them up for provisions after what she had just seen.

"Quiet, child," Michael said. "We were paid in shoes instead of money for the last work we did at the Basin. Look, we even got a pair for you." He held up black leather flats. He was about to hand them to her, when she knocked them out of his hand. They flew clear across the room.

The look of horror in her papa's eyes made Elisabeth go weak in the legs. Her hands started to sweat profusely.

"How dare you!" he howled.

Where she found her courage, she didn't know, but she forced herself to be heard. "How dare I?" she said. "Look at you. You haven't been around for over a month. I have to look after both Mama and Hanna. There's no more food. You knew the victualling was ending and you brought shoes?" Her voice was so shrill, she didn't even recognize it.

"Elisabeth." It was Christian. "Papa..."

"Leave this house at once!" Michael pointed to the door.

"Gladly." Elisabeth turned and stomped out, Petie still in her arms. She could hear her mama weeping in the background.

****

The following day Christian went to see his sister, hoping to patch things up. He intended to speak on Papa's behalf, but his sister would hear nothing of it. She's as stubborn as Mama, he thought. He gave her what little food he and Papa had brought with them. She refused. He left it sitting on the table and reluctantly left, accomplishing nothing.

Strolling back on the road, deep in thought, he didn't notice his brother-in-law march up in front of him.

"Heads up, fellow."

"Hmmmph?"

"Christian! When did you return?"

"Yesterday."

"Anything wrong?"

"That wife of yours, she needs a good beating to keep her in line." Christian proceeded to tell the sordid details of the day before.

"Just leave her. She'll cool her heels soon enough. Come with me, brother." Georg sped off down the road with Christian frantically trying to keep up with him.

"Where're you going in such a hurry?" But it fell on deaf ears as his brother-in-law ran ahead. Christian noticed how unusually quiet things were today; nobody was milling about.

"We're almost there," was the first thing uttered from Georg's lips since they met twenty minutes before. Realizing they had passed through the palisade gates, Christian said, "Where on God's green earth are you taking me?"

Georg was about to answer, when they were met by Herr Henderick and Hoffman. They gestured to Georg with a stern nod, then, disappeared into an abandoned log structure. They followed the men through the doorway to throngs of people inside. This explained why there was no one mingling about the settlement. Most everyone was here. It was stuffy and hot with so many pressing up against each other. So many voices melted together that Christian couldn't make out any individual conversations.

"Order!" Hoffman bellowed. "Order!" A wooden gavel met the table with a loud boom. Again it reverberated throughout the room; a myriad of voices gradually quieted with only a few small mutterings left. All heads turned to the front of the room.

Hoffman didn't mince words and spoke about the petition he clenched in his hand. "Every man and woman has signed this in Halifax." He let go of the petition, a roll of paper that was so long it reached the floor. Hundreds of signatures appeared, most marked with X's. "This is why Herr Henderick and I are here today, to make sure every one of you support this document."

"I'm not doing anything till I know what I'm signing, Hoffman," said one old man. Christian was in too close range of the waves of sour breath as he spoke.

"You'll want to sign this one," Georg piped up. "Mark my words."

"We'll see," he answered, and to Hoffman, "What's this about?"

"Muhlig, I can't believe you don't know," said another. "There isn't a tavern here or across the harbour that hasn't had the pleasure of knowing your patronage, and not one drinking establishment has talked about anything else the past few days."

"That's because he goes in drunk and passes out. Not one word gets through that thick skull," another roared, setting the whole room ablaze with laughter.

"Order!" Down came the gavel again with a heavy boom. "Order! All of you by now have heard about this, with of course the exception of Muhlig here," he said, chuckling. Another ripple of laughter went through the crowd. "Herr Henderick and I need to present this with all of your signatures to Hopson tomorrow, so he can send it off to London by week's end when the *Betty* returns."

"I'll sign your petition, if you help me get the pay deserving to me from Bulkeley." A man named Treber shouted to Hoffman. "I've helped him distribute supplies and rations to you folks here, and Bulkeley said he would pay me two and a half shillings a day. He's now refusing to pay me one penny. I have two witnesses to attest to this."

Hoffman replied, "That you'll have to settle yourself, Treber. Right now this petition concerns all of us. And..."

"I'm in danger of debtors' prison, Hoffman. I was counting on this pay to settle my creditors. My family's food rations were cut off a month ago and any work I could even hope to get now would be for only two weeks before the winter sets in. What do you expect me to do?" Treber beseeched, almost on the verge of tears. "My wife and children are starving."

"All right, see me after the meeting and I'll see what I can do. In the meantime, will you sign?" Nodding, Treber walked up to the table and put an X by his name where Hoffman pointed.

"What makes you so sure that by signing this we will be assured of getting the fifty acres promised us?" Christian had been silent until now. "Look around us, the land is sterile here. It's way too rocky. And with the threat of Indian attacks, can we forget the massacre here just over a year ago?"

The voices agreed in unison. "The Governor doesn't know what to do with us. Maybe they'll send us back home, which is fine with me," said one. "I'd rather face the horrifying sea voyage knowing I'd be going back to something I know."

"The Government has spent too much time and money on us to send us back," Hoffman replied.

"I came with nothing. I was forced to sell all my belongings, with the promise that my family would receive all the necessary things when we arrived. I still have nothing," said another.

Others voiced agreement. "Where's the land to grow food for my children? I have no cattle!"

"They've used us. These were empty promises to settle Nova Scotia. They used us to their advantage over the French. They don't care about us. In fact, if they told us the real truth, no one would come here." By now, everyone was talking amongst themselves, ignoring Hoffman's pleas for silence.

Herr Henderick yelled for calm as he pounded the gavel on the table. Christian was sure it left deep indentations. "As far as I can see, all of us need to be heard, and the only way this will work is if everyone here signs this." Again, Hoffman waved the scroll in the air. "In answer to your question, Christian, I can't promise you that Governor Hopson will fulfil the promises due us, but you can't blame him. He's only taken office two months ago. If you want to blame someone, blame Cornwallis, whose been here for almost three years. Knowing Hopson as I do, he's the one who'll fight for us. And it's not going to work unless all of us sign. A dozen signatures is not going to do us an ounce of good," he said, raising his voice to make his point heard.

Treber spoke up again. "If you want to do some real good, Hoffman, get us some food. Those who just arrived this year have been helping some of us with a bit of their rations, but how much longer can they do that with their own families to feed? If the Government gave us the land we expected, we'd all be growing our own food by now, not reduced to begging. What does Hopson expect us to do? How are we to feed ourselves this winter? Have you thought about that?"

"I've heard enough of why they haven't settled us on any land. You know the real reason? There isn't any such earth to live on with so many savage Indians about," said one frightened woman.

"Then sign this." Henderick laid the scroll flat on the table. One by one a few strolled up, dipping the quill into the ink, either signing their names or making their mark.

"I'll sign this with pleasure," one volunteered. "I just arrived this summer on the *Betty*. My family and I were amongst the many quartered on St. George's Island with shelters that barely offered any protection from the wind or rain. We slept on bare boards with nothing but salt meat to nourish our empty bellies. I've already signed one petition and I'll sign another." He walked up to the table with his family and all made their mark by their names that Hoffman wrote for them.

"*Gut*," Hoffman said, as more followed to sign.

Georg beckoned to Christian, "Come." They both signed.

****

As the rain continued unabated, they ran back to get Michael. Every person mattered, and the more signatures obtained, the more leverage Hoffman would have when he offered it to Hopson. Surprisingly, they didn't have to win Michael over. The problem lay with Anna. The fever had broken, and her recuperation was obvious when she lashed out in anger after hearing that her son had signed the petition and Michael was leaving to do the same.

"You leave here, husband, then don't bother coming back," she hissed, turning her back to her family.

"We'll talk when I return, wife! This has to be done!" He disappeared through the doorway and into the pouring rain, hugging a cloak around his body.

Anna could hear thunder rumbling in the distance. Lightning streaked across the sky and lit up the dark room as she stood exasperated after they left.

She started to cry and angrily wiped the tears from her face. Ever since we arrived here, she brooded, there's been nothing but heartache. She thought back over the year to broken promises, relying on others for sustenance instead of themselves, and losing dignity through it all. Anna was a proud woman who merely wanted to discreetly live her life on her own land. No one could convince her that life here was or would be any better.

She fretfully glanced around her. A table and bench in one corner and two beds on the other side. By the hearth, she watched Hanna play with a wooden doll that Michael had carved before leaving the old country. What family does she have left? Stefan? Jakob? She let the tears fall where they may as her heart ached for her eldest. A night didn't go by where she lay in bed unable to sleep, fretting about him, wondering where he was. Her mind always came back to the same thing over and over again. They should not have ventured here. Now Michael is getting involved with something that she was sure couldn't do any good. All the convincing from her son and son-in-law wouldn't change her mind. Michael would be murdered in cold blood. She was sure of it. Then she'd be alone.

Anna lay on the bed and gave way to her grief, whispering Jakob's name. Hanna reluctantly tiptoed to her Mama and crawled into bed beside her, hugging as much as her little arms could possibly allow.

****

Hoffman couldn't be more jubilant. He was sure every man and woman in the settlement had signed the petition. Coupled with the signatures from Halifax and the isthmus, London couldn't ignore this dire situation. There were actually three petitions presented to Hopson the next day. One was from the Germans, the second in French from those who arrived this summer on the *Speedwell* and *Betty*. The third begged pardon for having offended against proper procedure when those who arrived on the *Alderney* and *Nancy* two years before wrote directly to their clergymen and friends in London without first consulting the Governor. They had complained of their dire straits and begged for an orthodox clergyman.

The petitions were dispatched to London, October 16.

CHAPTER 23

October reluctantly gave way to a cold and damp November. The fallen autumn leaves that littered the landscape were covered with heavy frost, painting the surrounding countryside icy white. Word from England wouldn't arrive before early spring with the winter now upon them. It was at least hoped that the petitions did make it to London without any storm mishaps across the Atlantic. But there was a snowstorm near the end of October that blew in from the ocean two weeks after the *Betty* sailed. Both sides of the harbour prayed that it had missed the tiny sloop. And again, the winter storm signified the closing of the public works until next spring.

Georg found it difficult to work at the Orphan House. Because of the heavy mortality of recent passengers from the last three transports that summer, a large number of children arrived in Halifax without parents. Some were lucky enough to be taken in by other families, but a great many were destined to live at the House and die there. The hardest hit were the children between the ages one and four.

Elisabeth never knew when her husband would return. Sometimes he would become so engrossed in his work that days would go by, until he could no longer stomach the demise of those so young, and wearily trudged home. There was only one other *doktor* at the House, and an assistant who had absolutely no medical experience. But any help given was desperately accepted. Lately, Georg was attempting to get home every day to bring the few rations he was able to scrape together, mainly bread and on the odd day, hot broth.

How long he was able to do so was in God's hands, or as long as the weather permitted him to cross the harbour.

It had been six weeks since the victualling ended, and Elisabeth's clothes were looser on her now thinning body. Her breasts were tender and produced less milk from her lack of nourishment. Any food her husband did bring home was rationed to Petie. Christian was bringing what little food he could smuggle out of the house without their papa catching him. They were also getting little rations from the Schmitt family, which were sporadic at most as they had ten mouths to feed. If Michael knew of Christian's deed, he would fly into a fit of rage. Elisabeth hadn't spoken to him in six weeks and relied on her brother's daily news of their mama's health.

Last night, because of fierce winds that made the harbour unfit to cross, Georg didn't make it home for the first time in three weeks. Christian had failed to show, and Elisabeth worried as she hungrily ravished a bit of barley that her husband had been lucky to get. She had saved it just for this very occasion, when neither of them were able to bring food. After feeding more to her son, she let him search hungrily for her breast. Her nipples were so sore from his constant suckling that they now just dribbled. He wailed at the top of his lungs, just as Georg wearily walked through the door. The sudden blast of cold air filled the room.

"Quick! Close the door, Doktor Gessler," she said as she covered the little one. Elisabeth noticed that he looked more weary and thinner than usual. Deep lines were etched around his eyes that she was sure weren't there two nights before. Without a word, he stripped off his cloak, and let it fall to the floor in a heap. He eagerly drew himself to the warmth of the fire.

"No food?" she cried out, following Georg's every move. He slowly shook his head. "And why not? With those children dying, there should be more food!" Georg turned and stared at her dumbfounded.

"I'm sorry," she said weakly. She didn't know if it was the hunger or the force of habit she had gotten into when talking to him. She had denied the emotion that stirred inside her those many weeks ago. She was determined not to let that passion surface again. If only she could get through this winter, Peter will be waiting at the end of it.

"We need food," she implored, laying her son in his cradle, which he'd almost outgrown.

"For God's sake, don't you think I know that? Everybody in this colony is crying for food. You act as if you're the only one starving here. Look around you, woman!"

"How dare you talk to me in that tone of voice." Petie started to cry again, so she picked him up and rocked him in her arms. "I'm not blind, you know. Do you really think I'm that selfish? I care only for him. He's not going to die like those at that House." Elisabeth noticed her voice rising to a feverish pitch as she competed with the wailing. She stopped her pacing. "I can't go on like this. Look at us! Take a real good look!"

The crying settled to a whimper. Laying him back down, she threw her shawl down and tore open the front of her dress. Georg winced at the sight of her ribs protruding and her red, swollen nipples. She picked up the child again and lifted the nightshirt to reveal a much thinner torso than he remembered.

"Are we going to make it through the winter?" Elisabeth's voice quivered. "It's only November! The worst of the weather isn't even upon us yet." Her eyes pleaded for her son, who stared up at her with tear-stained cheeks.

Georg held his wife. "I'm so sorry," was all he could say. He felt helpless. "Christian didn't bring any food either?" he asked softly. Elisabeth slowly shook her head.

Frowning at the baby, he couldn't help but remember the orphans. "I buried three more children today." She looked up into his eyes, which were bloodshot. "All under five years of age," he continued. Releasing her, he sat down with stooped shoulders. "We haven't been able to give them the nourishment they need to fight their diseases. They all arrived so sick from sailing in those death traps they have the audacity to call ships."

"What of the older children? I thought you said people were taking them in as apprentices."

"*Ja*, they are." He sighed. "In fact, a Mr. Burger came in today to pick up two more, a boy and a girl. The boy is to be apprenticed as a butcher and the girl as a servant. I was reluctant to give them up." He faced his wife. "This was the second time he came in for an apprentice. I don't trust him. There's been rumour going around that he beats them into doing his bidding."

Elisabeth remembered the ordeal Christian went through in Goppingen. "Did you ask him about the previous boy he had?"

"He said he ran away. Now, Mr. Schenkell I have no problem giving my children to." He always referred to the orphans as his own. "He's that blacksmith I told you about. He'll feed and clothe his apprentices, and even teach them to read and write."

"A much better life than at the House," she answered, and Georg nodded in agreement. "And by what you say about Herr Schenkell, they have a good chance in life when they reach twenty-one."

"The lucky ones become bonded to families like the Schenkells." He shook his head. "It's the dirt like Burger that disgust me." He was still for a moment. The wind howled outside as the frequent gusts slammed against the door.

"Thank God that the endless traffic of children has stopped, at least until the spring," Elisabeth replied.

"The worst was when the last two ships sailed into the harbour."

Georg stared off into the distance, then, turned to gaze at Elisabeth. "You know the casualties were enormous, but did you know that three ships including the *Pearl,* totalled over one hundred dead? And that includes the master of the *Sally,* the last ship to unload its sick and decrepit from its hull." He didn't wait for his wife to respond and stared off into the distance again. "The sight of the orphans who fell out of her holds was heart-wrenching to say the least." Quietly Elisabeth knelt down beside her broken husband and laid her head on his lap to hide her anguish.

The wind was so vehement now that they barely heard a rapping at the door. Elisabeth wiped her face with the sleeve of her dress, then, wrapped the shawl tightly around her. She opened the door, and Christian walked in, shaking the snow from his feet, Herr Hoffman behind him. "Blasted weather."

"Well, don't just stand there, get in here and shut the door before we catch our death," she said. She put her arms around her brother. His cold face against hers sent a shiver through her. "*Awch*, brother, you are so cold." She placed both her warm hands on his reddened cheeks. "Come and sit."

Elisabeth busied herself straightening the bench so that it was set directly in front of the dancing flames. She was steadily growing closer to her younger brother since the falling out with their papa. Christian was the only lifeline to Hanna and her mama.

"How's Mama today?" She sat down beside him as both he and Hoffman briskly rubbed their hands together then faced their palms towards the warmth. She was sure Christian was here with bad news. Of course, that didn't explain why Herr Hoffman was here too.

"No change." He paused, then, looked to Georg. "That's not why we're here."

"That was my question," Georg said as he sat down beside him. "The *Betty!* Is she in trouble?" Elisabeth echoed his concern.

"*Nein,* no word, but that's not why we're here either," Hoffman declared. "There's talk of resettling."

"What! Where?" Georg exclaimed.

"Musquodoboit."

"It's northeast of the harbour," Christian said, "and the report also mentioned maybe Shillencook on the east coast."

"What report?" Georg asked.

"Along with the petitions, Hopson sent a report to London on the *Betty* to propose moving the whole colony along here." Hoffman was showing a rough sketch of the coastline, pointing his finger where Musquodoboit lay, with Shillencook a little farther up the coast.

"I've heard of that place somewhere," Georg said, scratching his head. "Ah! Last summer I was talking with Herr Schenkell, and he mentioned that Conrad Korber took his family in the spring to settle there. Said he even harvested his first hay crop."

"Why haven't we heard of this before?" Elisabeth asked. "And why aren't we all there harvesting our own crops instead of starving here?"

"It's not that easy," Hoffman replied. "It might seem like a sound idea on the surface, but the proposal hasn't been thought through. There's no proper harbour for access to the sea and that area is abundant with marshes." He looked up, "And if the marshes freeze in the winter, we would have no defence against the Indians."

"But I've been hearing how fertile the land is around the Bay of Fundy—Minas, Piziquid." On hearing her husband mention Piziquid, Elisabeth's heart excitedly skipped a beat. Peter! It was strange that no matter how hard she tried, it was becoming increasingly difficult to see the minute details of his face. "In fact, didn't I hear a rumour that Hopson had brought it up at the Council meeting when he first arrived?"

"Not Hopson, Georg. It was Cornwallis' idea, and Hopson gave the thought up entirely. With the hostility the French had shown against us in the past, Council agreed with Hopson not to jeopardize the long-awaited peace that has finally settled amongst the Acadians. They don't want to offend them by settling us there, in the hopes that over time they'll eventually become British subjects."

"But there's another site proposed that's been sent to London," Christian added.

"Merligash, down here." Elisabeth and Georg followed Hoffman's finger as he pointed.

"Seems a long way, farther than this other place you mentioned." Elisabeth traced her finger back to the previous spot on the map.

"About eighteen leagues from here, only a day's sailing, depending on the weather. Not far at all," Christian piped up.

Hoffman added, "Where Musquodoboit doesn't have a harbour, Merligash does. A harbour that can only hold small vessels, but a harbour nonetheless. From what I can see, Georg, London has got to give the okay to this site. It has the best improvable land of any other along the coast, and with about four hundred acres of cleared land, it makes sense."

"Cleared land? Who cleared it?" Georg raised an eyebrow.

"The French." Hoffman raised his hand to stop his protesting. "I know what you're thinking. For whatever reason, nobody knows, they just abandoned the area over the years. Rumour has it that there's only one family there now, and Old Labrador."

"And who's that?" Elisabeth queried.

"His father was Acadian and his mother Indian. Labrador and his family have lived there for a long time near the head of the harbour."

"I don't know, Herr Hoffman," Elisabeth said, "it seems awfully risky to me. You talk of the French who don't want us, and now you say there are Indians living there." Elisabeth shook her head.

"Calm down," Georg said, covering his warm hand over hers. "He only said *one* Indian and *one* French family. And besides, I'm sure that Governor Hopson wouldn't put our lives in danger by sending us somewhere that wasn't safe."

She removed her hand and jumped up. "I'd rather starve here than be subjected to those redskins!" she said defiantly and walked over to Petie.

"What about Indian attacks?" Georg asked. He pointed to specific areas of the map. "Couldn't this be a canoe route from Piziquid, using the Panuke Lakes by this river?"

"That's the East River. You're right, but..."

"What's going to stop them from using other river routes, or blazing a trail through here to the settlement? After all, by what you just said, Merligash is not new to the French or the Indians."

"There haven't been any signs of Indian activity there for a few years now, and you're right, Georg, they're not going to send us to our graves, are they?"

Elisabeth answered for her husband. "Maybe, just to get us out of their hair. They brought us here on empty promises. I don't trust them."

"Come, Elisabeth. You're beginning to sound like Mama now." Christian grinned. She turned her back again, fussing with her son. "You can trust Hopson. He's for us, not against us. He just disobeyed strict orders from London."

"What's this, Christian?" Georg straightened his sore back from leaning over to study the map.

"I was talking with Herr Henderick about it last night. Hopson and the Council agreed that we can't subsist on the money that London wanted to distribute amongst the colony."

"Money!" Elisabeth's ears perked up. Georg echoed her thoughts, "What money are you talking about?"

Hoffman replied, "You didn't know? I thought everyone knew."

"I've been too involved at the House and haven't had much of any news of late. *Bitte.* Go on."

"Herr Kilby was given orders to ship casks of coins to be distributed to all of us instead of provisions."

"What was the value of the coins?"

"Oh, about 4,500 pounds."

Georg let a long whistle escape from his lips. "Well, when did this happen?"

"Before Hopson took office. In fact, Cornwallis received word from London not to open these casks in case they arrived before Hopson did. And none of it could be distributed anyway until the food stocks had been used up in Halifax. Each family was to get threepence per day to buy what is needed at the market."

"Why, that's nothing, Hoffman!" Georg said. "Threepence a day wouldn't buy half of what we need. Look at the Schmitt family, there's ten of them."

"And the prices are too high," Elisabeth piped in. "Mutton is sixpence a pound, and fish!" She raised her hands in frustration. "With living this close to the sea, fish is plentiful enough to be cheap, but it's not."

"That's because the price of labour is so outrageous," Georg answered, and to Hoffman, "So when do we see this money, as little as it is?"

"That's my point. As Christian said earlier, Hopson disobeyed the orders and Council agreed that victualling should be continued. He called it compassionate victualling."

"So if Hopson cares so much, where's the food?" Elisabeth could feel the tears coursing down her cheeks and didn't bother to wipe them. She was exhausted and didn't care anymore. "I don't know what to do, Herr Hoffman. I just know we're not going to make it through this winter. Do you see my son? He's skin and bones." she wailed. "The next time you see us, the crows will be feeding off our bodies. We're going to die..." She slumped down, giving in to her emotional outburst.

Hoffman fidgeted uneasily. Christian was about to walk over to his sister, but Georg rose first and gathered his wife into his arms. She leaned against him, sobbing. Lifting her tear-stained face, she hadn't noticed that Hoffman had slipped out quietly until she heard her brother speak.

"I'll be back tomorrow. Maybe I can manage to gather some scraps without Papa knowing. I know that the Schmitts gave us what little they could spare."

"Go away, Christian," Georg implored. "Don't you think I can look after my own family? I'll get what's needed here. I don't need your handouts." Seeing his hurt face, Georg called him back. "I'm sorry. I didn't mean it." Christian kept his back to them.

"Doktor Gessler is right, but not for the reasons he gave," Elisabeth said, her voice barely a whisper. "Christian, you've got to stop. Papa's bound to catch on. Knowing him as I do, he probably knows where every scrap of morsel is going. If unaccounted for, well, you know, Christian, the state of mind he's in now, God knows what he could be capable of."

Her brother slowly glanced back and forced a smile. He opened the door and walked out.

****

The next few weeks saw a mixture of weather, but certainly not as severe or as cold as the last winter. The snow that blew in from the sea the first week of November soon melted with the fog that rolled in after. Then torrential rains left the roads full of thick mud that froze again. It was now the fifth of December, and the fog hung thick in the harbour, threatening to envelop the land.

Feeling as if the room was closing in on him, Christian opened the door to breathe in the coolness. The damp air felt good against his face. His eyes were closed, but he opened them to the sound of weeping and the sight of Herr Konrad and his daughter cradling the youngest in the family. They carefully laid their small bundle into the back of their wagon. Others in the colony watched but continued to walk by, unfeeling to the scene being played out before them. This was a daily occurrence since the food supplies were now almost non-existent. Disease and lack of food took its toll on almost every family, leaving behind mere shadows of the survivors. Hopson had received some food from Boston, but it arrived rancid.

The wagon moved forward with only Herr Konrad and his eldest daughter, who had just turned sixteen last week. They were on their way to take the child for burial down at Warren's point near the water's edge. That was where everyone seemed to be burying their dead. Christian thought because it was nearer to the sea; nearer to the old life back home. Pity gnawed his heart as he stared at the ghosts of people he knew. He didn't notice Elisabeth walk up beside him.

"Sorry, dear brother. Didn't mean to startle you." Elisabeth was looking so much thinner these days. She started to reel backwards and he caught her before she toppled over.

"Here, give me my nephew. Go inside and sit," he demanded. Lifting Petie out of her arms, he noticed how much lighter he had become.

"Is he gone yet?" she said, meaning Papa.

"I wouldn't have told you to go in," he said with an impish grin. She managed a weak smile. "And besides, I told you he was leaving this morning early."

Over the last couple of weeks, Christian had been keeping Elisabeth abreast of Anna's health, which had recently deteriorated. Because Papa rarely left her side, Christian would seize every opportunity to sneak his sister in without Michael's knowledge. The only worry was Hanna squealing, but to everyone's surprise in this charade, their little sister thought it a game. Anna hardly spoke at all and when she did, it was only about Hohctorf or Jakob. Two weeks ago, as her depression worsened, she wouldn't talk and the fever returned with a vengeance.

Elisabeth went immediately to the bedside. Hanna sat beside her. Anna's eyes were closed and no one really knew if she slept or was just deep inside her thoughts.

"Mama," she whispered, "it's me, Elisabeth." She gently laid her hand on Anna's bony arm. Her cheeks were sunken and dark circles lay under her eyes. It had been five days since Elisabeth's last brief visit with her, and she didn't recognize her.

"Mama," she uttered again. When Anna opened her eyes, she barely turned her head to the voice beside her. She stared blankly over her daughter's shoulder. Placing her hand under Anna's chin, Elisabeth gently turned her head to face her.

"It's me, Mama. Elisabeth." Even though their eyes met, Anna's eyes were empty mirrors.

Hanna whimpered, "Beth, is Mama going to die?"

Elisabeth held her tiny sister close and glanced up at Christian. "How long has she been like this? I can't believe how much she's changed."

"I know. The fever broke again a couple of days ago, and Papa thought that she'd be up again like before. But she just lays there staring into space. I don't even think she knows we're here."

"Why didn't you call me over before this?" Christian raised

an eyebrow at her and she knew what he was thinking—Papa. She looked back at Anna, her eyes were closed again. "I must have Doktor Gessler..." she started.

Christian put his hand up. "Georg was here last night and there's nothing he can do." Elisabeth remembered that her husband came in late last night, interrupting her sleep briefly, then he was gone again before she rose this morning. Between the House, neighbours, and friends desperately needing his skills, she hardly saw him. "He said she's just given up hope. The only thing we can do is keep her as comfortable as possible."

"Will she die?"

"That's up to her." Christian started to cry softly, something Elisabeth had never seen him do. He always seemed to have such a hard core about him, even through his experience with Onkel Gottlieb. Without a word, she turned away and focussed on Anna, leaving Christian to his sorrow. Embarrassed, he roughly wiped his eyes dry with the palm of his hands and knelt down beside the bed.

"Jakob?"

"It's Christian, Mama." To his sister next to him, he said, "I've got to find our brother. Maybe it'll bring her back. If she just saw him again, maybe, just maybe..." His eyes grew big at the thought.

"You can't. It's too far. He was seen there a year ago. He could be anywhere now. Besides, you've got to stay here. I don't want to lose you, too." She couldn't bear to lose the only one of her family who had been her saviour. She loved Hanna, but she was too young to understand what was going on. "You can't leave here, Christian. I won't let you."

"But Jakob could be our only hope. I spoke to Herr Henderick yesterday, and he said he could help me. We can start at Winter Cove and go from there. You know, where Papa and I worked last summer."

"Winter Cove! You know that Indians have been seen there on that footpath. Runners have disappeared trying to make it to Fort Edward in Piziquid."

"Well, if not there, Henderick said we could take the Shubenacadie."

"Then you've already made up your mind," she said.

"Don't think I've just thought about this now. I've been struggling with it for a long time. I now know it's the right thing to do. Don't you see? We've got to grasp at this one last hope."

"Don't do this to me, Christian. I honestly cannot bear you leaving."

"I'm sorry, but you can't stop me." There was a slight quiver in his voice.

"I'd better be going before Papa gets home," Elisabeth said, carefully lifting Petie up. "Be good, Hanna," and she leaned down to kiss her tiny sister. She looked longingly at her brother. "Don't you leave before saying goodbye."

"I promise."

CHAPTER 24

"Has he gone mad?" Georg asked, when Elisabeth told him. "I can't believe you can sit there and be so calm about it. Didn't you try and talk him out of it?"

"Believe me, Doktor Gessler, I'm not calm. There's just no changing his mind. It's set."

"And who did you say was going to help him?" Georg stood up to face her.

"Herr Henderick."

"Can he be trusted? My God, the dangers they're putting themselves into. They could be captured by Indians, or worse still, murdered." He sat down again and glared into his wife's eyes. "It's insane to travel in the winter."

"Herr Henderick feels it best to go now. The winter hasn't been cold enough to freeze the Shubenacadie. They'll canoe up the river."

"Why would they take that route?" Georg looked away and stroked his chin.

"Because of me." Elisabeth waited for her husband to respond. With his eyebrows knitted together, she continued, "This summer I found out that Jakob was living in Piziquid."

"Who told you that?"

"Peter." The word hung between them like an icy fog. She said it with defiance, but inside she felt weak and intimidated. It was the first time she felt sorry to say his name to her husband.

"So, when did Christian tell you this," he said, donning his coat.

"The day before yesterday. Why? Where are you going?"

"Where do you think, woman? I'm going to talk him out of this preposterous idea." He slammed the door hard behind him.

****

"It's too late." Michael sat in the dark room, hunched over in a chair beside his wife. Hanna was sound asleep in her bed. "He left this morning before sunrise, said he was meeting Herr Henderick but didn't say where." Georg read the pain in his eyes.

"We've got to stop him." Georg started to leave, but Michael pulled him back. "Whatever the real reason is, it will be perceived that he deserted to go over to the French. Why, Hopson will..."

"Hopson!" Michael gave an exasperated shrug. "He's smart enough to use the desertions over the past few months to his advantage."

"What makes you say that?"

"Georg, it's as plain as the nose on your face. He'll be able to use the fact that they're losing settlers to the French to get the high and mighty off their asses and do something with us! You see, Georg, what Christian has done is actually helping us in a strange and bizarre way."

"We can round up some men at first light: Hoffman, Schmidt..."

"Leave him be. It's too late; they've had a day's journey on us." Michael's voice was low and unfeeling. "Besides, he's a man now and old enough to make his own decisions. He's got his own mind and," he gazed up at Georg, "I don't care any more." He sighed, his shoulders hunched more profoundly into despair.

"Michael!" Georg couldn't believe what he was hearing. "You

don't know what you're saying. Why, just the other day you said how Christian was so much older than his sixteen years. How he was the more mature of your two sons. How can you sit there and say you don't care?"

"How do you expect me to react? Look at what's happened to my family. I haven't seen my eldest son in almost two years, now my youngest has taken it upon himself to make sure I don't ever see him again."

Georg started to protest, but resisted.

"With Stefan dead, and Margaretha..." He pondered for a second. His voice lost control momentarily but then quickly regained composure. "Two years this past October. May God rest her soul." He closed his eyes. "Now your wife has become the inconsiderate, ungrateful daughter that she is. She's so different from her sister."

Michael straightened, picked up his pipe, and gave it one strong hit against the side of the table in anger, or was it frustration? Georg couldn't tell. "Hell, if I didn't know any better, I would swear Elisabeth was born with a silver spoon in her mouth, a spoiled willful child." Georg just nodded in agreement.

"I come to a new world to improve our lot, and look where it has got us. Such atrocities we've suffered." He angrily rubbed his eyes. Rapidly blinking, he looked to his son-in-law and said, "I pray for Jakob every day. I'll pray for Christian now, and I'm constantly on my knees begging him to bring my Anna back." His voice softened when he spoke of his wife. Georg couldn't help but notice that he never mentioned praying for Elisabeth.

"Jakob." A weak whisper floated from the other side of the room. Michael turned to her with tenderness. Georg moved to check on her.

"It's okay, Georg. She's sleeping. A day doesn't go by without her calling out to him. Oh God, if only..." Michael turned his back to him and almost keeled over. Georg caught him before he could strike his head against the stone. "I'm fine."

"When was the last time you ate?"

"I don't remember. Two, three days. Whatever I have I give to Anna and the little one." He gestured toward Hanna, who was still sleeping soundly.

"God damn it! This can't go on anymore. We can't survive on the little sustenance we're being given. I'm sick and tired of the dead and dying!" Georg was mentally distraught.

"We shouldn't have come," Michael muttered. "This was a mistake to think things would be better over here." Michael laid his pipe down. "Nothing but heartache for daring to dream of a better life. I've brought this down on them."

"Michael!" Georg grabbed his arm to force him to face him. "You can't talk like that. You did the best you could under the circumstances. You know things could only have gotten worse back home, not better. For God sake's, man, your wife's life was threatened for a few measly *kreuzers*." Georg released his arm when he knew he had Michael's full attention. "I know it looks dark now, but it'll get better, I'm sure of it. You've got to admit that Hopson is a much better administrator than Cornwallis. For the past few months, the French have been quiet. And he's doing everything in his power to get food to sustain us through to spring."

"Hmph," Michael grumbled. "What food? It's been two weeks since that rumour ran about the colony, and we're still waiting for it. Just yesterday, I saw Isaac's wife and children begging on the steps of Hopson's house. A pitiful sight it was, Georg. They were so thin." He half turned away, staring over at his wife. "Empty dreams, Georg, all empty dreams."

Elisabeth had said that Michael hadn't been the same since Margaretha's death, but as far as Georg could see since first meeting him, he was still the epitome of strength for his family.

But, too much had happened in the last two years to test any man's faith. He couldn't let him down. Michael needed him now.

"Don't give up on those dreams. It's what will see you through this. As soon as spring comes, I'm sure we'll be making ready for a new life in Merligash or Musquodoboit. Better land that's already been cleared to grow our own crops. We'll regain our dignity and self-reliance."

Georg couldn't tell if what he was saying reached him. Michael didn't give a shrug or acknowledgement. Instead, he knelt down beside his wife. "She may not live til spring to see the promised dream." Georg stood beside him wordlessly. He prayed he could give Michael the comforting words he needed and give him the hope he wanted. "Please don't give up," was the only encouragement he could muster.

****

No matter what Hoffman said or how often he said that Christian couldn't be any safer with Nicolaas Henderick, Georg would not be convinced. He explained it was putting more people at risk to send a posse out to find them. Hoffman finally won the argument. A lack of food in the colony meant there weren't any able-bodied men to search for them anyway.

The long days poked by. Elisabeth and Georg both realised that any remote word about Christian and Henderick wouldn't reach them now till spring. They wanted to believe in the false hope that they might make it back in the new year, with Jakob.

Michael never went out now, as Anna was not long for this world. He refused to leave her side. Elisabeth hadn't seen her mama since Christian left, and now relied on reports from her husband, who cared for Anna daily. He couldn't do anything at this stage, but being there might give Michael hope.

Michael teetered from the depths of despair when Anna would be taken from him, to the fragile hope that she might survive. It was only on the former emotion that there was a remote chance he could be convinced to allow his daughter in the house. But to have the least bit of hope for his wife meant his stubborn pride wouldn't allow it, no matter how convincing Georg's arguments were. The situation between the two of them had gone much too far. Georg was sure that it wouldn't take much to convince himself to knock their two stubborn heads together. There were a couple of instances when he had had enough and attempted to drive home his points, but Michael refused to let his guard down, leaving Georg defeated and frustrated. But in Michael's weak moments, Georg would always attempt again.

Georg felt deep pity for Elisabeth. Unbeknownst to her, he could hear her crying softly to herself in a fitful sleep. He wanted so much to hold her, to soothe her, but he always held back. He had once told himself he would never give up on her, and as long as there was a God in heaven, he wouldn't. But the situation he was living in was enough to try the patience of the saintliest of saints. He promised himself that he would eventually wear Michael down and end this pointless charade.

One particularly dreary day, about a week before Christmas, Georg had looked in on his patient before going back to Halifax. The skies were dark with one great mass of clouds, and he could hear the sleet pelting down on the roof with a tedious beat. Anna had worsened during the night, her breathing was erratic, and the coughing that had suddenly shown up a couple of days before was growing more severe.

The little food there was wasn't nutritious. The kind Frau Schmitt was doing the best she could to spare some of her rations. They had arrived this summer, so they were still on the victualling list. She would gladly bring some bread and a bit of salted meat. The meat would have to be boiled and made into a soup for easy swallowing. Michael needed to blame something for Anna's declining health, and this was something he could sink his teeth into. Georg knew it wasn't the food, though it played some part. The real reason was that Anna had lost her will to live, and the weaker she got, the easier it was to die.

Walking through the doorway, Georg could see on Frau Schmitt's face that the end was close. Her eyes glistened with unshed tears as she quickly donned her coat and slipped out without a word. Hanna was in the corner playing with her doll, not able to completely take in all the grievous events. In her mind, Mama was sick, but she'd get better and no one tried to dissuade the child into believing otherwise, least of all her papa. Georg didn't need to examine Anna; her shallow breathing, sunken black eyes, and extremely thin torso were enough to tell that she wouldn't last another day. One look at Michael convinced him he knew. He hid his face from view and picked up Hanna. "Papa, you're hurting me," she squealed, as he hugged her tightly to his chest.

"You've got to let Elisabeth see her." Michael ignored him, and Georg's frustration got the better of him. "For Christ's sake, you can't refuse your daughter to see her. She's dying!" Still no word. "The pigs have more sense in their tiny brains than you do right now. You'll regret this for the rest of your life, and you don't have the intelligence to see through that thick head of yours." He shook his head. "To hell with you, Michael. I'm getting my wife. It's the right thing to do and you know it, by God!"

Before slamming the door behind him, he could hear Michael cry with obvious pain in his voice, "What have I done?" Disheartened,

Georg felt nothing towards Michael.

****

Eyeing each other like two tomcats, they didn't speak. At least Georg got Elisabeth inside without any resistance. He was sure that Michael realised he truly had no choice in the matter. Without taking off her coat, she rushed to the bedside and a whole stream of emotions rushed to the surface: anger at herself for not insisting that she be allowed in, pity for Papa's actions, and sadness at how lonely he would be with only Hanna now to comfort him. She felt sorry for Mama as she lay there with her eyes closed, not even aware that her daughter was beside her.

Without looking up, she said, "Doktor Gessler, isn't there anything you can do? Surely there must be some herbs or potions to help her," she spoke softly.

Georg sat Petie beside Hanna. He knelt down beside her while Michael watched from a distance. Slowly shaking his head, he said, "When she's coherent enough to take some liquid, she loses it as fast as she takes it."

"Well, what about food? Frau Schmitt brought some meat..."

"No good."

"Mama? It's Elisabeth."

"She may wake up later. She slips in and out of consciousness."

"I'm staying," she said, as she stared over at her papa. He stood watching her with a grim look on his face. "I'm not leaving Mama's side. Not now." Michael turned his back and tended to some soup that was left over.

"If the weather doesn't worsen, I'll be back tonight. Before I go though, I'll bring Petie some bedding and set you up. Michael?" Georg cast an unsure gaze to the sad figure slumped over in the corner of the room. He responded with a slight nod.

****

As daylight dimmed and night fell quickly, the sleet had turned to snow and the wind whipped the large flakes around the log house. Elisabeth was sure that her husband wouldn't be able to make it back tonight. Through Frau Schmitt's generosity, Hanna was allowed to stay over at her place, away from the dismal atmosphere that filled the little dwelling. Even though the fire in the hearth emitted great warmth, there was a distinct chill in the air. Michael had busied himself all day silently stacking wood and carving something that Elisabeth couldn't determine. When she asked, she was answered with a grunt and a shrug.

Anna didn't wake all day. For most of the time, Elisabeth watched patiently by the bedside hoping for some movement, but there was none. At one point, she thought she had stopped breathing. She waited a few anxious seconds until she heard a gasp for air, then the rhythmic, rattled breathing continued again. Petie slept peacefully, and as it was getting late, Elisabeth could hardly keep her eyes open herself. Not wanting to give in, she started pacing back and forth. She soon set herself on the bench and rested her back against the wall. She watched her Papa talk in inaudible private whispers to Anna.

Suddenly, a tremendous crash blew the door open. Doktor Gessler stomped in dripping wet. Elisabeth must have fallen asleep where she sat. Her back was stiff and she could hardly move her neck. Giving a shiver, she pulled the shawl tightly around her shoulders. Suddenly noticing the hearth, she was angry at herself for allowing the fire to get so low.

"It's pouring out. The snow turned to rain before sunrise. The ferry stopped running so Hoffman was kind enough to take me across. I swear that ferry is idle more than it is working." Georg slipped his coat off, and as he shook it, hundreds of droplets bounced onto the floor. "How's Anna?"

"Still holding her own," Elisabeth yawned. "I can't believe it's morning already. It seems like I just sat down when you burst in." She walked over to her mama, rubbing her arms vigorously to drum up some warmth. Michael stood and stretched beside her. Anna's eyes were still closed and her breathing was more laboured. Elisabeth turned away and busied herself, blowing into the embers until the fire caught again.

Leaving his in-laws alone, Georg followed the heat and rubbed his hands vigorously. Glancing over his shoulders to make sure Michael was out of earshot, he said, "Your mama won't live to see tomorrow."

Darting her weary eyes from Doktor Gessler to each of her parents, Elisabeth replied, "We have to let Papa know."

Georg shook his head. "In his heart, I'm sure he knows."

Throughout the day the three of them took turns sitting with her. As the daylight shortened and the shadows lengthened, Elisabeth sat once again, watching Anna's chest rise up and down. Elisabeth would hold her breath until she saw it rise again slowly.

"Mama?" Elisabeth didn't want to give up. "Wake up, Mama." Slowly, Anna's eyes opened. She turned to her daughter, but the eyes looked past her. "Margaretha?" She was barely audible.

Rushing over, Georg stood at the foot of the bed, while Michael knelt down to grip his wife's hand. "Anna! Anna! Look at me," Michael cried.

"It's Elisabeth." She leaned over, moving her hand in front of her eyes to force Anna to focus on her. For a brief moment, Anna did stare blankly at her with a weak smile, then she slowly turned to meet her beloved husband's eyes. Smiling, she closed them so gently. Elisabeth watched her chest. It didn't rise again. She waited as seconds turned to one minute, then two. Elisabeth stood in shock, motionless. No tears came.

Georg watched Michael lift his wife from the bed. Her arms hung limp on either side of him, while her head rested against his big chest. He walked to the bench and sat down and began to rock her back and forth.

"Oh God! What have I done to you, *mutter*? What have I done?"

****

Reverend Tutty had returned to England after falling ill with consumption, so Reverend Breynton officiated over the service. Michael carried a weeping and exhausted Hanna in his arms, while Georg and Elisabeth stood with heads bowed. The Schmitts were there, all ten of them, and a few of the surrounding neighbours. The air was damp, and Elisabeth drank in what little warmth the sun radiated. Up until now, the winter was fairly mild with no hard frost in the ground.

Michael wanted Anna to be buried on a hill, so he made sure that her grave faced the ocean, looking towards their homeland. From where she stood, Elisabeth could see dozens of seagulls as they stilled their wings to let the wind gently carry them over Cornwallis Island.

After the funeral, they all walked back to their homes. Michael was left alone by the grave, shivering in his despair. Frau Schmitt offered to take the children back to her house. Elisabeth gladly consented. She was feeling weaker today, and welcomed Georg's arm to help her. After a few minutes into their walk, they heard a commotion from the direction of the Kilby house. People were running from different directions with empty sacks.

"Hey! What's going on?" Georg asked, trying to stop one man who rushed by them.

"Food! Hopson has started the rations again."

"What!" Georg exclaimed in amazement. "Stay here, Elisabeth, it'll be safer. I'll come back for you."

She sat down on a nearby hewn log and watched her husband disappear through the throng. It wasn't long before he was back with two sacks hanging to the ground with the weight of its contents. Opening them up, Elisabeth found oatmeal, flour, small casks of molasses, and bread. "Oh, thank God," was all she could exclaim.

Hungrily, she broke off a large chunk of bread and shoved it into her mouth. She dipped another piece into the molasses; the whole inside of her mouth tingled as it watered profusely, sending a shiver through her body. "Oohhh," she cried, closing her eyes. Georg laughed out loud. Glancing up at him, she couldn't help but share his amusement at what she must look like. It felt so good.

"Come, let's get this home. This is only part of it! I'll take the cart back and fill it up with the rest of the supplies."

A week later it was Christmas, and even though there was the lack of customary festivities, the general atmosphere of gaiety was more profound after the food was distributed. But they later found out that the molasses they received, along with the rum and vinegar, should not have been distributed. Criticism ran rampant about how Hopson had the food allocated. Children received the same amount as adults, allowing families with small ones to get more food than those without. Petie received the same amount of food as an adult, and Elisabeth was targeted by angry neighbours. She was forced to help those who lived with no children.

She and Georg also heard that Hopson had used the coins that he received in the fall to buy the provisions from the merchants in Halifax. He then portioned it out amongst the settlers that arrived a year and two before those whose rations had stopped. Those supplies were meagre to say the least, and new stock wasn't to be delivered in winter. But Hopson had managed to accumulate enough provisions to start the 'compassionate victualling.'

A black cloud still hung over her papa's house. The food he received was met with empty gratitude. The rations were, in his mind, too little too late. Hanna was back with Michael and, surprisingly, he allowed Elisabeth into the house to help with the cleaning and preparing of the meals, even though hardly two words ever passed between them. Hanna talked enough for the both of them with her diligent merry chatter, Elisabeth thought. For her seven years, she seemed to have become wise since their mama died. She had a sense of peace about her.

One day Hanna said she knew Mama was happy now with Margaretha and Stefan in heaven. It was enough for her to make sense of the death. She soon snapped back to her natural cheeriness, though Elisabeth wondered if it was forced for their papa's sake.

As the weeks sailed by, Hanna, completely unaware, had been able to break through to Michael. It happened one foggy day in February. The snow that had fallen the week before was melting fast as the low clouds drifted in from the harbour with wisps of gray mist. It made it all the more depressing and close. Elisabeth dreaded the thought of having to go to her papa's house to endure another difficult encounter. She busied herself all morning with the tedious chore of simmering fat with the lye she made on Tuesday. It took all of three hours, starting before sunrise. It was still only mid-morning when the salt was added. She knew this was an excuse to delay her visit, but she still put all her energies into the task at hand. In the afternoon, after pouring the soap into the wooden moulds that her papa carved last year, she changed her mind about going and quickly dressed herself and Petie. Georg was at the House again, and he wouldn't be back until late that night. Upon stepping outside, it was a relief to see the sun trying to break through the fog. The brightness made her eyes squint.

She found Hanna in one corner, chattering away at her wooden doll as if she expected it to answer back. Her papa sat motionless. Only when Hanna would remind him that she was hungry would he force himself to give her some food.

After boiling meat for the broth, Elisabeth asked, "Papa? You're not going out today?" Even Elisabeth found it hard to refer to the grave. Not even looking up, he shook his head, so she went back to her task of stirring. What happened next occurred so fast, Elisabeth found it difficult to fathom what took place.

There was a high pitched scream from Hanna, then yelling. Michael sprang from his chair, toppling it over as it clattered against the wall. Elisabeth had just turned to catch sight of him snatching her sister before she fell into the fire. Elisabeth had been so engrossed in her stirring that she hadn't noticed Hanna was so close to her.

"My God! What happened?"

Michael stood there clutching his youngest as she wailed more from fright than anything else. "Hanna must have tripped," Michael said, his voice shaking slightly.

"Oh Hanna, thank God you're all right," he said, checking her all over after they sat down. Calming his youngest down was harder after she saw her doll engulfed in flames, the dress she was wearing incinerated from the heat.

"She's dead like Mama," she wailed. Elisabeth swallowed hard, her eyes burning as they started to water.

"Shh, my *liebling*. Papa will make you a new one," he soothed, wiping her tears. Hanna now was hiccuping through gasps of breath.

"I promise. I'll even get a piece of wood right now." He carried her over to the wood pile and asked her to help pick a piece out. "And this doll will be more beautiful than the first one." Hanna smiled at him through her tears as she hiccuped one more time.

After several minutes of deciding which piece of wood was best, Hanna sat on her papa's lap and watched him as the shavings started to fly. It was the first time Elisabeth had seen him respond to Hanna so tenderly.

"Papa," Hanna said, her tears drying on her cheeks.

"*Ja*?"

"Frau Schmitt says that you shouldn't feel bad if you don't go see Mama." He continued carving without acknowledging her statement. "Mama is alive, Papa."

He stopped and turned her around to face him. "What are you talking about, child?"

"Frau Schmitt says that Mama is alive right here," and she pointed a chubby forefinger lightly on his heart. "And you shouldn't feel sad."

Elisabeth turned away and continued stirring as she felt her own tears hot on her cheeks.

"Don't cry, Papa," she heard Hanna whisper. "You have me."

****

Michael was on the mend now, paying closer attention to his youngest. She now gave him a reason. Elisabeth and he weren't any closer, but he was willing to engage in conversation with her when she visited. As spring approached, he was mentally stronger, though he never brought up Anna's name again. He still went to the grave, but not as often, and he sometimes took Hanna. When they returned, Elisabeth noticed a spring in his step and a twinkle in his eye as he clasped Hanna by the hand. It was almost as if they had a secret between them, she thought one day, watching them from her doorway. Especially when she would catch her papa slip a wink at Hanna, who would squeeze both her eyes tight in return, thinking she was copying him. It was refreshing to see the change in him.

There was still no word if Christian and Herr Henderick had made it to Piziquid. As Michael's strength returned with each passing day, he would also ask Hoffman if there was any news of the pair. When he saw Georg, he always took the opportunity to remind him to ask anyone he saw at the House. As the days grew longer, the snow melted, and April brought unusually warmer weather. It was over four months now since the two of them had left.

Also, the letters and petitions that were dispatched in October had not been answered. Herr Hoffman kept them informed when Council met with Hopson. Without word from England, the Governor still wanted to proceed with the out-settling. He assumed that his last dispatch to the Board on December 6–advising of the necessary supplies needed to establish themselves–would be concurred upon.

The Council agreed that preparations should be made immediately, so there would be no delay when the supplies eventually did arrive from England. Hopson decided to write to the Board again on April 3, explaining how dependent they were on receiving the provisions in time to out-settle the colonists. In the meantime, he received a reply from his December letter, which stated that even though they agreed with the move, they drastically revised the required supplies that Hopson thought was necessary.

"As soon as the *New Casco* is ready, she's sailing for England with another one of Hopson's dispatches. This will explain just how drastic the situation is with the desertions," Hoffman said one evening, when he was visiting Georg and Elisabeth.

"Just how much did London cut the provisions?" Georg asked.

"Don't know exactly. However, I heard Hopson say that he has barely enough for two months in Merligash."

"So, it's Merligash for sure then."

"Musquodoboit's been scratched for the very reasons I said months ago."

"Anything more on our debts?" Georg interjected. It was on everyone's minds nowadays. There was talk that work would soon be ordered on George's Island since the weather was warmer.

"I did hear that Council is meeting next week on that very issue. Seems Hopson is frightened of more desertions if we're forced to work out the debts on the Island. He's about to suggest that we work by job, rather than permanently on the Fort they want built. And," he said, stopping his listeners with a hand gesture, "if we still refuse the work, they'll suggest something menial like repairing the beach."

"Sounds to me like they're asking for a lot of trouble. There should be some incentive other than paying off the debts. I know I'd refuse if I was out-settling soon."

"That's it, my friend," Hoffman agreed. "Council will probably promise continued victualling if we're willing to work." Georg nodded in agreement.

Elisabeth was listening but not really taking it all in. Mending some long-needed clothes, she sat with her needle and thread, occasionally watching over Petie who was playing contentedly with some small pieces of wood. Her mind drifted off to his *fater*. The long awaited spring had finally arrived, the time that Peter promised he'd be back. Thinking back to last summer, she thought that spring 1753 would never come. In the beginning, she dreamed about him daily. But through the winter, there were days when she never thought about him at all. She didn't want that to happen, but it just did. With Mama dying, Christian leaving, and then her son needing her attention, there was too much to occupy her. As the stretches of not reflecting on him lengthened, the dimmer her image of him became.

But now it was April. Her heart would skip a beat when she thought that any day now Peter would come back to her. Her and Georg lived together amicably now, hardly ever quarrelling. They would discuss the days' events like friends. He was always pleasant with her, never attempting anything sexually, for which she was relieved. Or she would tell herself that. Sometimes when he was near her, she could smell a male sensual aroma about him that stirred her innermost feelings. This was a sensation that had never been probed with Peter.

Nein, she thought to herself. I can't go to Merligash, not before Peter returns.

"Ambush! Ambush!" Elisabeth could hear shouting outside. Georg and Hoffman were up before she could comprehend what it was all about. Picking Petie up, she ran out after them. People were running towards a young boy who kept shouting, "Indian attack! Ambush!" and waving the familiar single sheet of paper, 'The Gazette.' The crowd grew larger as hands scrambled to read the news. Usually the news was old, and even then wasn't that interesting, Elisabeth thought. Judging from the scene that played out before her, this was different.

"What's going on?" she heard Georg yell.

"There was an Indian attack on the Shubie two months ago. A couple of days ago, they found a soldier half dead outside Halifax. He was mumbling that he escaped an Indian camp where he was taken after the ambush."

Elisabeth's hand quickly covered her mouth to stifle a scream. Pictures of Peter and Christian flooded her mind with horrid scenes of what could have happened. Her words stuck in her throat as she listened to a man she didn't recognize unravel the story.

"How many were killed?" she heard Hoffman ask frantically. Elisabeth knew he thought of Henderick and Christian.

"Don't know. They couldn't get much from the soldier, being on death's door as he was. He talked about two or three scalped and about four or five others taken prisoners." The bald man pondered what he had just said, "Maybe more!" he added.

Elisabeth thought it couldn't be Christian and Henderick. It was just the two of them on the river. However, that didn't mean they couldn't have met up with others. "Oh my God!" Her voice seemed to scream the words. Staring at Georg with wide, fearful eyes, she exclaimed, "Christian! My God, what will we tell Papa? This will kill him."

"Stop it, Elisabeth," he said firmly. "We don't know. It could be anyone."

"It makes sense. They were probably on their way back. Maybe Jakob was with them. I know, I just know they've been killed. I just know it!"

"Georg, take your wife home," Hoffman ordered. "This is no place for her, and besides, she could get hurt. The crowd's starting to get out of hand. I'll get some more information and meet you back at the house." Georg nodded as he guided her away from the mob.

It seemed liked hours before Hoffman returned, and with no more news than what they had found out earlier. The soldier who was found had died within a couple of hours, but not before he spoke of the attack by about a dozen Mi'kmaqs. Three were taken prisoner and two murdered. One of them was a young boy. "That's all they were able to get out of the soldier."

****

The next few weeks Elisabeth lived in a daze, wondering if Peter and her brothers were murdered or captured. No more news came. As April gave way to May and there was still no sign of them, the more she dreaded the obvious outcome. Papa surprised everyone and took the news calmly and without emotion. Every day, they anxiously waited for even the smallest bit of information, but none came.

Meanwhile, the harbour was busy with the new arrivals of various sloops from New England for the out-settling to Merligash. They were full of such provisions as lumber, livestock, and bricks. On May 21, in the early hours of the morning, all those moving to the new settlement assembled at St. Paul's Church in Halifax. A few days before there were orders posted to all those out-settling to stop working for any private employers. Everyone was told to prepare themselves to leave at a moment's notice.

On Monday morning, only those men who were entitled to lots met at St. Paul's. Michael, Georg, Hoffman, and Schmitt were among the many that showed up. It was announced then that Lieutenant-Colonel Charles Lawrence would be the best man to orchestrate the new settlement. Because Hopson would be returning to England later in the year to seek out medical help for his troubled eyes, Captain Patrick Sutherland was appointed Lawrence's understudy. Lawrence would be replacing Hopson at his departure, and Sutherland would slip into the running of Merligash.

It was a long morning Elisabeth spent waiting for Doktor Gessler to come home with any news of the meeting. Unlike most women in the community, she was halfheartedly organizing their departure. Even though there wasn't much to pack, as they hadn't accumulated much in the way of material things, it was still difficult to get geared up for the new adventure. She had it set in her mind she wouldn't leave until Peter and Christian came back safely but, as each day flew by, illusion gave way to reality. Doktor Gessler had made it quite clear he was going with or without her. She thought this was a scare tactic just to get her to move with him. She still hadn't completely made up her mind. Sense told her to go, while her dreams, which now seemed to be more ghostly than real, screamed at her to stay.

Michael decided to go to Merligash to make a new life for him and Hanna. Doktor Gessler had told him that Christian would know where to find them if he returned.

In the middle of the afternoon, the men returned, each holding a card with the number of one of the lots of land in Merligash. Over five hundred lots were drawn, each receiving a town lot, a garden lot, a three hundred-acre and thirty-acre lot. At one point, Papa corrected her. "Lunenburg, Elisabeth, not Merligash," and explained that Hopson had renamed the settlement. As excited as they both were, Elisabeth found it difficult to rejoice with them and excused herself. She wrapped her shawl close to her. Closing the door behind her, she barely heard something about Hoffman being named as one of the officers for the Lunenburg regiment.

Her mind wondered about many things. Before she knew it, she found herself standing in front of her mama's grave. There was a crude wooden cross with a batch of mayflowers tied together, lying partly upright. She figured that Hanna must have picked them yesterday and brought them on her visit with Papa. Elisabeth missed Mama terribly and wished she had been able to talk to her about Peter.

Glancing around, she stared at the large expanse of ocean beyond Cornwallis Island. She pushed her thick hair off her face as the wind insistently but gently blew it across her eyes. Beyond that was home. Home, so long ago, where everything seemed less complicated. Home where she could run to Mama's bosom for safety and be assured of a comforting hand.

Bending down, Elisabeth lightly traced the words that Papa

had lovingly carved into the cross, "May God Protect." Until now, she was so ashamed of not being able to weep for her. But today, kneeling on the grass amongst the crosses, her emotions poured out of her. It was the first time she was able to cry over her death. She was startled to hear her name called. Spinning around, she thought her eyes were playing tricks through her tears. She was assured of the voice when he spoke again.

She stood up to face him. "Jakob?" she cried, stunned, and ran into his open arms.

Part 3

CHAPTER 25

"The place of fir and spruce."

"Hmm?"

"The Mi'kmaq! They had another name for Dartmouth, and the place of fir and spruce is what it means." Looking down at his sister, Jakob realized what two years had done to her. It wasn't so much the time he figured, but what she had lived through. She was not the baby sister he remembered. "You're really not listening are you?" he jibed.

She gently shook her head, glanced at him and smiled. They were standing on the deck of the *Endeavour.* What should have been a day's sailing to their new home turned out to be more than a week. They had boarded the sloop early in the morning of May 29, and today being June 7, the first flotilla was finally on their way to Lunenburg.

Master Trivett had just announced that if the winds were good they should be anchored by tomorrow morning. Up until now, the weather had been against them. On the first day, the wind had died before they even left the harbour, and they had to anchor off Point Pleasant. Another delay came when the last three ships had to disembark at least sixty-five persons because they were overloaded. By the time they were dispersed onto other vessels, the wind had changed and, with the driving rain, had to anchor in at Mauger's Beach. There they were stuck for one week along with even more troubles.

Mr. Waite, master of the *Swan,* disembarked three children that were put on board by mistake. Their parents were still in Halifax. Then unrest reared its ugly head when the passengers couldn't get to their food. Michael had said that because they were expecting to make the trip in a day, the crew put all the food rations in the hold with the baggage. But the next day, Elisabeth and Jakob stood on deck with their sister and Papa watching the crew quickly distribute casks of food that were ordered from Halifax.

Throughout the pandemonium, there was a bright light. On the *Swan,* a baby was born. Doktor Gessler and another surgeon on board, by the name of Baxter, were quite pleased with themselves to announce the birth of a boy.

Yesterday, everyone was on deck so all the holds could be cleaned and freshened. A very drastic change from the horrible smells they endured on the Atlantic crossing.

It was dusk now. The sun had just sunk beyond the horizon amid the brilliant hues that streaked across the sky. There was a stiff breeze pushing the sloop to its final destination. Georg was below tending to the few that were seasick while Papa stayed with Hanna, waiting for her to fall asleep. Since Anna's death, she had developed a terrible fear of being left alone.

Turning to Jakob, Elisabeth said, "Did I ever tell you how good it is to have you back?" She linked arms with her brother.

"Every day." He smiled, closed his eyes, and slowly breathed in the fresh salt air. He could feel the wet spray on his face as the small vessel cut into the waves.

"You've changed, Jakob," she said, looking up into his emerald eyes. It was like having a new brother. He didn't talk as much, and he certainly wasn't as quick to anger.

"We're all different now," he replied. She wanted so much to know what had happened the past two years, but he refused to talk about it. Papa took him back with open arms, no questions. Elisabeth knew the old Papa wouldn't have, but because he had lived through so much sorrow, he just forgave his eldest of all past iniquities. However, she wasn't so sure of how she felt about the new Jakob, though it certainly felt good to have him stand beside her like this. He never spoke of Schutze and denied ever seeing Christian. Jakob, however, did admit to hearing of the Indian attack on the Shubie. He believed the rumour that all were murdered. This forced Papa to make his final decision in coming to Lunenburg. This, she thought, was another reason why Papa embraced Jakob so quickly. He believed he only had one son left. Elisabeth was not so quick to believe Christian was dead. She refused to give up.

In Hopson's eyes, Jakob was a deserter. How he was able to get back on the victuals list was a complete puzzle to Elisabeth. All she knew was that Herr Hoffman had a hand in it. Georg said one evening when they were preparing for their departure that because Hoffman was one of the militia officers, he was able to have Jakob commissioned to protect the new settlement. Of course, in return for his freedom, he was denied any lots of his own.

The night before they finally sailed out of Halifax harbour, a runner brought disastrous news that three hundred Indians lay in wait not far from Piziquid. The opposition to the new settlement was about to move towards Lunenburg as soon as the ships set sail from Halifax. Hopson had sent a dispatch back with the assurance of it being intercepted, informing the perpetrators that the sailing was indeed delayed. The last few days it weighed heavily on everyone's minds if the ruse had worked. Of course, the delays turned out to be real after all.

Elisabeth shivered.

"Chilly?" Jakob wrapped his long arms around his sister.

"Nervous."

"You're just excited about this new adventure. It's to be expected," Jakob said.

"Not that either. I'm worried that the Indians will be waiting for us when we arrive."

"I'm sure they won't. Basically the Mi'kmaq are a very gentle people."

Elisabeth attacked her brother, manoeuvring out of his arms. "They're savages! How can you call men who scalped and murdered innocent people, gentle? Or have you conveniently forgotten what happened two years ago?"

"They attacked in self-defence, Elisabeth."

"What are you talking about? No one attacked them. Those heathens descended on those poor unsuspecting souls in the middle of the night. Caught them totally by surprise."

"Elisabeth! Stop it! They're not heathens, nor are they savages. Put yourself in their shoes..."

"I'd rather not! *Danke*." She turned her back on him and stared out to sea.

"Let me finish, will you? What if you and your ancestors lived on land for generations, then suddenly someone sweeps in and steals it from you with nothing in return. How would you react?"

"Well, I guess I'd be angry," she replied, glancing back at him. "But that doesn't give them the right to kill."

Jakob continued to defend, even though he knew his sister wasn't convinced. "What do you expect the Indians to do? With the constant shoving and prodding, they fought back the only way they knew how. You want proof of how peaceful the Mi'kmaq are? The Acadians and the Indians respect each other while absorbing each other's cultures. If you ask me, the British should have learned from the French and there wouldn't have been all this bloodshed."

"But what about the new treaty that was signed four years ago?"

Elisabeth asked.

"Ha! That so-called treaty has done nothing but humiliate the Mi'kmaq."

"Jakob, just who's side are you on, anyway? And how do you know so much?" Elisabeth thought she could force him into revealing what happened to him, but he was just as tight-lipped as ever.

The crew began ordering the few on deck to go below, as it was now getting late. "We will be anchored at Lunenburg by tomorrow morning if all goes well," Elisabeth overheard one of the crew say to the passengers. Excitement coursed through her veins, along with the fear of the unknown. She watched her brother cautiously.

****

Early the next morning, Elisabeth and Georg awoke to the loud splash of the anchor and the pounding of feet above their heads. Along with everyone else in their berths, they quickly dressed. The commotion of bellowing orders echoed throughout the ships that were now moored in a small harbour. Dozens of noisy seagulls circled above them amid the elation of her fellow passengers. Everyone clamoured on deck, pushing and shoving to catch a glimpse of their new home. Not all the ships that left Halifax arrived together, and it was another couple of hours before Elisabeth would slowly see them drift in one by one.

Placing her hands on the heated wooden railing, Elisabeth surveyed the wilderness in front of her. She could hardly breathe with people pressing in behind her. A bit back from the shoreline was a hill steeper than the one in Halifax. It was covered with rugged brush and small trees. Not a single dwelling was in sight. Elisabeth could hear the gradual increase of discontent around her as everyone stared at the mass of tangled shrub and undergrowth. Where was the four hundred acres of cleared land that was promised? Surely they must be mistaken and landed in the wrong harbour.

"More broken promises," one disgruntled passenger voiced. "The French abandoned this years back," one of the crew yelled, as he scrambled down the rope that hung loosely over the side of the ship. He said it so coldly, with no compassion for what they had been through in Dartmouth, that Elisabeth hated him for saying it.

In the late morning, all those who were fit to bear arms were ordered ashore, leaving behind the women, children, and elderly men. This militia group had been decided on at the meeting last month at St. Paul's. Elisabeth had known her husband would be one of them.

She watched anxiously as the group slowly disembarked one by one, disappearing onto the shore. Everyone fretted whether Hopson's ruse to delay the Indian march had worked or not. There wasn't much anyone could do but anxiously wait until the men arrived safely back on board. Elisabeth strained her eyes, squinting against the sun's brightness, watching for any slight sign of danger. This new concern for her husband's safety surprised and shocked her. She convinced herself, and an overwrought woman who stood beside her weeping, that they were safe in numbers and the experienced rangers were with them.

The two of them watched together as the men formed three groups. One walked off along the beach, the second climbed the hill, while the third scouted the top of the ridge.

"No sign of any Indians," Georg exclaimed, when they returned later in the afternoon after spending about four hours on shore. Hoffman and the other captains had returned, but to the *Albany,* where Colonel Lawrence had located his headquarters. There was a general sigh of relief when the others listened. Everyone was talking at once while the women held their small children and closed in around their husbands, hanging onto every word they said of the day's events. What was it like and when could they go ashore were the questions most asked.

To Elisabeth, Georg said, "We've a lot of hard work ahead of us. The land's irregular and you can see where the French had cultivated, but it's now completely overgrown. It doesn't look like it at first glance, but this area will be easier to clear than the thicker brush of alder and evergreen surrounding it. You see that ridge, Elisabeth," his hand swept the horizon, "well, beyond that is mixed with thick woods, interspersed with some low brush and patches of grass. There are lots of weeds where the land was once ploughed."

"When can we go ashore?"

"Not yet. You're safer here. The first things we're going to build are the blockhouses to protect us against any attack." Elisabeth's eyes widened. Georg relaxed her fears, "I overheard Lawrence say that it looks like Hopson's ruse worked. There's no sign..."

"It's only been one day!"

"I'm sure the rangers would have seen some clues in their scouting today, and besides, don't you think the Indians would have attacked us as soon as we stepped on shore? Especially, while we were exploring the woods? It's the perfect ambush." Sighing, he put his arm around his wife and held her close. "Everything's going to be fine. We'll all be carrying muskets, something we didn't have in Dartmouth."

"That's not the same thing and you know it, Doktor Gessler. There was a palisade around us with the blockhouses already built and armed men guarding daily."

Georg was about to reply to that, when he saw Hoffman and a couple of others climbing the ropes from the small craft below. Scrambling to the top of the deck, Hoffman jumped down and landed not far from where they stood. "Three a.m. tomorrow morning we start," he said, a broad smile spreading over his face as if he couldn't wait to get started. He then hurried away to tell others.

"What's he talking about?"

"To take the timbers, tools, and other equipment to start building the first blockhouse."

"You're going back! What if the..."

"Now, Elisabeth," he laughed, "you're paranoid. The sooner we get started, the faster we can get everyone on shore and set up safely." He paused expectantly, "You're not worried about me, are you?"

Elisabeth looked at her husband in astonishment. She dismissed the issue with a wave of her hand as if he spoke insanely. She quickly walked away to go below. To her frustration, Elisabeth could hear Georg chuckling to himself.

A few hours later, after putting Petie down to sleep, Elisabeth returned to the deck to watch the unloading of the timbers and other equipment into boats that were readied to go ashore at high tide. Upon returning to her bunk, she lay awake listening to wood scraping against the side of the ship as they loaded the boats, the gentle splash of the water as the oars dipped in and out, and the orders distantly echoing in the still night as they unloaded onshore. With the slight listing of the ship, Elisabeth drifted off to the waves licking the hull as if they were beckoning her.

The next morning, she awoke with a start. Petie was sitting up alongside her, but besides his crying, the place was dead calm. Hanna was sitting up quietly playing with her doll in the berth across from her. Papa had left Hanna with her while he was with Georg, Jakob, and the others. She strained to see the other berths; they appeared empty, though it was difficult to see clearly in the dark. There was very little light filtering down from the hatch that was open above.

She handed Petie a piece of bread to chew on, something she

always kept on hand to quickly pacify him when he awoke. She quickly dressed herself, then took her sister and Petie up on deck. A fog bank drifted throughout the ship, and Elisabeth could not see the top of the masts. A heavy mist fell, immediately wetting her face and hair. She put her son down and, holding his hand, walked to the edge of the ship. There were some passengers mingling about, but certainly not the usual crowd. The hill on shore could barely be seen. Long, eerie fingers of murky haze slowly claimed it, leaving the shoreline barely visible.

Elisabeth couldn't believe what she saw. Most of the women and children were on the beach walking about, appearing and disappearing in and out of the mist like ghosts. How could she have slept through all the commotion?

"If you're looking to get off this vessel, you can forget about it."

Elisabeth turned to where the voice was coming from. An elderly man stood before her. She had seen him on board the last few days. His brown face, deeply wrinkled, was stark against the coarse white hair that hung in disarray. Elisabeth could see that one of the buckles that fastened his breeches at the knee was hanging loose over his dirty stockings. "Pardon me?"

"I said you won't get off now. You're too late."

"What're you talking about?"

"For the last hour, some husbands have been helping their families to shore. No boats left now." He spat on the deck in front of her. It made her empty stomach churn at the glob that lay there, and she stepped back. "You can be sure that the Colonel knows nothing of this, and when he does, there'll be hell to pay." He spit again, this time over the railing. She held Petie and Hanna tightly against her as the old man strolled past without a further word. It started to rain hard, so she quickly ran below to look for more food.

It poured all day, and that evening Colonel Lawrence managed to get everyone who wasn't allowed on shore back to the ship safely. Georg, Jakob, and Michael arrived with the other armed militia, while about fifty men remained on shore for safety. Wet and tired, they talked about the day's events and how most of it was spent carting the lumber up the hill to where the first blockhouse would be built. Despite the downpours, they managed to load up more lumber from the ships and cut a path through the woods from the top of the hill to the back of the harbour.

The weather cleared the next morning, and this time all were allowed on shore. There were strict instructions that four large timber tents be built for protection until the town plots were surveyed. Once on shore, Elisabeth set Petie on the sandy beach with Hanna. Squinting from the bright sun, she could see four of the sloops that had brought them, their naked masts standing stark against the cloudless blue sky. The quiet, peaceful nature, as they floated on the shimmering water, brought a stillness to Elisabeth's being. Farther out, Elisabeth watched as about eight or nine vessels sailed out of the harbour on their way back to Halifax to bring the second wave of passengers. In all, a little over half of the immigrants who landed at Halifax were settling here at Lunenburg.

Others were still being disembarked on shore as Elisabeth grabbed her son and sister, one in each hand, and started to walk down to the shoreline following the crowd. It soon became a state of confusion. Overseers were trying to contain some sense of order to distribute to each person a quota of building materials from the neatly stacked lumber that lay on the beach. The old man that spoke to Elisabeth yesterday was grabbing whatever timber he wanted, ignoring the orders and inciting others to do the same.

"I'm going up that hill and building my own cover. I'm not about to set up in the same tent as some of the scourge that I've had the privilege of living with the last few days." He grabbed a few pieces, which dislodged the rest of the neat stack and it came crashing down.

The overseers could certainly contain one old man, Elisabeth observed, but there was a sudden lunge for the lumber as men and women seized what they could. Children ran behind their parents as they left to find a place to set up temporarily. Some of the remaining men tried to talk sense into those that were stealing, while the overseers were running around seizing what they could before there was a mass exodus away from the shore.

"I'm not sleeping with them," one woman remarked, referring to a very poor family whose clothes and shoes were torn, and the children always dirty and smelly. "I don't want my son to catch whatever disease they carry," she said, gripping her small boy close to her.

Three of the overseers ran up the hill to stop the raid and managed to halt some of them. Others continued on to claim a spot. "Stop!" one of the overseers bellowed. "Stop! Now!" One let a musket fire into the air. As the puff of smoke hung above his head, he put his arm up to fire again. Elisabeth grabbed Petie, who started to cry from the sudden shot. Hanna leaned against her leg for comfort. People who had run helter-skelter immediately ceased what they were doing.

"You don't have to live together under one roof! Colonel Lawrence has given orders that you will all be divided into four different classes. That should satisfy some of you," he yelled out maliciously. Some of the other overseers moved near the lumber that now lay in disarray on the sand. They made it clear they would shoot anyone who stole more.

Slowly, the settlers made their way back to the beach with the timber, except the old man. Elisabeth noticed he sat down on his supply, defiantly refusing to move. The overseer ignored him and marched back down the hill following the others.

Early the next morning, Colonel Lawrence assembled the settlers after hearing of the problems the day before. Tension was still thick amongst them. Elisabeth and Georg noticed everyone had already started to form their own units. The Colonel stood partway up the hill so everyone could see him. He was a striking man, Elisabeth thought. His colourful uniform displayed the large fringed epaulettes on his shoulders, and wide cuffs went halfway up his forearm. His square jaw was accentuated by his dark hair, which hung in a braid down his back. When he spoke, his voice was deep with authority, and a hush came over the crowd.

"It has come to my attention that some of you have taken to wandering about in the nearby woods. I cannot stress enough how dangerous this is, not only to yourselves but to the rest of the settlement." The Colonel paused every so often as Herr Zuberbuhler translated to the Swiss, and Herr Hoffman to the Germans. Sebastian Zuberbuhler was appointed one of the Justices of the Peace before their departure from Halifax.

"You are aware of the daily perils of Indians, so let me assure you that there is safety here, *if* you do not foolishly roam about. Stay within the confines of the areas that my overseers have outlined to you."

Elisabeth could hear rude utterings amongst a couple of men beside her.

"Now, what occurred yesterday afternoon was senseless and unwise. Strength is in numbers, and everyone's safety will be jeopardized if you repeat the stunt some of you just pulled." Elisabeth listened as Hoffman translated. "I have a regular detachment of rangers posted on the southeast summit," he continued, pointing in that direction. "There's a corporal's guard at the head of the harbour, while others remain where you embarked on shore." Another pause.

Elisabeth watched as the Colonel leaned over to Captain Sutherland as the translations ensued.

"We cannot afford any more delays. The faster we develop this town, the safer it will be for you and your families. In a few days, the second flotilla will be arriving." Another pause for translation. "And finally, if I see anyone threatening our accomplishments here, that person will be struck from the provision list and immediately sent back to Halifax without delay."

Sutherland followed Lawrence up the hill as the translators spoke. Elisabeth could hear more grumblings but only from a small handful. The speech seemed to have struck a cord in almost everyone. Those who were appointed to work on storehouses, putting up sheds, and stacking lumber into piles quickly grouped together. Georg and Michael were in the party that were putting up the storehouse frames, and Jakob went with those that were building the blockhouse at the top of the hill.

During the speech, no one noticed the dark clouds that suddenly rolled in and with them came heavy rain and wind. Elisabeth picked up Petie, and with Hanna scrambling behind her, ran for cover. They huddled with other women and children in one of the roofed tents that had an unfinished side, but at least the roof gave some sort of crude protection. There were some who refused to be under the same roof with the sordid, and preferred to stand out in the elements. They wouldn't even allow their children to step inside.

The rain didn't clear for another couple of days, which not only hampered the building of the storehouses and blockhouses, it delayed the departure of the remainder of the sloops. Finally, on June 13, all left the harbour in clear weather, with the exception of the *Speedwell,* which was holding dry stores on board.

Watching as they left, Elisabeth felt alone, even though she was surrounded by so many people. The thought of the ships in the harbour had been comforting. Now that they were gone, she felt abandoned and vulnerable. She decided to keep herself busy with the other women: keeping the fire going, cooking meals, and washing clothes.

Tending to her family left her little time to dwell on Christian and Peter. However, at the end of the day when all was quiet, she wondered if their fate had dealt them life or death. She couldn't bear to think that Christian was one of the murdered. Anger swept over her when she thought of Peter not keeping his promise, but it soon turned to grief if he had also been killed by those savages. The daily chores were a Godsend to keep her mind occupied. She kept the plates filled with nourishing stews when the men returned after their day's labour.

"We're to start the palisade tomorrow morning at first light," Georg said, after filling his stomach with hot food.

Jakob was smacking his lips and nodding in agreement. Michael sat with Hanna on his knees, listening to the events of her day. "There's a lot more to cover than Lawrence thought."

"How's that?" Elisabeth queried, looking up at her husband after watching Petie amuse himself on the blanket at her feet.

"From the front to the back of the harbour and across the neck of the peninsula is going to require about three thousand pickets now. Herr Rundle said he'd do it at forty shillings per hundred, but it would take him a fortnight. Lawrence rejected it, saying he could do it cheaper if fifty of us crossed the harbour there to cut the pickets."

Elisabeth's anxiety showed and she protested when they told her the three of them had volunteered. Even though Papa said the militia would be there to protect against any attack, it still didn't allay her fears. Drops of rain were now splashing on Elisabeth's head. It was raining again, now even harder. The building they were in hadn't been completely finished, and it came in through the wide spaces in the roof.

****

Like everyone else, Elisabeth found it impossible to sleep that night. The rain never once ceased to let up. If you didn't get soaked by the unfinished tent roofs, then you were drenched by the lashing rains that blew in through the lack of walls. She was irritable and weary from the dampness and wet. Her threadbarren shoes couldn't withstand the puddles and streams of water gushing down from the hillside. When morning broke, Hanna and Petie were soaked through to their skin, and Elisabeth was only too glad to give them over to a kind girl who offered to care for them. She helped the other women rummage through what dry food they could find to cook breakfast. By this time, the rain had slowed to a fine drizzle, and Elisabeth could see a welcome brightness on the horizon as the rising sun tried to break through the thick fog.

The disgruntled men refused to cross the water to cut the pickets in the woods, causing further delays. Sympathetic to their needs, Major Rudolf appealed to Lawrence on their behalf to wait until noon so they could dry themselves out, much to everyone's relief. But as the morning dragged on, Elisabeth could hear increased arguments around her, not only amongst individual families but also amongst the men Jakob was in charge of.

Earlier on, Georg and Michael had left with Herr Geldart and a handful of others to help the soldiers mount the guns in the blockhouses. She could hear her brother's voice barely audible above the din that grew closer. From where she stood, she could see a large crowd of men running down the hill to where Captain Sutherland and Major Rudolf were assembled on the beach in their small tent.

Dropping the ladle back into the pot, she glanced to where her sister and son were playing just outside the tent. They were safe with two of Sarah's older children, so she ran towards the growing crowd.

"Come, Sarah!" The two of them had become fast friends last night in the wake of the rainstorm, and she was glad of it. Elisabeth saw in Sarah someone she could rely on and talk to when needed. There was ten years between them, Sarah being the oldest. Yet Elisabeth felt closer to her than her long-time friend Kristina. The two of them ran across the beach towards Sutherland's tent. The sun had been out for the last hour, slowly drifting from behind one billowy cloud to the next, but the sand was still wet and clammy beneath Elisabeth's bare feet. Her shoes were useless in this environment. The grains of sand would sneak in, leaving her with the task of constantly emptying them every few steps. So, like others, she opted to leave them off.

"We're tired of it," she heard one gruff voice yell, and another, "Do your own damn work!"

Drawing closer, she could barely see over the sea of heads as they crowded around Sutherland's tent. Sarah was taller and Elisabeth kept nudging her friend to tell her what was going on.

"Shush!" Sarah snapped. "Listen. I can't see all that well, either." She grabbed Elisabeth by the hand and they wove themselves through the crowd to run partway up the hill for a bird's eye view of things.

Elisabeth could see Captain Sutherland standing outside the tent with Major Rudolf at his side. The Captain was trying to quiet the crowd so he could talk. Difficult though it was, he still managed to say a few words. "I promise you, as soon as the defences are secure, the town lots will be drawn and you can start..."

"I'm sick of working for the lot of you and not for me," said one irate young man. He seemed to Elisabeth to be ready to hit

Sutherland, who stood directly in front of him. He complained about paying off the passage for his family and the lack of food in Halifax. In frustration, he swung his left arm at Sutherland, just missing him as he pulled back.

The crowd broke out into numerous complaints. Elisabeth and Sarah could only hear bits and not entire charges. Sutherland frequently turned to Rudolf to translate. Out of the corner of her eye, Elisabeth caught Hoffman running along the beach and around the crowd, pushing his way to the front. It became quiet for a span of a few seconds, then, the crowd erupted once more into a wave of criticism. She could see Jakob move towards Hoffman as he shoved his way between two men who blocked him. Hoffman leaned over to talk to Sutherland.

"What's he got to say for himself, Hoffman?" one old man spoke up. Elisabeth recognized him as the one she met on board the morning before they were allowed to disembark. More angry voices quickly erupted.

"You've got to be patient," Hoffman started in their native language. "The blockhouses and palisade are for everyone's protection. If..."

"Go to hell, Hoffman!" another one screamed. "I'm sick and tired of living in these conditions. I want to get a dry roof over my family's heads, get my land tilled and ready for next year's crops." Everyone shouted in agreement.

Hoffman had been finding it difficult over the past couple of days to give them incentive to keep going when they felt they weren't working for themselves. It was hopeless to convince them otherwise, as he understood their grief. He could see they were disillusioned and weary, and unless the go-ahead was given for the town lots immediately, it was clear work would be impossible from anyone.

"We've been here a week now and what have we got to show for it?" Jakob said loudly, turning to the crowd as they responded into an outburst that echoed across the harbour. It was obvious to Elisabeth her brother was one of the instigators. He was able to easily incense everyone, knowing their tempers the last couple of days. She thought he had changed, but she could see it wasn't true as he stood in the thick of it.

Jakob turned to Rudolf. "I speak for my friends, and we refuse you any more work on the pickets or the blockhouses until the town lots are set up and our homes built."

Elisabeth could see that old man again as he stepped in beside Jakob in defiance to the officers. His white hair was a sharp contrast to her brother's flaming red hair that gleamed as the sunlight caught it. She glanced at Sarah, who knew her every thought. Sarah knew about the old man Elisabeth met on board. They both deemed him untrustworthy, and she was sure her friend feared the connection between the two.

There was silence, except for the odd whispering here and there throughout the throng as Hoffman conferred with the two officers.

Rudolf spoke up. "It's decided that by next Tuesday you'll be on your lots and can begin building immediately." Jakob held up his hand to quiet everyone, the Major wasn't finished.

"You must promise…" Rudolf screamed until their joyful shouts were silenced. "You must promise that as soon as your families are safe in the confines of your newly-built houses, you are to continue to assist in the finishing of this colony's defences."

All shouted in agreement, overjoyed that they had accomplished a success they at first thought impossible. Jakob had proven to them that justified demands wouldn't be refused. Elisabeth watched as Jakob and the old man were received back in amongst the crowd with slaps on the back and thankful gestures. She was perplexed at how fast Jakob had become their leader, winning their affection in so short a time.

****

"Who is that man?" Elisabeth asked Jakob when the crowd dispersed and Sarah made her way back to the children.

"Of whom do you speak, my dear sister?" he quipped.

"Don't play coy with me, brother. The old man who was standing next to you."

"*Awch*, you mean Simon Gauer." He looked at Elisabeth, knitting his pale eyebrows together. "Why do you want to know?" He stopped walking and faced her.

"I don't trust him," and she told him of that morning on the *Endeavour.* He dismissed her with a careless wave of his hand and sped up the hill. Elisabeth ran to catch up. "Jakob," she called, trying to stop him with her hand. "Trouble always seems to find you."

"What trouble?" He stopped but didn't turn around. "If you're talking about what just happened, you're barking up the wrong tree." Then slowly he turned. "Only good came out of that meeting."

"I wouldn't exactly call that a meeting, Jakob Heber. It could have turned out wrong, very wrong, inciting a riot! People could have become hurt or killed!"

"You're being foolish." Jakob dismissed his sister again with a frustrated sigh and walked away.

"I'm telling you, don't get involved with this Simon or you may regret it," she cried after him. "He might be another Schutze."

Jakob stopped for a moment with his back still to her, then, "Humph," he shrugged, and continued on his way.

CHAPTER 26

On June 17, Reverend Moreau read the first service. When he had just finished his homily, Elisabeth could see the second flotilla on the horizon. Everyone ran to the edge of the shore, enthralled, as about a dozen sloops drifted in with their huge canvases billowed out against the wind. Everyone scrambled up and down the shore shouting and waving at the fleet, knowing that some of their friends and family were on them. It wasn't until later in the evening that all were disembarked and reunited. This sailing had more passengers than the first flotilla Elisabeth arrived on.

Because of the agreement that the town lots would begin on Tuesday, Lawrence had persuaded about four hundred to dig the trenches and cut the pickets. By the promised day, Elisabeth and Georg staked out their own town lot. Similar to Halifax, the streets were laid out horizontally, parallel to the waterfront. The cross streets ran up the hill from the shoreline. Each horizontal lot was forty feet wide, which Elisabeth and Georg received in Moreau's division. Michael and Jakob shared a larger lot of forty-eight feet, not far from them in Strasburger's section, but on one of the streets that ran vertically from the shore. The whole town plot consisted of forty-two blocks, with each block sub-divided and labelled with the letters of the alphabet.

The heavens opened up their wrath again, pouring rain down on Lunenburg. The small settlement had been drenched every day for the past two weeks. Elisabeth thought it would never stop. They were surrounded by huge puddles where the ground had become over-saturated, and streams of what seemed like rivers developed, gushing down the slopes toward the harbour. Even bigger pools of water were left at the bottom. Everyone had moved all their belongings to higher ground, storing them in a crude makeshift lean-to, to keep them as dry as possible. Some crowded as much as possible into the tents where they slept, until their houses were built.

Georg had built a small shelter for Petie to play in. Keeping an eye on her lively toddler was making it impossible for Elisabeth to make a difference in helping her husband build their house. Four square walls now stood vertically strong. They consisted of small trees stripped of branches and nailed together by horizontal strips of board.

"We're not going to have enough lumber to build the roof," Elisabeth said, exasperated, as Georg hammered a nail too close to the edge and it splintered. He cursed under his breath, seemingly about to let out his frustration on his wife.

"There'll have to be enough," he said. "Hand me another nail." He drove it in with such force, Elisabeth was sure the end of it must be sticking out the other side of the pole. "There's at least five hundred boards. That's enough." He hammered the last nail in place for the frame.

"We should have had more. If it wasn't for those greedy people stealing, we should have had the usual seven hundred boards."

"Don't harp on it, Elisabeth. We're lucky we got this much." He knew she was about to answer back with the same tired argument of how Lawrence should have forced those to return the stolen goods. He gave her a sidelong glance. She backed down and remained silent, to his relief.

Elisabeth heard Georg's stomach growl. It was difficult to fathom they had just eaten about an hour before. It seemed like the rations were mostly eaten in the first half of the week, with hardly anything left for the remaining few days. Georg ate more of their rations to keep his energy up through the hard labour. He splashed through the mud to where the boards lay. "Grab that end, Elisabeth."

The rain had stopped as suddenly as the downpour came. Elisabeth had a small light of hope that she felt yesterday and the day before that this was finally the end of the wet weather.

Briefly scanning the sky as she dropped two long boards on the wet ground, she could see more dark, ominous clouds building in the distance. By the end of the day, her dress was soaked and clung to her even wetter petticoat, while the bottom of her hem was caked with mud from her feet kicking up the sopping mess. Georg was no better off. His torn stockings were a filthy brown, almost matching the dark wet of his breeches. Stained with large murky sweat marks, his thin shirt stuck wet to his skin. The holes in the bottom of his shoes left no protection from the environment, and a nasty feeling of slushiness was left between his toes as he walked. Elisabeth's shoes were no better off, and she had thrown them off days ago, walking about in bare feet.

Resting her hands at the small of her back, Elisabeth painfully straightened up and looked over to where her son sat quietly for a change, playing with a piece of discarded wood. Far off, she could hear the distant rumblings of thunder. Every so often a flash of lightning would streak across the sky.

"Georg! Georg!" Elisabeth could see Jakob running towards them. Georg wiped his face with the tail of his shirt.

"Georg! You must come quick," Jakob said breathlessly. They had not seen much of each other lately with everyone eagerly erecting their houses.

"What's wrong?" Georg asked. Elisabeth rushed over to where the two were standing.

"It's Hanna, she's sick."

"When did this happen? How long?" Elisabeth was bombarding her brother with questions before he had time to answer.

"She's not been well the last couple of days, and just this afternoon..."

"Why didn't you come sooner?" She ran to grab her son. By the time she turned back, her husband and brother were fast on their way down the hill.

****

Michael and Jakob's house was more complete than theirs, though it still remained unliveable. Hanna was still in one of the tents on the beach. Carrying Petie hampered her speed, so Elisabeth arrived just as Georg finished examining her sister. Hanna was asleep on the cot, her face shining with fever, her damp black hair in disarray about her tiny face. Michael sat on the edge of the bed. While her lifeless hand lay in his, he continuously rubbed the back of it with his thumb.

"I don't think it's anything serious, Michael. We just have to make sure the fever comes down. Keep her covered in this blanket, and don't stop the cool cloths on her forehead," Georg said, squeezing out the last remaining droplets of water.

"What's wrong?" Elisabeth whispered. Putting her son down on his feet, she knelt beside her sister. She looked so small and helpless.

"With all this blasted rain, it's what everyone's been getting: diarrhoea." And to Michael, "You should have come to me when this started. It has gone on too long without any treatment. That's why the fever."

"It started the day before yesterday. I thought nothing of it because she didn't lose her appetite. It's only today that she's refused to eat." He stared down at his daughter. "She'll be okay, won't she?"

Since Anna's death, Michael had leaned on Hanna for everything despite her eight years. It was a crime to have so much happen to a small child, Elisabeth thought.

"I can't have this turn into dysentery," Georg answered.

Michael's face became even more distraught at the mention of the word.

Georg quickly added. "I'm sure we caught it in time. Jakob, I want you to gather some oak leaves. Boil the inward rind, and have her drink as much as you can get down her." Jakob nodded and left. "I'd rather give her blackberries, but they're not out for at least another month. The oak leaves will have to do."

For the next few days, Michael was pitiful to observe. He was visibly distraught, and had wondered aloud if God would take yet another precious one from him. Jakob continued to raise their house, while Michael stood vigil over Hanna, cooling her down, changing the sheets, feeding her the medicine when she woke. He wouldn't let anyone near his precious child. At nighttime, Elisabeth would listen to him read to her from the family bible by the light of a small candle. One particular evening, she caught him staring at the names he had recorded in the family bible.

After four days, Hanna recovered. She was back to helping where she could, while Michael helped Jakob resume building. She even looked after Petie while Elisabeth recovered from her own bout of diarrhoea. More people were coming down with it, which kept Georg busy. He now had less time to spend on finishing their roof.

Throughout the settlement, people were grumbling about the little rations and the work that had yet to be done. Lawrence had been unable to get anyone to work on the east and west blockhouses, since all were so intensely involved night and day to get a house built; not to mention the sickness and rain that had hampered the work the past two weeks.

Thank God, Georg exclaimed, when he arose one morning to a cloudless sky. No rain! Before starting his day, he had promised Michael he would look in on him. He was complaining of stomach cramps again, and everything he ate ran through him. He also thought he'd drop in on Elisabeth's friend Sarah, who was also sick. Now that the rain had stopped, maybe the diarrhoea would also, he thought, as he gathered the herbal medicines he needed.

He bid farewell to Elisabeth, who was up before him, scrubbing clothes in the large tub outside. She would help with the roof when he returned from his rounds. As he climbed the hill to Michael's house, he could hear the joyful chirping of birds swooping and gliding from one half-finished house to the next. Georg thought things were different this morning. There seemed to be a jumbled noise of hammers and boards banging together earlier than usual. Up to now the depressing weather had caused most of their neighbours to do everything they could to drag their feet to their labours. Georg, too, felt a little lighter in his step as he arrived at his destination.

Michael and Jakob had finished their house yesterday and slept in it last night for the first time. Outside, he found Hanna attempting to start a fire under a large black caldron that swayed slightly from an iron hook above. Exchanging morning greetings, she motioned for him to go inside to see Papa. She then disappeared around the corner with two buckets. Just as he was about to knock on the door, he heard low whisperings around the opposite side of the house. He peered around the corner and was met with immediate silence. Jakob and Simon noticed their intruder and stopped talking. Georg thought he heard the word desertion but dismissed it quickly.

"Papa's inside, Georg." Jakob gestured with a nod of his head. Georg couldn't help but notice the boorish formality in his voice.

"What are you two up to?"

"It's none of your business," Simon said in a huff.

"It is my business, Herr Gauer, if it concerns my brother-in-law," Georg said, suspiciously eyeing his opponent. "Elisabeth was right, Jakob, you haven't changed." He turned to walk inside.

"What's that supposed to mean?" Jakob quipped. "If you think that..."

"What do you expect me to think, Jakob? You're hiding behind the house with Simon, who obviously thinks your conversation must be done in secret. I really don't want to know or get involved. What you bring on yourself, Jakob, is your own affair. Just don't bring your family into the mess you're in."

"I resent that, Georg Gessler." Jakob's fists opened and closed quickly, as they usually did when he was trying to control his anger. Simon noticed it and mercifully nudged him. Abruptly, Georg turned into the house.

He left more medicine, but not as much as his last visit as Michael was much improved. In conversation, he neglected to mention what he had witnessed outside. He figured Michael had enough frustration in his life without having to learn that his eldest was probably involved with something shady. Georg had no trouble agreeing with Elisabeth that Simon was untrustworthy and needed to be watched carefully. Catching the two together like he did left room for suspicion.

He left Michael in good spirits as he stepped out into the hot sunshine. With a brief goodbye, he closed the door behind him. Hanna was nowhere to be seen, but Jakob appeared suddenly from around the corner.

"Aren't you just a wee bit curious, Georg?"

"*Nein.*" He continued towards Sarah's house, when he saw Hanna returning. Waving to her as he passed, he quickened his pace. Jakob caught up to him, falling into step alongside. Before he could speak, Georg voiced his feelings, "I don't want to get involved, brother. What you do is your own business. Just don't let your family find out."

"This is ludicrous. You don't even know what we were talking about. And what you just said about not getting involved, well, you're so wrong. It concerns all of us."

"If it was that important, it certainly wouldn't have been done so secretively."

"The rations, Georg. Did you know the soldiers get two pounds more bread a week than we do, and half a pound more of meat?"

Georg stopped. "Jakob, tell me something I don't know." There had been much discontent over this, especially when most family's weekly rations were frequently used halfway through the week. In most cases, the entire bread allowance was gone by Wednesday, after being distributed on Saturday.

"Doesn't that bother you?"

"We make do. We have to. Now, if you don't mind, I have a patient to see." He quickened his pace, forcing Jakob to run again to catch up.

"You know you're as bad as Papa, Georg. You don't want to make trouble. Well, things aren't going to happen by themselves. We have to make them happen."

He stopped dead in his tracks. "We? Listen, Jakob, you haven't told me anything new about what's amiss between you and Simon. If you're not going to say anything, don't waste my time."

"What if I told you that Lawrence paid two deserters to stay."

Georg knew that a handful deserted the night before last, and two were caught, then jailed on the *Albany.* He couldn't blame them for wanting to leave after so many disappointments and drowned expectations. For some, it had been four years waiting to get what was promised them. And it was still so slow in coming to fruition. They were tired of the anticipation. Of course, the ones that were deserting were the single men. He looked back at Jakob warily.

"How much?"

"Twelve pence each."

Georg couldn't believe his ears. No one got paid for their labours on the public works, so if this spread throughout the colony, it would cause a mutiny, with dire consequences. After building their homes, most had still refused to work for the benefit of the whole community, even though Lawrence spouted the voice of reason about the importance of defence. This could cause more to desert, and with the likes of Jakob and Simon inciting them, it could easily be done. Georg wasn't about to add fuel to the fire by condoning his brother-in-law's views.

"Lawrence must have had good reason for doing so."

"You're mad." Jakob's eyes lit up with angry frustration. "How can you defend him?"

"What good is it to have our houses built, then be murdered in our sleep by Indians? They'd have no problem ambushing us without any forts or a palisade to protect us. These should have been finished by now. That comes first, then, we build for ourselves."

"In Hohctorf, we were promised fifty acres, which I have yet to see. In fact, forget that, in Halifax, we were promised three hundred acres. The lot we have now is unfit to grow even a weed. It's so steep and stony. And barring that, even if the land was serviceable, there's been too much rain to plant the hardiest of seeds."

"All in good time, Jakob."

"All in good time?" Jakob mocked him. "Are you blind? It's been two years since we arrived in Nova Scotia. How much longer are you willing to wait?"

"You seem to forget that the Government owns us. Most of us

are indebted to pay the passage over here."

"Ha!" He gave a sarcastic grunt. "That's right, Georg. *Some* of us. You've nothing to worry about. You were lucky they needed a *doktor* and had your passage paid for."

"At least I'm sticking it out here, helping where I can, trying to make a life for me and Elisabeth. I don't run away from my problems." It was too late now to take it back.

"What the hell do you mean by that?" There was a vindictiveness in Jakob's voice that came through loud and clear. Georg ignored the comment and instead walked ahead. This was not the time or place in which to dredge up the past.

"Explain yourself, damn you!" Jakob screamed after him.

Georg sighed heavily, acknowledging Jakob's anger. "What's to explain? Rosina died at your hands, and you didn't have the guts to face up to it. Unfortunately, your way of solving things is to run away." He could see Jakob's face had coloured instantly as he spoke.

"Do you even realize what you've put your family through? Do you?" He raised his voice to a high, agitated pitch without realizing he had done so until he noticed some sidelong glances from passers-by. Stepping closer to his brother-in-law, he said what he longed to say and what others wouldn't dare to even whisper in private. "It doesn't matter how you look at it, Jakob, you murdered Rosina."

Jakob's face went beet red with outrage. He stared down his accuser, half grinning.

"Your family has given you the benefit of the doubt and forgiven you, but I can't." He knew he wasn't getting through to him.

"Go ahead, Georg, give me your best shot," Jakob pointed arrogantly at his chin, turning his face into the sun. "You know you want to." He twisted his head back to him. "*Awch*, you're a weak little bastard like Papa."

"You come waltzing into Dartmouth expecting to take up where you left off, as if nothing's happened. I know about your dealings in Piziquid with Schutze, helping the French hand over ammunition to the Indians. How do we know you're not a spy? Do you have a runner, Jakob, sending messages to the enemy? Is that why Schutze never came back here? He's waiting for word from you to send an army of Mi'kmaq from the East River to silently murder us? Is that it? They want this land for themselves..."

"You bastard! You're talking gibberish. Do you think I'd risk my family for the likes of Schutze?"

"Ha! You never cared before for your family's feelings, or you wouldn't have..." He stopped as they were creating a scene. People gave them curious stares as they slowed their pace to watch them.

"You'd better keep your voice down. You wouldn't want everyone to know your brother-in-law's a murderer, would you now?" That devilish grin appeared on Jakob's face again.

"Oh really! I'd say you'd better watch *your* step, with Simon attempting to stir up a mutiny." When Jakob laughed at him, he was determined to drive the point home. "I'm sure the Justice of the Peace would be glad to hear of your escapades in Hohctorf."

"You can't threaten me, Gessler. Zouberbuhler has no authority to arrest me. I'm a fugitive from Hohctorf, not England. We're not British subjects."

Georg couldn't believe that Zouberbuhler would harbour a murderer if it was known. He was about to retort furiously when a commotion echoed up from the shoreline. Jakob sped off toward it as if he knew exactly what was happening. Georg ran after him.

During their heated discussion, Georg never noticed that the clamour of hammering and building had ceased, leaving only the sounds of children playing. With the shore in view, he stopped to catch his breath. Georg could see a gathering of men and a handful of women interspersed here and there observing the scene. He couldn't see any of the soldiers nearby or any sign of Lawrence or Rudolf, only Simon shouting as the crowd grew in size. Running again, Georg found himself in the midst of it, becoming jostled from all sides by angry citizens. He couldn't see Jakob, who quickly disappeared into the multitude.

"Where is this place you speak of?" One gruff voice yelled. Georg recognized him as a close neighbour, who lived just two houses down from him and Elisabeth.

"St. John's Island. Not only is there cleared land, but you'll get a cow, a calf, and a breeding sow."

"What's going on?" Georg queried to someone who had shoved his way past him.

Gesturing his head towards Simon, the stranger replied, "He says the French are encouraging a settlement on St. John's and..."

"Shsssh," another glared at them.

Straining to peer over the sea of heads, Georg saw Jakob step up on the platform next to Simon. It was Jakob who spoke next.

"Look around you. Major Rudolf is not concerned about us building homes for our families nor about our safety. Our labour is just a cheap way to build their forts, which the soldiers should be doing themselves while we put up our houses. Do you want to be indebted to those bastards for the rest of your lives?" A resounding *no* ripped through the crowd. Simon's voice then overpowered Jakob as his fist punched the air, "The British wanted us here to influence the French. Well, let's prove them right and support them by settling on St. John's. Every family will receive three years' provisions." More agreement from the people encouraged them to say more.

"How much longer do we have to slave working off our debts?" Jakob bellowed. "Isn't two or three years long enough?"

"How about four years?" Georg couldn't see who said it, but

he could hear staggered comments throughout, sympathizing with his plight. Jakob answered back in full volume to be sure everyone heard. "The little clothes we have are fast wearing out. Most of us are now in bare feet with no new shoes in sight."

That's why the two of them were sneaking around Michael's house, Georg thought. It wasn't about the deserters at all. They're trying to incite this colony to vacate to St. John's. For the life of him, he couldn't see what was in it for Jakob.

Simon started reciting, "St. John's! St. John's!" which was eagerly met with cheers from the crowd and similar chanting. "St. John's! St. John's! St. John's!" rang in Georg's ears as the monotonous words grew louder.

Suddenly, shots reverberated in the humid summer air. Georg could see Lawrence running through the crowd, then jumping onto the platform, waving his gun high above his head. The crowd was surrounded by rangers carrying muskets, elbowing their way through trying to break up the mutiny. A handful surrendered, but most stood their ground. One brave young man even dared volunteer information to Lawrence of what Simon and Jakob were preaching.

"The next time this happens, I'll let my gun speak for itself and you won't live long to tell it, whether it be here or on St. John's." Lawrence spoke venomously.

After a screaming match amongst the three of them, with a few from the crowd trying to side with Simon, the end result was a threat from Lawrence to cut both of them off the list for lands and rations. When others voiced their determination to get to the Island with their families, Lawrence immediately said, "You wouldn't have enough provisions to make it. If starvation doesn't get you, the Indians will." And that, Georg noticed, seemed to silence the lot of them. The mob begrudgingly drifted back to their homes. Still, a handful remained loyal to Simon and Jakob as they lingered behind. With the threat of jail or having their lands and rations revoked, they too gradually dispersed, leaving the ringleaders standing alone.

****

When Georg returned, Elisabeth couldn't help but notice how despondent he was. After repeated prodding, she gave up, thinking it was just the attempted mutiny this morning. Elisabeth was aware of her brother's involvement earlier in the day, but to what extent she did not know. For now, Elisabeth decided not to increase her husband's obvious irritation.

Instead, she and Michael helped Georg finish their roof, which took until the later part of the afternoon. After Michael left, Georg went to the back of the house and attempted to survey what land they had to make serviceable. As much as he hated to admit it, Jakob was right. He was so busy building shelter for his family and tending to the sick that he never really noticed how bad the land was. It slanted steeply back from the house and from what he could see nothing but stones littered the ground. Wanting to prove his brother-in-law wrong, he proceeded to dig up the rocks, throwing the small ones to the side. The larger ones, he grunted and groaned around them, digging until they loosened enough to roll away.

Elisabeth observed her husband as the sweat poured down his back, his hair stuck in long wet strands. With the sun still up, there was still a few hours of light left. Even though it was now early in the evening, the heat was still at its optimum, and the humidity made it that much worse. It was amazing to Elisabeth, how Georg laboured so hard for the good of the three of them, knowing that any day she would leave when Peter showed up. She thought he was either incredibly naïve, or stupid. She still couldn't bring herself to call him by his Christian name, but remarkably, it was becoming more difficult to suppress the sweet pangs of tenderness Elisabeth was now feeling towards him.

Ducking back inside, Elisabeth tucked Petie into his bed, then, returned to toil beside her husband. Georg briefly eyed his wife kneeling in dirt, digging her hands into the soil as she discarded the stones. Elisabeth returned his smile.

Later, as soon as the sun relaxed and disappeared beyond the horizon, they both turned in, falling asleep immediately once they hit the bed. She was completely oblivious to the usual prickling in her back from the mattress that always irritated her. In the middle of the night, she never even heard Georg get up until he had lifted the latch on the door. At first she thought it was morning, but she could see the pitch black of the night when the door opened.

"Where are you going?" Before he could answer, she heard a shot echo in the still night.

Panic stricken, she bolted upright and ran to her son. "Stay here and don't open the door," Georg told her. "I'll be back." As he closed it behind him, she heard another shot and loud voices. The next hour felt like an eternity. She found herself frantically worrying for Georg's safety. There were no more shots, but the jumble of voices she heard increased in volume. They weren't distinguishable, then they quickly died away to silence.

Too terrified to move, she sat on the floor hugging her son to her breast. Except for his rhythmic breathing, the calm now outside was deafening. She could feel her heart thumping hard in her chest, not knowing if Georg would enter or some savage Indian. Earlier in the afternoon, two Indians were seen near the woods. Elisabeth stared at the door. Finally, when he did return, she surprised herself by falling into his arms, crying.

"It's okay. Everything's fine. Nothing to worry about," he cooed, caressing her back. "One of the rangers heard something in the woods and fired his musket prematurely. It turned out to be a bear. Hoffman, Creighton, and Steinfort went off with a few soldiers and could find no evidence of the Mi'kmaq. Come, you're shaking from the chill." He guided his wife towards the bed. Georg lifted her head between his hands and stared down at her tear-stained face. He pressed his lips to hers. For a moment, he stopped and raised his head so that their lips were barely touching. To his relief, his wife sought his lips in return, parting them, exploring his mouth with her sweet tongue.

An inaudible moan escaped Elisabeth's lips when Georg's hands lightly searched every inch of her body. He softly bit the nape of her neck, and her back arched with the sheer enjoyment of it. Despite the callouses on his palms, his tenderness exquisitely overwhelmed her as he caressed her small breasts under the nightdress. She weakened as he moved down, firmly stroking her belly in sensual circles. Slowly, he slid her nightdress over her shoulders letting it fall to a pillowy heap around her ankles. Her brown nipples hardened at his touch. Covering her buttocks with his gentle hands, he pulled her body closer as he continued to cover her with soft kisses. Elisabeth could feel an impassioned heat between her legs and wanted so much to give herself totally to him. Teasing her, he fondled her everywhere but the intimate private spot where she could feel an uncontrollable fire sweep over her like the cresting and ebbing of ocean waves. The room was incredibly hot despite the cool summer breeze that gently swept in through the window. When she thought the delicious aching was too much to bear, he finally fed her spoiled innocence with the tip of his circling tongue. Digging her fingers into his shoulders, she couldn't help but cry out as the motion became more intensified.

Georg lifted her, and carried her to their bed. As he lay on top, she felt a hardness pushed between her legs. In all this passion, visions of the pain she experienced with Peter the last and only time flashed through her mind. But no matter how much she wanted her husband at that moment, the twinges of fear were becoming foremost in her memory. She suddenly resisted his advances.

Softly cooing her to trust him, Georg tenderly slipped between her legs and inside the moistness. There was no pain, only delicious desire as the intensity grew with his rhythmic movements. Elisabeth found herself grasping his buttocks for harder thrusts. Georg's arousal was equally as sinful, grunting as each thrust became deeper until he could contain his passion no longer and exploded within her. Wanting much more, she eagerly motioned her need for him to continue until she too experienced such intense passion that she cried out Georg's name, savouring each wave as it crashed in upon her very soul.

They didn't move. They lay quietly, entwined in each other's arms.

CHAPTER 27

Elisabeth never knew such happiness could exist. After their night of lovemaking, her desire was now impossible to hide. She could no longer deny her growing love for Georg. But in the dark recesses of her mind, Elisabeth was torn if Peter returned.

As the hot summer days melted away, no more was heard of Simon and Jakob's escapades. Most of the colony soon forgot about it—nothing serious, they would quip. But there were others, Elisabeth and Georg included, along with Lawrence and Rudolf, who realized the seriousness of trying to defect. The threat of reneging their land and shipping them back to Halifax, for the present, kept the two at bay. But their daily activities over the past few weeks were watched closely by the soldiers.

One incident with another petition shed suspicion on Simon and Jakob, when they accused the local government of defaulting on the promises the British Government had laid out for the colony. Lawrence responded by saying the accusations were utterly false. He threatened imprisonment for the ringleaders, and anyone else who signed any other petitions. For the most part, things quieted down considerably, except for the usual thievery throughout Lunenburg which was dealt with promptly.

The palisade surrounding the colony had finally been completed in early August. A small log house was also built at the end of it. The picket line ran from the front to the back of the harbour, across the neck of the peninsula, beyond the western edge of the town. The Star

Fort, named because of its pentagonal shape, was occupied by the regular troops, with smaller blockhouses at the ends of the palisade. The blockhouse located at the eastern end housed armed settlers, along with the ammunition. Every able-bodied man was forced to take their turn at guarding, armed with muskets.

It was agreed that those assisting in the construction of the defences were paid one shilling. Elisabeth became very frugal in saving what she could. She hid the money in a battered tin box behind a loose brick in the hearth. Food rations were to continue for a full year, and were increased through successful beseeching on Lawrence's part. To Elisabeth's relief, they received an additional two pounds of bread per week, with molasses.

The more Elisabeth and Georg became acquainted with the countryside, the more they enjoyed their new home. The house was finished, and like their neighbours, they had a separate garden lot. The land their house occupied was much too rocky and steep for planting, so the days spent toiling to improve it were fruitless. The garden lots were east of the town and were easily accessible. Every day, while the men laboured to finish the blockhouses and palisade, Elisabeth and other women, with their children, exhausted themselves clearing overgrown brush and various debris from their lots. Just before summer's end, the land was ready to be tilled for next year's crops. Every night, Elisabeth's aching feet were scratched, bloody, and sore.

Despite the hardship, she felt a sense of well-being. Everyone had pulled together for the good of the community. She felt that finally her life was beginning to take shape. There were no more incidents of deserting, except a ranger and two soldiers under Warburton escaped in a boat belonging to Captain Rous. Two were caught and held in irons at the king's prison, which Georg, Jakob, and Michael had helped build. Eventually, they were sent back to Halifax for court martial. Elisabeth never heard of their fate or if the third one was ever found. She thought that if the soldiers couldn't find him, he was probably captured by the Indians. There were others that deserted from the colony, but Georg had opined that they were best without them.

Towards the end of August, four ships brought in thousands of bricks for more building. One priority was the storehouse. Jakob and Michael helped by digging out a cellar to protect the food. Everyone had agreed it was cheaper to build a proper storage than to lose the precious meat in the hot weather.

During the summer, Reverend Moreau had conducted his church services on the beach. In the inclement weather, everyone gathered in the crude wooden tents that were once used as temporary shelter when they first arrived. More lumber and nails had arrived in August, and everyone willingly gave their labour to building a church. It was up in no time and erected in the centre of the town.

September came and went. Under the new command of Colonel Sutherland, there was no hint of threat from the Indians. Colonel Lawrence returned to Halifax to finally replace Governor Hopson. Georg and Elisabeth were busy gathering and cutting firewood for the winter. So far, the autumn days were warm but gave way to cooler evenings. The countryside was wrapped in reds, golds, and yellows as the trees turned, then discreetly shed their leaves. Elisabeth's feet were so hardened and calloused by the labour of the summer that when new shoes finally arrived, she was reluctant to wear them. Her feet felt so restricted she promptly threw them off, placing them in the corner by her bed until the weather forced her to don them again. Expensive they were too, she thought, three and a half days' labour Georg had sweated on the palisade.

Soon after the shoes arrived, a petition was presented to Sutherland asking for livestock. As anxious as everyone was to have hogs and cows, which was a step closer to their long-awaited independence, Georg felt they wouldn't see any until the spring. The fast approaching winter would make it unsafe for crossing by water and impossible by land.

"Besides, where would we put them? They've only started surveying our farmland," Georg exclaimed one warm day towards the end of October. Both he and Michael sat wiping the sweat from their brows after chopping stacks of firewood all morning. Michael had volunteered to help his daughter and son-in-law stock up for the winter. Even though they lived in close proximity, they hardly saw each other. The frantic activity had intensified to prepare the colony before the snow blew.

On this day, Michael had left Hanna outdoors scalding clothes in a large caldron. Jakob refused to join him. Since that mutinous day in July, Jakob and Georg never spoke, except for a chilled nod of the head when they met in the street. Georg still suspected his brother-in-law of clandestine meetings with Simon, and was just as glad not to have to engage in what would probably be strained conversation anyway. He never discussed the meeting he had with Jakob that morning. If Elisabeth knew anything through the local town gossip, she never let on. And neither did Michael. In their eyes, Jakob could do no wrong, or they refused to believe otherwise.

"Have you been to the Northwest range?" Michael said, continuing to wipe around his face and the back of his neck.

Georg shook his head while he picked up his musket to clean the outside of it. "*Nein,*" he said not even looking up as he polished it hard. "I've been to the First Peninsula where the surveyors are dividing up the land, just west of the town." Georg pointed when he noticed that Michael had knitted his brows. "I think most of the lots are along the shoreline. There's great farmland along the LaHave River I've got my eye on."

"Anything we get is God-given, and we should thank Him that our prayers are being answered," Elisabeth exclaimed. She yanked a small object from Petie's tiny searching hands before it found its way into his mouth. "And don't you go looking at me like that, Georg Gessler. From what I can see, any acre we get, whether it be on LaHave River or on the Second Peninsula, I'll be happy. It's all good land, rich and fertile."

Georg smiled at her and winked.

Michael shook his head at his daughter. "Don't talk about things that don't concern you. Leave such things to the men." Elisabeth's face flushed with anger, and instead of starting a full-fledged confrontation with her papa, she bit her tongue. Georg tried not to laugh and vigorously rubbed a dirty spot on his gun.

"*Ja*," Michael started, as if he was already in mid-thought. "We should be receiving fifty acres, not thirty that the surveyor-general is laying." He took out his pipe and started stuffing it with tobacco from a cloth pouch he withdrew from his pocket. Shaking his head, he said, "It's not right. I don't blame my neighbour Mathew for being upset."

"They can't give us the original fifty. As it is, the thirty acre lots are far enough from town. God, if they were any bigger, it would take days to travel to your plot if you received the one farthest from here," Georg said laughing. But Michael failed to see the humour in it.

Putting aside his weapon, Georg said, "Look, Michael, you seem to forget what we were originally promised and what brought us here. Sixty acres in total. Look around you. You've got your house with a garden lot and will soon get thirty acres plus three hundred. We've got nothing to complain about and you shouldn't be listening to Mathew. He likes to cause trouble."

Shaking his head again, Michael responded, "We're still not on our land yet. I'm just tired of it, Georg." His breathing seemed to be heavier as he inhaled deeply on his pipe. "They're sweetening the pot. And like bees, we're attracted to the honey. The two-year delay stripped us of our dignity. We couldn't even sustain ourselves. Our meagre rations weren't even fit for mice. Anna starved to death and we almost with her." Michael's eyes stared off into the distance.

"You know that Anna wouldn't have survived even if the rations hadn't stopped."

"She would have if I hadn't brought her here." His voice was distinct but dark, and low with guilt.

"Michael, you have to release this bitterness. It's eating away at you. I shouldn't have to tell you again what you were up against. You're smart, you can see that."

Georg's voice was sarcastic. "Think what it would've been like if you stayed...with Rosina dead." He was somewhat relieved he said it now. "Even though we both know Jakob left right after it happened, the Council would've hounded you." Michael didn't look at him. "Could you really live like that?"

"It was an accident. They could never prove who killed her."

"We'll never know that for sure, but how would you expect the Council to handle it? There were witnesses in the tavern who saw him rush out after hearing him speak about her."

"Just circumstantial, Georg, and you know that. Anyway, he's safe here."

"Maybe."

"It isn't just Jakob. I'm tired of working for the Government. I still have to pay off Anna and Christian's debts. I'm a fool for emigrating under false pretenses."

"How can you say that?" Georg shook his head in disbelief.

"*Nein*," Michael glared at him, "you look. There were barely enough materials to build this house, and the land behind it isn't fit to grow one potato. Our garden lot isn't big enough to sustain a small family, let alone a large one. And the land they said was cleared…" he grunted a chuckle.

"This isn't like you, Michael. You're being influenced by Jakob and blinded by his foolish and mindless insinuations of the Government."

"He has opened my eyes." Michael stormed off.

Georg didn't stop him. It was useless to talk sensibly to him now. It was plain to see that Jakob and Simon had been wearing him down. He was furious at the thought of it. His immediate instinct was to pay his brother-in-law a visit.

****

"I don't give a tinker's damn what you do! You can go to hell for all I care, Jakob Heber, but keep your vile and cantankerous ideas to yourself." Georg had waited outside until Michael left the house. Hanna was visiting with Elisabeth, so it was just the two of them in the dark room. It had been raining all morning and no light came through the window. There was one lit candle on the table. It was difficult to see Jakob's expression, even though Georg was only inches from his face.

Jakob was much bigger in stature than Georg, but bursting in on him made it that much easier to grab him by the front of his shirt and pin him up against the wall.

"Get your ratty hands off me!" Jakob struggled to free himself. He froze when he felt a sharp object digging into his side. "What the hell are you grumbling about?"

"Michael! As if you don't know. You've slowly but surely poisoned your papa's mind into believing what you and Simon are preaching. How many more have you corrupted? Huh!" He shoved the knife across his throat.

"You can't threaten me. You haven't the guts to shove that in me. You're a *doktor*, not a murderer."

"Well, Jakob," he hissed, "at least one of us is suitable enough to live here." Suddenly Georg found himself on the floor doubled over in agony. Simon had snuck in from behind and kicked him in the small of his back, sending his knife flying through air. It hit the floor and bounced out of his reach. In a forward thrust, Georg attempted to grab it back but was stopped short when a heavy muddy boot came crushing down on his hand. Georg could barely make out the features of Simon's face glaring down at him. "Let me have him, Jakob."

"Let him go." Jakob latched onto Georg's shirt, almost ripping it as he pulled him up and shoved him towards the door. He threw the knife at Georg's feet.

Shoving the weapon back into its sheath, Georg then lunged at Jakob and hit him square on the jaw. He reeled back against the wall. Simon grabbed Georg from behind and twisted his arm across his back. Simon whipped the knife from its sheath and pressed the cold blade against the warmth of Georg's neck.

"Put it away, Simon. I'll have no bloodshed here," Jakob said, barely able to straighten up as he rubbed his chin. To Georg, he snarled, "You'd better get the hell out of here before I change my mind, you bastard."

When the knife was released from his throat, Georg quickly twisted himself free from his attacker. "You haven't heard the last of this."

"And neither have you, my dear brother," Jakob retorted with a scornful smile. "I'll prove you wrong and everyone else here in this bloody colony." He spat blood on the floor. "You'll see." But he stopped short when Simon gestured to him, shaking his head. "Now get the hell out of here," he shouted instead.

Georg stormed out, slamming the door behind him. He was puzzled by Jakob's statement.

CHAPTER 28

As the weather turned suddenly colder towards the end of November, snowflakes began to lightly coat the countryside, leaving a sense of serenity and quiet. But with the first signs of winter, there were indications of more unrest. Jakob and Simon added fuel to the fire when talk was spread about not receiving everything that the British Government had promised. Georg and Elisabeth had refused to listen, not wanting any part of the rebels' foolish causes.

At first, when Georg had told her of his encounter with her brother a month ago, and what he and Simon could be up to, Elisabeth had refused to believe him. For days after, it was tense between the two of them as she stubbornly rejected his accusations. Finally, after talking with Jakob, she couldn't ignore it any longer. He had blatantly attempted to win her over as well. Back in her own house, she snubbed her husband, wishing not to speak of it.

One late December afternoon, Georg had returned home exhausted from clearing a road to their thirty-acre lot that they had only been given a few weeks before. Up until now, they had been blessed with decent weather, and it looked like they weren't going to have a severe winter. It was colder but not frosty enough to make it impossible to work on the roads. They didn't receive the land on the LaHave River that they had hoped for, but were given a good plot nonetheless. In fact, Michael was one of the lucky ones who got Georg's desired lot. He had just returned home to an inviting fire with Elisabeth busily preparing supper, when Michael pushed open the door without knocking. "It's true!" he exclaimed, not even closing the door behind him and rushed over to where Georg was seated.

"Papa, for God's sake, it's not summer," Elisabeth said, slamming the door shut and shoving the iron bolt in its place.

"What's true?" Georg asked. Despite Jakob's influence, Georg was still on speaking terms with Michael, even though he did his best to sway him from his son's convictions.

"The letter that Petrequin says he has." Michael sat down, huffing and puffing. "It's all over Lunenburg that the Government ordered us all kinds of things we've never received."

"Hold it, Michael, you're not making any sense. What things are you speaking about?"

"Well, for one thing, the food," he replied. His laboured breathing was slowly returning to normal. "A pound of bread and a pound of meat with peas, oatmeal, butter, rice, molasses, and a pint of rum per person."

"We get that now."

"Per day?"

Elisabeth sat herself down beside Georg, listening more intently now.

"And they were to supply us with new clothes and housekeeping utensils. How would you like brand new spoons instead of using smelly seashells that you've picked up off the beach? You barely got enough lumber to build this house, let alone to construct the scantiest of furniture."

"Where did you hear this, Papa?"

"John Petrequin. His cousin in London wrote him asking if we received all this." Michael stopped and leaned in closer as if he was frightened of being overheard. "We were also supposed to get five pounds in money to cover our passage here," he said, rapping his forefinger hard on the table.

"Rubbish! That can't be true. It's got to be lies. I don't believe he even has a cousin in London. And even if he did, how can he be writing to him? John can't even read and write. It just doesn't make any sense."

"Remember the ship that sailed in about a month ago with more provisions from Boston?" Georg nodded. "A sailor brought him the letter, says he knew his cousin. He read him the contents."

"So where's the proof now? Where's this letter?"

"At the moment, he's refused to produce it."

"Doesn't that tell you something, Michael? It's all a ruse to get everyone stirred up for nothing. Maybe he's trumped up this scheme to force the Government's hand into giving us more so the riots and desertions will stop." Georg gave his wife a sidelong glance. "If you ask me, stay out of it. It can only lead to danger."

"Listen to him, Papa." Elisabeth laid her hand on his arm.

He shrugged off his daughter's hand. "I *have* listened. Well, you'll find out on Sunday."

"Sunday?"

"He promised to show the letter then."

"That still doesn't prove anything. Where did John's cousin get this information? It's not as if it was signed by some Government officials."

"There is! Petrequin says the letter has three signatures with an official seal beside each one."

"Until I see it, I'm not convinced."

****

"Tie his hands!" Jakob ordered. Simon obeyed, wrapping the rope tight around John Petrequin's wrists, which were squeezed tightly behind his back. Jakob nudged Petrequin ahead of him with his musket at his head. He shoved him out to a jeering mob, shouting at him to produce the letter. It was Saturday morning, December 15, when they marched their prisoner to the eastern blockhouse.

Elisabeth shouted for Georg to come quickly as she watched the rebellious procession march up the hill towards the blockhouse. Others were peering out of their doors. Petrequin's wife could be heard screaming after the mob as she was repeatedly pushed back. "Stay here, I'm going to get Sutherland." Georg sped off down the hill.

John Petrequin was goaded forcibly up the steps, stumbling many times until he reached the inside of the blockhouse. He finally fell onto the straw that lay scattered throughout the room.

"Give us the damn letter, you scoundrel!" Jakob screamed. The prisoner stared back at him with eyes wide with fear. Simon translated it into his mother tongue, French, and shoved him back down when he tried to rise.

Petrequin was about to protest, when the door opened with a crash. Sutherland rushed in, demanding an explanation. From behind, Major Rudolf and Captain Strasburger barged in with the magistrate Zouberbuhler, who stood beside him. On the opposite side was Georg. He glared at Jakob with hatred. "I might have known it was you," he said.

"Traitor!" Jakob screamed. "You should be on our side, you simpleton."

Zouberbuhler translated Sutherland's questions into German and relayed their answers in return. In the difficulty of the situation, no one seemed to want to give a sensible account.

Petrequin reiterated profusely in French that he didn't know why he was being held against his will, so Sutherland released him. After a tense few moments as Jakob watched Georg and the other four depart with his prisoner, rage welled up in him uncontrollably. Running down the steps to the remaining crowd, he spurted orders. "You, Casper, take about twenty to thirty men with you and go that way." He pointed towards the Star Fort. "Martin, take the same amount of men with you and cut them off on the east side. The rest of you, follow me." He gestured to Simon and anyone else who was willing to follow. Jakob surmised that Sutherland would take John to the Star Fort for protection until everything calmed down. He knew just where to cut them off.

They skirted the settlement, keeping close to the palisade. They were able to hide amongst the tall bushes. As silently and as quickly as possible, they turned south toward the main road leading to the fort and waited there in ambush.

Soon Jakob could see the three of them walking with Petrequin. Zouberbuhler and Georg weren't with them. He waited for the opportune time before he shouted orders to surround them. Sutherland and the others stopped a few feet away, aiming their muskets. They surrendered when they saw they were outnumbered by about twenty armed men. The other two groups that Jakob sent off from the blockhouse showed up, completely surrounding the small party. Casper's troupe held Sutherland, Rudolf, and Strasburger at bay with guns pointed at their backs. Simon seized the terrified Petrequin.

****

Word of Petrequin's recapture spread quickly. A small, curious crowd soon grew into hundreds of angry citizens outside the blockhouse where he was being held.

"Come out, Heber, I want to talk."

Jakob stuck his head out of one of the blockhouse openings to catch Sutherland standing in front of the noisy crowd.

"You can say what you want right there. Don't come any farther or I'll shoot Petrequin," Jakob yelled as he saw the Colonel and Zouberbuhler trying to approach the steps.

"If Petrequin is withholding evidence, and if what you state is accurate, I promise you an honest hearing and will hold him for trial."

After Zouberbuhler translated, Jakob replied, "Not good enough. We want to see the letter and we want it now. If we release him to you, how the hell can I be sure you'll bring him to trial? Without the letter, your promises mean nothing." Jakob could barely hear Zouberbuhler interpreting.

Zouberbuhler then turned to the crowd and spoke for Sutherland. "Go back to your homes. We'll handle this civilly and bring Petrequin to court on your charges and force his disclosure of the document."

Jakob cried out to the crowd. "Don't listen to him! Don't forget whose side Sutherland is on. He doesn't want the letter produced. It contains promises that his Government ordered but didn't deliver. If anything, he'll release Petrequin and try to have the evidence destroyed. We want the letter!"

The mob howled and chanted rhythmically, "Letter! Letter! Letter!"

Jakob watched as Sutherland and Zouberbuhler left in frustration. Probably, he thought, to bring back reinforcements.

****

Petrequin screamed in agony as excruciating pain ripped through his body. Jakob had tied him down while Simon repeatedly placed a hot iron on the soles of his feet.

"Where's the letter?" Jakob demanded for the last time, trusting the pain would do the talking. When he didn't answer, Jakob banged his fist against the wall. They had strip-searched him earlier but found nothing. Abraham Zimmer, whose turn it was to guard for that night, suggested torture as the best means of extracting the desired information. So far, for the past two hours, nothing had worked. Petrequin was as tight-lipped as ever.

Jakob started dropping boiling water onto his face again.

As the prisoner winced in pain, he said in French, "I'll tell you nothing," and spat in his face.

"Hot irons, Simon!" Jakob cried, as he wiped the spittle from his chin. A shrill scream shot through the still night air as Petrequin lay writhing in anguish, sweat pouring from his face in the cold room.

"Zouberbuhler," he sputtered, and spoke some words Jakob couldn't understand. Simon leaned over him. The smell of his putrid breath repulsed him, and he quickly stood back.

"He says he gave the letter to Zouberbuhler."

Jakob untied him, but ordered Abraham to keep him prisoner. "We need more men to come to our cause. Safety in numbers, I say. They wouldn't persecute a whole colony." Simon nodded in agreement. Turning to Stahl, the sergeant of the night's militia guard, Jakob said, "I want you to round up as many as you can and make sure they're armed. We need to get Zouberbuhler." Stahl disappeared into the darkness.

About an hour later, there was a clatter of noise ascending the steps outside. Raising their muskets, they were greeted by Casper panting hard, sending a cloud of cold vapour as he breathed.

"They've got Stahl, and now Zouberbuhler's at Star Fort under protection."

"What!" Jakob lowered his musket.

"How do you know?" Simon yelled.

"I overheard Stahl confess to the Colonel that we were out to arrest Zouberbuhler, as Petrequin admitted that he had the letter. I saw Sutherland leave, saying he was going to protect Zouberbuhler at the Fort."

"Tie Petrequin back up!" Jakob told Simon, and clamoured down the steps.

****

Early Sunday morning, Jakob and Simon scoured the town, ordering people to join them. Some willingly grabbed their muskets and immediately fell into step with the growing crowd. Others refused, even with the threat of burning their houses. Michael refused. What started out harmlessly had suddenly turned ugly. He wanted no part of it. Michael was scared of what his son was capable of doing. He took Hanna to Elisabeth and Georg's until the worst of it was hopefully over. He had never seen such hatred before in Jakob's eyes.

"We want the letter!" Jakob demanded, as he, Simon, Casper and Zimmer stood in front of Sutherland. About ten soldiers were behind the Colonel with their muskets readied if any trouble erupted. He replied and Simon interpreted. "He says Zouberbuhler doesn't have the letter. Petrequin is lying."

Outside, the crowd was chanting, "We want Zouberbuhler! Zouberbuhler! Zouberbuhler!"

"Hear that, Sutherland?" Simon exclaimed. "I just have to give them the word and they'll be in here faster than the blink of an eye. You wouldn't have a chance."

"I can promise you this, Gauer," Sutherland remarked. "I'll assure you that Zouberbuhler stays in Lunenburg until I get word to Lawrence in Halifax." Simon translated to Jakob. Feeling they were finally being taken seriously, Jakob accepted the terms and addressed the crowd. The news seemed to settle them, knowing that something would be done.

****

Shots suddenly echoed in the stillness of the winter night.

Elisabeth leapt to her feet, dropping a shirt she was mending. "You're not going out there," she cried, as Georg grabbed his weapon. "You might be killed!"

He ignored her.

"Or it could be another uprising after Zouberbuhler's skin. It's not your turn for duty until Tuesday. Let the others on guard now take care of it!"

"If it has anything to do with today's mutiny, then, all the more reason for me to go. Sutherland will need all the help he can get." Georg fled as fast as he could into the night. More shots rang as Elisabeth shut the door and bolted herself, Petie, and Hanna securely inside. She worried about her papa. It was his turn on duty.

Running towards the noise, Georg met others racing from the lower blockhouse heading back to town. Upon reaching it, he found Simon helping Jakob up. There was blood dripping from a wound in his arm. The last remnants of what looked like a large crowd had dissipated quickly, leaving only Simon, Jakob, and a few stragglers. On the steps of the blockhouse stood about two dozen soldiers laying down their arms as everyone dispersed.

"We decided to take matters into our own hands. We didn't trust that Sutherland would go to Lawrence for help." Jakob shrugged off his brother-in-law's help to mend the wound. "Stay away from me," he cried, leaning heavily on Simon.

"That needs to be bound, now! You're losing a lot of blood."

"You're not the only *doktor* here."

Georg watched as the two of them staggered towards town, with

Jakob hunched over in pain.

The next day Georg heard that Sutherland sent Lieutenant Adams to Halifax seeking an urgent conference with Lawrence.

****

"You're finally awake." Jakob turned his head toward the dream-like voice in the distance. He blinked his eyes, trying to adjust his vision in the darkness. Simon was in the corner cleaning his musket, and beside him Petrequin was on the floor tied with his hands behind his back, asleep. At first he didn't know where he was or how he got there. Then, in an attempt to rise, a sharp pain shot through his arm down to his fingers. A horrific picture triggered in his mind. He remembered the shots last night, Doktor Erad pouring liquor into him and over his arm.

"How long...ahhhhh," he moaned, as he tried to rise again. Sitting on the edge of the bed, he felt weak. His arm throbbed, and he could see the white bandages wrapped around his arm stained with large blotches of dark blood. And he could swear that there were hammers in his head as it pounded so.

"You've been out for two days. You lost a lot of blood." Simon got up from what he was doing and poured rum into a cup, then handed it to Jakob. The smell of it turned his stomach and he pushed it out of Simon's hand, sending it splashing to the floor. Petrequin stirred slightly, but didn't awaken.

"God's breath, that's putrid."

"How's your head?" Simon grinned at him. "You drank enough for both of us. The dok' only gave you a bit to make it easier for him to operate, but you kept insisting on more. You don't remember any of this, do you?" Jakob shook his head slowly so as not to jar it. "Anyway, he finally gave into your insatiable thirst."

"What's been happening?" Jakob said suddenly, realizing how and why he was shot. "I see Petrequin's still with us." Jakob rubbed the back of his head, stretching it back and forth, hoping it would help somewhat. "Has Zouberbuhler produced the letter yet?"

Simon shook his head.

"I can't believe it. What's he got to prove by not showing it? With us outnumbering the soldiers, they haven't a hope in hell. Might as well just give it up." He grabbed a chunk of stale bread that was lying on the table beside him.

"Yesterday morning, another mass of people persuaded Major Rudolf to present himself to Sutherland with our demands to give over the letter or Zouberbuhler," Simon told him.

Jakob raised his eyebrows as he continued to tear hungrily into the bread.

"I didn't go. With you out like a fire, there was no one to guard Petrequin. But Casper told me that they demanded the Government supply us with a ship so we can sail our own deputies to deliver our grievances to the King in England."

"And?" Jakob listened intently.

"And Sutherland wouldn't recognize Rudolf as our spokesman. He said he'd only speak to someone we appointed from within. But he promised he would send word to Lawrence in Halifax that we demand a passage to England."

"What about the corporal who shot me last night...I mean Sunday. I suppose Sutherland's going to turn a blind eye to this." Jakob grimaced as he tried to lift his arm.

"He's keeping him under arrest until a trial is prepared later, but he's refusing to let Zouberbuhler into our hands. He says that if one of us ever needed protection, he'd do the same thing."

"And you believe him! I don't trust the lot of them. Sutherland's defending his own kind. He knows if he gave him over to us, and the letter was found, there would be a lot of questions to answer. Then he'd have the whole colony after his skin." Jakob stood up for the first time, then, quickly fell back again. Simon handed him some more bread and a jug of water to wash it down.

"Anyway," Simon started, "Casper appointed himself, along with Abraham and Daniel, and for the last twenty-four hours, they have been talking back and forth between us and Sutherland." He grabbed a jug of rum and started pouring it down his throat.

"And!" Jakob impatiently pushed his friend to continue.

Wiping his mouth with the back of his hand, Simon sighed, leaning his right arm on his leg. He dangled the jug from the loop with his forefinger.

"Tomorrow morning," Simon moved his head towards Petrequin, who was still sound asleep, "we're to bring him to the Fort so Sutherland can hear what he has to say."

"That'll do no good. On Saturday, Sutherland ordered his release because he couldn't make head nor tails of what was going on. He just might order us to free him again," Jakob opined.

"Don't think so. From what Casper's told me this afternoon, looks like Sutherland is determined to get to the bottom of things now."

Taking another long swig of rum, Simon banged the jug onto the table. "It's a start. To prove our own conduct the last few days, he's also willing to hear the evidence, so there is no choice."

"I'll reserve my judgment for tomorrow." Jakob lay back down, cradling his arm so as not to subject it to any more pain. His head had stopped pounding, and he was feeling a little better after eating. Simon's voice became fainter and fainter. He eventually drifted off.

****

The sun was shining brightly, making Jakob squint from the glare of the snow that had freshly fallen the day before. His headache had eased, but his arm still throbbed with every movement. When he and Simon arrived with the prisoner at the Star Fort, there were masses of people standing. Colonel Sutherland and Captain Strasburger sat at a square wooden table that appeared to have been set up just for the occasion. Zouberbuhler was nowhere in sight, but Hoffman was there to translate Petrequin's story.

Those who had waited for their arrival were edgy and anxious to get things started. Jakob could hear the jeers when they approached. Everyone had a musket in hand. Petrequin stood between Jakob and Simon, his hands still bound behind his back. He reiterated his story to Simon, who translated to the Colonel. The prisoner repeatedly accused Zouberbuhler of having the letter. Hoffman handed over a collection of statements of Petrequin's friends, describing what he had told them about the letter. At the request of the colony, Hoffman translated it into English for the Colonel.

Once all was told, and it seemed that Sutherland understood it, Jakob noticed the crowd calm down considerably. It was mentioned that Lawrence would be sending help immediately once Adams had explained the uprising on Sunday. For the next couple of days, Petrequin was kept under close guard, while the assemblies of people continued to meet. To Jakob's consternation, no further threats were pointed at Sutherland. The majority agreed, as well as Simon, to wait to hear from Halifax.

****

To Elisabeth's relief, she was able to ascertain that Jakob was physically out of danger from the wound. Georg had spoken to Doktor Erad to calm not only his wife's fears, but his own. Unbeknownst to Elisabeth, Georg had attempted to gain entry to the blockhouse to talk to Jakob. But on his brother-in-law's insistence, Simon stopped him with a musket pointed at his chest. He could hear that Jakob was not alone with the prisoner, but recognized the voices of Casper, Stahl, and Heirshman. Behind him in the distance, he could hear shouts. He didn't dare turn his head, lest Simon attempt to attack him. Not until Simon darted back up the steps, shouting that Monckton's men were approaching the blockhouse, did Georg dare let his guard down.

At sunrise, Lieutenant-Colonel Robert Monckton arrived with four ships with a further month's supplies, and two hundred soldiers to quell the uprising. It didn't take long for them to disembark onto shore, Georg thought, as he darted behind a spruce tree that stood strong and tall on the northwest corner of the blockhouse. In front and behind the soldiers ran a myriad of settlers shouting profanities and demanding justice now. They were in stark contrast to the disciplined army, who marched their way towards the blockhouse, with Monckton leading. At one point, Georg noticed some of the more hot-tempered rioters were pushed into the ditch as a warning for the others to back off.

Above his head, Georg could hear footsteps. Straining his neck, he could barely see the top of Jakob's and Simon's heads. The bright, clean reds and blues of the uniforms the soldiers wore were quite impressive as the brass buttons gleamed in the sunlight. Georg could see them much clearer now when they stopped just a few yards from the blockhouse. A handful of followers ran up to the bottom of the steps and stood as if protecting Jakob and Simon. At the top of the steps, Georg could hear Petrequin's voice yelling.

"Silence the bastard!" Simon screamed. Then, a loud smack and thud.

After what seemed like an infinite amount of time, Monckton

finally spoke.

"I'm Lieutenant-Colonel Monckton come on Lawrence's orders." He walked forward a couple of steps.

Jakob and Simon's protectors immediately raised their muskets. They stood defiantly eyeing their aggressor. Monckton gripped the hilt of his sword, making no attempt to withdraw it from its sheath. He stood equally as defiant.

"You're outnumbered! Lay down your arms!"

Simon spoke, but not before letting out a horrific laugh that almost sounded demented. "You think you can just waltz in here and simply take over? Look around you, Monckton. There's not one man in this colony that's not armed and ready to fight." Eyeing things behind him, Monckton could see yet more had surrounded his group with weapons aimed straight at him.

"I will get to the bottom of this. I promise that Petrequin will be dealt with harshly, and the letter will be demanded from him. Give him up!"

"If you wanted to get to the bottom of things, as you say, you'd know by now that Petrequin says Zouberbuhler has it," Jakob said with a derisive sneer in his voice.

"Zouberbuhler's house has been searched from top to bottom, and Sutherland and I are confident of his innocence. You have my word that Petrequin will not be released but will be kept under guard until all truth is known." He continued, "You obviously haven't gotten anywhere yourself, otherwise we wouldn't be here."

Georg nervously stared as Jakob turned to Simon to speak.

"You can have Petrequin," Jakob said, "and if he is released under your arrest, I'm sure you're well aware of the dire consequences." He pointed his musket, scanning the crowd that stood around the soldiers. "Look over your shoulder, Monckton. You'd be shot dead in your sleep." Jakob motioned for his protectors to lower their weapons.

He and Simon vanished into the blockhouse and reappeared with Casper, Stahl, and Heirshman carrying an armful of muskets and knives. Georg silently watched the settlers retreat as Monckton's men took over the building and arrested the prisoner. Even though a potential disaster was averted, the next few days proved grim.

In Georg's mind, Jakob displayed too calm of an exterior; a complete turn-around. He wondered if there was a diabolical scheme in the making. He was soon to realize his fears were justified. The night before, Jakob, Simon, and two dozen armed men attempted to steal Petrequin away. They were convinced he would be freed and all the evidence swept away so the Board of Trade in England didn't have to answer to any litigation. The near skirmish was brought to bay with a few arrests but no injuries. Simon was arrested, but Jakob escaped.

Georg soon learned that he was lying low at Heirshman's house, which was located closer to the shoreline. When Elisabeth discovered where her brother was, she insisted on seeing him. Amid her husband's profuse protestations, she ran down the hill and across a small meadow until she found herself on the doorstep of Herr Heirshman.

His house was a small logged structure with a small opening for a window, as were all the dwellings in Lunenburg. It was dark within. Elisabeth pounded hard on the door, and she almost lost her balance when the door suddenly flew open. Heirshman had a thick black beard that was so long it lay on his chest. "*Ja*!" he said in a gruff voice.

"I want to see my brother." She was now stomping her feet to keep them from getting too cold. She had left in such a hurry, she hadn't even taken the time to don a warm coat. She only had a thin shawl wrapped tightly around her.

"Elisabeth?" She could see Jakob peering from around the door over Heirshman's head.

"Jakob!" She pushed past the short stout man who obstructed her path, and flung herself into her brother's arms.

Jakob's response was less than cordial, as he pushed her back at arm's length. "What the hell are you doing here?" Heirshman shut the door and strode to the fire. He squatted down to stoke it, leaving the two of them out of earshot. Jakob jostled his sister to a wooden bench.

"Georg told me you were shot. Are you okay?" She could see through his shirt that his arm was still bandaged, and there were stains of dried blood on his breeches. By the fetid body odour, it was obvious he hadn't washed in days.

"I'm fine." Jakob's voice softened towards his sister. "Does Georg know I'm here?"

"He told me where you were." Taking his dirty hand in hers, she tried to persuade him to come home. "Papa needs you, Jakob. Please come home. I know he's forgiven you." Elisabeth was lying, but she would do anything to hold onto what was left of her family.

"*Nein*!" He spoke curtly. Heirshman gave a backward glance but resumed what he was doing. "I can't go back ever again. Papa thinks I can never change. Well, he's right." Jakob leaned forward, resting his one elbow on his knee. "I can't be like Papa, who just sits and watches the world go by. I've got to fight for what's right. And if it means dying, well so be it."

"It's not worth it. Georg says that people are wanting to talk peacefully now. Everyone's tired of fighting. They just want to forget about everything and get on with their lives."

"Don't you see, Elisabeth? Thinking that way you'll have people like Lawrence and Sutherland walking all over you. We have to get what's promised us. *Awch*, forget it. You'll never understand."

"You're right, I don't understand you, Jakob Heber! All your life you've stuck your nose where it doesn't belong. Look where it got Hans Beck. Six feet underground, not to mention you could've been killed, too. Mark my words, brother, if you aren't careful, you'll be there too. I can't take another death in this family," she pleaded, trying desperately to fight back the tears. "Just leave things be and come home." He continued staring past her. "What more do you want? You have a family that loves you, a house, a garden lot, thirty acres plus another three hundred."

"I don't have those things!" he grunted, half laughing.

"Papa's got them. Remember? I'm considered a deserter and accused of aiding the French. I have nothing." Elisabeth heard the bitterness in his voice.

"So that's what this is all about. You're not fighting for us but for yourself. You resent that you haven't got what is rightfully yours."

"I have every right to feel this way."

She laid her hand on his forearm. "Sometimes I think that if you never got involved with Schutze everything would've been different."

"What's he got to do with this? I've my own free will. I fell into his footsteps on my own accord. Both of us had the same strong views to help our neighbours, and not have the likes of Eugen, Hopson, or Lawrence take advantage of us. We've been treated like we were worth no more than a dog." He turned and gazed at her. "And you came across the ocean to a life that was no better; stripped of your dignity, almost starving to death. No land to sustain even the smallest of crops. Mama would've lived if those promises had been kept. We're still paying for our passages, for Christ's sake. And, for how much longer?"

"You have to forget all that and look to the future. We're getting our dues now."

"Go, Elisabeth! You're living in a dream world." He stood up and started for the door. "Go back to your family. Let me live my own life. If you don't want to fight, that's your business. That's not for me!"

"Damn you!" Elisabeth screeched. "Face up to reality. I don't believe there ever was a letter. Petrequin probably made it all up. You're being sucked into this like quicksand, with Simon Gauer pulling you down with him. I never trusted that man the day I laid eyes on him. He's as shifty as Schutze. Stay away from him! *Bitte*!"

Suddenly the door flew open, almost hitting Jakob and startling Elisabeth. It was Hoffman. "We've been disarmed! Everyone's laid down their muskets."

"What!" Jakob roared.

"Monckton assured everyone that the passage debts would be dropped if everyone turned over their weapons."

CHAPTER 29

"Forgive me! Pleeease! I beg your forgiveness!" Petrequin was on his knees before Monckton, Reverend Moreau, and a handful of deputies representing the colony. The painful ordeal over the past few weeks had left him a pitiful being. Monckton averted his eyes from the bony face that knelt before him. His sunken eyes were wide with terror and his face was covered in scabs. A cold and dirty skeleton of a hand clawed at him. "I beg the King's pardon!" Then, Petrequin collapsed, sobbing in a pitiful heap before his onlookers. Monckton coldly watched as the tears made tracks through the dirt on his face.

"Take him away!" Monckton waved his arm at Captain Steinfort, who, with the help of another deputy, lifted him up by each arm. Before he was dragged away, Petrequin turned and spit in Monckton's face. Wiping the wet glob from his cheek, Monckton shouted, "Get out of my sight, you imbecile! Now!" The steely cold glare from the prisoner was devil-like as they removed him.

"What do you think?" Reverend Moreau asked as Monckton sat down heavily on a nearby bench. Just after the disarming, Petrequin had admitted that his accusation against Zouberbuhler was false. He confessed he had only done it so Simon and Jakob would cease the torturing. Now he confessed that Hoffman was the one who read him the letter, not the sailor.

"Don't know," Monckton replied, still wiping the spit from his face with a stark white handkerchief.

"How can we trust him this time? He's changed his story so many times," one of the deputy's said.

"No, I do think he's telling the truth this time," Monckton said, throwing his handkerchief onto the floor. "Didn't Petrequin also say that some fellow settlers had asked him about the letter before he even had a chance to tell anyone else about it?"

"That's right. What are you getting at?" Reverend Moreau asked.

"Well, who do you think was spreading the contents of it? I certainly don't think it was Hoffman, otherwise..."

"I see what you're on about now. Because Petrequin can't read or write, Hoffman forced him to have someone else write the reply to the letter. It makes sense that the writer spread the contents of the letter around the colony. And..."

Monckton finished his thought, "That way nothing gets traced back to Hoffman. I think Petrequin was just a poor illiterate son of a bitch caught up in a seditious plot by Hoffman. He must have told Petrequin to say the letter was read to him by a sailor, and threatened him to keep his mouth shut."

Last week Monckton had sent Lawrence a dispatch relating his thoughts over the past few weeks. Initially he felt that the whole colony seemed to be involved in the insurrection, but he now wondered if just a few instigators had riled the people. Lawrence had relayed his suspicions of Simon and Jakob's involvement in the rebellion. He had based it on the earlier incidents last summer. Simon, after being arrested, had accused Jakob of a murder he committed in Hohctorf. This had formed a judgment in Monckton's mind of the type of character Jakob was. However, now it seemed it was Hoffman they should be after.

"Hoffman's the instigator of all this mischief. I'm beginning to think there never was a letter from Petrequin's cousin at all," Moreau deduced.

"Neither do I. It was all done to stir up mischief. Have you seen Hoffman?"

"I saw him near Heirshman's house earlier. We can start there," piped up one of the deputies.

"Right! You come with me," Monckton replied, grabbing his musket. "We'll get more soldiers along the way, and the rest of you find Jakob." He gestured to the other four. "Might as well bring him in, too."

****

Jakob sat alone in front of the hearth, stoking the fire with one hand and swilling back rum with the other. Hoffman had come to the house a couple of hours earlier to get Heirshman.

The two of them slipped away to the Star Fort with the intention of spying on Monckton's questioning of Petrequin. In Jakob's intoxicated state, they insisted he stay lest he give away their position.

Zouberbuhler had been released a week ago when Petrequin retracted his statement. It was on everyone's mind whether or not there ever was a letter, and, if in fact Petrequin, as uneducated as he was, could even dream up such a plot. But in Jakob's eyes he was guilty. He had the letter. If Simon and he had not given up Petrequin, it would have only been a matter of time before they had it for themselves. He threw the poker down, and his ears rang from the loud clanging as it bounced off the stone. Leaning his back against the table, he stretched his legs towards the heat of the flames.

Schutze suddenly popped into his mind, along with an image of Rosina. He had never meant to kill them. It was all an accident. No one knew about Schutze's demise. Jakob told no one what happened and left it up to whoever found his body in the woods to determine how he died. The French, who they were living with, probably found his decaying body. Maybe, he thought, one of the young girls found it while picking herbs one morning. Then, maybe not, as he remembered he had hidden the body well under piles of evergreen boughs and leaves from the forest floor. Of course, he pondered, maybe a wild animal found him first and carted his body away to be eaten.

He didn't mean to kill him. This thought kept churning over and over in his mind. But he had it coming. Jakob didn't trust him after he had found out he was selling ammunition on the sly and pocketing money behind his back. Schutze denied his accusation and it eventually led to hand-to-hand combat. He had thrust Schutze's head back repeatedly against a large boulder. Ultimately, he lay motionless, blood streaming from an ugly open gash. There they were, the two of them in the still forest with only the sound of a crow circling overhead. Jakob had concealed the body as fast as he could, stolen a canoe from the Indians, and paddled down river, portaging over land until he found himself in Dartmouth.

Jakob opened a second bottle of rum. He didn't like people to take advantage of him, and Schutze did that all too well; like Rosina, for whom he didn't have one bit of sympathy. That witch was better off dead. After all, she could have killed his sister. The rum was going down all too easily, and his eyes were growing heavy as he thought about Michael whom he despised for his faults.

Squinting at the empty liquor bottle, he picked it up and threw it against the wall, splintering it into tiny pieces. Staring at the half empty second bottle in his hand, he poured more down his throat. Most of it spilled over his chin and down his already soaked shirt.

Outside, he could hear voices. Thinking it must be Heirshman and Hoffman returning, he carefully picked his way to the door as his head spun like a top. But to his surprise, Monckton stood with three soldiers.

"Where's Hoffman?"

"He's not here," Jakob slurred. Without a word, Monckton pushed him aside with his musket, clearing the way for the rest of his men to enter and search. "What the hell! Get out!"

"We're not going anywhere until we find Hoffman, and as for you, Heber, you're coming with us." Monckton pointed the weapon at his chest.

"What?"

"You're under arrest for inciting a riot and torturing a prisoner."

"He's not here," one of the soldiers bellowed from upstairs.

Jakob quickly sobered up as Monckton stood in his brightly coloured uniform, pointing a gun at his heart. Glancing sideways, he eyed his own musket standing upright in the corner a few feet from him. During the disarmament a week ago, he had managed to keep his hidden. Unfortunately, it hadn't been loaded recently, and at that moment he could curse Heirshman for not allowing him to do so. But there was a bayonet strapped to the muzzle of the gun that could come in handy, Jakob thought.

Suddenly, he heard more voices outside. They were Heirshman's and Hoffman's.

"Stay away!" Jakob screamed. There was silence.

Monckton motioned to the soldiers to go after them. The diversion was enough for Jakob to grab his gun as they pursued the two outside, leaving him alone with the intruder. Each pointed a weapon at the other.

"Put it down!" Monckton said, raising his gun higher.

"You're not going to take me in."

Jakob let out a wild yell and lunged at him from across the room. Monckton's immediate instinct took over and he pulled the trigger.

The force of the impact knocked Jakob back against the wall. He crumpled into a lifeless heap.

****

"It can't be. *Nein*." Elisabeth screamed, covering her ears, refusing to listen to Georg's words. Then, "Oh my God! Papa! I must go to him." But her husband held her back.

"You don't want to see him now. The state you're in would do him no good. Hanna's there. She's the best medicine for him now. She pulled him out of his depression before."

Elisabeth couldn't take it, to be able to do nothing. "Where's Jakob? I must see him." She made a fruitless struggle to free herself from Georg's grip.

"Reverend Moreau took his body to prepare it for burial."

Losing her strength to continue to fight, she finally relented. Elisabeth quietly laid her head against his warm chest.

For the next few days she was in a daze. She so wanted to believe it was a terrifying nightmare from which she would be jolted awake. Papa had refused to go to the funeral. Thank God it had been a fairly mild winter, Elisabeth thought. She couldn't stand the thought of waiting until spring to lay her brother to rest.

In the aftermath of their grief, Elisabeth and Georg learned that Hoffman was arrested. He was confronted by Petrequin, who refused to alter his story in any way. Hoffman claimed his innocence, stating that Monckton had bribed Petrequin to make up this story. He was sent to Halifax to await trial in the spring, along with Petrequin to be on hand as a witness. The truth soon came out. There never was a letter addressed to Petrequin. Hoffman had used the letter to show that the settlers were ill-used by the government. Hoffman was charged with false and scandalous libel. Stahl and Simon were also taken into custody and shipped to Halifax.

As the winter months drearily slipped by into spring, Elisabeth and Georg grew closer than ever before. She found herself wanting to be with him constantly, and surprised herself by praying for the day that she could have his baby. Perhaps, a sister for Petie, who was almost three years old now and a great joy to both of them. Her life in Hohctorf seemed like a whole other entity that never truly existed. She hardly ever thought of Peter, and when she did it wasn't with the passion she first craved when she was waiting for him to return just a year ago.

Papa wasn't pulling out of his depression as easily this time, but Hanna pressed on with her love for him. She washed and fed him daily, with the hope that one day he would snap out of it. Hanna's maturity in her tender nine years never ceased to amaze Elisabeth. Each morning and evening, she would always find the time to read to him from the Bible. Hanna said one day that she could see a slight change in him when he listened to her. He seemed to find solace in certain verses. His favourite, she said, was chapter three in Ecclesiastes: "'To everything there is a season and a time to every purpose under the heaven,'" Hanna recited by memory. "No matter how many times I read that chapter to Papa, he still wants more. When he just sits there staring out of the window, Elisabeth, it tears my heart out."

Talking for about an hour, they never noticed Michael get up from his usual seat to pick up the worn book. His weathered and aged hands quivered as he gripped the sacred Bible. Sitting down again, he whimpered like a child.

"Papa, what's wrong?" Elisabeth rushed to his side and sat down beside him.

Michael had it open on his lap to the entries of family births and deaths. Slowly moving his fingers over the carefully printed names of Margaretha, Anna, Stefan, and Jakob, a tear dropped onto the page. It left a blurry smudge on Christian's name. Elisabeth couldn't believe that his name was printed there. All these past months, she held on to the hope, as slim as it was, that her brother must still be alive, and that one day he would walk through that door. She wouldn't let herself believe otherwise.

"Papa. Christian isn't dead. I know in here he's still alive." Elisabeth raised her hand to her breast. "Don't give up. He *will* come back."

Michael slowly moved his head from side to side as he gazed blankly at his daughter. His empty eyes scared her and without saying goodbye to Hanna, she fled out the door.

Not wanting to go home, she found herself running for the longest time until she found herself at Jakob's grave. His was among a few dozen who had died over the year. She felt at peace here on top of the hill, as the warm breeze teased her hair. She threw off her shawl and watched the men working their fields in the distance, tilling the soil to plant oats, potatoes, and turnips. Because of the open winter, the surveyors were able to finish cutting the roads to the farm lots earlier than expected.

Tilting her head upwards, she relished the sun's heat on her face. Georg was watching Petie, and she knew he would be worried about her. He promised to take her to their new farm lot. Picking up her shawl, she started back to the house. Halfway down the path, she heard footsteps but saw nothing when she turned back to look. Quickening her pace, the steps behind shadowed hers again. Still not seeing anyone, she broke into a run. The mud from yesterday's rain spattered onto her legs and the hem of her dress flew up past her ankles. For the third time, she nervously glanced back, and this time, she could see a man chasing her.

Concentrating on reaching the gate of the palisade, her short heavy breaths deafened her to the sound of the approaching footsteps. Her pursuer caught up with her and wrenched her arm back.

"Leave me be!" she screamed, too frightened to look at her aggressor. She managed to wriggle away from him.

"Elisabeth!" She stopped in her tracks and spun around, almost losing her balance. She was shocked at who stood before her. Peter wrapped her in his arms.

"Elisabeth! My love," he cooed, kissing her all over her face. He searched for her lips, but she pushed hard against his chest.

"How dare you!" She slapped him as hard as she could, and he grabbed her hand. "Let go!" All the pent-up anger came back before she could stop it. "Where have you been all this time? What happened? What..."

"Whoa! One question at a time." He tried soothing his stinging face. "You've gotten a little feistier since I last saw you." He gave a forced laugh.

"One gets like that when waiting patiently for your return. At first I was worried that something terrible had happened to you, then angry that you never did return."

"Elisabeth." He stroked her face and she leapt back. "I'm so sorry. A year ago, I was on my way back to you, when I met up with Christian and a fellow. *Awch*, I can't think of his name. Anyway..."

Elisabeth couldn't believe her ears. "Christian! You saw him! Where is he?"

He looked into her bright eyes and his face lit from within. "Don't know. On the day I met up with him and...Henderick, that's his name. There was an ambush; Indians killed Henderick as he was putting the canoe into the river...don't know why they spared us."

"Is he still alive?" Elisabeth was frightened to ask the question.

"He was before Christmas. I haven't seen him since. I managed to escape and have been dodging Indians for the past four months, barely living hand to mouth."

Elisabeth now scrutinized his face. His rough tanned face was deeply etched with lines around his eyes. His long, unkempt hair hung down his back in a tangled mass. It matched the rat's nest of a beard that now covered his face. The clothes he wore were soiled and torn, and on his arm he carried what looked like an animal skin.

"This," he pointed to it, "is what got me through the cold nights in the woods. Thank God it wasn't a harsh winter." He threw the skin to the ground and moved closer to her. She couldn't discern the smell that permeated his body, but it was pungent.

"Did you find Schutze?" She asked sarcastically.

"Someone got to him before I did. He was dead in the woods. His head was split open." Elisabeth recoiled at the sound of it.

"Elisabeth, I thank God He brought me to you."

She pulled away. So many feelings came rushing back to her in one mass confusion. Peter leaned in and kissed her on her lips, then holding her tightly, he frantically kissed her forehead. "I've come to take you and our son away," he whispered, and pressed hard on her lips, trying to pry them apart with his tongue.

Her head was spinning. A stranger stood before her, and what he was telling her to do was utterly unthinkable. She truly did love Georg. The love she had for Peter so long ago was immature, and what feelings she did have for him were now stagnant.

Staring up into his dark eyes, she didn't know him anymore and didn't wish to. All along she was trying to live for the past. This was the present, and she didn't want him in it. It was peculiar though; she still felt the old childish love for Peter. And deep down, she knew it would always be there. "Things have changed, Peter. I can't go with you."

"You can and you will, Elisabeth. Go and get our son. I'll meet you back here in an hour."

"I-I'm sorry." Her voice trembled. It was taking all her strength not to give into this mysterious hold he had on her. The old feeling was nagging her.

"*Bitte*. Don't do this to me, Elisabeth. I need you."

"Don't do this to me? Why did you ever leave me in the first place? That night I was willing to come with you."

"Don't talk ridiculous. You and Petie would have never survived. I did all I could to keep myself alive, let alone have a woman and a baby. And I don't even want to think what the Indians would've done to you." He attempted to hold her again, but she gently pushed him away.

"Pride took you away from me. You weren't satisfied until you got your revenge. And look where it landed you. You've lost us." Her voice sounded final and without feeling.

She stood on her tiptoes and kissed him on the cheek. She then held his rough hand to her lips, smelling a mixture of dust and wildness about it. She walked away, fighting back her tears. When she reached the gate, Elisabeth glanced back, but Peter was nowhere to be seen.

Upon reaching the house, her son was imitating Georg as he chopped wood. She smiled through her tears as she watched his small chubby arms swing in a downward motion as if he was holding an axe. Wiping her eyes, she ran to her husband. All the way there, she debated with herself whether or not to tell him what had just happened. Putting her arms around his neck, she said, "I love you, Georg, with all my heart."

"Hey, what brought this on?" He laid down his axe. "Are you crying?"

"Just happy I have you," she replied, and kissed him tenderly.

Georg grabbed her hand. "Come, I have something to show you." He lifted up Petie and the three of them started up the path.

It seemed to take forever going up one hill and down the next, over narrow and muddy makeshift roads. Finally, Georg steered her onto grassland, then up a small hill.

"There she is, Elisabeth. Our new home where we'll raise a dozen children." He beamed and put his arm around her.

She started to laugh she was so happy. As far as the eye could see, there was land full of wonderful grass, dirt, and bush. Off to the right of it, stood the most beautiful clump of trees, where she just knew their home would be built one day. Petie wriggled his way down from Georg's arms and dug his pudgy fingers into the dirt.

Pulling his knife out, Georg cut a clump of grass and plunked it into his wife's hand, dirt and all. "This is all ours. Tomorrow we start clearing the ground for planting." He gathered her up into his arms and kissed her passionately. "I love you so much."

Elisabeth never imagined she could be this happy again, and vowed never to mention Peter. The tears flowed freely once again, but not for sadness. She knew in her heart this was right.

SELECTED BIBLIOGRAPHY

Bell, Winthrop P. *The Foreign Protestants and the Settlement of Nova Scotia.* Victoria, B.C.: Morriss Printing Company, 1961

Bruford, Walter H. *Germany Eighteenth Century*. Cambridge, England: University Press, 1965

Carter, Jenny and Therese Duriez. *With Child: Birth Through The Ages*. Edinburgh: Mainstream Publishing, 1986

Craig, Gordon A. *The Germans*. New York: Putnam General Publishing Company, c1982

Forbes, Thomas Rogers. *The Midwife and the Witch*. New York: AMS Press, 1982 c1966

Leavitt, Judith Walzer. *Brought To Bed.* Toronto: Oxford Unversity Press; New York, 1986

Martin, John Patrick. *The Story of Dartmouth*. Halifax: Privately Printed for the Author, 1957

Meltzer, David. *Birth, An Anthology of Ancient Texts, Songs, Prayers, and Stories*. San Francisco: North Point Press, 1981

Mitford, Nancy. *Frederick The Great (King of Prussia)*. London: H. Hamilton, 1970

Mittelberger, Gottlieb. *Journey to Pennsylvania*. A personal 18th Century Diary

Oldmeadow, Katherine L. *The Folklore of Herbs*. Birmingham, England: Cornish Brothers, 1946

Old Blockhouse, Lunenburg, anonymous artist, ca. 1800; Nova Scotia Archives and Records Management, Laing Gallery,

Toronto, Ontario, Collection; Nova Scotia Archives and Records Management, Photo Collection: Places: Lunenburg

Paul, Daniel N. *We Are Not The Savages*. Halifax, N.S.: Nimbus Publishing, 1993

Pettigrew, D.W. *Peasant Costume of the Black Forest*. London: A & C Black, 1937

Ruland, Josef. *Christmas in Germany*. Bonn: Hohwacht, 1978

Sagarra, Eda. *A Social History of Germany—1648-1914.* London: Methuen, 1977

Thonger, Richard. *A Calendar of German Customs* . London: O.Wolf, c1966

Vann, James Allen. *The Making of a State-Wurttemberg* . Ithaca: Cornell University Press, 1984

Zinsser, Hans. *Rats, Lice and History*. Little Boston, 1963